DARKNESS TRIUMPHANT

BOOK THREE OF
THE CATMAGE CHRONICLES

BY
MERYL YOURISH

COVER ART BY JULIE DILLON

MAY PUBLISHING

THIS BOOK IS DEDICATED TO THE MEMORY OF PAUL KING,
WHOSE KINDNESS AND HUMOR IS GREATLY MISSED.

All rights reserved. Published by MAY Publishing.

ISBN 978-0-9881804-4-4

First printing December 2015

CONTENTS

ONE: SUMMERTIME

The early morning sunlight slanted through the window into Andy Cohen's bedroom, where he tossed restlessly as he lay dreaming. He was back in the cellar of Principal Saunders' house, lying on the ground after the can of turpentine exploded in the fire. Nafshi lay in her cage, bleeding to death. He tried to speak, but he had no voice. He tried to reach out to her, but his arm wouldn't move. On the night table beside his bed, his Magelight—Nafshi's Magelight—glowed.

The scene shifted. A large, long-haired tabby Catmage, Methuselah, called out Nafshi's name to the crowd, and she took her place with the rest of the Council. She lifted her head proudly as they cheered for her—the newest Council member. Nafshi's chest swelled with pride as Methuselah congratulated her. Her tail flicked briefly at her good friend Hakham as she settled down beside him. Standing in front of them, so happy the tip of her tail was vibrating, was a small black-and-white female, Zehira, one of Nafshi's closest friends.

Andy's breathing slowed as the dream ended, and he lay still. On his night table, the Magelight faded and blinked out. Andy stirred in his sleep, his feet pushing up against the large orange cat at the foot of his bed. Letsan opened his eyes, yawned, and flattened his ears, tail twitching. He leaped onto Andy's stomach.

1

CHAPTER ONE

"Hey!" Andy said, waking up and pushing Letsan off.

"Mind-voice, Andy!" Letsan reminded him. "Don't want your mother to hear you and wonder who you're talking to in a room with only a boy and his cats."

"Cat*mages*," Goldeneyes corrected from the pillow next to Andy. She rose and stretched. "We are not dumbcats."

"I'll just tell Mom you jumped on my stomach," Andy sent, annoyed. "She'd totally understand. Why did you wake me up like that?" He looked at the clock. "At six-thirty in the morning? Are you kidding me? Letsan, it's summer vacation!"

"You woke me up when you kicked me. It seemed only fair."

"I kicked you? You mean like this?" Andy said, swiping his leg at Letsan, who leaped effortlessly over it but misjudged his landing and fell off the bed onto the floor. Andy laughed.

Goldeneyes turned her gaze on Letsan, who jumped back on the bed and started grooming his shoulder.

"Honestly, sometimes I think Silsula's new kittens are more mature than the both of you," she said.

"Ow! I am cut to the heart," Letsan said cheerfully. "No, thinking about it, you're probably right. I am immature. I blame my upbringing. Yes, it was living with humans that forever changed me." He examined his paw and started grooming that, too.

"Since you're awake, Andrew, I may as well tell you that we received a message while we were at the Compound yesterday," Goldeneyes said. "We have been summoned before the Council. Letsan and I leave tomorrow."

"Again? Why do they want you this time?"

"They didn't say."

Letsan stopped grooming himself. "No doubt they want to discuss our failure to stop Saunders from getting the Tilyon," he said, his tone no longer cheerful. "And the loss of so many Catmages." Letsan's head drooped as he thought of the friends that had died in the battle.

2

Andy grimaced. He didn't like the reminder that the month before, they had failed on every level against Principal Saunders. The Catmages, led by Letsan's warrior brother Razor, had been defeated badly in their attack on Saunders' house to retrieve the eleven Magelights that Saunders had stolen two years ago after killing their rightful owners. On that same night, Andy and his best friends Mike and Becca, with help from Mr. Velez and his granddaughter Teresa, had failed to get to the Boston Museum of Natural History before Saunders. They'd been tricked by a copy that Saunders had put in place of the cat-shaped amulet, while Saunders left with the real one. Now he had eleven Magelights and the most powerful amulet known to Catmages. And their side had lost a dozen warriors.

"Well, at least they lost a few of their own," Andy said. "Dogs, too."

"Yes, but our spies tell us he's already breeding another litter of pups to replace the ones that were killed. Perhaps we can do something about them before they reach maturity. They're more vulnerable when they're young."

Andy was shocked at the casual tone Letsan used. He couldn't even think of killing a dog or cat—or a Catmage.

"We don't like to kill, Andy, but if it comes down to them or us, we don't hesitate to defend ourselves," Letsan said.

Andy sighed. "I'm projecting my thoughts again."

"Because you feel strongly," Goldeneyes said. "Strong emotions can make it hard to keep your thoughts to yourself." She glanced at Letsan while she was speaking.

"Oh, is that why you project your thoughts so much when I'm around?" he asked. "Your strong feelings for me?"

Andy grinned. Goldeneyes liked Letsan more than she let on, and they all knew it. He was the only Catmage who could get away with teasing her, and though she grumbled about his behavior, she spent more time with him than anyone but Hakham, her mentor.

She ignored the question. "We have time for one more lesson today. And since you're already up, we can start early."

3

CHAPTER ONE

Andy yawned, closed his eyes, and lay back down. "I don't want to start early. I want to go back to sleep." He pulled the blanket up and rolled onto his side, ignoring them. Letsan glanced at Goldeneyes. The tip of his tail trembled as his eyes narrowed. Their Magelights flashed as one, and Andy's blanket flew off him and fell to the floor.

"Hey!" Andy said, sitting up. "Not fair!"

"*Mind-voice!*" Letsan repeated.

"Since you're up, you may as well shower and dress," Goldeneyes said, not bothering to hide the humor in her voice.

"All right," Andy said. "But I'm going to remember this." He slid out of bed and picked up the blanket.

"Oh, dear. I do believe we've just been threatened by the mighty Son of Aaron," Letsan said. "Whatever will he do? Strike us down with his Magelight? Sear our ears with his angry words?"

"Smother you with a blanket?" Andy sent, throwing his blanket over Letsan, who was still on the bed.

"Not the fur!" Letsan said, emerging from under the blanket with his long fur disheveled and sparking with static electricity.

Andy laughed as he headed to the shower. "The Son of Aaron strikes again," he sent.

"At least he's using his mind-voice," Letsan said as he put his fur in order.

"That boy is starting to act entirely too much like you," Goldeneyes said.

Letsan stopped licking his fur back into place. "That's the nicest thing you've ever said to me."

The three of them went downstairs after Andy dressed. His mother was putting her breakfast dishes in the sink.

"You're up early," she said.

"I couldn't sleep," Andy said, yawning. "A big Maine Coon decided my stomach would be a good place to sit. Hard." He glared at Letsan.

His mother laughed. "You're a bad boy," she said as Letsan wound

4

around her ankles and purred. "Are you hungry? Would you like some breakfast?"

"Are you talking to me or him?"

"The cat. You can get your own breakfast. I have an early meeting today."

Andy opened the refrigerator and took out a bottle of orange juice. "I'll feed them, Mom. Go take care of your work stuff."

"Thanks, sweetie. Any plans for today?"

"A bike ride."

"I thought you might head out. Your lunch is in the fridge. Be careful."

"See you later, Mom. Thanks."

"Have a good day."

She waved as she went into the garage, and a short time later Andy heard her car leave the driveway.

Andy removed a box of waffles from the freezer. While the waffles toasted, he set out some chicken for Goldeneyes and Letsan. After they finished eating, he rinsed the dishes and put them in the sink. He glanced at the clock. "It's too early to call Becca and Mike. Should I have them meet me at the Compound? Mike has something new he wants to show Razor."

"Razor is leaving with us. He may not have time for anything else," Letsan said.

"I'll text them. If they show, they show." He took his phone from his pocket and sent a text, grabbed his lunch and some drinks out of the fridge and stuffed them into a backpack. Goldeneyes and Letsan waited for him by the garage door.

"You could have opened the door yourselves," Andy said.

"Waste of energy," Letsan said, yawning, "especially when there's a big, strong human nearby who can open it for you."

Andy shook his head and opened the door. "So are you running or riding today?" he asked as he pushed his bike through the door. Letsan jumped into the basket, purring.

CHAPTER ONE

"Lazybones."

"Not at all. We're helping you keep in shape, Andy. Zahavin and I are the Catmage equivalents of you lifting weights while you ride. You get stronger when you ride with us in the basket!"

"Um, not very much. It's not like I'm running with you guys on my back or something. You don't get human physiology, do you?"

"Of course I do. Those are arms," Letsan said, pointing one paw at Andy's arm. "Those are legs," he said, his paw moving down. "And that round lump on top is your head. What more do I need to know?"

Andy grinned. "Forget I asked. How about you, Goldeneyes?"

"If that big oaf would move over, yes, I wouldn't mind riding," she said. Letsan moved aside and she leaped deftly into the basket. Andy grinned as he closed the door and got on the bike, setting a steady pace toward the edge of town. It was a fine day for a ride.

Andy breathed deeply as he pedaled along the road. The trees were clothed in green leaves, crops grew in the fields, and the smell of new-cut grass permeated the air.

"I love this time of year," he said as they rounded a corner and took the road leading east. "The birds are singing, the grass is growing, everything looks beautiful—"

"And there are lots of flying bugs to chase," Letsan piped up.

Andy grinned. "You chase bugs?"

"Me? No, I'm far too mature for that."

Goldeneyes snorted.

"The kittens love to chase bugs," Letsan said, ignoring her. "I've been teaching Silsula's litter how to stalk their prey. And getting delicious snacks as they learn!"

"It's really gross that you eat bugs."

"It's in our nature. And they taste great. You should try one."

"I'll pass. So that's what you're doing when you're supposed to be working with Razor?"

"Oh, no," Letsan said. "My brother would have my ears if I bailed on any of his meetings. But Zahavin and I visit the kittens while you're busy with your lessons."

"I didn't know that," Andy said, glancing down at Goldeneyes. "You've never shown any interest in kittens before."

"They are my nieces and nephews," she said. "Of course I want to know if we have any more talents like Leilei or Nafshi."

"Of course," Andy said, keeping his voice bland and guarding his thoughts. He wanted very much to smile, but didn't dare. Letsan looked up at him and winked, a habit he'd picked up from living with humans. Andy cleared his throat and kept pedaling.

He stopped the bike on the road as they neared the small clearing that marked the beginning of the path to the East Woods Compound, wheeled the bike to the hedge where he always hid it, and followed Goldeneyes and Letsan into the woods. Andy nodded to the guards as they passed. He knew there were hidden guards as well. Razor had increased the number of Shomrim on guard duty since Principal Saunders had stolen the Tilyon. In the last few weeks, Andy saw a regular stream of newcomers to the Compound, most of them Catmages who had worked with Razor in the past. The two grey cats guarding the path were fairly new. Andy wasn't even sure he knew their names.

"Tovah and Shefah," Letsan said. "Brother and sister. Razor and I got to know them when we were in the Teaching Rings together."

"I'm projecting again, huh?"

"Mm-hm," Letsan replied. Birds flitted from tree to tree, chirping and singing. A couple of squirrels scrambled up a tree trunk as they passed. Letsan's tail twitched as he watched them climb.

"You just ate!" Andy said.

"Instinct," he replied as Andy raised his eyebrows. "We're still cats deep down, you know."

"Don't let Goldeneyes hear you say that."

"Do I look like I was born last week?"

Andy smiled. His phone buzzed in his pocket. He took it out and

7

read the text. "Mike and Becca will be here in an hour or so."

"I'll let the guards know," Letsan said. He concentrated for a moment and a green light flashed out of his Magelight and headed back the way they had just come. "There. Now they won't be attacked when they arrive."

Andy was shocked. "Would they really attack Mike and Becca? I thought everyone knows them by now!"

"He's teasing you, Andrew," Goldeneyes said. "We don't get many human visitors. I doubt there's a Catmage in the Compound that doesn't know Mike and Becca. But we've been told to inform the guards of all visits."

"Oh," Andy said, sighing with relief. "Not funny, Letsan."

"Actually, it was. You should have seen the look on your face."

"There's Silsula," Goldeneyes said. "And my newest nieces and nephews."

An orange-and-white Catmage who looked a lot like Goldeneyes walked slowly across the clearing, followed by four kittens. Andy grinned as the two orange kittens stopped to grapple and roll while the two tabbies kept up with their mother.

"Come along, sweetlings," Silsula said to the two stragglers. *Chirrup.* "Your Auntie Zahavin is here with Andy!"

The tabby kittens sprinted ahead, calling out Andy and Zahavin's names.

"What am I, a tree stump?" Letsan said. "No greetings for Uncle Letsan?" The tabbies leaped for him as soon as they got within reach. Soon all four kittens were tumbling over Letsan, who batted lightly at them as Andy watched, grinning. One of the orange-and-white kittens detached herself from the battle and trotted over to Andy.

"Andy, make me fly!" she said.

"Did you ask your mother?"

"*Ima*, can I? Please?"

"Not too high now," Silsula cautioned.

SUMMERTIME

Andy sat down cross-legged and placed his hand, palm up, on the ground.

"Get on my hand, Ranana."

The kitten climbed carefully onto Andy's open hand and sat down. He picked her up and closed his eyes. His Magelight glowed, and he opened his eyes, concentrating. Ranana rose slowly above his hand, hovered there for a few moments, and then rose a few inches more. Andy grinned as she mewed happily. "Look, *Ima*, I'm flying!" she said. "Look, I'm flying!"

"So I see, my dear. *Chirrup.*" Silsula watched carefully as Andy moved his hand back and forth beneath the kitten. Ranana floated slowly through the air in time with his hand.

"That is excellent control, Andrew," Goldeneyes said, purring.

Still concentrating, he smiled. "Want to do a loop?" he asked.

"Yes!" Ranana squealed. Andy moved his hand in a slow circle, and Ranana squealed happily as she floated through the air upside down. The other kittens stopped playing with Letsan as they noticed what their sister was doing. "Me too! Me next! No, me!" they shouted.

Grinning, Andy eased Ranana down to the ground, where she proceeded to leap happily around his feet.

Silsula padded over to them. "That was quite a display, Andy. Settle down, little ones. *Chirrup.* Ranana, what do you say to Andy?"

"Thank you!" Ranana squeaked. "Thank you, thank you, *thank you*! That was fun!"

He grinned. "You're welcome."

The other three were now fighting over who got to go next. "Maybe next time, dears," Silsula said. *Chirrup.* "Andy has a lesson now. Run along!" She nodded at Goldeneyes and Letsan. "It's good to see you, sister. We'll talk later. I have to bring these scamps to their first Teaching Ring!"

The kittens said goodbye as they followed their mother across the meadow. Letsan took his leave of them and went off to meet Razor. Andy was still smiling as he and Goldeneyes headed toward the end of the meadow where the older students held their lessons. He loved kittens. He glanced over at Goldeneyes. She could pretend otherwise, but she wasn't fooling him at all. Goldeneyes was watching the kittens with what could only be called longing. Being very careful to guard his thoughts, Andy allowed himself to wonder what her kittens would be like.

She shook herself. "I must meet Hakham. We've got a lot to do before I leave. Zehira will take over your teaching once again." She looked across the meadow. "And here she comes now."

A small, elderly black-and-white female Catmage came slowly toward them, stopping a few feet away and nodding a greeting.

Andy liked Zehira. She was a good teacher and she had a sense of humor, something that Goldeneyes could definitely use. "Wait until you see how much I've improved since our last lessons," he told her.

"Oh, she knows," Goldeneyes said. "We discuss your training often. Zehira is an old family friend. I've known her since I was a six-moon kitten training with Nafshi." Goldeneyes paused as she thought of her much-loved grandmother. "She had nothing but high praise for you, Zehira."

"And I for her. She was my oldest friend. Oh, the tales I could tell you." She laughed. "There was this one time when—oh, but wait. Perhaps I shouldn't tell you that story. I can tell you about the day she was voted onto the Council."

"I already know that story," Andy said. "You looked like you were about to bust with happiness."

Zehira glanced sharply at Andy. "How could you possibly know that story, or how I felt all those years ago? I've never even mentioned it to you!"

"Uh—I—I don't know," Andy said. "I just have an image in my head of you watching Nafshi when she became a Council member. She was standing next to Hakham. And Methuselah was there, too."

Goldeneyes looked as puzzled as Zehira. "Nafshi must have told him about it while they were captive in the Evil One's cellar," she said. "Andy said she talked for hours to keep him from being frightened. Maybe she shared her memories."

Zehira looked relieved. "That must be it. Nafshi was a good story-teller, though she was prone to exaggeration."

"You sure looked happy, though."

"That's enough about that. Zahavin, you should be off. Hakham wants you."

"I'll see you later, Andy. Work hard!" She hurried away.

"Now, Andy," she said, "let's see how much you've improved since we last worked together. Impress me."

Andy closed his eyes in concentration, made a fist, and lifted a large rock from the ground with his Magelight.

"It's a start. Now, put it down. I've got some ideas that are going to push your powers to the limits."

An hour later, Andy sighed with relief as Zehira told him to take a rest break. He retrieved his backpack from the shade of a tree, took out a bottle of water, and drank half of it before sinking down to sit against the tree. He closed his eyes in relief.

"Snack or no snack?" he said out loud.

"First sign of insanity is talking to yourself," Mike said.

"Hey, Andy," Becca said.

Andy opened his eyes and jumped up from the ground. "Hey, you guys finally got here," he said, smiling at Becca. "Whatcha doing with those?" he asked Mike.

Mike shrugged the aluminum baseball bat off his shoulder and tossed the bag of balls onto the ground. Several of them rolled out. "I'm going to show Razor ways to make his fighters more effective. Want to watch me play some ball?"

"Yeah! When? Now? I have more lessons this afternoon."

"I asked for some time with His Scarredness. I haven't gotten a response yet. Catmages aren't exactly good communicators, or haven't you noticed?" He shrugged. "Well, we can play some ball ourselves. Let's go get Patches and Leilei or some of the others."

CHAPTER ONE

"That's not how it works around here, Mike. You have no idea how strict they are about lessons. It's worse than school."

"School? On summer vacation? I'd freak!"

"Then it's a good thing you're not the boy chosen to wield Nafshi's Magelight," a gruff voice sounded in all their heads. Razor, a large, stocky orange Maine Coon with torn ears and a scar across his face approached, his rolling gait making him appear bowlegged. Behind him were two Maine Coons that resembled him, Letsan and his son Zohar. Ranged in a semicircle to the rear were several of Razor's warriors and captains of the Shomrim.

"Let's see if you've got anything interesting to show me, or if this is going to be a waste of our time."

"Razor, stop! Your heartfelt warmth is making me cry," Mike said, pretending to wipe away a tear. Razor stared up at him silently.

"Mike!" Becca hissed. "Shut up and show him what we came for."

"Okay." He took the bat and ball bag, moved away from the trees and faced the open field, which was somewhat smaller than a baseball field. "Let me show you something," he said. He took a ball, tossed it softly in the air, and hit it hard enough that it flew across most of the meadow, bouncing a few times and rolling into the woods. Some kittens tore away from a Teaching Ring to chase it.

"Oops, sorry, didn't think of that," Mike muttered.

"Fine," Razor said. "You can hit a ball a long way with a stick. How does that help us?"

"You guys pick up small things with your Magelight powers, right?"

"Yes."

"Well, what if one of you picked up, say, a rock. And another one used his Magelight to bat the rock at, say, a Wild One. In battle."

Razor's eyes narrowed. "By the First," he said. "You actually have a good idea."

Mike beamed. "Oh, Razor, I love you too." Everyone but Razor burst out laughing.

SUMMERTIME

"Letsan, Zohar, let's see you two try this. Katana, find us a stone."

In a few moments, the Catmages were ready. Letsan and Zohar stood a little way away from the others, Zohar to the right of his father. At a nod from Letsan, Zohar raised the stone over their heads. Letsan's Magelight flashed, a jet of light flew out at the stone, and the stone flew as if it had been hit by a stick. The Catmages cheered and the humans applauded.

"Way to go, Letsan! High five!" Mike said, running over and leaning down, hand extended. Letsan reared up on his hind legs and slapped Mike's hand with his paw. Mike beamed.

"All right, boy, you showed us something useful. One Catmage raises the stone, another bats the stone at the enemy. We work as partners, and each uses less energy."

"So Mike's idea can help the Shomrim?" Andy asked.

Razor grunted. "Yes. You can be sure we're going to practice this. But don't think this changes anything!" he said loudly to the assembled warriors. "When you're in the middle of a battle, and a large dog is about to clamp its jaws around your head, you're not going to have the luxury of wondering where you left your rock and whether or not your partner is ready to launch it. This could be a great opening gambit if we were fighting a standing battle. But how likely is that to happen?"

Andy's heart had leaped at the thought of his friends having another weapon to use against Saunders and the Wild Ones. But now he wondered if this trick would be useful at all.

"That's our Razor, pulling cold ashes from a warm fire," Letsan said. "You could at least let us get proficient in this new tactic before telling us it won't do any good."

"It's my job as head of the Shomrim to keep my warriors sharp and ready. Katana, Zohar, Ari, Arel—get your teams to the training ground and start working on this. I'll want a full report later today." He sat on his haunches as the others hurried away, leaving only Razor and Letsan.

"You did great," Becca whispered to Mike, who was looking crestfallen. "Razor has to be careful. He's already lost too many fighters."

13

CHAPTER ONE

"Becca's right," Razor said. "Your idea is a good one, boy. But I can't let my warriors lose their edge. Not ever." His Magelight flashed and one of the baseballs on the ground flew several feet into the air. It flashed again and the ball zipped away, flung through the air to land halfway down the field.

"Not all of us need an assistant," he said.

"Showoff," Letsan told him. "Hey, Andy, I'm going to put one up for you. Let's see if you can get the ball past Razor's."

"Sure!" Andy stood like he was holding a bat over an imaginary home plate.

Letsan's Magelight glowed, the ball lifted waist-high, and Andy swung while his Magelight shone brightly. The ball soared high into the air over the field and landed deep in the woods. Andy whistled as he watched it fly.

"Holy—" Mike said.

"Whoa!" Becca said. "That was amazing!"

Razor and Letsan glanced at one another.

"Good job, Andy," Letsan said.

Andy shrugged. "I guess. But it sure was weird how hard I could hit it with my Magelight," he said.

"Yes, it was," Razor sent privately to Letsan. They glanced at each other again. Andy didn't notice the exchange. "*Very* weird."

TWO: PLANNING STAGES

A large shorthaired cat scratched at the opening of the most expansive shelter in the Council Compound. The full moon rose behind the bayit, bright enough to throw a shadow behind him. The cat's fur was so dark grey it was almost blue, and his muscles rippled as he walked. His copper eyes blinked courteously at the two cats within. A plump grey female sat next to an even fatter black-and-white Persian with a squashed face, who lay on the ground with his paws tucked under his breast.

"What is it, Matanya?" asked Ruma, the female. "Kharoom has had a wearying day."

The British shorthair lowered his gaze and blinked. The sound of Kharoom breathing loudly through his nose seemed to fill the round shelter.

"Velvel wishes to see you, sir. Shall I send him in?"

"I am not so weary that I can't entertain a Seeker," Kharoom said, glancing at his mate. "Thank you, Matti. You may leave us."

Matti left to stand guard outside the door, moving a short distance from the bayit as a sandy-colored cat strolled in.

"You have a report for us, Velvel?" Ruma asked.

Velvel glanced back at the Shomrim guard. "Isn't that one of Razor's Shomrim?"

CHAPTER TWO

"Matanya is not one of Razor's," Ruma said. "He heads the guard here at the Council Compound. He is ambitious and forward-thinking. Talk to him yourself, and you will soon discover that he is tired of living in Razor's shadow. We have found many Shomrim who are dissatisfied with the, ah, *colorful* captain of our guard. Kharoom has very wisely asked that many of them be assigned to our personal security." She gazed fondly at her mate, who blinked at her with affection.

Velvel sat down and curled his tail around his legs. "They're not the only ones who are tired of Razor," he said sourly. The tip of his tail began to twitch.

"Did you come here to complain about how much you dislike the current guard captain, or have you something important to tell us?" Ruma asked.

Velvel took the hint. "I've spent the past few moons observing the Son of Aaron and his friends as well as the Wild Ones and their new Compound."

"And they have no idea you've been spying for us these many moons," Ruma said.

"No, Councilors. Each side is convinced I am with them." He yawned hugely. "The Wild Ones are far more challenging than Hakham and his Catmages. Hakham doesn't even know that Roah has set up a Compound on the opposite end of his very own wood, no more than a half a day's walk from his precious second home."

Kharoom snorted, but Velvel couldn't tell if he was laughing or just had difficulty breathing. "On the other hand, I must constantly watch myself around Roah. He's a sharp one."

"We remember," Ruma said sourly. "He grew up here, Velvel."

"I had forgotten."

Kharoom slowly raised himself to a sitting position. "Am I right in guessing that our long efforts are coming to a happy conclusion?" Kharoom asked.

"I believe they are, sir," Velvel said. "The Wild Ones will have much

16

more freedom in their new Compound. They won't have to hide their numbers from the local humans. This will enable them to move forward with their plans. But I fear for our friends in the East Woods if it comes to another battle. The Wild Ones' forces are growing every moon."

Kharoom snorted derisively. "Letsan and Razor have bragged many times of their skills. If they're so smart, they'll figure out for themselves that the Wild Ones are on their border."

"You are right, my dear," Ruma said. "But Velvel must keep us informed if they plan on moving against our friends. We don't want harm to come to so many good and innocent Catmages."

"Of course not!" Kharoom snapped. "I was merely remarking on their arrogance. You've seen what I've had to put up with, particularly from Letsan." His voice was sulky and his ears lay flat on his head as he spoke. "He has never shown me the respect I deserve."

"You have every right to be annoyed, Kharoom," Velvel said. "Everyone knows how Letsan belittles you. But you shall have your revenge on him. You shall have the glory of victory, both here and in the East Woods." He exchanged a glance with Ruma, who nodded. "We will not let the Wild Ones harm our friends. You have my word on that."

"I'd better," Kharoom growled. "I am responsible for *all* Catmages, not just the ones in this compound." Kharoom's loud breathing was the only sound for a long moment. Then Ruma strode over to him and rubbed her cheek against his. "You are so clever, my love. Your enemies won't stand a chance against you."

Kharoom purred softly as he glanced at Velvel. "You may leave. But I want you to stay in the compound until the Council meeting. We will need you in place after we take care of Hakham and his faction."

Velvel stood. "Yes, Kharoom." He left the bayit, blinking at them both. Ruma sat down next to her mate, her flank just touching his.

"If you keep impressing me this way, I may rethink my decision to stop having kittens," she said.

Kharoom leaned against her and licked her ear. "There will be time

17

to discuss that later, my dear. First, we take care of Hakham."

"Yes. I'm looking forward to the next Council meeting. I can't say the same for him."

Kharoom rose heavily and went to the door. He glanced up at the sky as Ruma joined him.

"Are you sure we're doing the right thing, my love?" he asked. "I don't want our Catmages harmed. We must take care of those Wild Ones, but we can't let them murder any more of our own."

"Don't worry about it, Kharoom. Niflah used to be one of us. I'm sure he can be reasoned with, especially after we remove Razor and Hakham. They have always been the burrs in our coats."

"And Letsan. Don't forget Letsan!" he said.

"No, dear. Letsan will be disgraced along with his master. I doubt he'll ever show his face around you again. Let him live his life in exile, far away in the East Woods, since he loves that *human* so much."

Kharoom let himself be soothed by her words, and by the shoulder she rubbed against his. "Yes. I have had enough of his insolence. I will live to see him punished for it." They turned away from the moonlight and went back into the bayit, settling in for the night. In a few moments, the bayit was filled with Kharoom's nasal snores.

Standing guard some feet away, Matanya watched Velvel stride quickly from Kharoom's home. Matti's hackles rose. There was something about Velvel that he'd never liked. But Velvel was a favorite of Kharoom's, and it was well known that he protected his favorites. Well, Matti was rising in Kharoom's favor. He would watch and wait. Unlike his mentor, Razor, he knew how to work within the politics of the ruling Council. Matti's ears twitched as he settled in for the night watch, listening to the sounds of the Compound all around him.

The bright moon illuminated Alef and Bett, two chocolate-point Siamese, as they trotted slowly down a winding path in the wood. Behind them were four young Wild Ones, their first litter from over a year ago. Three of them were chocolate-point Siamese like their parents. The fourth, the smallest, was a black-and-white tuxedo cat. He walked several feet behind the others. Alef looked back, saw Kel lagging behind, and slowed until he was abreast of him.

"Problems, boy?" he asked.

"No sir," the yearling said fearfully.

"Then keep up!" he snapped.

"Yeah, Kelev, move it!" Gimmel said.

"By the One, he's always so slow," said his sister Dalet. The third Siamese followed silently along, head held high.

"Hay," Alef said, "nothing to add?"

"Why should I waste my breath? We have work to do, *Abba*," he said. "We've got the West Woods Compound nearly ready to go, and it was done right under the Shomrim's stupid noses. If Kelev can't keep up on a simple march, he'll be the first to fall when we take on Razor and his Shomrim."

Bett purred loudly. "Our son is a wise and courageous warrior. You would do well to emulate him, Kelev."

"I'm your son, too," Kelev muttered.

"Not *my* son," Alef said viciously. The others laughed. Kel's sister's tail switched quickly back and forth as she waited for him.

"Aww. Is Kelev feeling lonely? Does little Kel want us to call daddy Roah?" Gimmel said. "What? No answer? Catmage got your tongue?"

Kelev did not respond to the taunts. He gathered his strength and pushed forward past Alef. As he came level with Gimmel, his Magelight flashed and a twig flew into her path, causing her to stumble. She growled and leaped at him. The others gathered around as the two growled, bit, and clawed. As in every previous fight, Kel was overpowered and had to back away and surrender. His siblings were all larger and stronger than he. Blood shone darkly on his cheek where Gimmel had scratched him. His brothers laughed and congratulated her. The three of them put their heads together, then turned and stalked toward Kel.

CHAPTER TWO

"Enough!" Bett said. "Leave Kelev alone. Back to the march! We have much to do once we get to the Compound." She and Alef took off quickly along the path, not waiting to see if the others followed. Their young ones would not dare disobey—they had all been marked by Alef's and Bett's claws at one time or another.

The young cats hurried after, Kel still in the rear. He quickened his pace, making sure to keep a good distance between him and his siblings. He'd show them. He'd show them all. He might be the runt of the litter, but he was as smart as any of them. Smarter. His mind raced as he tried to think of the best way to prove himself to his father. His real father, not the one walking beside his mother. Mother. Ha! She never lifted a paw to stop Alef and his siblings from picking on him. Roah was the one Kel needed to impress, not Bett. If Kel could show Roah his worth, he would never have to go near his siblings again—except to give them orders. Yes, that was it. He'd find a way to raise himself in Roah's eyes. Then his siblings could live in fear of *him*.

His family was nearly out of sight. Kel ran to close the distance and caught up just as they veered onto the path to the West Woods Compound. Kel knew much more about the world than his brothers and sister did. They wasted their time with the other young ones, playing or practicing with their Magelights. Kel practiced his spells, but he didn't waste his spare time playing. He spent as much time as he could around the older ones, listening to their conversations and learning what he could before they chased him away. Sometimes he hid in places too small for grown Wild Ones to fit and overheard things he wasn't intended to. Information was power. Kel learned much about his fellow Wild Ones and stored it all away for future use.

This Compound, for instance. Kel knew Roah had insisted on naming it the West Woods Compound to reflect the name of the Catmage Compound a few hours' walk away. It had also been Roah's idea to build the Wild Ones' camp near their enemies. Roah had insisted they establish themselves in secret, keeping their presence from the Catmages as long as possible. But it was Kfir, the fearsome warrior, who had found an abandoned building in town and posted several squads of Wild Ones there, where they could be called up quickly if they were needed. In the meantime, their main home would be within easy striking distance of the East Woods and then, well—Kel wasn't privy to the inner circle's plans, but he was fairly certain none of them were good for the Catmages. There would be a battle, and he would help the Wild Ones to victory.

Moving so close to the East Woods made it easier. Kfir and Roah weren't the only ones with good ideas. Kel was smart, way smarter than his siblings. Roah would discover his worth. Kel would leave this family that despised him and go where he belonged—with his father Roah and the other leaders of the Wild Ones. He could almost see it in his mind's eye: Standing next to Roah while the rest of the Wild Ones cheered. Kfir would acknowledge Kel's bravery and intelligence as his father beamed. And his brothers and sister would look on with envy. And fear.

The others were nearly out of sight again. Kel raced after them and took his place at the end of the line just as they reached their bayit. He moved to the farthest edge of the shelter, away from the others, and curled up to sleep the rest of the night. First, to learn the lay of the land. Then to put his plan into motion. He shut his eyes and went to sleep.

Stan Saunders sat at his kitchen table eating a late-night sandwich. A grey striped tabby sat on the table across from him. Around Stan's neck hung a thick gold chain. The chain held a small golden amulet in the shape of a sitting cat, its eyes two pieces of dark yellow amber. The tabby cat seemed to be looking into the eyes of the amulet.

"Why do you keep staring?" Saunders asked irritably. "You've seen it dozens of times since we took it from the museum."

"I know. But it is the Tilyon, Saunders! It represents the birth of my kind. Can't you feel its power? The First Catmage wore that amulet, and performed amazing feats with it."

"And yet, I cannot perform amazing feats with it. Why is that,

21

CHAPTER TWO

Niflah? How much longer must I wait to unleash the full power of this amulet? Am I going to have to replace you as my teacher?"

Niflah's tail started twitching. "We have been over this before. You resist my suggestions, refuse to practice the little things, and complain that you are unable to progress in your lessons. It is not the *teacher* who is failing at his task."

Saunders glared at Niflah. "I say it *is* the teacher who is failing. I shouldn't need to do the little things. I have the Tilyon, the most powerful amulet known to Catmages. Why is the power not flowing to me?" He brought his fist down on the table, causing his plate—and Niflah—to jump.

"We have never tried to train a human before, Saunders. You know that, too."

"Your brother is training a boy, Niflah, and that boy has learned how to wield his Magelight with far greater power than I." His lip curled. "A child. A child can do what I cannot!"

"Andy Cohen has a Catmage's aura," Niflah said. "He was born with the power to wield a Magelight. You were not."

"Niflah is right," Roah said as he entered the kitchen through the cellar door. The door closed behind him and he leaped to join Niflah at the table.

"You will achieve what you wish, Saunders. You have great strength of will. The boy learns at a faster pace because he has an aura. A Magelight does not work as well for those who do not have the *neshama*. We have learned this from your experience." Roah lifted his left paw and licked it.

Saunders frowned. "Bunk. Sheer bunk. I don't want excuses. I want results!" He gripped the amulet tightly in his hand and turned it to face him. "Glow, damn you! Glow!"

The amulet did not glow.

"May I try?" Roah asked.

Frowning, Saunders removed the chain from his neck and placed the amulet on the table. Roah touched it with his paw. The amber eyes glowed brightly in tune with Roah's Magelight. He felt a warmth spreading from the gem on his neck down to the tips of his claws. Roah gasped. "Never have I felt such power," he said. The paired lights glowed brighter, pulsing.

"Let me see," Niflah said, reaching eagerly to place his paw alongside Roah's. As he touched the Tilyon, his Magelight also glowed brilliantly. Saunders shaded his eyes.

"This is magnificent!" Niflah said. The lights pulsed as if in time with their heartbeats. They felt the warmth of the lights on their faces.

"That's enough!" Saunders said, grabbing the amulet. The lights faded abruptly, and a chill seemed to come over the room. Niflah and Roah felt a wave of disappointment. Saunders pulled the amulet over his head, glaring at them as he tucked it into his shirt.

"When I am finished with my sandwich, Niflah, we will continue our lessons. I expect to see some improvement. Soon."

Niflah nodded, distracted. Roah was breathing deeply, gazing at the amulet with awe.

"Did you feel that, Niflah?" he sent privately. "Did you feel the power of the Tilyon?"

"Yes. It draws me, too."

Roah's glance slid carefully toward Niflah. The two looked at each other and then quickly broke eye contact, their unspoken shared desire uniting them for the moment.

"On second thought, I think I need a new teacher," Saunders announced. "Niflah, you've had long enough. You have failed. I am no farther along today than I was last spring with eleven Magelights. Roah, since you are so adept at using the Tilyon, you will take over my lessons starting now. You will be available to me in the evenings when I get home from school."

Roah blinked at him. "I will be honored to teach you."

"Niflah, you can go out to the West Woods and help the others set up your new home. You've lazed around my house long enough."

Niflah looked at him sharply. "Lazed? I have been integral to all the

23

plans of these past few years," he said angrily. "Do not treat me like one of your servants, Saunders. Because of me, you have the Tilyon and the Council's Magelights. *I* was the one who drew Nafshi here. *I* was the one who gave you the Council!"

"Yes, yes, you have been invaluable. I didn't mean to belittle your accomplishments," Saunders said, his voice silky. "But your wisdom is needed at the Compound. Kfir is a good fighter, but not a real thinker outside the battlefield. They need a proper leader to get the Compound running well. Someone like you, not a thick-headed warrior."

Niflah was mollified by what he considered an apology. Saunders could be short-tempered, but he did always seem to defer to Niflah's expertise.

Saunders held back a smile as he gauged Niflah's mood. As always, Niflah went the way Saunders steered him. He had long ago learned to school his face from showing his emotions. When he discovered that Cat-mages could overhear what some people were thinking, he learned how to school his thoughts as well. The cats heard only what he wanted them to hear. They thought they were his equals. He almost laughed at the thought of an animal being equal to a man, even an animal that could think and cast magic. The cats were useful tools, and he needed them for now, but they were tools nonetheless. Niflah was still necessary, so he let the cat think that he was apologizing to it, when he was really only flattering it. Once again, Niflah bought what Saunders was selling.

"Very well, I'll go visit Kfir and the others. Will you give me a lift out there tomorrow?"

Saunders smiled thinly. "I'll run you to the edge of town on my way to school. Now," he said, leaning back and stretching, "I'm going to head upstairs. I will see you in the morning. Roah, with me, please. I want a lesson before I turn in."

"I will be right up. I need to confer with Niflah about the West Woods Compound."

"Don't be long."

"He doesn't know what he has in the Tilyon," Roah said after Saun-

24

ders left the room.

"No, he does not," Niflah said.

"The Tilyon," Roah said. "It could be a mighty weapon—in the right hands."

"You mean paws."

"Then we understand each other," Roah said.

"Yes. We understand each other perfectly. Go to Saunders and teach him. We will discuss this again."

Roah leaped to the ground and hurried out of the kitchen. As he ran up the stairs, he thought to himself that Niflah knew very well that the Tilyon could not be shared. It could only have one owner. This could only end in one victory. It would be his. He rounded the corner to the office. Saunders waited for him at the desk.

"Let us see how much you've learned without me, Saunders." Roah's Magelight flashed, and the door clicked shut behind him.

THREE:
AFTER SCHOOL SPECIAL

Taylor Grant walked nervously through the empty hallways of Co-reyton High School. He had no idea why Principal Saunders had summoned him. School had let out two weeks ago. Football practice didn't start for ages. Saunders had seemed happy with Taylor the last time they saw each other. He could have sworn the year had ended on a good note. What could he have possibly done wrong? Well, the answer wouldn't be long in coming. Taylor knocked on the office door.

"Enter," said the familiar voice. Taylor pushed open the door and saw the long, lean frame of the principal standing in front of a window, gazing out.

"You called me, sir?"

Saunders turned away from the window and sat behind his desk. A laptop computer and a small metal box with a combination lock were the only items on its surface.

"Mr. Grant," Saunders said. "Points for showing up promptly. You may sit."

"Uh, thanks," Taylor said as he sank into the chair in front of the principal's desk. Taylor was a tall, stocky boy with broad shoulders, but Saunders was taller still and seemed to tower over him even while seated.

"As you know, a few weeks ago I successfully retrieved the Tilyon, the amulet worn by the first Catmage." He pulled at the thick gold chain beneath his shirt and brought the amulet out so that Taylor could see it.

Taylor waited for Saunders to go on. He had learned from painful experience to speak as little as possible around him. Saunders paused and stared at Taylor long enough to make him uncomfortable. *I hate when he does that,* Taylor thought.

"I have been thinking. You haven't been an altogether terrible assistant, although you have much work to do before you can be really helpful to me."

Taylor perked up. "You want me to do something for you? Just name it, sir. Does it involve going after Cohen? It's summer, I can't get expelled." He grinned.

Saunders frowned. "You can't be expelled unless I *wish* you to be expelled," he said. "And when you talk like a fool, you make me think I'm making a mistake. Perhaps I can find another student to elevate to my assistant."

"No, please, sir. I can do it. Just tell me what you want."

Saunders reached out to the metal box and spun the combination lock. He raised the lid and removed a strong silver chain on which were strung five colored gems. The gems glowed as he lifted the necklace. Taylor saw a corresponding yellowish glow from the amulet that lay against Saunders' white shirt.

"I want you to learn how to use these," he said.

"The Magelights?" Taylor said incredulously. "You—you want *me* to have them?" His face lit with pleasure.

"To *borrow* them," Saunders corrected. "I'd like to see how you do with them first. My associates tell me that Mr. Cohen appears to be getting more adept with his Magelight. I think it wise to have you do the same. Who knows? You may even be of some use to me."

Taylor couldn't believe what he was hearing. He knew that Magelights gave their holders—usually only Catmages—magical powers. He knew the amulet Saunders was wearing was the most powerful Magelight that had ever existed, that it was thousands of years old or something. He wasn't clear on the details, but he knew the principal had spent the best part of last year searching for it. Now that he'd found it, Taylor guessed that was why Saunders no longer needed the Magelights.

"I'll do it, sir. I'll run circles around Cohen with them. Just tell me where to start."

Saunders smiled and put the Tilyon back inside his shirt. "I like your enthusiasm, Mr. Grant. You will be taking lessons at my home. And you will tell no one what you are doing."

"Of course not!"

"Further, until I see signs of progress and responsibility, the necklace remains in my house under lock and key. You will earn your place, Mr. Grant, or I will find someone else to take it." He placed the necklace back in the box and spun the lock again. "You will memorize the combination, and you will *not* allow the Catmages to learn it."

"They can count?"

"Most can't. Those who do don't understand numbers very well, and they don't seem to be able to grasp the concept of combination locks. But that doesn't mean they cannot learn, especially now that Mr. Cohen is in daily contact with them. These Magelights are your responsibility," he said, lifting the box and handing it to the boy. "Don't make me regret trusting you with them."

"No sir," Taylor said, rising. "You won't. When's my first lesson?"

"Today. Come with me. This time, I'll drive you. You will find your own way there in the future."

Saunders rose and strode on his long legs to the office door, Taylor hurrying to keep up. They walked quickly through the halls. As they neared the entrance to the parking lot, they passed Mr. Velez, the janitor, who was on a ladder replacing a ceiling light. Mr. Velez watched them pass. Taylor glanced away uncomfortably as their eyes met. He quickened his pace. Mr. Velez knew things about him that nobody outside his family knew, and it bothered Taylor that he did.

The janitor gazed after them thoughtfully as they left the building. The echo of the closing door faded in the empty hallway. He went back to repairing the light. When he had finished replacing the fixture, he climbed slowly down. Then he pulled his phone out of his pocket and pressed the keypad.

"Teresa," he said, "how would you like to invite your friends to dinner this week? I know you haven't seen them since school ended." He paused to listen. "Okay. Yeah, all of them, Mike, Andy, Becca. You call them and let me know when they can come."

Taylor could barely contain his excitement during the ride to Principal Saunders' house. He held the metal box on his lap as if it were the most precious object in the world. Five Magelights! Five! Wouldn't Cohen just freak when he found out.

The car stopped in the driveway, and he leaped out, racing around the side to open the door for Principal Saunders. Taylor followed him inside the dim house. The shades were drawn in nearly every room. Saunders led the way upstairs to an office.

"Where are all the cats?" Taylor asked.

"They are setting up their new home in the woods outside town. Niflah will be arriving shortly to give you your first lesson. You may take out the necklace now."

"Yes, sir!" Taylor said, putting the box down on the desk and turning the combination lock. He lifted the necklace carefully. Five stones— two green, two yellow, and one orange—were arranged in a semicircle on a strong silver chain. Taylor looked at Saunders for permission before putting it over his head. "Where did they come from?" he asked, touching each Magelight in turn.

"It doesn't matter," Saunders told him. "Their former owners are dead."

"Oh. How did they die?"

CHAPTER THREE

"The dogs killed them."

"With our help," said Roah as he and Niflah strolled through the door. "Saunders needed Magelights. We helped him gain them. We need things that only a human can give us. He helps us with that. We are partners." He leaped onto the desk and looked up at Taylor. "You will work with us too. Do as we tell you, and you will learn much. Disappoint us, and—" His Magelight glowed, making his eyes light up.

"Now, Roah," Niflah said, chuckling, "I think the boy is smart enough not to fall for your tricks."

Taylor held still, trying not to show that he was afraid of Roah, and hoping the Catmages couldn't read his thoughts.

Roah snorted. "You are too soft, Niflah. It is a weakness that your enemies will exploit."

"And you are too harsh, which is why I will be teaching the boy. Go pick on your warriors and leave the human to me."

"The strong take, and the weak are taken from, Niflah. You will see that when we finally defeat your brother, and you will thank me for pushing our warriors to do their best."

"That, my dear boy, is why you are in command of our forces. Whereas I am in charge of strengthening our warriors' capabilities."

"And I stand above it all," Saunders said with a thin-lipped smile, "making sure it is done right. Roah, come downstairs with me. I'd like to hear your report on the new Compound."

Roah jumped to the ground and the two of them left the room. Taylor stood uncomfortably, waiting for Niflah to speak, not knowing what to do or say.

"Sit. On the floor," Niflah said. Taylor sat down cross-legged. "Now, do you see that leaf in the planter by the window?"

"Yes."

Niflah's Magelight flashed and the leaf lifted from the dirt and floated across the room.

"Hold out your hand."

Taylor obeyed, and the leaf floated slowly above his hand, and then dropped.

"First, you're going to learn breathing exercises. Then you're going to learn how to float the leaf, if you're lucky. Are you ready?"

Taylor nodded, grinning.

"Good. Then let us begin."

Roah followed Saunders to the kitchen, relating the progress made in the new Compound. "And the best part is that the fools in the East Woods have no idea we're so close." He laughed harshly.

"The surprise will only last until our plans are in motion," Saunders said.

"Yes. But it will make things easier for now."

"We shall see. For now, since Niflah is occupied with his new pupil, let us go to the dogs and give them *their* lessons. They have improved much in the last few weeks."

"I told you they would. And Niflah still knows nothing?"

"Nothing at all. This is our little secret still, Roah. Though I don't see why you should care if it gets out in the open."

"I do not. But Niflah—as I said, he is soft. Sometimes I think his heart is not fully with us. I worry that he cannot escape his upbringing."

"Watch him carefully," Saunders said. "I do not tolerate dissent."

"It isn't as bad as that. But there are some things we should do without his knowledge. He is powerful, and he has many uses. We need him."

"Then we shall keep him, for now. But if he ceases to be useful…"

Roah paused as they reached the door to the cellar. He opened it with his Magelight before Saunders could reach for it, padding quickly down the steps as Saunders flicked on the light. "If he ceases to be useful, you can do what you want. I can rule the new Council just as well without Niflah." He stopped in front of a row of wire kennels. The six young Dobermans inside sat or lay alertly watching Saunders and Roah. Each of them wore a metal-studded leather collar, the center stud of each collar noticeably larger than the others.

"Good afternoon, my special ones," Saunders said in a silky voice. "How are we doing today?"

The dogs that were lying down rose to a sitting position, the stubs of their tails wiggling. Saunders surveyed the dogs and smiled.

"Time for another lesson," Saunders said. "We shall start with obedience training."

Roah's Magelight shone, and the dogs stopped wagging their tails.

Andy's mother pulled the car to the side of the road in front of a small white house with a neatly trimmed lawn. There were bushes on either side of the front door and flowers along the front of the house. An SUV was parked in the driveway.

"Fifty-seven James Street," she said. "Here we are. How are you getting home?"

"Mr. Velez said he'd drive us," Andy said.

"Should I go in with you?"

Andy shrugged. "If you want."

She looked at the clock on the car radio and sighed. "I should get home. I still have a lot of work to do on my project."

"Okay. See you later," he said, getting out of the car and walking to the door. His mother drove away as he rang the bell.

"Hi!" Teresa said as she opened the door. "Everyone's already here, come on in!"

He followed her through the foyer into the kitchen, where Mr. Velez was putting the finishing touches on a table laden with all the fixings for tacos. Mike and Becca sat at the table. Becca smiled as he came into the room.

"Andy!" Mike said. "About time. Come on in and see what I helped create."

"You helped cook?" Andy said skeptically.

"No, I helped by tasting everything to make sure it was all just right for everyone."

"And almost got his fingers cut off," Mr. Velez said with a snort.

"My grandpa and I made supper," Teresa said. "He's been teaching me to cook since I was little."

"Cool," Andy said, sitting down next to Becca. "Thanks for inviting us, Mr. Velez."

"Yeah, thanks," Mike said.

"I had my reasons, besides enjoying your company. But they can wait. Let's eat." He sat down, took a taco shell and started filling it. The others followed his example, Becca slapping Mike's hand as he tried to steal a plate of cheese away from her. They steadily ate their way through the laden plates until they were full.

"That was really great, Mr. Velez. Thanks again," Becca said. She got up and picked up her plate.

"No, sit down. I got to talk to you kids," he told her. "I'm happy to have you all here, but I asked Teresa to invite you so I could tell you something. Something big, maybe."

He told them about seeing Taylor and Saunders together in school. "I didn't hear nothing this time, but I seen what Saunders was carrying. It was a locked metal box. Now what do you think he carries in a locked box?"

"The Tilyon!" Andy said. "Saunders wouldn't want to leave it out of his sight, I bet."

"I don't know. But it's something important. And I think, well, I can't call you at home without your mother wondering why the school janitor is calling you. Then I thought it wouldn't be a bad idea to get to know Mike a little better since he's seeing so much of my granddaughter." He glanced at Mike, who grinned. "So I had Teresa throw a dinner party. You gotta tell those cats about this."

"Catmages," Andy corrected absently. "I will, Mr. Velez. Thanks."

"And I'll see if I can find out anything else. Maybe I can catch

Saunders talking to one of his cats again."

"You should be careful, Mr. Velez," Becca said. "Saunders can have you fired. Don't give him a reason to."

"Yeah, 'Buelo," Teresa said. "Don't let him hurt you, too."

Mr. Velez nodded. "Okay, okay, I won't do anything obvious. But if he starts talking where I'm working on something—"

"That's different. Take my cell number and text me if that happens," Andy said, handing his phone to Mr. Velez, who put his phone number in Andy's phone and gave it back to him. "Letsan and Goldeneyes aren't around right now, but I'll tell Razor or Zehira or someone. They'll know what to do."

"Give my love to Razor," Mike said. "And do it in baby talk. Then show me the scars after."

Andy laughed. "Sure, the next time I'm feeling suicidal I'll definitely do that."

Teresa rose to start clearing the table. The others followed suit, and soon after they went to the backyard, chatting and laughing while Mr. Velez finished up in the kitchen. Then he sat with them until it was time to take them home.

"This was great," Andy said as they followed him to the SUV. "Thanks!" Mike and Becca echoed his thanks as they got into the vehicle. Mr. Velez dropped them off one by one, until only Andy and Teresa were left in the back seat.

"You be careful," Mr. Velez said as he stopped in front of Andy's house. "That Saunders, he's a mean one. Never forget that."

"You too," Andy said closing the door. He waved to Teresa and went up the sidewalk to his front door, looking automatically for Letsan or Goldeneyes before remembering they were gone. The SUV roared off as Andy closed the door behind him.

FOUR: LEVELING UP

Jack Straight was putting the finishing touches on a quiz for next year's class when his office phone rang. He recognized Stan's number. He frowned and picked up the receiver, and before he could even say hello Saunders said, "In my office. Now."

Sighing, Jack walked quickly out of the room and down the halls of the empty school. He was about to knock on the door when it opened and a short, portly man stopped just shy of running into Jack on the threshold.

"Oh. Hello," he said.

Stan's lips thinned in a smile. "Robert Hunter, meet Jack Straight, our history teacher. Jack, Mr. Hunter is the head of the School Board." Robert reached out and shook Jack's hand.

"Pleased to meet you. Congratulations." His expression did not match his words. He looked rather put out, Jack thought.

"For what?" he asked.

Robert frowned slightly. Before he could speak, Saunders said smoothly, "Robert brings us the good news that you've been confirmed as the permanent history teacher here." He smiled crookedly. "And I am Coreyton High's new principal."

"Con—congratulations," Jack said, trying not to show his shock. "And thank you, sir."

Robert waved a hand in dismissal. "Don't thank me. Thank your principal. He was most insistent that we bring you on full-time." He flashed a sour look at Stan that Jack caught. "We've heard good things about you. Make sure we keep hearing them." He nodded and walked quickly down the hall. As his footsteps faded, Jack's gaze turned to his cousin.

"How did you manage that?" he asked.

"I did Mr. Hunter a favor."

Jack's eyebrows rose. "It must have been a big one."

"It was. I didn't send his wife the photos I have of Mr. Hunter kissing another woman."

Jack's mouth dropped open. "How—what—you—"

Saunders smirked. "Oh, my dear, innocent cousin. You cultivate all the wrong friends for all the wrong reasons. Whereas I have a network of, shall we say, underachievers that I have kept in touch with over the years. You never can tell when you'll need someone followed. Or a copy of a valuable amulet made."

"You're blackmailing the head of the School Board?"

"I believe we have already established that."

"What did you do to Mrs. Barron?" he asked suspiciously, thinking of the teacher on maternity leave that he replaced last year.

"Oh, don't be so dramatic. I did nothing to her. No, check that—I did her a favor as well. She was given the opportunity to take a teaching job closer to home. A woman with a new child relishes that sort of offer. She couldn't wait to transfer schools."

Jack sighed with relief.

"I know how much you've always wanted to teach high school. This goes on the ledger. You owe me for your job." Saunders smiled smugly.

Jack looked away, uncomfortable at the thought of owing Stan for anything, and especially uncomfortable at the way he was hired for the teaching post. "I didn't ask you to do this. I don't owe you for it."

"Oh, but you do. You have achieved your heart's desire. Doesn't it feel wonderful?"

Jack flushed at the sarcasm in Stan's voice. "I could have gotten here on my own."

"Possibly, many years from now. But here you are, in the present, teaching history at Coreyton High. Since you never once offered payment for your upkeep after you moved into my family's home all those years ago, we shall have to consider well what you will do to repay me for this."

"Your mother was happy to have me there!" Jack said. "You're the only one who had a problem." He thought of the many times his cousin had punished him just for being—well, just for being in his aunt and uncle's home. "Our mothers were sisters. When are you going to get over it? My parents *died*. What was I supposed to do, go to an orphanage?"

Saunders grinned slowly. "That would have been my choice, had I been consulted. But since they took you in, my parents might have taken your house as payment for your keep."

"Gee, I'm so sorry they kept it for me so I could live in it once I was grown," Jack said. "My bad!"

"No wonder you get along with these children so well. You sound just like them," Stan said. His grin widened as Jack's face reddened. "Well, not that this hasn't been lovely, but I have many things to do. I'll let you know when I need your assistance. Now get out."

Jack bit back a reply, turned on his heel, and stalked out of the office. Leave it to Stan to take what should have been a wonderful event—getting a permanent position teaching high school—and turn it to ashes by knowing he'd gotten it through blackmail. If only Jack could get out from under his thumb. "Someday," he muttered as he went back to his office. "Someday."

A few days after Goldeneyes and the others left for the Council Compound, Andy and Zehira stood near the edge of the main field of the East Woods. It was a hot, humid morning, and the Catmages who weren't studying were sleeping in the shade—some under trees, some in the woods, some in their homes. Andy had been working for the last hour without a break.

He sweated profusely as he used his Magelight to float a large branch about three feet above the ground.

"Now let it down carefully," Zehira said.

Andy lowered his hand slowly, his Magelight flickering. The branch wavered and nearly fell. It was almost as thick as his leg. It felt as heavy as if he were holding it in his arms, and it was getting heavier by the minute.

"Slowly!" she snapped. "You're moving too fast."

"I can't help it, it weighs a ton!" Andy said. He tried to stop himself, but the branch fell to the ground with a loud crash. Several Catmages within earshot leaped up from their slumbers, fur fluffed out, then settled down again when they realized what had woken them.

"Oops," Andy said. "Sorry!"

Zehira stared up at him unblinking.

"I don't see why I have to do stuff like this," Andy said. "How is this going to help us against Saunders? Oh, gee, look, Andy can lift a tree branch with his Magelight. Whoopee!"

"Sit," she said.

Andy sat down heavily in the shade of the oak tree. He felt like he'd just run a mile.

"Andy, how does one learn something?"

"I don't know. You go to school, or you get a teacher."

"No, I'm not talking about that kind of learning. I'm talking about the *act* of learning. How do humans learn to read?"

"Well, first you learn the alphabet, and then you put letters together into words and then you read. Why, are you planning on learning how to read?" He grinned at her.

"No," Zehira said sternly. His grin disappeared.

"What was the first thing you learned how to float?"

"A leaf."

"And look at you now. That branch is heavier than many Catmages put together."

"Yeah, but I can barely hold it."

"And yet, you can lift it. This time last summer, could you have lifted that branch?"

"Oh. No. Oh! I get it. It's like weight training. You start out with a smaller weight and build your way up. Like this," he said, turning toward his backpack sitting a few feet away in the shade. Andy concentrated, balling his fist, and then he waved his arm toward his body and the backpack flew up off the ground and landed at his feet.

"That's part of it," she said. "You are also learning control. Look how easily you retrieved your backpack. You couldn't do that last summer, either."

"I get your point. But can we stop now? It's lunchtime," he said. "I'm hungry and thirsty and tired, and I need a break."

"All right," Zehira said. "You may eat and rest. I think I'll do the same. I will meet you back here later."

"See you," Andy said, reaching for his lunch. He leaned against the tree, munching on his sandwich and wondering where Goldeneyes was and how she was doing. He ate and drank his way through everything he'd packed except for the extra water bottle, which he left for the ride home. Then he stretched himself out in the grass, leaning back with his arms beneath his head. Within minutes, he was fast asleep and dreaming once again of Nafshi.

Methuselah sat next to Hakham on a fallen log. Below them on the ground, Nafshi waited expectantly.

"This is your last chance to back out, Nafshi," said Methuselah. "There is no shame in admitting this is not yet your time."

"Master Methuselah, I have prepared for this. I am more than ready. Can't let Hakham have all the fun," she said. "It's bad enough he beat me to this."

The grey tabby chuckled. "Why do I think this is going to be the first and last time I ever beat you at anything?" he said.

"Because it will be."

CHAPTER FOUR

"Very well, Nafshi. You have prepared for this. You know what is at stake. Come back to us as a member of Avdei Ha-Or. We will wait here for you."

Nafshi nodded at them, turned, and headed down a path that led into the deep part of the forest. Hakham looked at Methuselah.

"Master, will she succeed?"

"I'm sure she will. She comes from a line of powerful Catmages. But the ceremony of Avdei Ha-Or has led to tragedy for many."

"I know," Hakham said, his voice full of worry.

Nafshi laughed to herself. Neither Hakham nor her master realized she could hear their thoughts as well as if they'd projected them to her. Well, she'd come this far. She wasn't about to let anything stop her. The power that would come after she embedded her Magelight near the great artery in her neck—she couldn't wait to experience it. Methuselah had worked her hard, but no harder than she worked herself. She was ready. There. There was the grove where the ceremony took place. And sometimes, where Catmages failed and died.

"Not this Catmage," Nafshi said loudly. She took her place in the circle of trees, closed her eyes, and began to concentrate. Her Magelight glowed. She could feel its warmth. She pictured the metal clasp opening, and the gem sprang free from her collar and floated near her throat. She breathed deeply and did as she was taught, feeling the blood pulsing in the vein. Nafshi steeled herself for the next step.

Whoosh. Whoosh. Whoosh. She could feel the thumping of her heart resonating in her neck.

Whoosh. Whoosh. Whoosh.

Now!

With a piercing scream, Nafshi separated the skin and muscle near the artery. The Magelight flew into her neck, and the skin closed over it. Nafshi had just enough energy left to cast a healing spell before she collapsed.

LEVELING UP

Andy woke with a start. His heart was racing, and he was drenched in sweat. The dream vanished as he sat up.

"You don't look very rested," Zehira said as she approached.

Andy jerked around at her voice.

"You're very jumpy, Andrew. What's wrong?"

"I was dreaming."

"About what?"

"I—I don't remember. Something painful."

"Well, you're awake now. We have time for another lesson before you leave. Are you ready?"

Andy breathed deeply, willing his pulse to go back to normal.

"Yeah, just give me a minute." He took a long drink of water. Then he nodded to Zehira. "I'm ready."

"Good. Let's get back to lifting large objects."

Andy concentrated, closing his hands into fists.

Whoosh. Whoosh. Whoosh. His blood thrummed in his ears. He moved his arm. The branch flew off the ground, soaring over Andy's head and hanging there. The young Catmages in the nearest Teaching Ring cheered. He concentrated and let the branch float slowly to the ground.

"Wonderful! Excellent, Andy!" Zehira said. "What did I tell you? The more you practice, the better you get at it."

Whoosh. Whoosh. Whoosh.

The blood roared in Andy's ears.

FIVE: KHAROOM'S TRIUMPH

Ruma and Kharoom lay at ease inside their bayit. They had just eaten well of several fat mice their servants had brought them.

"I must say, a cycle on the Council has not dimmed my appreciation of its advantages, my dear," Kharoom said, breathing heavily through his rather squashed-looking nose. "It's so lovely not to have to hunt for ourselves anymore." He panted slightly. The heat and humidity of the day permeated even the shady dome of twigs and grass. "You don't think I'm eating too much these days, do you?" he said, glancing at his stomach.

"You look as handsome as ever, my dear," Ruma said. "None of us is as sleek as we used to be." She licked her right paw and began washing her face.

A short-haired orange female Catmage walked up to the door and stopped outside. "Hakham and his Catmages have passed the guards," she told them. "Shall I summon the others for the meeting?"

Kharoom rose heavily. "Please do," he said. "Today's meeting will make up for that disastrous vote from last summer, eh, Tigra?" The Catmage who had brought the message nodded and trotted away.

Ruma turned her attention to the other side of her face. When she finished, she stood and joined her mate. "It took very little effort to persuade that one to our side," she said. "You were right when you said that everyone has a price."

Kharoom purred softly. "They will never underestimate me again," he said.

"Yes, you have always been undervalued by Hakham and his allies. Today, though, we will finally set things right. And our society will be the better for it."

"Ruma, you have always believed in me. I couldn't have done this without you by my side." He waddled over to her and licked her ear.

"There will be time for that later, my love. Let us get to the broken tree."

"You're right again, Ruma. I want to be there when Hakham and Letsan—" his tone made the name an epithet—"arrive. Oh, this Council session is going to be fun." Together, they went down the path.

"I'm getting really tired of being summoned to the Council every summer," Letsan grumbled as he followed Hakham and Goldeneyes down the trail that led to the Council Compound. "I'm especially tired of the long walk."

Razor snorted loudly. Letsan paused, turned, and the two orange Maine Coons stood facing each other. The rest of the party halted as well.

"If you have something to say, brother, say it," Letsan said.

Razor's tail switched. He glanced at Katana and the other Shomrim who surrounded them. "We're wasting our time here," he said. "The last two Council sessions were jokes. All they did was talk. We should be spending our time recruiting more warriors. We got our tails handed to us by Roah and the Wild Ones, and Saunders has the Tilyon. Talking will achieve nothing."

"We have no choice," Hakham said. "Are we a society that follows laws and procedures, or are we dumbcats, fighting one another for dominance and females?"

"Laws are overrated," Razor growled. He glanced around and lowered his mind-voice so that only Letsan, Goldeneyes, and Hakham could hear him. "And there's something off about the Council. I've been hearing things. Trouble is brewing. Kharoom is ambitious."

43

"And stupid," Letsan said. "You're worrying for nothing, brother. Remember, I spent moons in his Teaching Ring as a youngster."

"I remember. And I think you misjudge him," Razor said. "Never underestimate your enemy."

Letsan laughed. "Brother, you worry too much. Believe me, Flathead is as incompetent a Council member as he was a teacher. We have nothing to fear from him. Come on. The sooner we get there, the sooner this is over with." He brushed past his brother, followed by Goldeneyes, leaving Razor and Hakham gazing after them.

Razor growled softly. "Kharoom is up to something, Hakham. Beware."

"I will, my friend. But I still must attend this meeting." Hakham followed the others. Razor grunted softly and padded after them. He and Katana exchanged glances.

"This is going to go badly for us," he said.

"I hope you're wrong, sir."

"So do I."

Hakham and his group reached the Compound. They saw students and teachers scattered around the shady areas, napping through the midday heat. Goldeneyes watched a mother lying on the ground while her kittens played on wobbly feet, falling frequently. A pang of yearning hit her, and she breathed deeply and pulled her gaze away from the kittens, hoping no one had seen her staring.

"Where is everyone?" she asked. The last time they'd been summoned before the Council, hundreds of Catmages had been in attendance.

"It is not a public meeting this time," Hakham said grimly. "And I fear it may not go well. Razor is not the only one worried about today. I've had some troubling messages from our friends on the Council. They tell me Kharoom has used this time to seek allies and strengthen his position."

Razor growled. "Just get me alone with him, Hakham. I'll have him seeing things your way in no time."

"While I greatly appreciate your loyalty, Razor, I cannot allow you to intimidate a fellow Council member," he said wryly. "Kindly control yourself in this meeting. We can't afford to alienate the other Councilors. Letsan, if you are asked to speak, you will treat Kharoom with the respect he deserves as a Council member."

"Hakham, you know he doesn't deserve a shred of respect!"

Hakham turned to stare at Letsan, ears drawn back, his voice cold. "Your issues with Kharoom do not concern me. You *will* treat him with respect. Are we clear on this, apprentice?"

Letsan blinked at Hakham and dropped his gaze. "Yes, Master."

"Good." Hakham started across the Compound. The others followed silently, the only sound their soft footfalls on the earth.

"Where is the meeting?" Goldeneyes asked, hoping to thaw the chill that had fallen on the conversation.

"In the woods by the broken tree. It is a good place to meet during the heat of the day."

"It would be better to meet at night during the summer heat," she pointed out.

"Zahavin, the time is set," he said sharply. "All of you, stop wasting my time with foolish chatter. Be silent and let me concentrate!"

"I have a very, very bad feeling about this," Letsan sent privately to Goldeneyes. "I've never seen Hakham so worried. He hasn't told us everything."

"No," she agreed, "he hasn't." They exchanged anxious looks. Razor stumped along, keeping his thoughts to himself. But his hackles were raised, and his tail switched from side to side.

"A *very* bad feeling," Letsan said.

They reached the broken tree shortly. Two Shomrim stood guard along the path. Others were scattered around the woods. Razor recognized Matanya, a big British shorthair, and Ufara, one of his favorite captains. He nodded at them as they passed. Kharoom, his mate Ruma, and several other Council members had arranged themselves along the tree trunk. Keres and Talma, two very heavy Catmages, sat on the ground below. The rest found places nearby. Hakham stopped below Kharoom. He leaped onto the tree into a small space between Kharoom and Tigra, forcing them to move aside to make room for him or be pushed off the trunk.

"Nice move," Razor said privately to his brother and Goldeneyes. "The old one has some life in him yet." He took his place near the Council. His warriors waited a respectful distance away. Goldeneyes and Letsan settled themselves on the ground not far from Hakham.

"Well, we are here," Hakham said. "Let's get on with it, Kharoom."

"Greetings to you, too, Hakham," Kharoom said smoothly. "Your manners, as always, are impeccable."

Hakham stared at Kharoom, who held his gaze, unblinking. "Let us get straight to the point, Kharoom. Why have you brought us here?"

"For the same reason we brought you here last cycle. We want you to stop training the human boy and destroy Nafshi's Magelight."

"You lost that vote," Hakham said. "The issue was settled."

Ruma spoke up in a sweet tone that didn't match her laid-back ears and twitching tail. "It is a different time, and these are different circumstances. A human has found the Tilyon. We fear that he might also steal Nafshi's Magelight from the boy. And so we would like to take another vote to see whether the Council agrees with us. You are free, of course, to make your case for the boy."

"Oh, you're giving me a chance to speak before you make your proclamation?" Hakham asked acidly.

"My dear Hakham, there's no need to be uncivil," she continued in the same tone. "You know we would never vote on an issue without the full Council present, as you taught us last summer." She and Kharoom exchanged glances.

Goldeneyes gazed at Letsan. "So that's what this was about," he said to her. "They've spent the past cycle convincing the other Council members to vote their way." His hackles rose.

Hakham could barely contain his anger. "Civility is not the issue, Ruma. The issue is defeating the Evil One!"

"That is an issue for another day. For now, the subject is whether or not to train the human," Kharoom said. "You will see, Hakham, that the Council shares my concerns."

Hakham surveyed the other Council members. Some of them looked quickly away as he glanced at them. Others looked nervous or angry.

"Yes, I see, Kharoom. I see very well what you have done in my absence." His tail swatted against the tree trunk. "Let us vote. All those who stand with Kharoom, stand with him on this tree," Hakham said, leaping to the ground. "And let all those who vote with me stand firmly on the earth." Adin and Benzi dropped to the ground. Dar looked at Hakham uncomfortably and stayed where he was. Sharonit gazed steadily at Dar for a long moment. Then she dropped to the ground with the others.

Letsan held back a snort of laughter as he watched Keres and Talma struggle to their feet and try to leap onto the tree trunk. After a few moments of watching them try, Hakham said, "That's enough. You two may sit next to the tree and be counted with Kharoom. And thank the One that you live in this Council Compound, where you are unlikely to face dangers you might have to flee quickly."

"You shame them, Hakham," Kharoom said.

"They shame themselves with their gluttony! Do you think we don't know that you no longer hunt your own food, but have servants bring it to you? Are you housecats, enslaved to a human master, waiting on their favor for handouts? Or are you Catmages, independent, powerful, with a history as old and grand as the Tilyon? Kharoom, you and Ruma are heading down the same path as Talma and Keres. There may come a time when you will need to be quick and light, and you will wish that you had not been so greedy."

Kharoom's hackles rose. Hakham glared steadily at him. The two faced each other silently, tails lashing.

"Hakham," Letsan interjected, "you are stealing my material and I'd like it back when you're finished. If Flathead starts hating you instead of me, what am I going to do for entertainment at the Council sessions?"

Kharoom shifted his angry gaze to Letsan as some of the others chuckled.

Hakham lowered his hackles. Letsan's comments had hit the mark and made him realize he was letting the younger Councilor get the better of him. He calmed himself and waited for Kharoom to settle down.

"You have no idea what you would do by forbidding us to teach the Son of Aaron," Hakham said. He looked at the Council members allied with Kharoom. "We must band together if we are to defeat the Darkness that is rising. I have spent the past two cycles fighting Wild Ones and the evil human that aids them. We are not winning! We have lost many good Catmages, and every Catmage is needed for this fight. I beg you, do not do this. Andrew Cohen has the aura of a Catmage. He wields Nafshi's Magelight with increasing skill. And he is the Son of Aaron, who will help us defeat the Evil One. Razelle foretold it! Will you weaken us now, when our strength is most needed? Will you go against the Council Prophet's last prophecy?"

Nobody spoke after Hakham finished. Few of the Council members even looked at him. Goldeneyes felt helpless. There was no crowd to sway this time, and no assistance from undecided Council members. It was obvious that Kharoom had planned this long ago. No wonder he wanted a private meeting. He needed to make sure that none of his new allies were influenced by popular opinion. They may be unable to meet his eyes, but Kharoom's allies were not swayed by Hakham's speech. It was obvious he did not command the votes he had last time.

Levana, Adin, Sharonit, and Benzi ranged themselves in a ring behind Hakham. Kharoom looked extremely pleased with himself. His group was clearly the greater of the two.

"We underestimated him," Goldeneyes said privately to Letsan. "This is a disaster."

"Worse," he muttered.

"The will of the Council is clear," Kharoom said. "You will stop teaching the human to use a Magelight. You will take Nafshi's Magelight from him and bring it to us so that we may destroy it. Then you will receive instructions from the Council on how to proceed against the human who has the Tilyon—if it even *is* the Tilyon. We have only your word for that."

Goldeneyes caught herself growling at the insults Kharoom heaped on her master. "You dare accuse Hakham of lying?" she shouted.

"Quiet, Zahavin," Hakham said. He looked from her to the Council. He held Kharoom's gaze until the other Catmage looked away. "My word used to be good enough for all of you," he said, looking angrily at the other Council members. "I am not mistaken. It *is* the Tilyon. We have felt its aura. Even from afar, it is unlike anything you have ever experienced. If you doubt me, come back with us and see for yourselves."

"We will stay here, Hakham. You will go back to the East Woods Compound to do as the Council commands," Kharoom said. "I want you back here before the next moon waxes and wanes."

Hakham laughed. "Are you now the leader of the Council, Kharoom? Did I miss that vote?"

"Not yet, but perhaps we should do that next," Kharoom said, his eyes flashing. "Times change, old one. New blood is needed."

The Catmages nearest him spoke out in agreement.

"Your time has come and gone, Hakham," Ruma said sweetly. "It is not your fault. You have lived a long, full life. I fear, though, that your age is affecting your judgment. It is time to let younger, stronger Catmages take the lead." She did not bother to stop her tail from switching.

Hakham stared at her. She met his gaze.

"I see," he said. "If you are not careful, Ruma, you and Kharoom will break this Council, not unlike the tree that lies fallen beneath your paws."

"There is no need for dramatics, Hakham," Kharoom said. "The Council is not broken. We have told you what we want. Go back to the East Woods and bring us Nafshi's Magelight."

"No."

CHAPTER FIVE

Kharoom took a step backward in disbelief. "No? *No?* You are defying the Council?"

"That is exactly what I am doing. I resign. I will not accept your authority any longer."

There was a shocked silence. Ruma leaned toward Kharoom, clearly speaking privately with him. His eyes narrowed. "If you will not do it, then Zahavin will retrieve the Magelight," he said.

Goldeneyes laid back her ears and shook her head. "I most assuredly will not. I stand with Hakham."

"Razor!" Kharoom shouted. "You will take your Shomrim and retrieve Nafshi's Magelight."

Razor rose from where he had been sitting. He stepped forward and looked from Kharoom and his allies to Hakham. He turned his back on Kharoom, closed the distance between himself and Hakham, turned to face the Council and sat.

"I'm with Hakham. You're an idiot. I quit."

Letsan laughed out loud. Kharoom glared at them all, his hackles raised and his tail whipping furiously.

"What? You're not going to assign me to the task, Flathead?" he asked. "Please? I do so much want the pleasure of saying no to you."

Levana, an all-white female Councilor, stepped forward. "If Hakham goes, I'm going too," she said.

"No, Levana. The Council is much the better with you on it," Hakham said aloud. "Even Kharoom acknowledged this when he voted for you."

"Now is not the time for foolish sacrifices," he sent privately. "I need eyes and ears on the Council."

She nodded curtly and stepped away from Hakham.

Ruma narrowed her eyes at the old tabby. She moved closer to her mate and rubbed her shoulder against his. "Calm yourself, my dear," she said privately. "Show them who is in command." Kharoom's tail stopped switching.

"You will learn that leadership is about more than having a title,

Kharoom," Hakham said. "Or servants," he said disdainfully. "Servants! No Council member in living memory has ever made use of servants as a privilege of office. You are too lazy to hunt for yourself, and too foolish to see the damage you are doing. Loyalty may be bought, but it will not last unless it is earned. It's not too late. Rescind your order about Andy and Nafshi's Magelight, and I will return to the Council. These are difficult times. All of us are needed. We must work together to defeat the enemy."

Kharoom's voice was cold. "You heard your instructions. You choose to resign. Very well, then, Hakham. You are no longer welcome at the Council Compound or anywhere else. You are banished. All of you are banished!" he shouted.

Hakham and the others laughed. Even some of the Council members on the tree joined in.

"Why are you laughing? Do you think banishment is amusing?"

"Letsan, would you like to do the honors?" Hakham asked.

"It will be my pleasure to teach my former teacher," Letsan said. "Kharoom, had you actually paid attention in the Teaching Rings, you would know that a Catmage may only be banished for breaking one of the Seven Laws. And that can be done only after a trial and conviction. You may be head of the Council, but even the great Kharoom must abide by our laws."

"As resigning from the Council and refusing Council orders do not constitute breaking the law, we will come and go as we please," Hakham said. "It happens that I no longer wish to be here. There are much more important events happening in the East Woods Compound. So once I and my companions are rested, we will leave this place."

"Then go! Get out!" Kharoom shouted.

Now it was Hakham's turn to be angry. His Magelight flared, and electricity crackled along every inch of his fur. "Kharoom," he said, his voice dripping with contempt, "you have spent the last cycle working against me, and by doing so you have been working against the interests of all Catmages. The Evil One has risen. He has murdered dozens of Catmages, including most of your predecessors on the Council. He has attained the Tilyon with the intent of turning it into a powerful weapon. I showed you all Razelle's prophecy at the first meeting of this reconstructed Council. She said we cannot succeed without the Son of Aaron, and Razelle was never wrong. If I didn't know how utterly incompetent you were, I would suspect you were working with our enemy. But alas, you are simply doing what you have always done—trying to gain renown without expending the effort to achieve it. As always, you have only managed to make yourself smaller."

There was a shocked silence. None of the Catmages present had ever seen Hakham so angry. All of the Council members but Ruma edged away from Kharoom. But Hakham glared only at Kharoom, his tail whipping angrily, his hackles raised. His mind-voice seemed to get even louder.

"Do not get in my way, Kharoom, or you will learn why I was chosen to be the head of this Council while you were still suckling at your mother's breast. I will tell you this only once."

Kharoom dropped his gaze, unable to bear Hakham in his unbridled fury. His tail was curled around him, its tip trembling. Ruma watched Hakham warily, ears twitching. After a long moment, Hakham's Magelight flickered out, his fur settled, and he turned his back and trotted quickly away down the path that led to the Compound. The others followed hastily, leaving Kharoom and his allies dumbfounded.

Goldeneyes and Letsan traded glances as they trotted after Hakham, afraid to speak until Hakham said something. He said no word until they reached his bayit. Razor settled himself to guard the door, but Hakham shook his head and told him to come inside. "Leave Katana and the others on guard."

"Now what?" Letsan asked.

"Now we return to the East Woods Compound. Levana and the other Councilors must be my eyes and ears on Kharoom and Ruma. I will need regular communications. We'll discuss details later." He sighed and sat down heavily. Goldeneyes noticed that Hakham seemed tired. The fur around his muzzle was getting whiter. Her master was showing his age.

"Now what?" Razor asked.

"There isn't much to be done here," Hakham said. "We rest, eat, and leave."

"We're going back to the East Woods?"

"You are. Letsan and Zahavin are going to accompany me on a visit to a friend."

"We are?" Letsan asked.

Hakham ignored him. "Razor, I don't have to tell you to be careful, do I? You've made an enemy today."

Razor laughed harshly. "I'm always careful, Hakham. Kharoom doesn't frighten me."

"Good. And if you pick up a few recruits for us on the way home, I'm sure it would drive Kharoom into another frenzy."

Razor grunted. "I'll see what I can do. Flatnose did steal a few of my best Shomrim for his own guard duty. I'm betting the ones who were around him the most will be the most likely to want to leave his presence." He laughed harshly. "Most of my warriors can't stand him." He rose to leave, bumping Letsan on the way out the door. "Take care of yourself, brother," he said. "I'll see you back at East Woods."

"Don't lose any more of your ears on the way home," Letsan said.

"And you watch that precious tail of yours."

Letsan laughed as Razor left the bayit, twitching his scarred and slashed ears as he went.

"And now?" Goldeneyes asked.

"Now, Zahavin, we rest through the heat of the day and leave this place tonight. We've a long way to go."

"Where are we going?" she asked.

"To see my teacher, Methuselah. I'm sure Nafshi told you many stories about him."

"He's still alive? But he was Nafshi's teacher. He's even older than—" she stopped, embarrassed.

"Older than I? Yes. He taught us both. Methuselah is the oldest living Catmage that I know of, and he has a store of knowledge that few other living Catmages can imagine. That is why we are going to seek him out. We have questions. He may have the answers."

Letsan sighed. "Another long journey. Andy was right. I've gotten fat and lazy."

"You'll get a chance to walk it off, I assure you," Hakham said, eyes twinkling.

"But not for another few hours." Letsan curled up on the ground and yawned. "By the One, I will never forget the look on Flatnose's face. Remind me never to make you that angry, Hakham."

"Never make me that angry, Letsan."

"You've been around Letsan too long," Goldeneyes said.

Hakham laughed and lay down near the wall. "Count yourself lucky that I don't spend much time with Patches."

SIX: METHUSELAH

A week after the disastrous Council meeting, Letsan and Goldeneyes sat in the shade of a tree on a quiet street, panting. Hakham stood on the sidewalk in front of a small cottage, head tilted, listening.

"Fat and lazy is right," Letsan muttered to Goldeneyes. "All this walking has made me wish that Catmages could ride bicycles like humans."

"Or cars," Goldeneyes said wearily.

Letsan laughed. "I would give my right ear to see you in a Catmage-sized car, riding around the neighborhood."

Hakham glanced back at them. "Come," he said sharply. They followed him onto the low porch in front of the door. They could hear voices inside.

"I thought we were going to see your master. You didn't say he lived with a human. Now *another* human knows of our existence?" Goldeneyes asked. "Just how long have you been violating the First Law?"

Hakham's eyes flashed as he turned to her.

"I neither owe you an explanation nor have time for one, Zahavin. Either be quiet and follow me, or go back to the East Woods Compound alone."

Goldeneyes stopped in mid-step at Hakham's response. She felt like an errant kitten in the Teaching Rings. She and Letsan glanced at each other in shock.

CHAPTER SIX

Hakham paid her no further attention. His Magelight glowed and the door latch clicked. He nudged the door open and slipped inside. Letsan and Goldeneyes followed him into the house, and Letsan used his Magelight to close the door behind them. They paused just beyond the door in a central hallway, marveling. Floor-to-ceiling bookshelves overflowing with books lined the foyer. They could see through the open doors on either side that the rooms were also filled with books. Books lay on chairs, on tables, on every spare surface they could see. As they followed Hakham through the house, the voices grew louder.

An old man with a grey beard and a fringe of grey hair around his head was standing opposite a long-haired mackerel tabby, whose back was to the door. The old man held a dark blue sweater out to the cat. His face was flushed. "Look at this! Look what you've done!" the man said, shaking the sweater.

"*I* didn't do anything," the Catmage said. "*You* sat down on the sofa."

"Of course I sat down on the sofa. It's my sofa! Why shouldn't I sit on it? It's for sitting, not shedding. *You* left your cat hair all over my sofa! Do you have to shed all over everything I own? You're a Catmage! Use your magic to do something useful, like cleaning up after yourself when you lie on my sofa!"

"If you had leather furniture, you wouldn't have to worry about cat hair."

"I don't want leather furniture. It makes my *tuchus* cold in the winter and sweaty in the summer. Why can't you be considerate for a change and pick up after yourself instead of leaving your fur all over my things!"

"Pick up after myself? I don't even see it until you point it out to me."

"That's because you're completely inconsiderate. I don't leave my hair all over your things."

"You don't have a whole lot of hair to leave. Except when you trim your beard, and it winds up all over the sink."

"Not *the* sink. *My* sink! Mine! You shed all over the house. *My* house. I'm retired, I should be enjoying life, not picking up after a Catmage who's too lazy to pick up after himself!"

"Well, I can't stop myself from shedding. I'm a cat, or haven't you noticed?"

"How convenient. *Now* you're a cat, but God forbid I should call you a cat instead of Catmage. The last time I did it was six weeks before you stopped whining about it."

"Six weeks? Ridiculous. I don't hold a grudge that long."

"Six weeks. I called you a cat on Thanksgiving Day and you barely spoke to me until after New Year's."

Hakham started laughing. The old man stopped arguing and turned his gaze toward the newcomers.

"Another Catmage? Who are you? Who let you in?" the man said irritably. He peered at Hakham. "Wait, I know you. Hakham, isn't it?"

"Hello, Harry," Hakham said. "I take it Methuselah forgot to tell you we were coming?"

Harry frowned. "Of course he did. Why should he tell me we were going to have visitors? It's not like I pay the bills around here. No, I'm just someone who puts out food and cleans up cat hair."

"Oh, dear, I did forget to tell you, Harry."

Harry snorted. "Wonderful. More Catmages to shed all over my things." He looked at Hakham and the others. "Who are these?"

"These are Letsan and Zahavin," Hakham said, indicating the orange tom and Goldeneyes in turn.

"Hello, Master Methuselah," Hakham said as the tabby turned to greet them.

"You—you're wearing glasses!" Letsan said.

Methuselah wore a small, gold-framed pince-nez across the bridge of his nose. He tilted his head and curled his tail over his back. "Well, don't *you* have a keen grasp of the obvious. One of your students, Hakham? I'm not very impressed with his deductive abilities."

"Hey!" Letsan said. "I didn't travel all the way from the Council Compound just to be insulted by an old Catmage. I could have stayed where I was and been insulted by my brother."

Methuselah chuckled. "Your brother, eh? And who might that be?"

"Razor."

"Ah. I've heard of him. A Catmage of few words. I like the ones that don't talk so much."

"Glasses are for humans. You're a Catmage," Goldeneyes said coldly.

"They help me see better," Methuselah said. He chuckled. "You remind me of your grandmother. Nafshi said the same thing the first time she saw me wearing these."

Her tone changed immediately. "You knew Nafshi?"

"Yes, and the first time she saw me with these she laughed and told me I looked like a cross between a Catmage and a raccoon, and that it flattered neither species."

They all laughed. Goldeneyes dropped her head and blinked at Methuselah. "I'm sorry I insulted you."

He chuckled. "Don't be. Your grandmother insulted me regularly, and she and I were the best of friends. We kept in touch until just near the end."

"You saw her before she died? When?" Goldeneyes asked eagerly.

"I saw her a few months before she was kidnapped by the Evil One," Methuselah said gently. "I was very sorry to hear of her passing." He paused, his tail twitching slightly. "I will be happy to talk to you about her another time. But I think there are other things to discuss now. Why are you so late, Hakham? I expected you weeks ago."

Harry cleared his throat. "No, it's all right, don't mind me. I'll just stand here like a dummy while you all conduct your business and ignore me. I live to watch my retirement checks support Methuselah and his fur-shedding friends."

"Oh, pshaw. Your mortgage was paid off ages ago, I require far less heat than you, and what I cost in upkeep I more than make up for in companionship and razor-sharp wit," Methuselah replied.

The others laughed again, and even Harry joined in.

"Thank you for your hospitality, Harry," Hakham said. "It is good to see you again. It isn't just Methuselah I'm here to see. We need wisdom from both of you. But first, if you don't mind—we've traveled a long way and could do with a rest. And a meal, if you would be so kind."

"Hear, hear!" Letsan said.

"All right," Harry said. He led them into the kitchen, which held a small table with two chairs, a water and food dish for Methuselah, and still more overflowing bookshelves.

"Why do you have so many books?" Letsan asked.

"Because I'm a librarian," Harry said. "Didn't Hakham ever tell you about me?"

"No. We didn't even know Methuselah was still alive. You must be—"

"Forty-one in the fall," Methuselah said. "I'm so old most Catmages can't even count that high."

"You can count like a human?" Goldeneyes asked.

"Well, I'm not like other Catmages, my dear. Eighteen is as high as any of the best of them can count, but that's only because it's the number of claws on our paws."

"That's an interesting number," Harry pointed out. "You know, eighteen in Hebrew numerology is *chai,* the number for life. I never really thought of how it related to cats before."

"I can count," Goldeneyes said, sounding offended. "Andy's been teaching me."

"Ah, but there's more to me than simple mathematics, my dear," Methuselah said. "I'm the Catmage librarian. I'm the *Safran.*"

"The *what*?" she said incredulously.

Harry chuckled as he bustled around getting plates and canned tuna for his visitors. "That's why I got him the glasses. He's so old he needs them for reading."

"You can *read*?" Goldeneyes asked in the same tone.

Methuselah looked amused. "This is one of your best students, Hakham? She's not very quick on the uptake, is she? What about you, Letsan? Catmage got your tongue?"

"I—I don't know what to say, sir," Letsan replied. "I've never met a Catmage who could read."

"I've told neither of them," Hakham said. "At first there was no need, and then there was no time. You don't come up in general conversation, Master."

Methuselah chuckled. "Ah. Well, then let me give you the short explanation," he said. "The advent of the age of literacy in humans made Catmages realize they had a serious shortcoming when it came to passing along information. We can't write. And let's be honest: Without opposable thumbs, we'll never be able to. Oral histories are simply not the best way to pass information to successive generations. No matter how hard you try, information will go missing. A case in point: we lost the Tilyon."

"It's not lost anymore, sir. It's been found," Letsan interjected.

"*What*? The Tilyon has been found? This is wonderful news! This is amazing! Where is it? May I see it? Have you seen it? Is it truly as powerful as the old stories say?"

"We don't have it," Letsan said glumly. "Saunders got to it first."

"What? This is terrible! The man who murdered Nafshi now has the Tilyon?"

"That's partly why we're here, Methuselah," Hakham said. "I'll give you the full story later, but do go on."

Methuselah twitched his ears and continued.

"It's like this—if a scholar dies without passing on his knowledge, that knowledge dies with him. Who knows what spells we lost during the thousands of cycles that have passed since the First's powers awoke? Our ancestors finally got tired of losing knowledge. They decided to find a human who could help us write down our histories so we'd never again lose important knowledge." He paused to straighten the pince-nez with his paw. "It was probably the most difficult thing we had to do since the First learned how to wield the Tilyon and pass along what she knew to her children. Those who proposed we join with humans had to spend many years convincing the Head Council of the day that it was worth violating the Secrecy Law. But we had other problems. The search took place during the time when many Catmages were murdered by humans who thought we were witches' familiars."

"Well, they weren't far off," Harry said. "You do have magical powers."

"Yes, but we weren't using them to harm humans!" He glared at Harry. "The first Safran found a wise man, a religious scholar, Reb Zalman, who was already steeped in the Oral Law of the Jews, the descendants of the Hebrews. It was Reb Zalman who helped the Safran organize our histories and commentaries. He was most intrigued by the Seven Laws and their similarity to the Ten Commandments. It is told that he and the first Safran would spend many hours discussing the resemblance of—"

"Forgive me, master, but we don't have time for a lesson," Hakham said. "You can tell us the tales of the Rebbe and the first Safran some other day."

Letsan shot Hakham a look. "It seems there is much you haven't told us, Hakham."

"I have led a long life," Hakham said stiffly, "and at no point have I ever felt obligated to explain myself to you."

Letsan blinked and quieted.

"Oh, yes. My apologies, Hakham," Methuselah said. "Well, to get to the point, ever since we have found humans in each succeeding generation who are willing to help us set down and pass on our history. Harry is the most recent of our human librarians, and a very good one he is, too."

Harry beamed at Methuselah's praise.

"Obviously, humans are longer-lived than we, so sometimes a librarian will work with two or more Catmages, depending on his age when he is chosen. In fact, now that I think of it, it's probably time that both of us started looking for our replacements. We're not getting any younger."

"Is that why we're here, Hakham?" Letsan asked. "Surely you're not thinking of asking Zahavin or me to become the next Safran!"

"No. We are here because the Evil One has the most powerful weapon known to Catmages. We must utilize every resource we have in this battle."

"And what if Methuselah has no information that will help us?" Goldeneyes said.

"Then we still will not have come here in vain."

"About that food," Letsan said, interrupting Hakham's train of thought. "I can't think on an empty stomach. Are you just going to stand there with your hands full of delicious-smelling fish?"

Harry smiled and put the dishes down for the guests.

"Let us eat quickly and then retire to the study," Methuselah said. "We've a lot of work to do." He looked up at his friend and blinked. "Thank you, Harry. You have always been there for us when we need you, and we appreciate it. You're a good man." He stepped over to Harry and rubbed against his leg.

Harry sighed as he saw cat hair sticking to his pants. "Cat hair," he muttered, "always with the cat hair!" Grumbling, he brushed off his pants and went to the refrigerator to get himself something to eat. A few minutes later, Harry was finishing his tea and sandwich while the Catmages cleaned themselves. He pushed back his chair, rose, and put his plate in the sink.

"I think I know where we might find an early mention of the Tily-on's powers," he said, walking down the hall. The Catmages followed.

Hours later, open books lay scattered all over the floor, the sofa, and Harry's desk. "This is useless," Harry said, shaking his head at the book he was holding. "This is the fourth retelling of the same story, all of them reporting unhappily that the Tilyon was lost to Catmages, and none of them saying anything about its powers!"

"I think we expect too much of our sources," Methuselah said. He sat next to a yellowed, hand-written leather-bound volume, yawning as he looked down at the pages. "Don't forget that many centuries had passed between the time the First received her powers and the time our ancestors decided to write down our history."

"How many years, exactly?" Letsan asked.

"It's difficult to say, since we don't know the exact time of the Exodus," Harry said. "It's much easier to say how long there have been Safrans."

"How long?"

Harry shrugged. "A few hundred years. Sometime during the seventeenth century, your ancestors sought out a human to help them record their history."

"I don't know how long a hundred is," Letsan said.

"A hundred cycles of the sun is about four or five Catmage lifetimes."

"Do you know anything at all about the Tilyon besides what we all learned in our Teaching Rings?" Goldeneyes asked.

Harry shrugged. "Not really. Methuselah and I have rarely discussed the Tilyon, other than as part of the origin of Catmages."

"Then why are we here, Hakham?" she asked wearily. "Have we come all this way for nothing?"

"No," he said, "this journey was never a waste of time. There is more here for us than just books." He looked meaningfully at Methuselah.

"Oh, Hakham, must I? But I'm so very, very old," Methuselah said, "and so comfortable here."

"We need you. There are only a few of us, one fewer now that Nafshi is gone. The Darkness rises. It is your duty, Master."

Methuselah sighed. "But the East Woods is such a long way away."

"You're leaving?" Harry said. "Why?"

"Harry," Hakham said, "Methuselah is a Magus. He is one of the most powerful Catmages alive. These are dangerous times. We need his power and his wisdom if we are to defeat the Evil One."

Goldeneyes and Letsan exchanged shocked looks. No wonder Hakham wanted Methuselah to come back with them. A Magus was that incredibly rare Catmage who had reached the pinnacle of his or her powers. The Magi were also members of Avdei Ha-Or, the secret organization of Catmages who embedded their Magelights next to the great artery in their necks. Nafshi and Hakham were the only Magi that she knew of, and Letsan the only other member of Avdei Ha-Or. She had seen both her grandmother and her mentor channel extremely strong magic. Now the long journey here made sense, even if they discovered nothing about the Tilyon—if Methuselah was as powerful as Nafshi or Hakham.

Methuselah looked from Harry to Hakham, blinking.

"I have to go, Harry."

"Well, if you have to go, you have to go," Harry said. He started picking up books, closing them, putting them into piles on his desk. "It's probably for the best. I'll have a little more free time, and I'll be able to get the cat hair off the furniture." Mumbling, he picked up a pile of books and went into the next room.

"He's going to be lonely," Methuselah said. "We've been together for a very long time."

"I'll get my granddaughter to come stay with me!" Harry called from the other room. "I managed to live an entire life before I met you. I'll survive a few weeks while you're gone."

"It may be more than a few weeks, Harry," Hakham said.

Harry came back in the room, the books still in his arms. "So, it'll be a few months, then. All right. I'll get to work on cataloging those really old books that we've been putting off. When are you leaving?"

"In the morning."

"So. Where are you going?"

"To the woods outside of a town called Coreyton."

"Coreyton! That's hours from here by car. It will take you weeks to get there! I won't have it. You're too old to walk that far, Methuselah. I'll drive you."

"Harry, I'm liking you more and more every minute," Letsan said. "I'd show you how much, but I don't want to get any more cat hair on you."

METHUSELAH

"You see?" Harry said. "There's a *polite* Catmage—one who thinks of others besides himself," he said, frowning down at Methuselah.

"It would be much nicer than walking," Goldeneyes admitted.

"Thank you, Harry, we appreciate the offer," Hakham said. "If you don't mind, we need to leave in the morning."

"Fine, fine, tomorrow morning it is. Anything else? Breakfast in bed, maybe?"

Letsan laughed, yawning. "Just bed, thanks. Mind if we use the sofa?"

"Why not? You can't get any more cat hair on it. It's already covered!" Grumbling, he put the books down on a nearby table and went through the house, turning off lights behind him as he went to bed. Methuselah gazed after him.

"He's not fooling me," he said softly. "Harry is going to miss me just as much as I'm going to miss him. This is not an open-ended offer. I won't leave Harry alone forever."

"We won't ask you to, Master. But we need your wisdom and your powers to recover the Tilyon."

"Well, we'd better get it back, then. You three make yourselves comfortable here. I'm going to stay with Harry tonight."

He walked softly down the hall. They heard the bed creak as he joined Harry, and soft murmuring coming from their room.

"Another Magus," Letsan said quietly. "That makes two for our side. The Wild Ones have none."

"No. But they have the Tilyon."

"But they can't use it properly. Saunders has no aura."

"We'll get it back," Goldeneyes said as she settled herself for sleep. "With another Magus on our team, how can we fail?"

Letsan leaped onto the sofa and lay down next to her, their flanks touching. They were asleep before Hakham could join them.

Hakham was already awake when Goldeneyes woke, yawned, and stretched.

65

CHAPTER SIX

Sunlight streamed through the east-facing window, and birds were chirping outside.

Letsan stretched and leaped to the windowsill, where he watched the birds flit from branch to branch. "If Harry doesn't want to offer us breakfast, I'm going to catch my own," he said, yawning. "They look fat and tasty."

"No need to trouble the local bird nests, young one," Methuselah said as he padded into the room. "Harry is fixing us breakfast now."

"Good," Letsan said, jumping to the floor. "I'm definitely ready to go home."

Half an hour later, they watched while Harry locked his cottage. He opened the car doors and waited for them to get inside. Methuselah and Hakham sat together on the front passenger seat.

"Try not to shed too much during the drive," Harry said, closing the rear door. "And don't tear the seats!"

"We'll do our best, sir," Letsan said from the back seat, turning his head away and trying not to laugh.

He and Goldeneyes spent much of the ride standing on their hind legs with their paws on the base of the window, watching the scenery. Harry was a slow, careful driver who didn't mind answering their questions about the towns they passed and the things they saw outside their window. Methuselah and Hakham said little. Goldeneyes suspected they were having a long private conversation about the events of the past year.

"We are indeed, and you need to rein in that projection, Zahavin," Methuselah sent privately. "You can't afford to get careless. I think you and I are going to have some private lessons. Yes, I would very much like to see how much Nafshi has taught you."

Goldeneyes looked toward the front seat. "I would be honored, sir."

They reached the East Woods around lunchtime. Harry parked his car on the shoulder of the road. He stopped the engine and got out, opening the back door.

"Well, here you are," he said. "I'd offer to come with you, but it's lunchtime and I don't particularly care for eating mice and birds."

Letsan laughed as he exited the car. "You don't know what you're missing. Mice are pretty tasty!"

"I'll pass," Harry said sourly. "Well, Methuselah. This is it."

"Yes." Methuselah looked up at Harry, then he wound around Harry's legs, purring. "I'll miss you, old friend. You take care of yourself!"

"I'll miss you, too," Harry said, leaning down to scratch Methuselah's ears.

"Letsan! Goldeneyes!"

They turned at the sound of their names. It was Andy, riding down the road toward them.

"Andy!" Letsan called, running to meet him. Andy pulled up short and Letsan leaped into the basket, where he perched on his hind legs to rub his face against Andy's while Andy stroked him.

"Who's that?" Harry asked.

"Andrew Cohen, the boy in Razelle's prophecy we told you about last night. He bears Nafshi's Magelight. Look to his wrist."

"He has a Magelight?" Harry asked.

"Yes," Methuselah said. He closed his eyes. "Nafshi's aura is still strong within it."

"You can sense an aura without casting a spell?" Goldeneyes asked. "I thought that was something you were born with, like a Seeker."

"Mostly it is, but it can be taught. I can show you if you like."

"I would like that very much, Master Methuselah."

Andy reached them, looking curiously at the old man and the long-haired tabby.

"Uh, hi. I'm Andy Cohen." He held his hand out to Harry, who shook it.

"Harry Mendelson. And this is—"

"Methuselah. Yeah, I know."

Methuselah looked sharply at Andy. "You know? How on earth

could you know me when we've never met?"

"We haven't?" Andy said, kneeling down to scratch a purring Goldeneyes behind the ears. "But I know your name. And what you look like. I remember you from somewhere. Are you sure we haven't met?" He smiled at Goldeneyes. "I missed you."

"We missed you too, Andy," Goldeneyes said.

Hakham and Methuselah shared a puzzled look.

"Later," Hakham sent to him privately.

"Are you staying?" Andy asked Harry. "Are you coming to the Compound? The path is kind of tricky, do you need me to help you?"

"No, I'm too old to be wandering through the woods," Harry said. "I'm going to find someplace to have lunch and then head back home. I'm only here to save this old Catmage a ninety-mile trip."

"Which way are you going?"

"North."

"Try the Coreyton Diner about ten minutes down the road. Good food, decent prices."

"Any chance you can come with me and keep me company?"

Andy shook his head. "I wish. I have lessons. Zehira gets really mad when I'm late. But thanks for the offer."

"Time to go, Methuselah," Hakham said. "We'll meet you at the entrance in the woods. Andy, follow us, please." He led the rest of them to the hedge where Andy hid his bike.

Andy looked toward the road and saw Harry pick up Methuselah.

"If that isn't a hug, I'll eat my tail," Letsan said.

"He's a big softy," Hakham said.

"Which one?"

"Oh, go on ahead," Hakham said. "Methuselah and I will meet you at my bayit. Andy, you'd best run along to your lesson."

Hakham watched the others go, then waited until Methuselah joined him. They stayed where they were until they saw Harry get into his car and drive away. Methuselah sighed.

"Don't worry, you'll see him again," Hakham told him.

"I'd better." Methuselah watched until the car drove out of sight. "How could the boy know my name?"

"I don't know. We've never mentioned you to him. Perhaps Nafshi told him about you? They spent a good deal of time together when they were trapped in the Evil One's house."

Methuselah gave a little grunt. "Maybe. Something tells me that we need to keep an eye on that boy."

Hakham laughed. "That's all we've done for the past few cycles. Zahavin and Letsan practically live with him. And when they're busy, he comes here for lessons."

"Is that why you want me here? To teach the boy?"

"No. I'd like you to work with some of our more promising Cat-mages. There are a few worthy candidates. Some of them may even have Magus capabilities."

"Zahavin for one, I assume?"

"Yes. She's nearly ready for Avdei Ha-Or. And there is one other of Nafshi's line that you should see, a great-granddaughter. There are a few more who would benefit from your tutelage."

"I'll need to examine them all."

"Of course."

"Then let's get started. I'm hungry again."

"I hope you haven't forgotten how to catch your own meals," Hakham said, eyes twinkling. "We don't have humans around to feed us three or four times a day. But if you can't, I'm sure we'll find some young ones that will be happy to catch something for you."

"Hmph. I'm not so old that I can't still beat you to that dead oak tree," Methuselah said, racing off as he spoke. Hakham chased after him and soon caught up. They reached the oak at the same time and pulled up breathlessly, laughing. Then the two old Catmages trotted down the path together.

SEVEN: MATTI

Two days after Hakham and Razor left the Council meeting in chaos, the Catmages of the Council Compound gathered on the main
meadow. Kharoom had tried to suppress the news, but the word that
Hakham and Razor had resigned in fury raced around the Compound.
Even the kittens in their first Teaching Rings knew about it. The residents
learned, however, not to discuss it in front of Kharoom and his allies. Catmages spoke in hushed voices of Hakham's fury and Razor's rejection of
Kharoom's demands. There was a fair amount of unhappiness. Razor may
not have been overly friendly, but he was trusted and popular. Word had
it that the Council would be presenting both a new member and a new
captain of the Shomrim. The gathering filled up quickly.

The early morning sun threw long shadows across the grass. Matanya stood in front of the Council at the edge of the field, arranged in their
traditional semicircle. His lieutenant, Ufara, stood behind him with a team
of Shomrim. She was a tough calico who had been with Matti for many
seasons. He glanced at his honor guard. Some of his favorites were missing.
Razor had recruited a few of the best Council Shomrim before he left, to
Matti's disappointment. Well, he could always have his Seekers bring back
some good candidates from other Compounds. He made a mental note to
speak to Ufara about that.

MATTI

He glanced over at the new Council member chosen to replace Hakham. Yeshana, an ancient calico cat, sat at the far end of the semicircle. One rumor had it she was related to Kharoom and was only chosen because she would be loyal to him. Another said she was too old to really know what was going on, and would vote as Kharoom directed. Matti didn't care if the rumors were true or not. What mattered to him was knowing how she could help him with his goals. One of those goals was about to be realized. He was not only present to guard the thirteen Council members, he was about to be invested as the new Captain of the Shomrim. The big British shorthair's chest swelled with pride. Until this summer, he didn't think he had a butterfly's chance in a bayit full of kittens of seeing Razor leave the guard. He liked and respected Razor, but the grizzled warrior never could learn to get along with those in power. If it had been Matti who was chosen to retrieve Nafshi's Magelight ... well, an order was an order. And speaking of order, it looked like Kharoom was finally ready to begin. He raised himself to his feet and padded a few steps to the front of the semicircle, the leader's position that most had only seen Hakham in. Matti glanced quickly at the crowd and saw more than a few Catmages shift uncomfortably. Kharoom was oblivious. He had finally gotten what he wanted, and it was obvious he was having the time of his life.

"Thank you all for coming," Kharoom said to the crowd. "We would like to welcome Yeshana, our newest Council Member, who takes Hakham's recently vacated seat on the Council." Silence greeted that announcement. Yeshana was unfamiliar to many members of the Compound. Hakham had been a fixture on the Council since before most of the resident Catmages were born, and was friendly and approachable. Yeshana was taciturn and solitary. Few approved of the change.

"I would also like to make an announcement. Following Hakham's resignation, the Council has elected a new head. They have asked me to lead us through these dark times."

There was a low murmur at this.

"Do not be afraid!" Kharoom said. "Yes, these are troubled times.

71

But now the Council speaks with one voice. And with the wisdom of the other Councilors"—he glanced at Ruma—"and the help of our loyal Shomrim, we will come together and defeat the enemy who has risen to challenge us!"

The crowd cheered politely.

"There is another reason we are gathered today. As you know, Razor has been dismissed for insubordination. Today, I'm happy to announce that we will invest Matanya in his stead. Everyone welcome the newest Captain of the Shomrim."

The cheering was louder this time, led by the members of the guard. But not everyone joined in. Heads turned in the crowd. Kharoom's words contrasted with the story that had gone around. Several of the Council members glanced at Kharoom. Matti held himself still, knowing full well that Razor had resigned and Kharoom was lying to the assembly. But he knew better than to contradict a superior, especially in a public gathering such as this. Matti was surprised to see Yeshana shoot Kharoom a look, though. Perhaps she was neither as senile nor as firmly in Kharoom's camp as he thought.

Kharoom went on when the cheering stopped.

"The Council unanimously approved Matanya as the new captain. He has served well and faithfully since he was barely out of the Teaching Rings. It is with great pleasure that we place the safety of this Council and our Compound in his hands."

There was another pause as the crowd cheered. Matti was popular and, unlike Razor, sociable. He faced the crowd and stood at attention, waiting for the cheers to die down. Feeling the eyes of all thirteen Council members upon him, he proudly raised his head.

Kharoom spoke over the noise. "We know that Matanya will be a great leader. Captain, the Shomrim are yours."

Now Matti was surrounded by his warriors, who crowded in trying to bump shoulders or heads or lash him with their tails. A chant began, picked up by the crowd.

MATTI

"Matti! Matti! Matti!"

"I thank you all, Councilors, for this great honor. I serve with pleasure, and will defend our people to the death!"

The crowd roared again. When the sound died down, Kharoom spoke.

"As our business is concluded, this meeting is adjourned. Captain Matanya, please escort my mate and me to our quarters."

The assembled Catmages left the meadow in small groups, chattering contentedly, their fears at losing Razor soothed by his replacement by Matti.

Matti signaled Ufara closer. "Take the Shomrim to the practice field. I'll be there when I can."

"Yes sir," she said. "And Matti—congratulations." She flicked her tail at him as she passed, making Matti wonder if she was going into heat. That was something he'd enjoy looking into later. But for now, he had official business and couldn't just please himself.

He marched smartly in front of Kharoom and Ruma as they made their way to their bayit, the crowd parting for them. Matti noticed that none of the other Catmages ventured to talk to either of them. That was another change Kharoom had encouraged. The Council Catmages were used to Council members who made themselves available to all and sundry. Hakham would stop and chat with the least little kitten who approached him. Kharoom was more distant, more prone to enjoying what he called the perks of the office. Where Hakham had called himself a servant of the Catmages, Kharoom strove to show that he was their leader. But how Kharoom conducted his business was not important unless it concerned Matti and his Shomrim. It was not his job to tell the Council how to lead.

When they reached Kharoom's home, Matti stopped and waited politely by the entrance.

"Come inside, Matanya," Kharoom said. "I know you've only just been appointed captain, but we have a task for you. We want you to go to the East Woods Compound."

"I thought Razor was going back to East Woods, sir."

"No doubt he is. But that Compound is still under our rules and laws. You will take command from Razor. If he wants to be an outcast, let him. But he will not take some of our best warriors with him."

"He already did, sir. I gave you their names yesterday."

Kharoom gazed at Matti unhappily.

"Then you will retrieve them. Their job is not to do Razor's bidding. Their job is to serve the Council!"

"Yes sir, but—but what about the Evil One? The Wild Ones? What about retrieving the Magelights and the Tilyon? I thought you might like to hear some of the plans I've been considering. I don't understand—"

"It is not your job to understand, Captain," Ruma said with a baleful stare. "Your job is to protect your fellow Catmages and serve the wishes of the Council."

"Now, now, dear, there's no need to get upset. Matanya has the right to ask questions that concern the actions of his Shomrim."

Ruma glanced at her mate. "Of course. Please continue."

"We are working on other ways to defeat the Wild Ones, Matanya. We are not yet ready to share our plans with you. Rest assured, we shall take care of getting the Council Magelights and the Tilyon back as well. But for now, we wish you to go to the East Woods and put their Shomrim in order."

"Yes, Kharoom," Matti said, blinking at the two of them. "When shall I leave?"

"Immediately."

Matti hesitated.

"Do you have any further questions?" Kharoom said sharply.

Plenty, Matti thought. But he said aloud, "No, sir. I'll stay the remainder of the day to instruct my Shomrim, and I'll start for the East Woods first thing in the morning. I'll leave Ufara here to guard the Council."

"That will do."

MATTI

Ruma settled down next to Kharoom and purred softly. "We will send you further instructions by the full moon. We expect to hear of the great progress you've made by then."

"I shall await your orders," Matti said.

"Good. And may the One Above Us All bless your journey."

Matti blinked once more and took his leave. He regretted having to leave so soon. His warriors had spent many moons getting ready, and now he had to leave most of them behind. He'd expected to stay in the Council Compound for quite some time, building up new relationships with the Council and his Shomrim. He wanted to present his ideas to retrieve the Magelights and Tilyon to the Council, but later, after he'd had time to discuss them with his captains. Going to the East Woods so soon, and without giving his input, was unexpected. Oh well, it would give him a chance to prove himself. Razor wasn't going to like this. Neither would Hakham, he was sure. But orders were orders, and rules were rules. One way or another, Matti would get what he wanted. He usually did.

The rest of his guard was on the practice field in ordered groups, each squad leader running their team through drills. Matti kept his warriors in top form, and made sure not to neglect physical combat training. Catmages almost never fought one another with tooth and claw, but you could never tell when a strange dumbcat or dog would wander into your territory and jump you. The rest of his training routine involved mandatory daily Magelight drills. These were dangerous times, and he'd not see the Council suffer a repeat attack like the one that destroyed Kharoom's predecessors. There were also the matters of the stolen Magelights and the Wild Ones.

Matti observed the squads quietly from the edge of the trees for a while. It was a good way to watch them perform without the pressure of knowing their war leader was watching. He made a few mental notes, then strode into the middle of the field, calling the Shomrim to attention. They assembled in ranks quickly, squad leaders in the front row. Ufara took her place next to Matti.

He informed them of his new orders and noted with pride that not a single one of his warriors gave any indication that they were surprised by the news. Soldiers, every one of them, he thought.

"Some of you will come with me to the East Woods," he told them. "We must be prepared for anything. Ufara will be in charge while I'm gone. I know she'll do a fine job until I return." He glanced sideways at his lieutenant, who stood proud and still, as his second-in-command should.

"I'll want the squad leaders at my bayit after practice. They'll inform those of you who will be traveling with me. The rest of you will continue to do your job. We will protect the Council!"

"We will protect the Council!" they echoed.

"Ufara, with me." He turned and strode back the way he had come, Ufara falling in behind. When they reached his bayit, they settled themselves comfortably.

"Well, that was unexpected," Ufara said. "I thought you'd have moons to get used to being the new captain of the Shomrim."

"So did I. Instead, I get to tell Razor things he's not going to want to hear."

They laughed. "I don't envy you," Ufara said. "Do you think he'll go for your ear or just give you a nice scar across your face?"

"He can try," Matti said, rising to his hind legs and hitting out with his front paws. "I think I can take him. But we both know he won't fight me. At least, not physically."

"Good," she said warmly. "I like your face just the way it is."

Matti strode over and licked her ear. "So, when do you go into heat again?"

"Not any time soon. I want to stay in the Shomrim, not take time off to have another litter."

"Really? Because I'm pretty sure I can talk you out of that."

She groaned. "Oh, Matti, not again."

"I think there's something wrong with my eyes, because I can't take them off you."

MATTI

Ufara reached out to slap him with her paw. He ducked out of the way. "I thought we'd gotten past that," she said.

"Never."

She slapped the ground with her paw. "Sit." He sat. "Captain Matanya, we need to discuss what you want me to do with the Shomrim while you're gone."

He sighed. "So, you're going to be that way? All right, Ufara. I'll want you to implement some of the things I'd planned to do myself, but now that I'll be gone—"

"Just tell me what you want, sir. The Shomrim will be ready on your return."

"Good. Here's what I had planned for the next few moons."

The next morning, Matti was on the road with a dozen of his best warriors. Half of them were the second in command to his squad leaders. This mission would be a great opportunity to judge how ready they were to lead squads of their own. Matti glanced behind. His Shomrim ranged in a loose arc within a few feet of each other, slipping in and out of the shadows as they marched in the smooth lope that would bring them to the East Woods in the rising and setting of a few suns. None of them had ever been there before. Matti wondered who else he would find at the Compound besides Razor and his missing Shomrim. He knew Razor had been recruiting for several cycles now.

Matti looked to his left at the only non-Shomrim traveling with them—Velvel. When Matti had reported to Kharoom and Ruma to take his leave, Kharoom had ordered him to take the Seeker with them since they were all going to the same place. "And this way there's no chance you'll get lost," Kharoom added, only half-joking. The words still rankled. Was he the head of the Shomrim, or was he a kitten fresh out of his first Ring? Matti guarded his thoughts carefully. It wouldn't do to let Velvel know how unhappy he was both with the order and with his company. At least Velvel wasn't a chatty companion. They bent to the trail, saying little.

The company rested during the heat of the day, hidden in a copse near the human road they would walk beside to the East Woods Compound. Matti's soldiers took turns keeping watch. Velvel offered to take one, but Matti politely declined. "My Shomrim are used to guard duty," he said. "It's our job."

"Suit yourself," Velvel responded, yawning. He curled up and went to sleep. Matti chose to stay awake for the first watch, eyes and ears open for the sound of human or animal. They heard and saw nothing worse than birds and squirrels.

The next two days of travel were much the same. The most dangerous animal they met was a fox, who watched them carefully but fled when Atzel sent a Magelight arrow into the dirt between its paws.

In the late afternoon of the fourth day, Velvel announced they would arrive at the East Woods shortly. Matti stopped his squad and gave them a quick look-over before allowing them to go on.

"We want to be at our best for this," he said. "I want to make a good impression on Hakham and the elders of the Compound."

"Not to mention Razor," Atzel said.

Matti laughed. "Well, we won't be getting any compliments from him no matter what we look like, especially when he learns why we're here."

"He's a soldier first and last, sir. He'll do what's right."

"I'm sure he will," Matti said with a confidence he didn't feel.

A short time later, Velvel led them to the winding path that would bring them to the Compound. A pair of grey tabbies rose from the ground and blocked the path.

"We recognize you, Velvel, but who have you brought with you?" the larger one asked. "Why didn't you send us a message you were bringing more warriors?"

"You received no message because none was needed," Matti said brusquely. "I am Matanya, your new captain of the Shomrim. The Council sent me to get this Compound in order. These are the warriors I chose to aid me in that task. Instead of questioning your superior officer, you will stand aside and let us through."

The tabbies looked at each other and moved aside.

"I'll expect reports from every guard shift," Matti said. "You'll be informed of the new schedule as soon as I've gotten the feel of this Compound."

"What about Razor?" the smaller tabby asked. "We're supposed to report to him."

"What are your names?"

"Teriya. This is my sister, Timura."

"Well, Teriya, Razor is no longer head of the Shomrim. I am. You will report to *me* now. Is that understood?"

The tabbies glanced at one another again. "Yes sir," Teriya said.

"Then get back to your guard duty," Matti said, brushing past them. Velvel hurried to catch up to Matti. The warriors followed them down the winding path that led to the Compound. They reached the meadow and saw the Teaching Rings breaking up and students leaving, some walking sedately, some leaping around like the kittens they were.

"It looks like we've come at a good time," Matti said. "Atzel, bring the squad to attention."

"Yes, sir!" Atzel said, signaling to the other warriors. At his command, they broke into a trot and headed for the center of the field, where they quickly moved into formation, waiting silently for their commander. The students who had been wandering away from the field stopped to watch the newcomers. Matti waited until he was sure he had the crowd's attention, then sent a silent signal. The Shomrim fired a series of light daggers straight up in the air, where they burst into small needles of colored lights, falling harmlessly back to earth. The buzz from the Catmages watching the show pleased Matti. The crowd parted and, as Matti expected, Razor headed his way.

"How sweet. Your Shomrim can fire off colored sparkles," Razor said. The big Maine Coon was flanked by Hakham and Letsan. A number of Razor's warriors ranged themselves behind. "I'm sure they'll terrify the

Wild Ones in our next battle. Or were you going to use the lights to distract them and attack while they're still oohing and ahhing?"

"I'm sensing a touch of hostility, Razor," Matti said cheerfully. "Get up on the wrong side of the bayit this morning?"

"That's not hostility," Letsan said. "It's his normal tone." He ducked as Razor lashed his tail at him.

"Welcome, Matanya," Hakham said. "To what do we owe the pleasure?"

"Council business. They sent me to take over the Shomrim in this Compound."

"That's going to be a problem," Razor said, "because these are my Shomrim now." He moved forward until he was only a few inches away from Matti. Matti held his ground and sent a silent command to his warriors to keep them still. He met Razor's glance and held it.

"The Council has the right to determine the head of the Shomrim."

"Of the Council Shomrim, yes," Hakham said. "But our Compounds have always been independent. They have no jurisdiction here."

"I've been commanded by Kharoom—"

Razor laughed harshly. "Say no more, Matti. That fool no longer has power to command anything of me."

"Nevertheless, I was given an order to come here and take control of the Shomrim."

Razor studied Matti carefully. "We can always use more fighters. You're welcome to stay. But you won't be taking my warriors." He laid his ears flat back on his head and raised his hackles. Matti braced himself for a fight.

"Just a moment, Razor," Hakham said. He stepped between the two, forcing them to back away from one another. "Matanya, we have our own Council of Elders here. I will convene it and you can make your case. But I warn you, I don't think you'll win."

"Why not?"

"Because I am the head of the Elders, and most of the Council are my friends. I have no intention of taking command away from Razor."

"It's kind of like what happened at Kharoom's Council meeting, only with the opposite result," Letsan said, chuckling. "Sorry, Matti, but you won't win this vote."

"He won't," Razor said. "But I have a better way of settling this. I'll fight him for it. Winner takes the Shomrim."

Matti's heart leaped. There'd be no better way of proving himself to the Shomrim at this Compound than beating Razor in a fight. "I accept," he said. "What are the rules?"

"This is absurd," Hakham said. "Razor, there's no need for violence. The Elders—"

"I agree with Razor," Letsan said. "These times call for the best war leader we have. The Shomrim deserve no less. They will follow the winner without question."

Hakham's gaze swept over Matti and Razor. He surveyed the crowd and turned back to Letsan. "A fight it is, then. The rules, Razor?"

"No Magelights. No teeth. No claws. Strength against strength. What do you say, Matti?"

"Agreed. Now?"

"Unless you're too tired from your travels. I can give you a few hours to rest."

Matti held Razor's gaze. That was clever. Matti would lose face if he accepted. "Now is fine. Lead the way."

A thrill of excitement went through the crowd as the news traveled quickly from mind to mind. Catmages ranged themselves in a wide circle around an area contained by the Shomrim of both captains. Soon the fighting ring was ready. Razor and Matti faced each other in the middle. Hakham stood next to them. He broadcast his voice to all assembled.

"Matanya and Razor, on my mark you will begin. The first Catmage to draw blood loses. This is a battle of strength and strategy, not Magelights and claws. The fight ends when one of you is completely dominated by the other." Hakham paused and moved outside the ring. "If there is any question, you both agree to stand by my rulings. Are there any objections?" Neither Matti nor Razor spoke. "Then begin!" he cried.

Razor and Matti circled slowly, studying each other carefully. Suddenly Matti leaped. Razor rose to his hind legs and met him with a crash. The two fell to the ground and rolled quickly, growling softly. Neither could gain the advantage. They drew apart and went back to their circling.

"You're not as fast as you used to be," Matti said.

"And you talk too much," Razor growled, leaping in mid-word and forcing Matti to jump aside. But Razor expected that, and contorted himself in midair to land on Matti's hind leg. Matti stumbled and fell to the ground. Razor leaped and Matti rolled over to meet him. In one quick move, Matti was beneath Razor, both hind legs poised to gut him. Razor held himself stock-still, hind legs splayed as he stood over Matti.

"Looks like I win," Matti said.

"Look at your throat, boy," Razor responded.

"I can't, you big oaf. You're on top of me."

Hakham and Letsan hurried over. Letsan started to laugh.

"What on earth are you laughing at? I won!" Matti said.

"Brother, extend your claw just a bit so Matti can understand what's so funny."

Razor did so, and Matti felt a claw touching his throat.

"It's a tie," Hakham said. "Razor's claw sits on top of the great artery that gives us life. If this had been a true fight, you'd have died at each other's claws."

The crowd cheered for Razor. He leaped away from Matti, who rolled over and shook the grass from his coat.

"Well, this is a problem," Matti said. "The fight didn't resolve anything."

"Indeed it did. Since you were unable to beat Razor, you will present your case to the Elders, and you will abide by our ruling."

Matti blinked at the old tabby. "Yes, Hakham. In the meantime, my warriors need quarters. And I could use a drink."

Razor grunted. "I'll show you the stream. Zohar, find our visitors a place to stay."

Matti followed Razor to the stream for a drink as Zohar led Matti's warriors away. "You're awfully quiet," he said.

Razor grunted. "There's not much to say that I haven't already said. Matti, you're a fool to work for Kharoom. He's out of his depth and too hungry for power to see how much damage he's doing."

"He's the head of the Council, Razor. We are soldiers. We do what the Council demands."

"No. We serve all Catmages, not just the Council. When the Council's decisions conflict with what's best for our people, we no longer serve the Council."

"That's where you and I disagree, Razor. I don't think the Council is wrong."

"Then you're a fool, too. Here's the stream."

Razor waited until Matti had drunk his fill, then led him to Hakham's bayit. The Elders were ranged in a semicircle within. Matti and Razor sat before them as they would at a Council meeting.

Hakham said, "Matti, these are Methuselah, Zehira, and Silsula. Letsan you know. I have told the Council what you want. Have you anything to say?"

"Only what I told you. The Council notes that East Woods is a Compound of loyal Catmages and must abide by our Laws."

"By our Laws, yes," Zehira said, "but not by Kharoom's dictates. Who is he to rule over us?"

"I can only tell you the orders I was given. I did not ask Kharoom his reasons for them."

"Perhaps you should have," Hakham said. "Matanya, these orders worry me. Compounds have been autonomous since the Great Council was disbanded thousands of cycles ago. We work together when there is need, but we bow to no Catmage. Does Kharoom wish to lead, or is he trying to rule?"

"I don't know, sir. I only know what I was told. I came here to retrieve the Shomrim who have joined Razor, and to take command from him and lead them myself."

"And what do you want, Razor?" Zehira asked.

"I'm keeping my command. Matti took a long walk for nothing."

"With all due respect, Hakham, if you are under no obligation to obey Kharoom, then the Shomrim in this Compound should also be allowed to decide for themselves who they wish to follow," Matti said.

Razor growled. "They already did. They came here of their own free will."

"And they may leave here of their own free will. Council, I ask only that you give me the same chance Razor was given. Let me talk to the warriors and let them decide what they want."

"He has a point, Hakham," Silsula said. *Chirrup.* "The Councilors are only advisors. As long as a Catmage abides by our Laws, she is free to do as she pleases."

"What say the rest of you?"

"He is right," Zehira said.

"That is our way," said Methuselah.

"Sorry, brother, but I agree," Letsan said.

"As do I," said Hakham. "All right, Matti. You may try to persuade our Shomrim to join you. But you will not be taking command here. Razor heads the East Woods Shomrim. You may not disrupt his training, or the teaching of our younger Catmages."

"Thank you, Elders. I will abide by your requirements."

"And Matanya—you have until the full moon to make your case. If you can't get a good number of Razor's warriors by then, you will go back to the Council Compound and leave us to manage our own affairs."

"Yes, Hakham."

Razor grunted. "You won't steal my warriors away, Matti."

"I guess we'll just have to wait and see."

"I'll show you where your Shomrim have been housed," Letsan

said, forestalling another staring match between Matti and Razor. He led Matti past the Teaching Rings to the northern edge of the field. "We have a few empty bayits together that you and your warriors can use. But I have to tell you, I think you're wasting your time. Razor has been recruiting warriors for two cycles. I don't think they're going to follow you back to the Council Compound."

"Then Razor has nothing to worry about, does he?" Matti said. "Thank you for showing me here. Doubtless we'll see a lot of each other in the days to come."

"Doubtless," Letsan said. He turned and headed back the way they had come.

Matti watched him leave. Then he called his fighters to attention, pleased when they came quickly out of the bayits and lined up in good order.

"Are we rested? No? Too bad. We have work to do. I've got a group of warriors to impress, and you lot are going to help me do it."

EIGHT: SUMMER'S END

The week before school started, Jack Straight sat in his classroom working on lesson plans. He had to admit that even though he hated the way Stan got him his teaching position, he was happy to be teaching permanently at the high school. He picked up the printout for his tenth grade AP history class list, and his smile disappeared. Jack crushed the paper in his fist and stalked out of the classroom and through the open door of the principal's office. His cousin looked up from his computer, eyebrows raised. Jack didn't wait for him to speak.

"What on earth are you thinking putting Taylor Grant in my AP history class? I doubt he's ever gotten above a C in the subject in his entire school career, and that was in regular history classes! How do you expect him to keep up with the demands of my advanced course?"

Saunders lifted his chin and stared at Jack. "You will put him in the class because I need him to be there. You don't need to know anything more."

"Oh, stop it!" Jack said. "That's not going to work this time. I'm not taking on a kid who will clearly be in over his head. He'll flunk out!"

Saunders raised himself from the chair. He crossed the room, closed the door, turned back to Jack, and leaned against the door, arms folded.

"Well?" Jack asked.

Saunders crooked his finger. "Over here."

"Damn it, Stan," Jack said as he closed the distance between them, "stop playing these stupid games. This is a boy's life we're talking about. If Taylor flunks my class, he's off the football team." He stopped just out of arm's reach from Stan. "Football is one of the only things he likes about school. You can't take it away from him."

"I said here," Stan said, pointing to the floor in front of him.

Jack sighed and moved forward a few steps. "Are you going to discuss this, or do we have to play yet another one of your power games?"

"Oh, it's not a game," Stan said. In one swift motion, he grabbed Jack by the arm and throat, turned on his heel, and pushed him up against the door he had just been standing against.

"Do not *ever* speak to me in that tone again," he said between clenched teeth. He tightened his grip painfully on Jack's arm.

Jack snapped his mouth shut, holding back a cry of pain as his elbow bashed painfully against the door. He struggled to free himself.

Saunders laughed. "You never learn. You will do what I require or you will suffer the consequences. Mr. Grant will be in your class. And you will see to it that he does not fail. You will tutor him yourself if you have to. But you will keep him in your class the entire year."

A wave of anger passed over Jack. "Not this time," he said through gritted teeth. "No more. NO! MORE!" He struggled, trying to push Saunders away. His free arm pulled at the hand Saunders had wrapped around his throat. Jack's watch scraped painfully against Stan's wrist, startling him and making him loosen his grip. A few drops of blood welled out of the scratch. Jack pushed Stan away, but his elation was short-lived. Stan's face darkened, his brows closed down, and he clenched his fists. A bright yellow flash soared from beneath Stan's shirt, and suddenly Jack felt a pain like a hot knife slicing along his left cheek. He cupped his cheek in his hand. It came back wet with blood.

"What—what did you do to me? I'm bleeding!"

Stan started laughing happily. "It appears the Tilyon reflects my mood. I was thinking about slapping your face, and it did it for me. And drew blood! Even better!"

Chills went down Jack's spine.

"I wonder what it will do when I actually *think* of the punishment you deserve. Shall we see what I can accomplish when I put my mind to it?"

The Tilyon glowed.

"No!" Jack said fearfully, blood running through his fingers. "No," he repeated softly, defeated. "I'll do it. I'll make sure Taylor passes."

Stan turned his back on Jack and returned to his desk.

"You know, Jack, I've thought a lot about what happened at the museum. So many ... coincidences. For instance, how did those children and their Catmage allies know where to find me? You and I were the only two people that knew the location of the Tilyon."

Jack licked his lips nervously. "Those are three of the smartest kids in the school. The Catmages have been watching you nonstop. Why would you think they wouldn't have set two watches on you the night you went to Boston?"

"I notice you're not denying telling them where I went."

Jack looked Stan straight in the eye, took a deep breath, and said, "I never told those children where the Tilyon was." It was technically true. He had never mentioned its name, just which museum had something they might be interested in seeing.

Saunders eyed him suspiciously. He sneered and nodded at the door. "Go clean yourself up before you stain my carpet. And Jack—"

Jack paused at the door.

Saunders voice was icy. "Don't ever challenge me again."

Jack hurried out of the office to the nearest bathroom. He stared at his cheek in the mirror. A long, thin slash cut diagonally across his left cheekbone. It really did look like he'd been cut with a knife. Jack washed his face and held paper towels to the cut until the bleeding stopped. He went back to his room for a first aid kit and then to the nearest bathroom.

On the way he ran into Mr. Velez, who was holding a crumpled piece of paper.

"Mr. Straight. The principal give me this to give to you."

It was the class list. "Thank you," Jack said taking the paper and folding it into his pocket.

Mr. Velez' gaze drifted to his cheek.

"What happened to your face?"

"I, uh, I wasn't watching where I was going and ran into a metal cabinet," Jack said. "Hit the corner. It has a sharp edge."

Mr. Velez' eyebrows rose.

"Excuse me, but I really need to take care of this."

"Okay," Mr. Velez said, shrugging. "See you later, Mr. Straight."

"Thank you again."

Jack hurried down the hall. Mr. Velez went in the opposite direction. Once he reached the bathroom, Jack cleaned the cut once more, put the bandage on, and looked in the mirror. Anger overwhelmed him. He took the class list from his pocket, unfolded it, and ripped it to shreds, letting them fall to the floor. Then he went back to his classroom to design a tutorial program for a student he knew was incapable of passing his class.

Andy was clearing the table from breakfast when he heard the front door open. Goldeneyes and Letsan watched him from their perch on the windowsill.

"I'm in the kitchen," he called. Becca walked through the door.

"What are you looking so happy about so early in the day?" he asked, yawning.

"It's not that early. It's after nine," she said.

"Yeah, but you weren't woken up early by a couple of Catmages who decided you needed to have a lesson the second your mother left for work."

"School starts in a week. We're not going to have as much time for lessons. We can't waste the day," Goldeneyes said.

CHAPTER EIGHT

"So you're definitely going to the Compound today?"

"Yeah. Why?"

Becca grinned. "Because I thought of a way we might be able to mess with Principal Saunders. I did a little research last night. He needs a kennel license if he breeds more than two litters of dogs per year."

"So?" Andy said. "What makes you think he doesn't have one?"

"Oh, he does. But that's not the only thing I found out. Do you know what a commercial kennel is?"

"No."

She took a piece of paper out of her pocket and started reading. "A commercial kennel is a kennel maintained for boarding or grooming dogs or cats. We can't get him on the dogs, because what he's doing is legal with the right permits. But if we were to, say, let the town clerk know that Saunders had a houseful of cats that he doesn't have a license for..."

"Becca, that's brilliant!"

"Yeah, I'm pretty happy about it myself." She glanced at the two Catmages.

"This will cause trouble for Saunders?" Goldeneyes asked.

She shrugged. "Maybe. I hope so."

"Then let us cause him trouble, by all means," Goldeneyes said happily.

Andy started laughing. "Let's do it now! Are they open yet?"

"Should be. It's after nine."

"Here," Andy said, handing her the phone. "Be my guest."

Goldeneyes, Letsan, and Andy listened avidly as Becca called the town clerk and told her that one of her neighbors had a lot of cats, and she wanted to know if it was legal. Andy could barely suppress his laughter as Becca played innocent said she could only guess, but that she'd seen at least a couple of dozen different cats all around number 19 Oak Street. And yes, it had been happening for months. Andy nearly lost it when Becca asked if having all those cats around wasn't some kind of health hazard. Finally, Becca thanked the woman and hung up the phone.

"Well?" Andy said.

"She said she'd look into it, and that if she couldn't find a commercial license, she'd send someone around to check on the cats."

"What will happen if they go to the house and find the nest of Wild Ones?" Letsan asked.

"I'm not sure. Maybe they'll fine Saunders, or give him a citation. Best case scenario is they make him get rid of his cats." She grinned that lovely, double-curved smile again. "The Wild Ones would have to leave."

"That would be so great," Andy said.

"They'd just set up house somewhere else," Letsan said.

"Yes, but it would be an irritant," Goldeneyes pointed out. "Just imagine having to move our entire Compound."

"No thanks," Letsan said. "That's too much work to even think about." He leaped down from the window, yawned, and stretched. "Speaking of Compounds, isn't it time to head to our own? Becca, are you coming today?"

"Sure. I've been reading up on battle tactics and strategy and I'd like to share some ideas with Razor."

"He'll like that. Don't tell him I said so, but I'm pretty sure you're one of his favorite humans."

"Gee, what a compliment. He only knows three of us, and he can't stand Mike."

"Darn. I was hoping you wouldn't have noticed that."

"We can chat later," Goldeneyes said as she jumped to the floor. "Let's get going. I'll ride with you, Becca." She and Letsan followed Becca out the door.

Andy collected his bike from the garage. He waited for the Cat-mages to jump into the baskets, then he and Becca headed down the street to the route out of town.

"Here's hoping Saunders gets a nasty phone call today!" Becca called.

"Me too. They have to get him in trouble for having too many cats

91

on his property. We have something going for our side, for a change."

Laughing, the two of them sped down the street.

When they reached the Compound, Goldeneyes told Andy to find Zehira for his lesson today.

"Class with Methuselah?" he asked.

"Why else would I not be teaching you?"

"Wait, you're still in class?" Becca asked. "Don't Catmages ever stop training?"

"Most do. Those who want to continue to grow and improve do not." They passed the Teaching Rings as the morning sessions broke up. Silsula saw them, spoke briefly to another Catmage, who took charge of the kittens leaping around her, and headed toward them.

"Good morning, all!" she said cheerfully. "Ready for another class, sister?" *Chirrup.*

"You're in the class, too?" Becca said, surprised.

"Indeed. Am I not also of Nafshi's line?" She struck a haughty pose. Andy and Letsan laughed.

"There are three scions of Nafshi in Methuselah's class," he said. "Here comes Leilei."

"Yes, and only two of your line," Silsula teased.

"Three," Letsan said. "You forgot Zohar."

"I wonder if we can count Patches as a tie-breaker," Silsula said, glancing at Goldeneyes as she did so.

"Certainly not!" her sister said, causing the rest of them to burst into laughter.

"I guess I'm on my own for the next hour or so," Becca said. "Razor's going to be too busy to discuss strategy."

"But I am not," Hakham said. "Come with me. Let's go find Matanya and some of the captains." Everyone headed off to their separate destinations.

Back in Coreyton, Stan Saunders sat at the kitchen table enjoying a second cup of coffee. He thought about his altercation with Jack the day before. There would be no more complaints from his cousin. Today he would have Roah show him a few similar tricks. He remembered that he'd managed to open a wound that Roah had given Patches last year. The principle must be the same. Stan had thought about punching Jack, and a cut appeared on his cheek—right where his fist would have landed. Perhaps he should find a cat on which to practice his newfound skill.

The phone rang, interrupting his train of thought.

"Hello?"

"Mr. Saunders, it's Barbara Hutchins at the town clerk's office. I thought you'd like to know that a girl called here earlier complaining about a large group of cats on your property."

"A girl? Did she leave her name?"

"No, but she sounded like a kid, maybe high school age. Mr. Saunders, what should I do about this?"

"If she calls back, you will tell the girl that you sent an investigator and he saw no signs of cats on my property. Tell her she must have been mistaken."

"Yes, Mr. Saunders."

"And Barbara, thank you. You'll be getting a nice little gift in the mail this week."

"Thank you, sir."

Saunders hung up the phone. A young girl, eh? It had to be that nuisance, Becca Jefferson. Andy's friends were becoming almost a big a problem as he was. Perhaps it was time to do something to set them all on edge. And he had just the thing. Yes, Taylor Grant was coming along nicely. It was time to have him shake things up a bit. Mr. Grant was due for a lesson today. He'd talk with him afterward. Try to make trouble for him, will they? He'd show these children that they were seriously overmatched.

"Roah!" he snapped. "I need to talk to you about Mr. Grant."

Moments later, the cellar door swung open and Roah came into the kitchen. He jumped onto a kitchen chair and waited.

CHAPTER EIGHT

"How is the boy coming along with the Magelights?"

"He is doing well. He took to it right away."

"Good," Saunders said with a twinge of jealousy that a child should have mastered skills that he struggled with. "I see you learned how to teach him better than you taught me."

"No matter. He is learning quickly. He can levitate objects skillfully."

"What kind of objects?"

Roah chuckled. "Everything from human writing instruments to small Catmages. Kelev was extremely displeased to be the subject of our experiments. The boy did not even drop him."

"Good. Perhaps you should start teaching him offensive spells."

"We have a structure to our lessons, Saunders. We will stick to that structure with Taylor."

Saunders frowned. Once again, the cat was getting above itself. He guarded his thoughts carefully and checked his temper.

"Work harder, then. Push Mr. Grant's limits. I want him ready to take on those children when I need him to."

"Yes. He will be a help to us when he is fully trained."

"In the meantime, I want to show him off on Parents Night. Mr. Cohen and his friends need a little shaking up."

"It will be done. Is there anything else?"

"No."

"Then I will go back to training the dogs."

"You do that," Saunders muttered as Roah leaped off the chair and opened the cellar door. Saunders took his cellphone from his shirt pocket and pressed a button.

"Mr. Grant. Come to my house this morning. I need to speak with you." He hung up the phone and took a sip of coffee. "Children need to learn their place," he said.

On their last night together before school, Andy, Mike, and Becca sat on

Andy's porch and compared schedules. They were still in AP history and Spanish together, and Andy and Becca continued in the same English class.

"Teresa's in my math class again," Mike said, grinning. "Also AP history and English."

Becca shook her head. "I can't understand how you can be disciplined enough to be a straight-A math student and then turn around and get detention for acting up."

Mike shrugged. "Math is easy. Comedy is hard."

In spite of herself, she laughed along with Andy and Mike. "If you'd just learn to tolerate authority a little better, you'd probably not have to spend so much time sitting in detention."

"Hey, I'm actually looking forward to the first day of school," Mike said. "It's all the days that follow it that I can't stand."

"So what's Ms. Morris planning for the theater club this year?"

Mike raised his head in mock arrogance. "You'll just have to learn with the rest of the peons, my dear. I am an actor, not an usher."

"So you'll be second spear carrier to the left this year instead of third?" she asked, grinning.

Mike clutched his chest. "Ow! Cut to the heart! You know I'm first spear carrier material."

The front door opened, and Andy's mom came out with a tray of milk and brownies. "One last summertime snack before school starts," she said.

"Thanks, Mrs. C.," Mike said, reaching for a brownie and stuffing half of it into his mouth.

Becca shook her head. "He gets older, but he never matures," she said, grinning as she took a glass of milk and a brownie. "I'd excuse him to you but you've known him all his life. Thanks, Mrs. Cohen."

"Yeah, thanks Mom," Andy said.

Mike swallowed the last chunk of brownie and got to his feet. He nodded to Andy's mom and bowed with a flourish. "We thank you for the provisions, good dame," he said in his best British accent. "I am in your debt. You have but to name a favor, and it shall be yours."

Andy's mother laughed and shook her head. "Never change, Mike. Never change."

"Done, good woman!" he said brightly, bowing again.

Still laughing, she left the tray of brownies on the table next to them and went back in the house.

NINE: BACK TO SCHOOL

The first week of Andy's second year as a high school student was a lot less confusing than his first. He knew where all his classrooms were and happily greeted friends he hadn't seen all summer. AP History was his last class before lunch. Becca and Teresa were already sitting together in the classroom when he arrived. Andy took a seat next to Becca. To everyone's surprise, Mike showed up on time.

"It's Teresa's influence," Becca whispered to Andy.

Andy nodded. For two people who weren't officially a couple, they sure seemed to spend a lot of time together.

"I know, right?" Becca said.

"You heard me?" he hissed. "But—I was just thinking that."

"Uh-oh. Andy, you need to be more careful," she said softly.

"I thought I *was* being careful."

"Careful about what?" Mike asked.

Mr. Straight came into the room and stopped Andy from having to answer. But Andy's jaw dropped open as he saw who came into the room behind Mr. Straight.

"What's *he* doing here?" Andy said out loud.

Mr. Straight ignored him. "Class, I'd like you all to welcome Taylor Grant. He'll be joining us this year."

CHAPTER NINE

Taylor looked over at Andy and smirked.

"Take a seat, Taylor," Mr. Straight said.

Taylor walked down the aisle and took the empty seat behind Andy.

"Looks like we're in the same history class again, Cohen," he said. "Maybe we can be homework buddies." His smirk grew broader. "We can work when it's *light* out. Maybe you can help me have a *light*bulb moment. Perhaps you'll be de*light*ed to help me."

"Shut up, Taylor or I'll knock your *lights* out," Andy muttered.

"Now is that any way to greet the new kid?"

Becca, frowning, raised her hand.

"Yes?" Mr. Straight asked.

"Mr. Straight, since Taylor is new to the AP class, maybe you should have him sit up front so he doesn't miss anything. You know how distracting it can be in the back sometimes."

"That's a good idea, Becca. Taylor, up here," Mr. Straight said, indicating the desk in front of him.

"That was genius," Andy whispered, grinning broadly.

"Yeah," she whispered back. "Let him try to bug you from right under the teacher's nose."

"Genius," Andy repeated. The glower on Taylor's face indicated that he did not agree. But he wasn't able to bother Andy for the rest of the period. Andy smiled brightly at him every time he turned around to glare. Mike snickered a few times and blew him kisses when Mr. Straight's back was turned.

When class was over, Mike stood up and said, "That was possibly the best class in the history of classes." He grinned hugely as Taylor passed them all, glowering. "See you tomorrow, Tay-Tay!" Mike called after him. The rest of them laughed, but they stopped laughing as Mr. Straight approached.

"I would have thought you'd be a little more sensitive to bullying, having experienced it yourself, Andy."

Andy was shocked. "What? But—but we weren't bullying him! You know how horrible he's been to me, Mr. Straight."

"Yes, I do. You hated it when he and his friends ganged up and picked on you. So what exactly did you all just do?" he asked, looking at each of them. "On Taylor's first day in a new class—a class he's going to have to work his butt off to pass—you were all laughing at him."

"That's not fair, Mr. Straight," Becca said. "Taylor started up with Andy the minute he came into class. We weren't bothering him. All we did was laugh at Mike when he cracked a joke."

"He called Taylor 'Tay-Tay'. He didn't crack a joke."

"Okay, well, you have a point, but it's Taylor!" Andy said.

Mr. Straight nodded. "Yes, I know. But perhaps the four of you might want to stand in Taylor's shoes once in a while and look at things from his point of view. This class won't be easy for him. I don't want you making it any harder. Are we clear on that?"

"Yes, Mr. Straight," Becca said as the others nodded.

"Good. Now get to your next class."

"Hey! Lunch! Let's go!" Mike said, rushing out the door. The others followed him, leaving Mr. Straight alone in the classroom.

The first Saturday after the start of school, Taylor Grant pushed his chair away from Principal Saunders' kitchen table toward the end of a Magelight lesson with Roah. Taylor closed his eyes and concentrated. The salt shaker rose slowly from the table, quivering in midair. Taylor opened his eyes and willed it to move in a circle. He smiled as it did exactly that. Then he let it down slowly. It settled to the table with a soft thump.

"That was very good," Roah said. "Your control is much better."

"Indeed," said Mr. Saunders from the kitchen door, where he stood, arms crossed, leaning against the doorframe. "I thought for sure you would be cleaning my kitchen floor again."

Taylor grimaced. The first time he'd tried to float it, he had knocked the salt shaker into a half-filled cup of tea that was on the table, spilling both. Saunders had made him mop the entire floor as punishment. He had graduated to much larger items, but Roah was testing his ability to move items with his Magelights today, not testing to see how much he could lift.

"When do I get to do more than make stuff float?" Taylor asked.

"When I say you may," Roah said. "For now, you will practice the basics."

"Principal Saunders, have I proven myself enough to show off on Parents Night?"

Saunders watched the boy and Catmage for a long moment. "Yes, you have. I think it will be good to make Mr. Cohen and his friends nervous. Worried people—and Catmages—make mistakes. And that's exactly what we want, eh, Roah?"

"As you say, Saunders."

"Thanks! Oh, this is gonna be great! I'll have Cohen so worried he's going to wet his pants!"

"Do not gloat before you have achieved anything," Saunders said. "You must first show me what you can do."

"No, sir. I mean yes, sir."

"Go home, Mr. Grant. Roah and I have things to discuss."

Taylor rose hurriedly and left the room. As the door closed behind him, Saunders said, "Call Kfir and his lieutenants. I want to go over our plans."

TEN: PARENTS NIGHT

The phone rang and Andy looked up from his book. His mother's work number showed on the screen. "Let me guess. You're running late again," Andy said as he answered the phone.

"I'm so sorry, sweetie, but you know how work can be."

"Yes, I do know. That's why I ordered pizza for us. It'll be here in ten minutes."

"I'll be there in fifteen. Thanks, Andy, you're a great kid."

"I know," he said, smiling. "See you when you get here."

He hung up the phone and whistled as he set the table for dinner. His phone buzzed. It was a text from Becca.

How late are you going to be this time?

We may make it on time. I ordered pizza.

Smart. But I won't hold my breath waiting for you guys.

Save us seats.

You know I will. Text me when you get there.

Here's looking forward to the most boring Parents Night ever.

That would be nice.

The doorbell rang. Andy put down the phone and went to pay the delivery man. He put the pizza in the oven. Any minute now … yep, there was the sound of the garage door opening. Shortly after, his mother hurried into the house.

"Mm, smells good. Angelo's?" she asked.

"Of course." They ate quickly and Andy smiled as he looked at the clock. Yes, they'd be on time for a change. He cleared off the table as his mother went through the mail for the day.

"Nothing but junk mail and bills. All right, let's go."

Andy texted Becca as they pulled into the school parking lot, asking where they were sitting. "This way," he told his mother, leading her through the crowded hallways to the gym.

Becca waved at them from across the gym. Her family and Mike's were holding enough space for Andy and his mother to join them. Becca's father pretended to faint as Andy and his mother walked up the steps of the stands. Becca's mother smacked her husband lightly on the shoulder. "Really, Jake?" she asked.

He clutched his chest. "Danielle, my heart can't take it. Rachel's on time!"

Rachel started laughing. "Okay, okay, I get it. Sometimes we're late."

"Sometimes?" Greg Murdoch, Mike's father, looked incredulous.

Becca rolled her eyes as Mike's mother poked his father in the side.

"Our parents, ladies and gentlemen," Mike said. "The role models on which we base our behavior!" Everyone laughed.

"Hey, there's Teresa. Teresa!" he said, waving. She made her way to them and Mike slid over to make room.

"Hi," she said.

"Let's assume we all know each other and skip the introductions," Mike said.

"We do all know each other, silly." She took a seat next to him.

"Then there's definitely no need for introductions!"

Shaking his head, Andy sat down next to Becca. "Wonder what Saunders is going to say this year," he said.

"Wait, we're supposed to listen to the speeches?" Mike asked. "Oh, so that's what I've been doing wrong all this time."

Andy was relieved that this year, Saunders was ignoring him. The last couple of years he had made it a point of staring at Andy during the speech. Then again, Andy wasn't as easy to intimidate now that he knew *why* Saunders was staring.

He glanced over at Teresa. Nights like this were still hard for her. Her mother, the former principal, had died over a year ago, shortly before school started. Andy was sure Saunders was responsible for the accident that killed her, but he couldn't prove it. Teresa seemed a little sadder than usual. Andy felt bad for her. Becca saw him watching Teresa and nudged him with her shoulder. The gesture made him feel better.

People all around were clapping politely as Saunders finished speaking. It was time for the parents to split up and pay fees and meet the teachers. They told the kids what time to meet them and where, then headed out of the stands.

"What should we do?" Mike said. "Go over to the auditorium again?"

"You know that's off limits," Becca said.

"So? We got away with it last year."

"I'd rather not," Teresa said.

"You guys figure it out and let me know. I have to hit the head," Andy said. "I'll be back in a bit."

He made his way down the stands and out to the empty boy's locker room. He was washing his hands when the door opened. Taylor Grant saw him and grinned.

"Andy Cohen! Just the guy I wanted to see," he said.

"Just the guy I never want to see," Andy replied. "Really, Grant, do you make a habit of following me into the bathroom? Because it's more than a little creepy."

Taylor ignored the dig. "Oh, you really do want to see me. You just don't know why. Ask me why. Go ahead. You're gonna love the answer."

"Grant, I wouldn't spit on you if you were lying on the ground in front of me covered in flames."

"No? What about if I was covered in light?"

"Again?" Andy said. "What is it with you and talking about light?"

"Lights, actually," Taylor said, grinning hugely. "Lots of lights. More than you, in fact." He opened his letter jacket to reveal a loose t-shirt. He pulled up the thick silver chain around his neck and displayed the Magelight necklace Saunders had given him.

"Lights, Cohen. Lights. Have you ever seen anything like them? Oh, wait, of course you have." He reached for Andy's wrist. Andy jerked his hand away.

Taylor put both hands on the Magelight necklace and concentrated. As he held them, the Magelights began to glow.

Andy's jaw dropped open in disbelief. "He gave you Magelights?" he asked incredulously. "Saunders gave them to *you*?"

"Got it in one. No wonder you get straight A's!"

Andy couldn't speak.

"Oh, he not only gave them to me. I'm getting lessons, too. Guess what I can do? No, wait, I'll show you." Taylor took a crumpled piece of paper out of his jacket pocket and held it on his hand. His brows contracted as he concentrated. The Magelights glowed and the paper floated above his hand.

"Looks like you're not the only one around here who can use one of those things," Taylor said, nodding at the Magelight on Andy's wrist. "Or are you still pretending that's just a piece of plastic?"

Andy glared at Taylor. "Yeah?" Andy said. "You can make a piece of paper float? Wow, I'm so impressed. What a scary hard thing to do."

"You want scary hard?" Taylor said, stepping closer. "I don't need Magelights to take you apart." He closed his hand into a fist.

Memories of the many times Taylor had bullied him rose unbidden to the surface. Andy flushed red with anger.

"You want to mess with me, Taylor? Just try it. I've got a lot more practice at this than you. And you don't have your stooges around to help today." He looked around the locker room and grinned. His Magelight blazed and a jet of light shot out. Andy jerked his hand upward, and a metal wastebasket in the corner zoomed through the air and dropped on the ground an inch away from Taylor, who jumped as it landed. The crash of metal on tile echoed throughout the room.

"Want to try something, Grant?" Andy said. "Go ahead. Or maybe you should just float a paper ball at me. I might get a really bad paper cut."

Taylor glowered. "You think you're such a big man now, huh Cohen? But just you wait. I have five Magelights. You have one. We'll see who gets the last laugh." He turned and stalked out of the locker room, slamming the door on the way.

Despite his bravado, Andy was worried. Taylor had five Magelights! Saunders had given his worst enemy *five Magelights*. What if he learned how to wield them properly? This was really bad. He left the locker room and found his friends waiting near the door.

"What happened?" Mike asked. "Taylor just brushed past us looking like he wanted to bash someone. Did you see him in there? Did he start something with you?"

"Yeah, I saw him," Andy said, frowning and motioning Mike and the others to come closer. He quickly told them what happened, looking around to make sure nobody overheard them.

"Well, it isn't too bad," Mike said. "I mean, if all he can do with five Magelights is float a piece of paper, that's good, isn't it?"

"That's how you start," Andy said grimly. "And then you work your way up to other stuff. No, this isn't good. It's not good at all."

"You need to tell Goldeneyes," Becca said.

"I know. But I can't do it here and now."

"Is she at your house?"

"No. She's at the Compound."

Becca's forehead wrinkled in thought. "Let's get out of here," she said.

"Where to? You said the auditorium is off limits."

"It is. But the art studio isn't. I think you should all come and see what I've been working on since school started."

"Becca, Andy doesn't have time to look at your stuff. He needs to send a message—hey!" he said as Teresa elbowed him in the side.

"Andy can find a private place to send a message if we go, knucklehead," she said.

"Oh." Mike grinned at Becca. "Sorry. Sometimes I'm a little thick."

Becca wasn't listening. She had already turned to lead the way down the halls to the studio. They passed some other kids and parents in the hallway, but most of the parents were still in the gym standing in lines.

"This way," Becca said as they neared the room. She went down another hallway and pointed to the door. "Boy's bathroom, Andy. There's a window. Go send the message. Mike, go in with him."

"Why?"

"Because sometimes using the Magelight exhausts him, and we don't want Andy falling and cracking his head open."

"Good point. I kinda like Andy's head the way it is."

"So do I."

Andy was hesitant.

"Becca, what if I can't send the message?"

"You can. You've done it before."

"But I don't know how I did it. I've only been practicing short distances. Those other times were emergencies."

Becca's expression grew stern. "Then it's about time you learned how to send a message the right way. Are you or are you not working hard with Goldeneyes and your teachers?"

"Yeah, but—"

"No buts. Get in there and send that message. Do *not* come out until you do."

Mike's brows shot up and he whistled. "Come on, man. We don't have much time." He pushed the door and held it open for Andy. Becca and Teresa looked at each other as the door shut behind them. Becca expelled her breath with a big *whoosh.*

"Do you think it worked?"

Teresa shrugged. "Well, you sure scared Mike and me, so probably."

"I really hope so," Becca said in a worried tone. "He can do so much more than he thinks he can. All he needs is a little more confidence."

"Maybe Mike can give him some of his," Teresa said. They grinned.

Inside the bathroom, Mike opened the window as Andy stood gazing at it, his right fist clenched.

"So how does this work?" Mike asked.

"I think about what I want to say, then think about who I want to say it to. Goldeneyes said I should think of it like I was giving someone a present with my voice in it. She says pictures work better than words, though."

"Well," Mike said. "Just imagine yourself recording a video and sending it off to Goldeneyes."

"Not bad!" Andy said. He closed his eyes and concentrated.

"Your Magelight's glowing," Mike said.

Andy opened his eyes. "I know. Please don't talk. It breaks my concentration."

"Sorry."

Andy tried again. He pictured Taylor in the Magelight necklace, then taking a video of himself with his phone. Last, he saw himself emailing it to Goldeneyes. He smiled as he mimed pressing the send button on his phone. As his thumb hit the imaginary button on the screen, bright light flared from his wrist. He opened his eyes in time to see a round message light zip out the window.

"You did it!" Mike shouted. "Awesome!"

"Quiet!" Andy said as the door was flung open. Becca and Teresa were smiling.

"I knew you could do it, Andy," Becca said.

"Congratulations!" Teresa added.

Andy was breathing hard, but he smiled happily. "Thanks. And I'm not that tired, either. Let's get out of here before anyone finds us. Is it time to meet our parents yet?"

Becca glanced at her watch. "Almost."

"Then let's go. Goldeneyes has been warned. She'll know what to do."

Principal Saunders reclined behind his desk, hands behind his head, smiling at the quiet knock at the door.

"Enter," he said.

Taylor came into the room grinning hugely.

"And?"

"He fell for it completely. Better than we thought, even."

"Explain."

"He picked up a metal wastebasket from across the room and dropped it right next to me. Practically hit me on the arm!"

"How heavy was the wastebasket?"

Taylor shrugged. "Just a few pounds. But it went really fast. I think he could have hurt me with it if he tried."

Saunders leaned forward and put his elbows on the desk, steepling his fingers and resting his chin on his hands.

"And you did as I told you?"

"Yeah." Taylor removed the paper wad from his pocket. "This was all he saw," he said, grinning as he floated the paper.

"Excellent. Now, Mr. Grant, show me what you can do with this." He pointed to an empty chair near the wall.

Taylor narrowed his eyes in concentration. The Magelights beneath his shirt glowed, and the chair rose above Taylor's head.

Saunders smiled. "Now lower it without breaking it, or you'll be spending time mucking out my kennels to pay for it."

Taylor lowered the chair slowly. Beads of sweat formed on his forehead. The chair thumped as it landed on the floor.

"Very good, Mr. Grant. Mr. Cohen and his friends have no idea how far along you are. You have done well tonight. You've shown me that my faith in you was not misplaced."

Taylor's grin broadened.

"Continue to show progress, and you may keep the Magelights. You know the penalty for failure."

Taylor's grin faded.

"All in all, Mr. Grant, you have done well. You may leave."

Taylor stood and left the room with a spring in his step.

ELEVEN: MESSAGE RECEIVED

A few weeks after he arrived at the East Woods, Matti sat in the sunlight watching his Shomrim at their exercises. He was pleased with the way things were going. After observing Razor and the East Woods Shomrim for a couple of days, Matti realized that the best way to get his warriors back was to let his soldiers speak for him. So he set up the same routines here that he had at the Council Compound, and he set his soldiers to mingle with Razor's and talk up their roles and responsibilities. Matti met privately with each of the Shomrim who had accompanied him from the Council Compound, and impressed upon him or her how important it was that they draw Razor's soldiers away from him. He had told them to mention that they had centuries of tradition on their side. Sure, Razor was a great leader, but he shouldn't be going against the Council's wishes. Matti himself brought up these points whenever he could, making sure not to raise them around Razor or Letsan. But there were other captains who would listen attentively. No Shomrim wanted to think of himself as breaking the rules.

And then there was simple envy. Matti's warriors were tough, disciplined, and obviously having a great time. Razor was surly and short-tempered and sparing with compliments. As Matti expected, the younger Shomrim were the most easily lured away. By the end of the first week,

Matti had doubled his numbers by recruiting some of the young ones and some latecomers to Razor's cause. And more were joining every day. But he still didn't have enough warriors to keep Hakham from enforcing his agreement and turning Matti out of the Compound.

Then one day, the last thing he expected happened. Zohar, Letsan's oldest son, came to Matti privately and made it clear he wanted to join his Shomrim.

"What about Letsan?" Matti asked. "Surely he wants you to stay with Razor."

"It's a difficult situation," Zohar said, looking away uneasily. "My father won't be happy. But I'm a grown Catmage and have been for some cycles. Letsan doesn't run my life."

Matti decided to test him further. "Don't get me wrong, Zohar. I want you aboard. But aren't you afraid Razor will accuse you of disloyalty?"

"It's not a question of loyalty. I love being one of Razor's warriors. But as you say, it's a matter of what's right. The Council made you head of the Shomrim. If we don't follow the rules, then we're no better than Wild Ones."

"If you want to join me, then you'd better make it quick. There's plenty of upward mobility for those who follow me. I could use a good squad leader like you in my Shomrim. But the openings are filling quickly."

"I understand, sir. But I have to speak to my father first. I don't want him to think I'm going behind his back. I'll see him as soon as I can and get back to you."

Matti watched Zohar go, elated. Razor's nephew coming over to his side would probably influence many more of Razor's fighters. Victory was assured. His Shomrim were turning into an army before his eyes.

Two days later, Matti stood before his soldiers on the training ground. They sat in neat ranks, waiting for him to speak. Just as he was about to start, a half dozen young fighters led by Zohar approached the gathering. They marched smartly forward and halted in front of Matti.

"Zohar reporting for duty, sir. My squad would like me to present them as your newest recruits."

Matti gazed steadily at the young Maine Coon, though he wanted to leap in the air and shout with laughter. Getting Razor's nephew to join him was largely symbolic. Getting Zohar's entire squad was a prize Matti had never expected. He contained his elation and spoke levelly.

"Thank you, Squad Leader Zohar. You and your warriors can take up positions next to Safam." Safam, a mostly black cat with white socks and a white mustache shape on his muzzle nodded and moved his squad over to make room.

Matti watched them march into position, happy and proud. It was time to send a message to Kharoom about his success. He would report back to the Council that he now had an army of Razor's Shomrim to call his own.

"Warriors," Matti said, noting that not an ear or whisker twitched as he spoke, "you have done well. You should be proud of yourselves. The Shomrim of the East Woods have blended perfectly with the warriors that marched with me from the Council Compound. Today we receive into our ranks our newest members, Squad Leader Zohar and his excellent fighters, swelling our numbers even further. Together, we will defeat the Wild Ones!" He paused and the assembled warriors cheered. "We will retrieve the Magelights, and we will avenge the Council!" The cheers grew louder. "Put your best paw forward, and stay tight and ready. Soon, we fight!"

The Shomrim cheered wildly, and Matti's chest swelled with pride as he stood before his army. *We're ready*, Matti thought. *We're ready*.

Roah and Niflah sat on the back porch of Saunders' house continuing a discussion that had begun shortly after they had removed the Tilyon from the museum. Roah wanted to know how much of what he had been taught was true, and how much was myth.

"We need to separate legend from fact," he said. "Much of what we were taught is no more than tales to tell kittens in the nursery. The Tilyon is real. Its power is real. What part of its history is real?" he asked.

"Of course the part about how the First received the Tilyon is real," Niflah said. "You felt its power. No Magelight ever created can come close to that kind of strength. It had to have come from the One Above."

"But what of the Tilyon's powers? Legend says this, legend says that—but legends lie, old one. You know this from hearing Saunders read his ancestor's journal."

"Yes, yes, we both know that Giles Corey worked with Wild Ones during the time the humans know as the Salem Witch Trials. We don't know that the journal lies."

"No. But the human judges accused his ancestor of witchcraft and executed him, whereas we both know he had no powers at all. It was the Wild Ones who held the magic."

"I see your point. But Roah, I know only as much of our history as you, perhaps a little more due to my being some twenty cycles your senior."

"There must be a way to be sure. Perhaps we can test the Tilyon ourselves. A message spell would be a good way to start."

"That's a wonderful thought!" Niflah said. "Let us go find Saunders and see if he'll lend us the Tilyon for an experiment."

They found him in his office poring over his ancestor's journal. He closed the book as they entered and put it back in its lockbox.

"I don't know why you bother locking it away," Niflah said. "We can't read it."

"I have always been one to put away my tools when I am not using them," Saunders said. "Or when I no longer need them." He glanced at Niflah. "What do you want?"

They leaped onto the desk and sat facing him.

"The Tilyon," Roah said. "We were discussing its powers. We would like to test them."

"Test them how?" Saunders asked suspiciously.

"I propose a simple experiment to start," Niflah said. "A message. It's easy to send your thoughts to another when you're in the line of sight, or not very far away. But over distance, the effort is much greater. Roah

113

and I think the Tilyon might enable us to contact a Catmage over a great distance without the exhaustion sending such a message entails."

"This intrigues me," Saunders said. "I should like to see if you're right. How do you propose we perform this test?"

"Velvel is at the West Woods Compound. We will try to communicate with him."

"Very well," Saunders said. "How?"

"When we touched the Tilyon with our paws, we felt its strength," Niflah said. "I shall put my paw on it and attempt to contact Velvel through the mind-voice only."

Saunders lifted the Tilyon over his head and placed it on the desk. He gestured toward the amulet. "Go ahead."

"One moment, Niflah," Roah said. "Make sure you include the two of us when you try to contact Velvel."

"Yes, yes, of course. Be quiet and let me do this." He moved over to the necklace and placed his front paw on the Tilyon. Niflah closed his eyes and concentrated. He called Velvel's name. The other two could hear him calling. The amber eyes of the amulet glowed in sync with his Magelight.

Miles away, in a bayit in the middle of the West Woods, Velvel jerked awake from a nap. "Niflah?" he said incredulously. They heard him clearly. "Where are you?" He yawned. "I was asleep, give me a moment and I'll come outside and meet you."

Niflah laughed. "I'm not at the Compound, Velvel. I'm in town, at Saunders' house!" He was so overcome with joy he leaped in the air. The moment he lost contact with the Tilyon, the communication ended.

"We were right!" Roah said. "This will be useful. *Very* useful," he said. He and Saunders exchanged glances.

"More than useful," Saunders said. "It was a two-way conversation. Your Magelight messages go only one way."

"This is wonderful! Thank you, Saunders! By the First, I feel like a kitten again!" Laughing, he leaped off the desk, ran down the hall and back again, and leaped back up from the floor, skittering across the desk mat and knocking over a pad and pen. At Saunders' frown, he settled down, using his Magelight to retrieve the fallen items.

"We can use this to stay in touch with the West Woods without worrying that my brother's Shomrim will see our messages flying past," Niflah said. "Oh, this is perfect. Perhaps we can teach you to send messages as well, Saunders. Yes, Roah, make sure you put that into your lessons."

"Calm yourself, Niflah," Roah said. "It is unseemly for one of your stature to act like this."

"Oh, *that* for my stature," he said, laughing. "The Tilyon is amazing. How can you not feel overwhelmed by its power every time you are in its presence?"

"There is a difference between feeling overwhelmed and acting the fool. We have proven the Tilyon is as powerful as legend says. Let us leave Saunders to his work."

"All right. I think I'll head out to the West Woods and tell Velvel he wasn't just dreaming that he spoke to me." Laughing, Niflah left the room.

Roah waited until they heard the downstairs door open and close. Then he spoke to Saunders.

"Communicating with the Tilyon will be extremely valuable," he said, "but not in the way Niflah thinks."

"Agreed. I believe it is time for another test of the Tilyon's powers. I can think of a much farther Compound I'd like to communicate with."

Roah sat next to the pendant. He touched it with his paw and concentrated. The amber eyes of the amulet began to glow. Roah closed his eyes. He could feel his body suffuse with warmth. His Magelight glowed in sync with the Tilyon. He thought about the Catmage he wished to contact. A black shape began to form in his mind as he reached out. Soon the shape coalesced into a dark, shadowy figure. Roah was transfixed. He could see the Councilor he was trying to contact, even though he couldn't make out features or colors. This was far more than he had ever achieved with a Magelight! Niflah was a fool for not realizing the Tilyon's potential.

"Can you hear me?" he asked.

CHAPTER ELEVEN

"Roah? I hear your voice. Are you here at the Compound? I did not give you leave to abandon your duties in Coreyton!"

Roah took a deep breath. "No, Councilor. I am still with Saunders. I am using the Tilyon. We learned today that it can send messages over distance. Apparently it can send messages over a very *great* distance."

The shadowy figure purred. "You have done well. You have done *very* well. What have you to report?"

"All is prepared. We are about to move our forces to the new Compound. We are ready for the next step in the plan."

"It will be taken care of. I must prepare things on this end as well. Have your warriors ready."

"Yes, Councilor."

"Keep me informed. It seems I won't have to send any more messengers. This is a much better method."

"Yes. I must go now." The effort to hold the communication open was getting to be too much for him. Roah removed his paw from the Tilyon, his sides heaving. He was exhausted. Apparently even the Tilyon required power from its user in order to work. But he could never have sent a message that far with a Magelight.

"Well?" Saunders said impatiently. "Obviously something happened, but I could see nothing."

"I could not include you in the conversation. Even using the Tilyon, it took all my strength to keep talking at such a distance."

Saunders rose and paced back and forth. "I don't care about that. What did you say? What did you hear?"

"The plans are in place. We are almost ready to strike."

"Good. Good. I grow tired of this constant interference from Hakham and his friends."

"We are all tired of it. And soon they will no longer be an issue. The Tilyon is far more powerful than I had ever dreamed." He looked at the amulet, purring.

Saunders stopped his pacing and frowned. "Yes, it is powerful. But

I have yet to harness much of that power!" He grabbed the necklace and opened the lockbox, thrusting the necklace on top of the journal and slamming the metal box shut. Then he glowered at Roah. "I expect you to work harder at helping me learn how to work the Tilyon."

Roah blinked at him. "It will be done."

Saunders opened a desk drawer, put the box in it, and closed it firmly. He stalked quickly out of the room. Roah remained on the desk, staring down at the spot under the wood where the Tilyon lay. He closed his eyes, and his Magelight glowed bright green.

Outside the office, halfway down the hall, Saunders looked back and saw the glow emanating from his room. His eyes narrowed as he turned back toward the stairs. "I think," he muttered, "I must keep a closer watch on things."

TWELVE:
COMPOUND METHODS

Andy was seeing less of Goldeneyes and Letsan during the school year because they spent a lot more time at the East Woods Compound. He could only get there on weekends since school started. It would be a lot easier if he could drive. He'd be old enough for a learner's permit on his next birthday. Unfortunately, his birthday wasn't until May, so he was stuck biking out to the Compound after work or on Sundays if the weather was nice.

It was a pleasant surprise to see Goldeneyes waiting for him on the porch as his mother drove him home from work Saturday afternoon.

"Oh, look, there's Goldeneyes," she said. "Where has she been? I don't remember seeing her around lately."

"She's been around," he said. "You probably just keep missing her. You do work a lot of hours," he pointed out.

His mother sighed. "Yes, I know. It's one project after another. Someday, I promise, they'll ease up."

"Well, I have Goldeneyes to keep me company," Andy said. He heard Goldeneyes laughing at him.

"You are such an awful liar, Andy. It's a wonder your mother hasn't figured things out by now."

"Not helping," Andy sent. Out loud, he said, "What's for lunch? I'm starving."

"Chicken salad sandwich for me, cold pizza from last night for you. Sit down, I'll get it."

"Cool! Thanks, Mom."

"You're not going to invite me to lunch?" Goldeneyes asked.

"Are you hungry?" he sent.

"As a matter of fact, yes."

"I'll just feed the cat," Andy said to his mother, ignoring Goldeneyes' complaints at being associated with dumbcats. "Serves you right for laughing at me," he sent.

They sat down to their meal. Goldeneyes finished her tuna and headed upstairs while Andy told his mother about the cases he'd worked on at the vet's that morning. He helped his mother clear the table and said he was going to his room to do some homework. Goldeneyes was sitting in the window, washing her face.

"Wait, I want a glass of water," Andy said out loud. He went back down the stairs and caught his mother with a puzzled expression.

"Did you forget something?"

"I want a drink while I work."

"Uh-huh. Do you always tell your cat what you're doing?"

"Uh, no. I was at Dr. Crane's all morning. I guess I just got into the habit of talking around animals." Andy filled a glass with water and hurried up the stairs, not daring to look at his mom.

"You're right, I'm a terrible liar," Andy sent when he got to his room, "and I think Mom's starting to wonder about you. We better be more careful."

"You could have just told her the truth. I wasn't around for a few days. Dumbcats wander from their homes, don't they?"

"I guess. You're the first cat—I mean, Catmage—that I ever had. I never had a dumbcat."

"As much as I would like to sit and listen to myself be compared to a creature that can neither think nor speak, we have work to do."

"Here? Now? I don't think we should have any lessons with Mom in the house. I told you she's already suspicious."

Goldeneyes sighed. "Andrew, someday you're going to let me finish explaining things to you before speaking, and on that day, I shall faint like a human."

Andy snorted. "You really *have* been hanging out with Letsan too long."

Her ears flattened. "By the One, will you be quiet and listen?"

He closed his mouth.

"That's better. You need to come to the Compound tomorrow. We have a project for you. It will be a great learning experience."

"So you don't want me there today? Good, because I have a ton of homework and I'm pretty tired from working with Dr. Crane this morning." He yawned. "I could use a nap, actually."

"So take one. I'll join you," she said, jumping onto his bed.

"Can't. I have a history paper to finish. But don't let me keep you from your beauty rest."

Goldeneyes had already curled up on her pillow. "You won't." She closed her eyes and was asleep in moments. Andy shook his head, grinning. Then he turned on his computer and got to work.

By the time he finished, the room was dim enough that he needed the light. Andy stood and stretched, yawning. One paper down, one more to go. He'd have to finish his English paper after they got back Sunday.

Sunday was another fine autumn day. The air was crisp and clear. The leaves on the trees were a riot of colors, and Andy passed a few farms selling pumpkins and apples. He breathed deeply as he rode. Maybe not being able to drive wasn't so bad after all.

All too soon, he was at the edge of the woods and putting his bike in its hiding place in a hedge. He nodded to the Shomrim on duty as he walked down the path. As he crossed the teaching area, he saw Leilei and

Patches with Goldeneyes, Letsan, and a large group of Catmages at one end. Branches and rocks lay scattered on the ground. Leilei caught sight of him and shouted hello. Patches leaped up and ran toward Andy. Laughing, Leilei followed.

"Andy! Andy! Andy! Patches is glad you are here. Andy will help Patches and Leilei. Will help us all. Right?" He bounded around Andy's legs in his signature four-legged hop.

"Help you with what?" Andy said, trying not to step on Patches as he walked.

"We're building a ma'on!" Leilei said excitedly.

"A what?"

"A ma'on! A dormitory!"

"There are too many Catmages in the Compound," Patches said. "No room to sleep. Patches gets in trouble when he moves in his sleep!"

"You're a restless sleeper, eh?" Andy said. "Why am I not surprised?"

They fell in step with him as he headed toward the gathering. Andy greeted his friends and nodded to the Catmages he was unfamiliar with. Now that he was closer, he saw a number of large stones set in piles. They looked too heavy for single Catmages to lift with their Magelights. Silsula waited for him near one of the piles.

"What do you need me to do?" Andy asked. "Pick up those stones and carry them somewhere?"

"Not exactly," Silsula said. "You're going to help us build the ma'on. You've never seen us create a Catmage structure, have you?"

"Nope."

"Then watch and learn. Stand back over there while we begin." She nodded at a spot a few yards away. Andy moved where he was told.

"Leilei, did you and the others finish mapping out the structure?"

"Yes, Silsula. Would you like us to pace it for you?"

"No, I can see it from here. Wait just a moment." Silsula went to stand with Andy. "Would you pick me up, please?"

Andy bent down and did as she requested. She twisted around in his arms until she was facing the structure. "Oh, that's much better. Yes, you did a wonderful job!"

Andy looked in the direction Silsula was gazing. He could see small channels dug into the ground in a long rectangle. It was about six feet wide and fifteen feet long.

"That will hold a lot of Catmages," he said.

"Exactly the point. If you don't mind, I'm just going to perch here," Silsula said, climbing out of his arms and moving to his shoulder.

"Uh, okay," he said, holding still. He was wearing a jacket, but he'd had some experience with Catmages forgetting how sharp their claws could be.

"Don't worry, sweetling, I'll be very careful. Though it would be better if you don't make any sudden moves," she said, laughing. *Chirrup.* "Stones first. Alef and Bett squads, begin!"

Andy recognized the group of young Catmages from seeing them regularly in the Teaching Rings. At Silsula's signal, Alef and Bett squads' Magelights shone, and stones lifted from the ground and moved slowly through the air. Andy marveled that though many stones were in motion, none of them hit any of the others. Soon there were circles of stone scattered inside the dirt lines that resembled campfire rings. The piles of rocks grew smaller and smaller as they worked.

"Now," Silsula said, "Dalet squad, the branches."

Another group of more senior Catmages moved to the front. Leilei and Patches stood at the front of the group.

"Ready? The first one. Now!" Magelights flashed as one, and a tree branch about three inches in diameter rose in the air, straightened, and slammed down into the dirt at the corner of two drawn lines. The combined power of the Magelights drove it several inches into the dirt.

"Perfect!" Silsula called. "Hay squad, start working from the other end. Gimmel and Vav, relieve them when needed."

"What do you want me to do?" he asked. "I mean, besides be a platform for you to supervise from."

COMPOUND METHODS

"You're going to work with Zahavin," Silsula said. "We're putting you on medurah duty. We need large stones placed in the circles, and my sister thinks you can use the practice and exercise. Get those Magelight muscles strong!" *Chirrup.* "And here she is now." Silsula leaped down from Andy's shoulder. "He's all yours, sister."

"Come with me, Andy. I'll show you where we'll be getting the stones." She trotted into the wood, followed by Andy and a group of the Shomrim.

"Whats a medurah?"

"It's like a fireplace."

"Catmages don't build fires, do they?"

"No, but a large structure like a ma'on sometimes gets cold in the wintertime, even when it's filled with Catmages. So we heat the stones with our Magelights to warm it."

She stopped at a dry stream bed, where Andy saw a number of large rocks that would be impossible for a single Catmage to lift. He kneeled down near one of them.

"Do you want me to bring this back to the ma'on?" he said, grabbing hold of it and pulling.

"No, Andy. I don't want you to exercise your arms. I want you to exercise your Magelight. You'll work with Zohar, Matti, and me. Today we're going to see how well you work with other Catmages."

"Uh—a little help, then?" Andy said. "I don't know how to work with anyone else."

"It's easy, Andy," Zohar told him. "We all try to do the same thing at the same time. Surely you work with humans that way."

"I guess. You mean like helping move something heavy. Yeah. Everybody grabs hold and lifts."

"Then you know how to do this," Matti said. "On my mark, concentrate on lifting the stone with your Magelight. On three, everyone. One, two, three!"

Four Magelights flared in unison, Andy motioned upward with his hand as the stone rose from the stream bed.

"Now," Goldeneyes said softly, "keep focusing on the stone and we'll walk it back to the ma'on."

Andy walked behind the Catmages, hands out as if he were holding the stone in them. He could almost feel the weight in his hands as they directed the rock until it hung in the air over one of the rings of stone.

"Now," Goldeneyes said, "drop it!"

The stone fell with a thump. Matti and Zohar cheered.

"Well done!" Goldeneyes said.

Andy found himself breathing hard. His arms were as tired as if he'd used them to carry the rock. "That was no picnic," he said.

"That's why we do it in groups," Matti said. "Are you ready to get another one?"

"Yeah. Let's go!"

They went back and forth several times, passing other squads of Catmages at the same job before Andy was ready to call it quits. On their last pass, Andy saw that the ma'on now had all the stone rings filled as well as nearly all the wooden pillars set into the dirt. He sat down near his backpack and pulled out his water bottle.

"Building a Catmage house is hard work!" he told Goldeneyes, who was resting beside him.

"Yes, a ma'on is a huge undertaking. You're doing very well today, Andy. It's good to see you moving forward so easily. Nafshi would be proud."

Andy grinned. "Thanks."

"It's good to have you helping us today. I'm proud, too," she said, purring.

Andy's brows rose. "Thanks!" he said again.

The rest of the work on the ma'on was finished fairly quickly. Catmages old and young brought twigs and small branches and used their Magelights to weave them into the sides of the building. They left openings along one side for doorways. Finally it was finished, and the kittens and

124

younger Catmages ran squeaking and screeching in and out of the ma'on while the older ones looked on indulgently.

"Andy, Andy, come inside!" Ranana called, running in and out of the nearest entrance.

He smiled at her. "I'm pretty sure I can't fit in those doorways," he said.

"Oh. Well, make them bigger!"

"No, sweetling," Silsula said, "you'll just have to play with Andy outside."

"I can stick my head in and take a look," he said. Ranana squealed with joy and ran back and forth while Andy kneeled down and peered through an entrance. Inside, the shouting and laughing was very loud. He couldn't help but join in the laughter. Ranana stopped running and sat down next to Andy, sides heaving. He backed out cautiously and reached down, raising her up near his face. She purred and rubbed her cheek against his. Andy smiled and looked over at Silsula and Goldeneyes.

"I love this place," he said.

THIRTEEN: FRENEMIES

Roah padded down the hall to the office where Saunders waited for his next lesson. They had had several lessons since he had used the Tilyon, but Saunders would not allow him to use it again. He seemed suspicious of Roah's motives. Roah closed off his thoughts as he went through the door. Saunders, he knew, was adept at reading the people—and Cat-mages—around him.

"Right on time," Saunders said.

"I am always on time. Let us begin."

The morning sun traveled across half the desk during their lesson. Saunders cried out in triumph when he managed to put a long scratch in the metal lockbox that held the Tilyon and his journal.

"Ha!" he said happily. "Look at that scratch. It's as good as metal on metal. Go ahead, try to scratch it with your claw. You won't be able to make a mark."

"No thank you," Roah said sourly. "I have no desire to break my claws. You did well today, very well."

Saunders grinned at the compliment.

"Now that we are done, I should like to send another message to the Councilor," Roah said.

Saunders' grin vanished. "No," he said curtly.

"Why not?"

"It isn't necessary."

"There will be no messenger. They are counting on us to contact them for further instructions. We must proceed with the attack soon. We are ready."

Roah realized his mistake when Saunders slammed his chair backwards as he rose, his brows drawn together in anger. "I take instructions from no one! No one, do you hear?" he shouted. "*I* will give you instructions. And my instructions are to wait until I tell you that you may use the Tilyon."

Roah blinked up at him. "Yes. It will be done. If there's nothing else?"

"No. Get out!"

Roah jumped to the floor and trotted out of the room. He would have to find a way to use the Tilyon without Saunders' permission. He went down the stairs and left the house, heading out to the West Woods to find Alef.

Patches sat on the edge of the meadow in the Compound, waiting for Leilei to finish her lesson. For the first time in his life, he felt like he truly belonged somewhere. Everyone was kind and generous, and the kittens loved playing with Patches as much as he loved playing with them. Best of all, the Catmages here weren't mean. Patches had made friends.

Zehira blinked at Patches as she left. Leilei started toward him, but he couldn't wait. He ran full-tilt toward her, leaping over her and hopping stiff-legged back until he was close enough to rub shoulders. "Leilei is finished with lessons! Leilei can play with Patches now! Look what Patches has brought, Leilei!"

She laughed. "I don't see anything, silly. I think you forgot whatever I'm supposed to play with."

"Patches did forget! He left it across the meadow. Wait, Patches will get it!" He sat on his haunches and his Magelight flashed. A small pink sponge ball came barreling along a few inches above the ground heading straight for the both of them. Leilei didn't flinch, even though the ball's trajectory made it clear it was about to hit her in the face. Her Magelight glinted, and the ball shot off at an angle away from them both.

"My turn!" Patches said, pushing the ball up instead of zooming along the ground. Leilei laughed again and let the ball fall to the ground and start bouncing. They bounced after it until the ball rolled to a stop and the two of them stood panting happily.

"What was Leilei learning with Zehira today?" Patches asked.

"Never you mind," she said. "If you don't want to continue your studies, that's fine, but don't expect me to give away my secrets." Leilei sat with her nose in the air, affecting an attitude she didn't really feel.

"Patches does not want to learn any more magic. He learned enough from Nafshi. Does not want to remember what Roah taught him."

"Oh, Patches, I'm sorry. I didn't mean to remind you of that," Leilei said, rubbing her face against his. "You're here now. You never have to see the Wild Ones again."

Patches brightened at the thought. "No. Patches is with good Cat-mages now. Patches likes East Woods! I will stay here forever!" He leaped up, hopping toward the trees. Leilei sent the ball flying toward him. Patches knocked it aside. It rolled into the wood and disappeared in the thick underbrush.

"Patches will get it!" he called. He trotted in the direction of the ball and found it half-buried in a pile of leaves. He was about to pick it up with his Magelight when his ears twitched. Something was in the wood, watching him.

"What are you waiting for, Patches?" Leilei called. When he didn't answer, she came after him. "What's wrong?" she asked as she came alongside.

"Quiet," he sent privately. "Something is in the wood. Not a bird. Not a squirrel. Something like us."

"A Catmage?" she asked.

"No. Wild One. Patches can feel it. It is familiar."

Leilei remembered that Patches was that rare Catmage who could sense another Catmage's aura without having to cast a spell. She growled softly and looked carefully around.

"Come out!" Patches shouted. "We know you are there! Show yourself, or Patches will get Razor!"

"Patches not very subtle," Leilei murmured.

There was a rustling in the leaves and a small black-and-white tuxedo cat came hesitantly forward, trembling. He lay down on the ground and blinked up at them.

"Who are you? What are you doing here?" Leilei said brusquely. Her tail lashed.

"I mean you no harm. I was just looking."

"Looking at what? Bad Wild One! You are spying on good Catmages. Patches does not like spies!"

"You're Patches? I heard about you. You got away. I wish I could get away."

Leilei watched him suspiciously. "Get away from who? From what? Who are you?"

"My name is Kelev. But I hate that name. Call me Kel."

"Why is Wild One named Dog?" Patches asked. "That is a stupid name for a Catmage."

Kel laughed harshly. "My parents chose it because they hate me."

"Hate you?" Leilei asked, shocked. "How can your parents hate you?"

"Well, my real father doesn't. But my mother's mate hates that I was born."

"Who are your parents?" she asked.

Kel dropped his gaze to the ground in front of him. "Alef and Bett. Bett's my mother. But Roah is my father."

Patches and Leilei growled, their hackles rising.

"You *are* a Wild One. Patches was right!"

"No! I mean, yes, I am, sort of. But I hate them! I want to get away like you did, Patches. My brothers and sister pick on me all the time. Alef made them all hate me. And my real father, Roah, doesn't care if I live or die. I can't stand any of them. I want to be around Catmages like you, Catmages who are nice and friendly. Please don't tell on me. Please!" His whole body shook as he lay on the ground, blinking.

Patches and Leilei glanced at each other.

"Wild Ones were horrible to Patches," he told Leilei privately. "Patches believes Kel."

"Well, I don't know," Leilei said.

"Look at the scratches on his face," Patches said. "They are mean to him."

His half-healed scratches looked painful. Leilei's heart went out to the young Wild One lying on the dirt in front of them. "That still doesn't mean we can trust him. He shouldn't even be here! How did he get here without being noticed?"

She directed her thoughts at Kel. "How did you get past our guards?" she asked.

"There weren't any guards," he said. "I walked along the road, then I went into the woods to look around. I heard you two playing, so I stopped to watch. I—I wanted to see if it was true that there was a Catmage Compound out here, or if it was another lie the Wild Ones told me. I just wanted to be around Catmages who wouldn't be mean to me."

"They talk about us? What do they say?" Leilei asked.

"Not much," Kel said. "All I heard is that you have a Compound in the east woods. Do you need to know more? Because I could find things out for you." Kel blinked rapidly at her. "I want to stay, but I can't. Not yet. They'd come after me. They'd kill me if they knew I was talking to you. I have to be back before dawn. They won't miss me until then."

"No!" Patches said. "Not let them kill him. Wild Ones are mean. We must help Kel. Think of something, Leilei. What can we do?"

"Both of you, be quiet and let me think," Leilei said. They watched as she lashed her tail and paced back and forth. Kel's trembling stopped, but he still blinked and did not meet their eyes. Finally Leilei stood up and walked over to Kel until they were face to face.

"I'm sorry, Kel, but we don't know you, and we can't take any chances. You're going to have to come with us. We'll take you to Hakham. He won't let anyone hurt you. But you can't just wander into our Compound without anyone knowing about it."

Kel licked his lips. The trembling started again. "Are they going to hurt me? Please don't let them hurt me. I didn't know there were supposed to be guards. I didn't see any."

"They won't hurt you. But you have to come with us. Patches, lead the way."

Kel followed Patches as Leilei walked carefully behind him, alert and watchful. As they neared Hakham's bayit, Kel moved more and more slowly. His head turned from side to side as if he were looking for a place to hide.

"We won't let them hurt you," Leilei said. "Calm yourself."

Katana was on guard by the door of the bayit. "Who's this, Leilei?" she asked suspiciously. "I've never seen him before."

"His name is Kelev. He says he wants to leave the Wild Ones."

"He's a Wild One spy? And you brought him here, to Hakham's bayit? Leilei, have you no sense at all?" Her Magelight flared.

"Don't hurt him!" Patches shouted. All of the Catmages within range winced at the volume. Hakham, Razor, and the Elders came out of the bayit.

"Patches, explain yourself," Hakham said sternly. "You are interrupting an important meeting."

Patches cowered down. "Patches is sorry. Patches did not mean to shout. Katana was going to hurt Kel. Hurt him like Roah used to hurt Patches." He started mewling like a kitten. Leilei explained how they'd found Kel and brought him here.

"Where did you leave the road? How did you get past my guards?"

Razor growled. "You will show me and I'll have the ears of the guards who didn't stop you."

"If I show you, will you let me go?" Kel squeaked. "I swear by the First I mean you no harm. I can help you. I told Leilei and Patches. I can tell you things about the Wild Ones."

"He can help," Leilei said. "He must know a lot. Roah is his father!"

"And we're just supposed to trust you?" Letsan asked. "A son of Roah?"

Kel stopped crouching and sat up at the sound of his father's name. "So what if Roah's my father? I hate him! He abandoned me. He lets Alef and all the other Wild Ones pick on me. They're not my family. Tell me what I can do to help you. Let me prove myself."

"How?" Razor asked.

"I bet you didn't know that Roah is setting up a compound in these woods. How do you think I got here? We're only half an afternoon's walk away. I was trying to get away from my littermates for the day. I didn't know I was near your compound."

The council stood in stunned silence as Kel's words sank in. An entire enemy compound, created under their very noses, and they knew nothing about it? This was news that shocked them to the core. At last, Razor's ears twitched.

"Katana, how is it that we have no news of something this major?" His tone was like ice. "That house is being watched day and night, and not one of our spies has managed to discover it?"

"I'll find out, sir," she said. "You'll have a report right away." She trotted quickly away.

"So what do we do with Roah's son in the meantime?" Letsan asked.

"If I'm not back by dawn, they'll start looking for me," Kel said.

"We'll see about that," Razor said. "First, we find out if you're telling the truth. Then we decide what to do with you—little dog."

"Call me Kel," he said. "I hate my stupid name!"

Razor let out a bark of laughter. "So, you have some backbone.

132

Good. But you're going to stay under guard until we figure out what to do with you."

"Take care of it, Razor," Hakham said. "The rest of us have business to discuss." He and the others went back into the bayit.

Razor looked at the young Catmages. "Come with me, all of you. Patches, stop fretting. Nobody's going to hurt anybody. Yet. Leilei, get these idiots under control or I *will* call my Shomrim to help."

"Patches is not an idiot!" he said. "Razor is mean to Patches."

"Yes, Patches, I'm mean to you. I'm mean to everyone. Now Kel here is going to take me to the point where he came through our woods and show me the hole in my perimeter. The First help any of my Shomrim that missed you slipping past them."

"I got past your guards," Leilei said. "I waited until they changed shifts. They were distracted because the guard going off watch had to report to the guard coming on duty."

Kel brightened. "That must be what happened with me, sir. I swear I didn't see any guards. They must have been changing places and left a space where they couldn't see me. There's no need to punish anyone on my account."

Razor grunted. "We'll see. Show me," he said. "And don't even think of running off. If you think Roah is rough on you, just try going against me."

Kel trembled as he moved in front of Razor to lead them to the place where he'd slipped into the Compound. He went quickly back the way he had come, stopping within view of the road. "Here. Here's where I came in. There weren't any guards."

"There still aren't," Razor said, growling softly as he surveyed the edge of the trees. He looked back toward the Compound and his Mage-light flashed. An orange message globe shot out and disappeared into the wood.

"We'll wait here until my Shomrim arrive. Looks like Kel has done us a favor. We had a hole in our perimeter. He found it. Now we seal it."

The three young Catmages waited uneasily with Razor. Kel glanced back and forth between Razor to Patches and Leilei, meeting none of their gazes.

"This is boring," Patches said to Leilei. "Tell Razor he should let Kel go. He showed us a good thing."

"I'm not telling him anything. Keep quiet and wait."

Kel crouched, blinking at anyone who looked at him, shaking from time to time. The afternoon passed slowly. Patches and Leilei napped. Kel sat or lay quietly, waiting for something to happen. At last Katana appeared with Atzel, one of Matti's Shomrim who shared guard duty with Razor's squads.

"We surveyed the west woods, sir," Katana said. "Kel was telling the truth. There's an entire Compound of Wild Ones—males, females, kittens—where he said it would be."

"How close did you get?" Razor asked privately.

"Close enough to cast an aura spell, far enough that their guards didn't get wind of us."

"How many are there?"

"A fair number, but not as many as there are here, sir."

"Good."

"Matti wants to see you, Razor," Atzel said. "He's gathering our captains and the Council of Elders to discuss the new compound."

"I'll be there. But I still haven't decided about Kel here. What, my young Wild One, shall we do with you?"

"Kill him," Atzel said indifferently. "He's one of them."

"No!" Leilei and Patches said together. "He didn't do any harm," Leilei added. "He can't help who his parents are."

"She has a point," Razor said. "As far as I know, the only thing Kel did wrong was trespass in our woods. It's not like the Wild Ones don't know we're here."

"They do know, sir," Kel piped up. "They've known for ages. I tell you, if you spare me, I will be your eyes and ears in their compound!"

FRENEMIES

Razor gazed at Kel unblinking as the young Wild One crouched in front of them.

"I will spare you, Kel—this time. But you had better prove your worth to me. Keep your eyes and ears open and your mouth shut. Find out what you can about their battle plans, about where Saunders keeps the Tilyon, about anything you might think is remotely interesting to me. You will report to the guard on duty here, and only here. If we find you anywhere else, you will be killed."

Kel cowered.

"I expect you to have something worth hearing when you do return."

"You will, I swear by the First!" Kel said. "You'll see. I can help you."

"We shall see," Razor growled. "Now you can leave." He and the others walked Kel to the road and watched as he crossed it and disappeared into the woods.

"I hope you're not making a mistake," Katana said.

"So do I."

They turned and slipped back into the woods. Atzel settled himself in for guard duty.

Two days later, the half-moon was high in the night sky as Roah hurried inside the back door, through the kitchen, and up the steps of Saunders' house. He never moved slowly unless he was hunting. Time was precious, and he had many things to accomplish. He had just set in motion the events he calculated would move him closer to his goals.

"Ready for your lesson?" he asked as he strode into the office where Saunders awaited him. The Tilyon was on the desk next to the open lock-box.

"I should hope so, considering it was scheduled for this time," Saunders said. "I want to learn how to fire those jets of light that burn."

"Then we shall try. You must concentrate deeply on the Magelights

135

within the Tilyon. Their fire will be your fire. Make them glow, and take them inside you until you can feel their heat."

Saunders frowned and stared at the Tilyon. He concentrated and the eyes began to glow. Saunders narrowed his eyes and kept staring.

"I don't feel anything," he said.

"Keep trying."

Roah watched silently for a few seconds more. Then he sent a one-word message: "Now."

Downstairs, Alef sat on the back porch railing. His Magelight blazed. Shortly afterward, a rabbit pushed its way through a hole in the fence near the dog yard. It hopped straight for the chain link fence that surrounded the kennel and crashed into it. Dog collars jingled as the sleeping Dobermans awoke. They started barking as the rabbit leaped again and again into the fence. The dogs nearest the rabbit opened their jaws and tried to bite it through the fence, barking and howling.

The back door of the house next to them slammed against the wall as their neighbor charged onto the porch. "Saunders!" Mackie thundered. "How many times have I told you to keep those damned dogs of yours quiet!"

Alef jumped down from the railing and moved quietly into the house, shutting the door softly behind him. He went into the darkened dining room and jumped onto a windowsill to watch the dogs. As soon as Alef let go of it, the rabbit stopped leaping against the fence and instead began to run around the yard in a panic as the dogs kept up their barking. Alef made sure the rabbit did not find the hole in the fence, grabbing it with his mind and moving it away from the hole whenever it got too close.

Saunders heard the racket from upstairs and swore. "What are those dogs up to?" he said, dropping the Tilyon into the lockbox and racing out of the room.

Behind him, Roah's Magelight flashed and just managed to stop the lid from closing. Roah waited until he heard Saunders exit the house to open the box fully. Then he leaped onto the desk and put his paw on the

Tilyon. The rush of power energized him. He could practically feel his fur standing on end. He concentrated on the Council Compound, and soon he could see a shadowy shape.

"It took you long enough to contact me again," the muffled voice said.

"It is difficult. Saunders is possessive of the Tilyon. I had to resort to trickery."

"We must do something about that when we can."

"Yes, Councilor. I am working on it."

"Anything else?"

"Kfir grows impatient. He says his warriors will go stale if we don't move soon."

"Then he will be pleased to hear that you will attack on the next full moon."

"That is good. Kfir is not the only one tired of waiting. Any further orders?"

"Kill Razor and Letsan. Hakham too, if you can manage it."

"We will do our best," Roah said, ears flat. "I must go, Councilor. The dogs have stopped barking."

"Don't fail me, Roah."

"I shall not."

Roah took his paw off the Tilyon and the image faded. He flipped the lid closed and dropped wearily to the floor and waited for Saunders to return. He took long, controlled breaths. By the time Saunders came back, his breathing would be normal.

Outside, Saunders had found the rabbit. He noticed Alef in the window and ordered him outside to get rid of it. Once the rabbit was gone, Saunders quieted the dogs. Whining, they went back into their kennels.

"Make sure they stay there, and keep them quiet!" Saunders told Alef. "Why didn't you stop them in the first place?" he asked.

"I didn't know why they barked. I waited for you to stop them. Had I known there was a rabbit—"

CHAPTER THIRTEEN

"Oh, never mind. I need to go talk to Mackie before he calls the police." Saunders hurried through the house and over to his next-door neighbor's house, where he checked his impulse to shove Mackie up against the wall and instead stood on the porch and listened to his neighbor complain about his son being woken yet again.

"I'm sorry," Saunders said, barely controlling his disdain. "A rabbit got in the yard. You can't blame the dogs for following their instincts."

"Yes, I can when those instincts are breaking noise laws. You keep those dogs quiet, Saunders. Or else!" He went inside and slammed the door behind him, shutting off the porch light.

Saunders stood in the dark, fuming. He strode quickly back to his house, the expression on his face boding ill for any Catmage unhappy enough to be in his path. He found none until he got back to the office. Roah sat in a chair next to the desk.

"You're supposed to keep those dogs quiet!" Saunders shouted as he came into the room.

"Not when they sleep," Roah said. "My responsibility ends when you put them in their kennels for the night. Alef told me a rabbit got into the yard. We will find the hole and block it up. Now, if you are ready for your lesson, we can continue."

Frowning, Saunders rounded the desk and sat down heavily. He picked up the Tilyon. "Fine. Teach me to make those burning jets," he said. The Tilyon's eyes glowed fiercely as Saunders gripped it tightly.

"It should be easier for you while you are in this mood," Roah said. "Let us begin."

FOURTEEN: HALLOWEEN

A ndy sighed as he looked in the mirror. "I don't care what Becca says, this costume is stupid," he muttered.

Mike, Teresa, and Becca had decided they should all come as characters from the Broadway play "Cats." Andy was going as Mr. Mistoffelees. Mike in particular thought it would be absolutely hilarious for Andy to dress up in a cat costume.

"I look ridiculous," he said. "It's a good thing Razor will never see me in it."

"Oh, that gives me an idea," Letsan said. "I'll have to show my brother just what you look like in that costume. Just let me concentrate hard so I don't forget this moment. No, wait, even better, take a picture with your phone. You can show it to him next time you're at the Compound. Come on, Andy, you look great."

"You show Razor what I look like and you can sleep the entire winter at the Compound. No more soft, warm bed for you," Andy warned.

"You're bluffing."

"Try me."

"All right, all right, my brother doesn't need to know you look like an idiot. Well, some might argue that he already thinks—"

"Watch it," Andy growled.

CHAPTER FOURTEEN

Goldeneyes paused from washing her face. "Now, children," she said, "if you can't play nice, I'm going to have to separate you."

"You sound like my mom," Andy said.

"Zahavin wants to laugh at you just as much as I do, Andy. She's just trying to be nice."

Goldeneyes stared at Letsan.

"Before you guys get into a fight, remember that my mom's home," Andy said. "No zapping allowed."

To his surprise, Goldeneyes laughed and settled back to grooming herself.

"You're in a good mood tonight."

"That's because we're not going to have any trouble tonight. You're going to your dance, Letsan and I are staying here, and no one is going to that horrible house."

"Good," Andy said. "I'd like to make it all the way through this Halloween dance without a problem. It's not like Saunders can surprise us with his Magelight necklace like he did last year."

"And we already know he has the Tilyon," Letsan said.

"Don't remind me," Andy said, groaning.

The doorbell rang and Andy started. "Becca's here! I got to run!"

"I'll come with you."

"Why, you want to laugh at Becca, too?"

"I'd never laugh at that lovely girl. I just want to see how much better she looks as a cat than you do."

"Thanks for the vote of confidence," Andy said. He picked up his phone and wallet, slipped them into his pocket, and headed out the door, followed by Letsan.

"Have fun," Goldeneyes said, licking her paw and starting on her left ear.

Andy and Letsan raced downstairs. Becca and her father were in the kitchen talking to Andy's mother. Andy stopped dead as he came through the door. Becca looked fantastic as Grizabella.

"You look great!" he said. "Hi, Mr. Jefferson."

Becca smiled that wide, lovely, double-curved smile. "You look pretty good yourself."

Andy shot Letsan a look. "Ha!" he sent.

"She has to say that. She's your friend," he sent to both of them.

"Oh, be quiet," Andy muttered out loud as Becca smothered a laugh.

"What's that?" his mother said.

"Nothing. You guys ready?"

"We're waiting for you, Catman," Mr. Jefferson said. "If you're ready, let's go."

"Okay. 'Bye, Mom."

"See you later, sweetie."

"Good night, Mrs. Cohen."

"You look great, Becca," Letsan told her, winding around her legs. She smiled at him and leaned down to scratch him under the chin. "Thanks," she whispered softly. They followed her father out to the car.

Letsan trotted up the stairs after Andy left. He leaped onto the bed, yawned hugely, and stretched. "I'm thinking a nice, long nap," he told Goldeneyes.

"That's not a bad idea at all," she said and leaped off the windowsill onto the bed. She curled onto the pillow and dropped her head on her paws. "Here's to an uneventful night."

"So, no funny business this year, right, Andy?" Mr. Jefferson said as he pulled the car onto the street.

"Nope. We're just going to dance and eat and drink the night away." He grinned at Becca, who nodded. The ride passed quickly after Mr. Jefferson started reminiscing about previous Halloweens. The three of them were laughing about Andy's first grade robot costume when they pulled up to the high school.

Mr. Jefferson dropped them off at the front door of the school and waved goodbye as they headed inside. Andy and Becca walked leisurely through the crowd, searching for their friends.

"We could text Mike and Teresa," Becca said.

Andy shrugged. "Nah, we'll find them. Let's just walk around and enjoy ourselves for now." It was nice just being with Becca. Mike was a great guy, but he tended to be a whirlwind of activity and chatter. This way, they could talk to each other without being constantly interrupted.

They stopped at the snack table and picked up some food and drinks, then found a spot near a pair of closed doors, where they stayed and observed their fellow students' costumes. Andy was rolling his eyes at a group of sparkly vampires when Taylor and his friends found them.

"Oh, isn't he just the cutest thing?" Taylor said to Pete and Tommy, who laughed on cue. "He loves cats so much he's becoming one. Want some milk, Cohen?"

Pete and Tommy meowed, then guffawed. Becca frowned.

Andy glared at Taylor, who was wearing a black shirt, red bandana, an eye patch, and a leather necklace with five colored gems. Becca gasped as she realized he was wearing the Magelights publicly. Taylor grinned at her reaction. Andy and Becca exchanged glances. He smiled grimly.

"Nice necklace," Andy said. "Did you make it yourself or did your mother do it for you?"

Now it was Taylor's turn to glare.

"Too bad they don't let us carry real swords," Pete said. The three of them were dressed as pirates. "Bet we could have a lot of fun with those."

"You're such a moron," Andy said.

"Who's a moron?" Mike asked, pushing past Pete and pulling Teresa by the hand to join Andy and Becca against the doors. "I mean, there are three of them here to choose from. Wait, never mind. No need to choose. They're all idiots."

Taylor closed his hands into fists.

"Try it," Mike said. "Please do. Oh, hi Mr. Straight!" he said, waving to a spot behind Taylor. Taylor and his friends turned, and Mike laughed again. "Whoops, made you look! No Mr. Straight, but there are plenty of other teachers around. Please. Try something. I want to see you all in detention until Christmas."

Taylor's eyes narrowed. "I won't forget this, Murdoch."

"Yeah, yeah, we know the drill. Later, loser." Mike held his thumb and forefinger up to his forehead in a backwards L. "Go walk the plank or something."

Taylor glanced around, motioned to Pete and Tommy, and disappeared into the crowd.

"Thanks," Andy said.

"Hi, Teresa," Becca said.

"Hi back."

"Good timing," Andy said.

"Don't mention it," Mike said. "So, let me see you two. Turn around!"

They twirled as requested.

"Not bad. Not bad at all," he said.

"Your costumes are really good," Becca said.

"Gus and Jellylorum at your service," Mike said, bowing.

"Please don't start singing," Andy said.

"Nah, not tonight. Tonight, we dance! And I think they're playing our song. Come on!" He grabbed Teresa's hand and pulled her toward the dance floor. Andy and Becca followed suit.

Earlier that day, Razor and Matti had sat together in the late afternoon sun outside Razor's bayit. One of Matti's Shomrim approached.

"Captain, Velvel is outside the Compound by Guard Station Vav. He says he has a message for you."

"Bring him here," Matti said.

"Velvel?" Razor asked.

"The double agent I told you about. Razor, the Council has set a lot of things in motion since you left. One of those is having eyes and ears on the inside the Wild Ones' compound."

Razor growled at the reminder that a Compound had been set up right under his nose. That's why they'd had to double the guard perimeter.

"If he's such a great spy, why didn't he tell us about the Compound while it was being built?"

"I don't know. Ask him."

"Do you trust him?" Razor asked.

Matti shifted uncomfortably. "I have no reason not to."

"So you *don't* trust him?"

"It isn't that, Razor. I've always had an odd feeling about him. But he's never done anything to make me dislike him, and my feelings about a Catmage are no reason to mistrust him."

"Yes, they are. My feelings have kept me alive more than once. Listen to your instincts, Matti. If you don't like him, there must be a reason for it."

Matti shook his head. "I don't think so. He's been reporting to Kharoom and Ruma for at least a cycle. He's a loyal Catmage."

Razor was about to respond heatedly when Zohar and Velvel arrived. He bit back his words as Matti spoke.

"What news?"

"The Wild Ones have left the house fully unprotected. They've moved into their new home. The last of them left two nights ago."

"So? The dogs are still there. And so is Saunders," Razor said.

"Ah, but you didn't let me finish, Razor. Tonight is the night that Saunders has to stay late at the school for another of those human rituals. The house will be unprotected except for the dogs, and they're locked in cages when Saunders isn't home."

"What ritual?" Razor asked.

"The one where humans dress up and stand in a big room jumping up and down to music."

"That's a dance," Razor said. "Andy was talking about it the last time he was here." He turned to Zohar. "Our watchers will know. Send a message to Hanit. Find out if this is true. Report back as soon as you hear."

Matti bristled at the way Razor took command, but now was not the time for an argument. "We could have used a little more notice, Velvel," he said. "Why did you wait so long to tell us?"

"I couldn't risk contacting you until now. I have to be very careful coming and going. If they suspect I'm working with you, I'm dead. I told Roah I'm off on a journey to recruit more Catmages."

"What happens when you go back to them empty-handed?" Razor asked.

"I won't. But I'll make sure I only give them a kitten or two who will be of no use to them for at least a cycle or more."

"You shouldn't be bringing them any. Wild kits belong with us."

"If I don't bring them recruits, they will find another Seeker to do their bidding," Velvel said, his ears flattening. "Gestures like these keep me on the inside, where I can pass vital information to Kharoom."

Razor grunted. "Sensitive little thing, isn't he?" he sent privately to Matti, whose ears twitched. "Doesn't like to be criticized."

"He never has," Matti sent back to Razor. "Try not to offend him so much that he loses his train of thought."

"Why didn't you tell us about the Wild Ones building a Compound?" Razor asked, ignoring Matti's suggestion.

Velvel looked steadily at Razor. "They've been getting more and more secretive and suspicious," he said. "I'm not allowed to come and go without permission from Roah."

"So Roah thinks you're out seeking half-breeds."

"I said as much before," Velvel said irritably. "Do you think I'm lying?"

Zohar returned before Razor could respond. "Velvel's information checks out, sir. Hanit hasn't seen any Wild Ones at the house for several nights. He thought it was because they were keeping out of sight. When we sent the message, Hanit did an aura check. There are no Wild Ones anywhere in the house, only Magelights."

CHAPTER FOURTEEN

"The Magelights!" Matti said. "Then we can retrieve them tonight. No Saunders, no Wild Ones—only the dogs, and they're locked up. This is the chance we've waited for, Razor!"

"Yes, it is, but I don't like it," Razor said. "Something feels wrong."

"What?"

"It's too easy. The Evil One has never left his home unprotected like this. The Wild Ones have always been there."

"But the Wild Ones didn't have a Compound until recently," Velvel pointed out. "Of course they were always there. They had nowhere else to stay."

Razor stared at Velvel, who leveled his gaze coolly back at the big Maine Coon.

"Get rid of this fool," Razor sent privately to Matti. "We need to talk alone."

"Velvel, thank you for your report. Zohar, would you take him back to my bayit to wait? Razor and I need to discuss this."

"Yes sir," Zohar said.

"I wouldn't take too long," Velvel warned. "We may never get another chance like this. We don't know how long that house will be empty."

Matti said nothing until Velvel and Zohar left.

Razor paced in a circle, his tail switching. "I tell you, Matti, it's a trap. Your instincts are right about Velvel. Something about this reeks. Trust me on this. We tried to attack twice already on bad information and lost a lot of good Catmages. My gut says this is another one of those times."

Matti shook his head. "I have my orders, Razor. I am to retrieve the Magelights at any opportunity. This is the best opportunity we've had since the old Council was slaughtered."

"No! Don't be a fool," Razor said, stopping to face Matti. "Saunders isn't this careless. He wouldn't leave the Magelights unguarded."

Matti's ears flattened. "So now I'm a fool who should defy Council orders because Razor has a bad feeling?"

"You're a fool if you *don't* defy their orders. They don't understand

146

the situation like we do. They're not here. Did they make you head of the Shomrim because you'll do whatever they say, or are you the head of the Shomrim because you're a good warrior?"

Matti growled softly. "Don't insult my integrity, Razor. I wouldn't take our fighters out if I thought I was leading them into a trap."

"Of course not! But you're not listening to me. This is my third autumn in the East Woods. I know the enemy better than anyone, and I tell you, I don't like the smell of anything tonight. Not Velvel's tale, not the Council's order, and especially not the supposedly empty house!"

Matti and Razor stared at one another for a long moment. At last Matti dropped his gaze and stilled his tail.

"All right, Razor. You win. I'll stand down for now. And I'll think of some way to explain it to Kharoom."

Razor laughed harshly. "Explaining anything to that idiot should be the least of your worries. Feel free to blame it on me. He'd love that."

"If that's all, then?" Matti asked.

Razor grunted. "Yes. Glad you came to your senses, boy." He yawned and stretched. "I've had a long, tiring day. I'm going to take a nap. Don't worry, Matti. You made the right decision."

"Yes. I have." Matti watched Razor enter the bayit, lie down, and curl up to sleep. He trotted down the path to his own home and found Zohar and Velvel waiting.

"Get the Shomrim ready," he told Zohar. "We're going to attack the Evil One's house tonight."

"So you settled Razor's fears?" Velvel asked.

"No. But we're going anyway. I am captain of the Shomrim now. Zohar, have you ever gone against Razor's wishes?"

"No, sir. Nobody does."

"Well, I do. We can either fight Razor or we can work around him. I see no need to have two battles tonight. We're acting on orders from the Council. I have good information that the house will be undefended. Gather the Shomrim secretly and get them ready. We'll form up on the north side of the wood."

"Yes, sir."

"Zohar," Matti said, "tell me truthfully—do you have any problems with what I'm about to do?"

"No sir. If tonight is our best chance, let's take it. I owe the Wild Ones for the last battle. I lost some good friends that night."

"Get your warriors ready. And don't tell anyone outside the Shomrim, not even Letsan."

"That won't be an issue, sir. He's in town."

"Good. That's one less meddler to worry about. You have your orders."

"Sir." Zohar nodded to Matti and Velvel and left.

"I'll head out too, Matti," Velvel said. "I need to find some wild kits to satisfy Roah. May the First favor you tonight."

Matti watched Velvel leave. He sat down and curled his tail around his legs, thinking. In spite of his words, he was worried about defying Razor. What if he was right? What if this really was a trap? But no, it couldn't be. Velvel was one of Kharoom's creatures. He had spent the last several seasons currying trust with the Wild Ones. No, his source was solid. Tonight, Matti would do what even the great Razor and Hakham could not achieve: He was going to retrieve the Council's Magelights—and perhaps even the Tilyon—from the Evil One. Matti rose and strode quickly to the rendezvous point. Tonight would be a night to remember. They'd tell tales of it around the firestones in the winter for many cycles to come.

When he reached the Shomrim and saw their neat, ordered ranks, the last of his doubts evaporated. "Split up. Stay under cover. When you get to town, go to your assigned areas and wait until the signal is given. Let's go, warriors!" he said, leading them down the road at a brisk trot.

Hours later, Matti lay under a car across the street from Saunders' house. The Shomrim had all made it into town without incident and hidden until nightfall. The guards reported no movement in or out of the house. There was no sign of Wild Ones. Shamir, their best aura detector, confirmed that several Magelights were together in a small area on the second floor of the house. Matti poked his head out from under the car and watched the clouds moving quickly in the night sky. "When the clouds cover the moon," he sent to his captains, "we go. You know your roles. The squads going inside will go fast and silent and get those Magelights. The rest of us will form a defensive perimeter." He waited while the captains notified their squad leaders. "Now!" he said as the moon disappeared.

Catmages hurried out of hiding places all around the house. The front gate swung open and two squads ran up the stairs, knocking the door open as they charged. The outdoor squads separated to each side of the house, some standing at the corners while others went down the alley to the rear. Matti stopped on the sidewalk in the middle of the front yard. So far, all was going smoothly. Then dogs barked and growled from around the side of the house.

"They're not locked up!" Zohar sent. "The cellar door was open and the dogs are free! We've been tricked!"

Shouts and yowling came from the backyard. "Wild Ones!" Atzel said. "They're coming through loose boards in the fence! They must have been waiting on the street behind! They're coming through into the yard! Retreat! Retreat! There are too many of them! And they have more dogs!"

"Razor was right! It's a trap!" Matti said. "Indoor squads, get out! Get out of the house! The rest of you, battle formation!" As the Catmages retreated and tried to form a defensive front, Matti thought frantically. Zohar said that Letsan would be in town tonight. In a flash, a globe of copper-colored light flew from Matti's Magelight. If only Letsan got the message in time!

As the sun set, Razor padded through the Compound. The nap had done him good. His mind and body were refreshed. A strategy for retrieving the Magelights had occurred to him as he was drinking at the stream, and he wanted to run it past Matti. After a few minutes of looking, Razor realized that Matti was nowhere to be found. Nor, he saw, were Matti's Shomrim.

"By the First's whiskers, that fool went to town after all! Damn it!" he said, his human upbringing coming out in his anger. "He's going to get himself killed, and my warriors along with him. Hakham! Hakham!" Razor raced grimly along the path in search of the old one. They needed to gather their remaining warriors, and quickly.

By the time it was fully dark, Razor, Methuselah, Hakham, and a dozen warriors were heading into town. Razor didn't dare take more. He couldn't leave the Compound undefended. This might be a ruse for the Wild Ones to attack them in their homes. He hoped they were worrying over nothing. Maybe the house really was empty, and Matti had the chance to get back the Magelights. But in his gut and heart, Razor knew that Matti had made a terrible mistake.

Letsan leaped awake as Matti's message reached him. "Zahavin! Zahavin! Matanya is in trouble. We have to go, now!" He shared the message with her and quickly raised the window with his Magelight. Letsan jumped onto the roof and to the ground, waiting for Goldeneyes to land. They tore through the yard and down the street.

"We need to tell Andy," she said as they ran. "He can bring help."

"How?" Letsan said.

"The man who helped us the night we lost the Tilyon. Velez."

Letsan thought it over as they hurried toward Oak Street.

"It can't hurt. I won't wait for you, Zahavin. Send the message and catch up with me."

"All right," she said, coming to a stop as Letsan trotted away. She concentrated and sent a message to Andy. It winded her, but not as much as it used to. "Nafshi said my power would grow as I got older," she said. "Thank the One she was right!"

Goldeneyes waited to catch her breath, then raced after Letsan.

Andy and Becca applauded with the rest of the students as the music ended. They moved off the dance floor and found a couple of chairs. Mike and Teresa stood nearby, chatting and laughing with their friends. Mike waved at a boy across the room.

"Hey, Teresa, there's Paul King and Vicki Reed. I need to talk to them about the play. C'mon, it'll only be a minute."

"Okay," she said, following him through the crowd.

"Alone at last," Andy said, grinning.

"Yeah, in the middle of half the school," Becca said.

"And yet it's so much quieter with Mike out of earshot."

"He does seem to fill the room, doesn't he?"

Andy was about to answer when a golden light zoomed along the ground and into his Magelight. He looked around quickly, but no one else had seen it. Andy gasped as Goldeneyes relayed Matanya's frantic call for help. "There's trouble!" he said. He scanned the room and rushed over to Teresa and Mike, Becca on his heels.

"Teresa! Teresa! Where's your grandfather?" he asked. "It's an emergency!"

"I think I saw him over there," she said, pointing at the far end of the room. Without another word, Andy turned and hurried through the crowd, Becca in his wake.

"Man, that's rude," Paul said.

"Yeah, sometimes Andy's like that," Mike said distractedly. He and Teresa looked at each other. "See you around, Paul. I got to go do something." He pulled Teresa after him. As soon as they were out of earshot, he said, "I don't know about you, but I think we should tag along and see what's up."

"Let's go," she agreed.

"Please, Mr. Velez, they're getting slaughtered!" Andy was saying as Mike and Teresa arrived.

Mr. Velez frowned. "You kids will get in trouble if you get caught out," he said.

"Let us worry about that," Becca said. "Mr. Velez, if we don't get

151

there soon—"

"They'll *die!*" Andy said. "Some may already be dead."

"What's going on?" Mike asked.

"Matti went to Saunders' house. They lured him into a trap. Goldeneyes sent for help. We have to go. Please, Mr. Velez!"

Mr. Velez and Teresa's eyes met and she nodded. "Grandpa, we should help," she said.

Mr. Velez frowned. "All right. Let's go. Mike, get out of here. When you're out of sight in the hallway, run to the locker room and grab a load of towels, as much as you can carry. My SUV is by the gym door. Wait for me there. The rest of you, leave separately. And *walk*. Saunders has been watching you all night. I seen him."

Mike nodded and left.

"Andy, you go stand near the door," Becca said. "Teresa and I will think of something to get Saunders' attention long enough for you to slip out."

"Mike's friends!" Teresa said. "They'll help." She and Becca headed off to find the theater troupe. A short time later, Paul was leading his group in raucous cheering that settled into shout after shout of "Huzzah!"

When they started leaping into the air with every "Huzzah!" Principal Saunders could be seen heading toward the noisy group, the frown on his face boding ill for them. Andy, Becca, and Teresa quickly made their way to the door behind Saunders, hurrying through the corridors toward the parking lot. They found Mike already in the SUV. They hurried into the car and Mr. Velez took off as they were fastening their seat belts.

"What are we gonna do when we get to the house?" he asked Andy.

"I don't know," Andy said worriedly. "I guess I'll figure it out when we get there. I have my Magelight."

"I have these," Mike said, uncovering a towel filled with rocks. "I picked them up while we waited for you to get to the car. Figured we could help a little." He separated them into three bundles and gave one to each of the girls. "And listen," he said, "don't be afraid to hurt the Wild Ones.

They're trying to kill our friends."

Mr. Velez glanced in the rear view mirror. "Make me a bundle, Mike. I used to be a pretty fair pitcher."

The SUV skidded to a halt in front of Number 19 Oak Street. Andy flung open the door and leaped out of the car, running to the front gate and throwing it open with a wave of his fist and the glow of his Magelight. He stopped short inside the yard. Catmages lay on the ground and porch, dead or wounded—Andy couldn't tell. Dogs and Wild Ones battled the last desperate stand of Catmages, bunched in a corner of the yard with Razor, Letsan, Hakham and Methuselah on the front line, the other Shomrim ranged behind. Goldeneyes and Methuselah, fur fluffed and eyes blazing, were at the point of the wedge of Catmages, firing jet after jet at the Wild Ones, who jeered as they tried to penetrate the shield of light Hakham held in front of them. Arrows of light flashed back and forth. The Wild Ones launched a flanking attack as Andy and the others entered the yard. An arrow of light hit Letsan, who was defending a wounded Catmage lying on the ground. Letsan grunted in pain and fired back at the Wild One, who dropped.

Andy's friends slipped around him and started throwing stones. A stone hit a dog on its hind leg. The dog dropped and Mike shouted "Got him!" Wild Ones turned to face the new onslaught and found themselves dodging stones, some finding their mark, others thumping against the house or the ground. The Wild Ones, their Magelights glowing, sent a flock of light daggers straight at Andy and his friends.

"Look out!" Andy said, reflexively raising his arm to deflect the blow. A shield flew out of his Magelight, deflecting the light daggers and covering Andy and his friends.

While the Wild Ones were distracted, Razor laughed harshly and picked up the fallen stones with his Magelight, flinging them accurately at the Wild Ones and the dogs. Other Shomrim saw what he was doing and joined in. The tide began to turn.

CHAPTER FOURTEEN

Andy stood in front of his friends as they attacked the Wild Ones, his green shield deflecting attacks. His mind raced, but he couldn't figure out how to split his concentration the way Hakham could. Either he went on offense or defense. Right now, defense it was. He pushed his shield out farther as a Wild One tried to sneak around Letsan's side. As Andy extended the shield, he saw one of the dogs about to close its jaws around Matti, who flung a feeble light dagger at it and tried to crawl away on three legs. It was obvious Matti was completely spent. The dog was about to kill him.

"NO!" Andy roared. He clenched his hands into fists, crossed his arms over his chest, and flung them out fiercely. A wave of green light arced from both arms, passing harmlessly over the Catmages and flinging down every single dog and Wild One in sight. It was as if a great wind had blown them over. The dogs yipped and whined and scrambled to their feet, running along the side of the house to hide in their kennels. The Wild Ones ran too, some leaping through the loose boards in the fence, some racing under the porch, a few running into the house. Neighbors' lights flickered on as the noise subsided. For a few moments, there was dead silence in the front yard. Mr. Velez and the others stared in awe. The Catmages who could still stand turned toward Andy, stunned at what they had just seen. Mike finally broke the silence.

"What do you want us to do?" he asked.

Andy couldn't answer. He stood where he was, panting, legs wobbling. Mike walked up and grabbed his arm, supporting him.

"We need to get inside the house," Razor said. "There may be survivors."

Andy swayed as he stood, breathing hard and sweating, his hands trembling. "I'll be fine," he said, gasping. "I'll go." He shook Mike off, tried to take a step, and fell to his knees.

"You stay here," Mr. Velez said. "Some of you cats come with me to tell the good ones from the bad."

"I'll go," Goldeneyes said. "Razor! You and Atzel come with us." They hurried up the porch steps and disappeared into the house. Mike frowned at Andy and ran across the yard to help the girls. Teresa got the towels from the car. She and the others eased the wounded Catmages onto them and used them as stretchers to bring them into the SUV.

Letsan came over and nudged Andy's hand. "Are you all right?" he asked.

"Yeah. I just need to catch my breath. Are you okay?"

"Yes. I'm going to have to grow back some fur," he said, looking balefully at a burn on his shoulder, "but we're okay. We got here after most of the fighting was done. Still, we're very glad to see you. That was some spell, Andy. How did you do it? Zahavin never taught you that. Have you been training privately with my brother?"

"No," Andy said. "I don't even know what I did. I just got mad when I saw all the Catmages down and bleeding." He looked around the yard. Mike, Teresa, and Becca were kneeling by various Catmages. Hakham, Methuselah, and the other uninjured Catmages were helping heal the wounded. Andy saw Matanya sit up shakily, holding his front paw off the ground. Mike carried a wounded Catmage gently out to the car and put him on the floor of the back seat.

"I have to help," Letsan said. "You stay here."

"I can help, too," Andy said.

"You can barely stand. Stay here," Letsan said firmly. Andy sat back and rested while the others gathered the wounded. When they were nearly finished with the Catmages in the yard, Mr. Velez, Goldeneyes, and the others reappeared. His arms were filled with towel-wrapped bundles. Andy rose to his feet with a questioning look on his face. Mr. Velez shook his head.

"I'm sorry, Andy. None of them left in the house made it." He laid the covered Catmages gently on the ground. Andy's eyes welled up with tears. Matanya bowed his head.

"This is my fault. Razor warned me. I—"

"We'll assign blame later," Letsan said. "Let's get out of here before those dogs decide to come out of hiding." He went over to the bundles on the ground. One of the blood-soaked towels had fallen open to reveal long, orange fur. Letsan pawed it open until it revealed the Catmage beneath. His son lay within.

"Zohar! Zohar! What are you doing here? You said you'd stay at the Compound. Zohar!" Letsan nuzzled his son's face. "They've killed my son!" He yowled in agony.

Andy stared down at Zohar in horror. He dropped to the ground next to him and cupped Zohar's face in his hand. Was it his imagination, or was Zohar still breathing? Andy wasn't sure.

"Letsan! Letsan, wait! I think he's still alive!"

Letsan stopped crying and put his ear to his son's body. He licked Zohar's ear. "I can barely hear his heartbeat. He's nearly gone."

Andy fought back tears. He couldn't watch another Catmage die. Not again. Not Zohar. Not another friend! An unbearable anger swept over him. No one else would die tonight!

Whoosh. Whoosh. Whoosh. He could feel his pulse thumping. *Whoosh. Whoosh. Whoosh.* Andy moved his hand to Zohar's neck, feeling for a pulse. Was he imagining it, or was it getting stronger? Before Andy could decide, his Magelight flashed, bathing Zohar's body in green light. Andy dropped to his knees, breathless again.

"I'm sorry, Letsan," Mr. Velez said. "I didn't know he was your kid." He bent down to pull the towel back over the Catmage. Zohar's side rose and fell slowly.

"He's not dead! He's breathing! Letsan, he's still alive!" Andy said. "We have to get help." He pulled his cell phone out of his pocket and keyed in a number.

"Dr. Crane, it's Andy. It's an emergency. I have five badly wounded cats that need your help. Yes, again. Okay, thanks."

"He'll meet us at the office. Let's get going. Matanya, let Mike carry you. Mr. Velez, I'll take Zohar."

Razor came running back from the rear of the house. "They're gone. The cowards all ran after Andy knocked them down. Let's get out of here." He looked around the yard. "I'll take the ones who can walk on their own back to the Compound. Zahavin, are you coming with me?"

"I'm going with Andy and Letsan," Goldeneyes said.

"Fine. Send me word later." Razor watched as they left the yard. He walked through the gate and stopped. His Magelight flashed and the gate slammed loudly, startling them all. The wood around the latch cracked and broke.

"Did you have to do that?" Andy asked.

"No, I didn't have to. I wanted to."

Andy bit back a retort. "Let's go, Mr. Velez."

"Andy?" Razor said as he was getting into the SUV.

"What?"

"You look like an idiot in that costume."

Andy rolled his eyes as Razor limped off, followed by the rest of the Catmages. He closed the door and gave Mr. Velez the address of Coreyton Animal Hospital.

"Let's get out of here," he said.

FIFTEEN: SECRET'S OUT

It was quiet in the car on the way to the vet's. Andy was exhausted. Goldeneyes spoke softly to the other Catmages, telling them about Dr. Crane and what to expect from a human veterinarian. Letsan sat next to Becca, who held Zohar in her lap. Matanya sat on the back seat, staring out the window, saying nothing. Even Mike was silent.

Dr. Crane and Maddie rushed out the door as Mr. Velez pulled up to the office. They helped the others carry the wounded cats inside. Goldeneyes and Letsan leaped quietly out of the vehicle and moved to the shadows near the building.

The reception counter became an impromptu triage area as they put the wounded cats, still in their towels, on the desk. Dr. Crane frowned as he examined Zohar. "He needs to go first. Prep him for surgery," he told Maddie. "He's got internal injuries for sure. I'll be right in." He turned to Andy as Maddie took Zohar away.

"While I'm waiting for Maddie to stabilize that cat, I would like some information. Two of these cats have crushed and broken legs," Dr. Crane said. "Dogs?"

Andy nodded. "Yeah."

"How did this happen?"

Andy shrugged. "I don't really know."

SECRET'S OUT

Dr. Crane looked at him steadily. "Andy, I will treat the cat in the operating room—the one with the crushed ribs and mangled leg and severe bites. I will tend to these cats as well. But I'd appreciate not being lied to anymore."

He continued examining the cats as he spoke. "Maddie!" he called. "I'm going to need four syringes of morphine!" He went back to his examinations and stopped, looking at Andy again.

"This is a burn. Andy, how did a cat get a burn like this along its flank?"

Andy looked away rather than lie again.

Maddie came out front holding a tray with bottles and needles. Dr. Crane started injecting the wounded cats.

"Do you think I didn't notice Goldeneyes hanging around outside?" he asked after the first two Catmages lay back in relief. "Or that I forgot about the cat that was nearly killed in a dogfight last year? Andy, this is the third year in a row you've brought me wounded cats, including one that was shot. I want to know what's going on."

Andy stared at the floor. "I can't tell you. I want to. But it's not my call," he said.

"Andy—"

The light on Letsan's collar flared and the door flew open. He ran inside, Goldeneyes right behind him, and leaped onto the counter. "I'll tell you, Dr. Crane," Letsan said. "After you've healed my son and these other Catmages, I'll tell you everything you want to know."

Dr. Crane's mouth dropped open.

"Are you going to help Zohar, or are you going to stand there looking like a fish out of water?" Letsan asked.

Dr. Crane shook his head. "You're—you're talking. You're a talking cat."

"I'm going to be a biting cat if you don't hurry up and help my son!" Letsan said, growling.

"His son is the Catmage in your operating room. You probably should go to him," Andy said.

"Dr. Crane, Andy will explain everything later," Becca said. "I know it's weird. It happened to us, too."

The vet looked at the others. Mike was grinning. Mr. Velez shrugged his shoulders.

"Oh—okay. Andy, does your mother know you're here?"

"No."

"Then either call her up or go home. The rest of you should leave," he said.

"I'll take them back to school," Mr. Velez said.

Andy looked at the clock. "It's only a quarter after nine. You guys go back to the dance. I'll stay here and help."

"Yeah, we better leave. I hope my dad doesn't show up early again!" Becca said. "Text me later."

Andy nodded. "Or tomorrow. I don't know how late we're going to be here."

"What about the dead ones?" Mr. Velez asked.

"Leave that to me," Dr. Crane said. "I'll take care of them."

Andy looked at Goldeneyes. "They need to be buried," she said. "We'll have to bring them to the Compound tomorrow."

"How?" Andy asked.

"I'll do it," Mr. Velez said.

"I'd really appreciate that, Mr. Velez. Thank you."

Dr. Crane reached into his pocket. "Andy will show you where to put them. Here's my card, Mr. Velez. Call me in the morning."

"I'll be right back. Andy, you be careful," Mr. Velez said. "The rest of you, get in the truck." They said goodnight to Andy as they left.

"Thanks, Mr. Velez," Andy said. "You helped save my friends. I owe you."

Mr. Velez nodded and followed Teresa and the others out the door.

Dr. Crane turned to Andy. "I'll call your mother. If she says it's okay, you can stay here and I'll drop you off home when we're done."

"That's great, Dr. Crane. Goldeneyes and Letsan want to stay, too."

"Of course they do. A pair of talking cats would absolutely want to be at a vet's office," he said, shaking his head. He picked up the phone and dialed. "Hello, Rachel? It's Tom Crane."

Andy's mother said he could stay. Mr. Velez came back with the fallen Catmages. Andy felt another wave of sadness as he showed Mr. Velez where to leave them and saw him out. He stood by the entrance, his head bowed against the glass door. He felt a touch at his legs. Goldeneyes leaned against him.

"We have to stop Saunders," he told her. "Somehow, some way, we have to stop that man from hurting another Catmage."

"We will," Goldeneyes said, eyes blazing. "But for now, go help the doctor." Andy nodded and followed Dr. Crane, who had finished administering the painkiller and was heading for the operating room, Letsan on his heels.

"Why is he following me?" Dr. Crane asked.

"I told you, Zohar is his son."

Dr. Crane frowned. "I don't think it's a good idea for him to watch. This cat's been badly hurt. I can't save his leg. We're going to have to amputate."

"What does 'amputate' mean?" Letsan asked worriedly.

"Cut it off."

"No!"

"It can't be saved. It's not just the bones that were crushed by the dog. The nerves and blood vessels are damaged beyond repair. If I don't cut off the leg, it could get gangrenous and kill him."

Letsan sat down with a thump, stunned.

"You can't stay," Andy told him. "Heck, I don't think *I* want to stay," Andy said.

"Andy, it will be hard, but you should stay and learn," Dr. Crane said.

Letsan lay down on the floor looking miserable.

"Let me take Letsan out of here first," Andy said. He reached down and picked him up. Letsan lay limply in his arms. "I'm so sorry," Andy whispered. "I should have been faster. I should have been there to help."

"I should have been a better warrior," Letsan said sadly. "Or Zohar should have been a better listener. I told him not to join Matti. I told him to stay with Razor." Andy carried him out to the waiting room and put him on the counter.

"I'm going to go back and help the doctor. Goldeneyes, keep an eye on him, will you?"

She blinked at Andy. "Letsan, make yourself useful. See if there's anything we can do to help the Shomrim out here. You're a fairly talented healer."

"I'm not that good. I couldn't save my son."

"That's the spirit," Matti said, breathing rapidly as he lay on the counter. The painkiller had dulled, but had not removed the pain from his broken leg. "It's everything I could hope for in a healer."

Letsan growled. "I get the point. Shut up and let me take a look at you."

There wasn't much to do with Matti. Letsan worked on his broken leg a bit, then he and Goldeneyes moved from Catmage to Catmage, calming them and helping to close wounds where they could. One more warrior had a leg so badly broken that Goldeneyes was sure it would be amputated as well, but she kept those thoughts to herself. Matti kept up a stream of jokes and encouragement to his Shomrim. Goldeneyes couldn't help but notice how much his attitude eased their fears. She was beginning to like Matti.

Razor and the other Catmages arrived at the East Woods Compound as dawn was breaking, many still limping from wounds received in the battle. Katana was on guard duty at the main path into the Compound.

"Double the guard on the perimeter," Razor told her. "Institute constant patrols, three Shomrim roaming the borders regularly. The Wild

Ones will be looking to exploit any weakness."

"Yes sir," Katana said.

"When you've given the orders, find someone to cover you for guard duty, and meet me at my bayit."

Katana nodded and trotted off to carry out his orders. Razor turned to one of the healthier of the Catmages in his wake. "Take Katana's place until her substitute arrives." The warrior took his position and the rest headed wearily down the path behind Razor. Silsula and a few other Catmages came running out to see if they could help.

"See to the wounded," Hakham said. "Methuselah and I will be resting at my bayit." The two old Catmages moved slowly past the others. When they reached his home, they went inside. Hakham sat down heavily. "That was a debacle," he said, "but even a loss as bad as we have suffered pales in comparison to something else we saw last night."

"So you noticed it too?" Methuselah said.

"How could I not? Andrew Cohen used a spell that Nafshi created, and he clearly has no idea what he did. That was a Magus-level spell. Only three Catmages in existence know of it and are powerful enough to use it. Two of them are sitting right here, and the third is dead. I am beginning to understand why Andrew's powers are so erratic, and so—powerful. And I am deeply concerned."

Methuselah's ears went back. "Hakham, no Catmage has ever used another's Magelight. I cannot believe I may be agreeing with Kharoom. Could he have been right? Is there, perhaps, a good reason we destroy them upon the death of their owners? So much knowledge has been lost to us over the depths of time!"

"What do we do about it, old friend?" Hakham asked.

Methuselah sighed. "I don't know. I've never come across anything that documents this phenomenon. And I don't relish the journey back to Harry's house to look through the library."

"Perhaps we're worrying for nothing. The power surges that Andy experiences have all been for the good of our cause."

"For now, yes. But what happens if that changes? Andy is tapping powers that we don't understand. What happens to that piece of your soul you put into your Magelight if the Magelight isn't destroyed after you're gone?"

"I don't know, Master."

"I don't either. But I think we'd better keep this to ourselves," Methuselah said. "And I'd best start keeping a closer watch on Andy."

"Yes. We'd both better watch the boy." Sighing, Hakham settled down to sleep.

Andy sat wearily on a chair in the back. Dr. Crane was nearly finished. The wounded Catmages lay sleeping in cages in the back. Letsan sat in front of Zohar's unlocked cage. Matanya was with him, his broken leg set and in a bright blue cast. His had broken when a Wild One directed a stone back at him. "Couldn't duck fast enough," he admitted sheepishly as his left front leg was being set. He refused Dr. Crane's offer of anything to dull the pain.

"No medicine. My Shomrim will be confused and frightened when they wake in those cages," he said. "I must be here for them."

"Suit yourself," Dr. Crane told him. He shook his head. "I can't believe I'm talking to a cat."

"Catmage," Goldeneyes said.

"Catmage." He shrugged and called Maddie, who was filing charts in the other room, to help Andy put everything back in order for the next day's work. When the clinic was clean, Goldeneyes and Andy went to the lobby and sat down to wait for Dr. Crane to take them home. Andy reached out from time to time to stroke the side of her face. He said goodnight as Maddie left, pulling on her coat and waving as she went through the door. Finally, Dr. Crane came and sat next to them.

"Will Zohar be all right?" Andy asked.

"He's a strong, healthy young—Catmage. He had some serious internal injuries. We fixed most of them. His spleen was crushed and had to be removed."

"Like Leilei's," Goldeneyes said.

"Yes. And we amputated his right front leg."

Andy bowed his head.

"Andy, I know this sounds hard, but he'll be just fine on three legs. Plenty of cats and dogs get along fine with amputation. And they're up and about a lot faster than you'd think. They're very strong and adaptable."

"But these are Catmages, not plain cats," Andy said.

"They're still cats. They have the exact same bodies. I saw that when I operated on Zohar. And speaking of Catmages, it's time for you to tell me everything. Start from the beginning. I want to know how you met a talking cat—"

"Catmage, Doctor," Goldeneyes said. "We are Cat*mages*. Cats are the ones that won't talk back to you when you insult their intelligence."

"Cat*mage*, then," Dr. Crane said, holding back a grin.

Andy yawned. "Don't you have to take me home soon?"

"Your mother isn't expecting you at any given time. So before we leave, you can tell me what's going on, and you can fill me in on the things you didn't tell me the last couple of years. I want to know everything there is to know about—" he paused and smiled at Goldeneyes—"Catmages."

Half an hour later, Andy sat in the front seat of Dr. Crane's Jeep, his head nodding. Goldeneyes was on his lap, her paws on the door, looking out the window. Dr. Crane glanced over at them occasionally.

"I can still barely believe it. But here I am, talking to a Catmage. Wow. Just—wow. Hey, are there any other animals that can talk?" he asked.

"No," Goldeneyes said. "Perhaps someday I will tell you our history. But tonight, we have a tired boy who needs to get home."

"I'm not that tired," Andy said, yawning.

Dr. Crane smiled. "Uh-huh. Well, make sure you sleep yourself out before checking on your friends tomorrow."

"All right."

He yawned again when Dr. Crane dropped him off, waving goodbye as he drove away. Andy turned off the porch light and walked quietly up the stairs. His mother's bedroom was dark. He kicked off his shoes and changed into his pajamas, brushed his teeth quickly, and climbed into bed. Goldeneyes leaped up after him and took her place on the pillow next to him.

"We have to stop Saunders," Andy sent. "I'm getting really tired of seeing Catmages die."

"So am I, Andrew. So am I."

SIXTEEN: UNDER MY SKIN

Rachel Cohen eyed Andy over her morning coffee. Yet another cat emergency had consumed her son, and once more he was not telling her the whole story. The brief explanation he had given her earlier did not satisfy her at all. She frowned as she tried to decide what to do about it. Well, at least this time he didn't get into a fight or disappear from detention. And he was with an adult, so the out of bounds issue wasn't as serious. Rachel had met Mario Velez a few times when dropping off Andy, or when he brought Teresa over. He had it rough, trying to raise his granddaughter on his own. Rachel knew exactly what it was like being the single parent of a teenager. Mario seemed to be a good man.

Andy, she noticed, was being extra quiet as he finished his breakfast.

"Tell me more about what happened last night," she said.

"A bunch of dogs attacked Letsan and his friends. Letsan got away and found me so I followed him to the fight and found a whole lot of injured cats. And some dead ones." His throat closed and he blinked quickly, turning his head.

Rachel watched Andy as he spoke. He still wasn't telling the truth, she was sure of that. She wondered if she should challenge him and learn what had really happened last night. She frowned.

"Zohar—he's the big orange one that looks like Letsan—he lost his leg. So did another one. Doctor Crane had to amputate them. He—he wanted me to watch."

"And did you?"

"Yeah. He said it would be a good learning experience for me. It was, I guess. But it was, well—"

"Grim?"

"Grim. Yeah. Grim is the right word." Andy bowed his head.

No, she wouldn't question him this morning. He was hurting badly. But sooner or later, one way or another, she was going to get the truth. For now, she'd let things be.

"What kind of name is Zohar?" she asked.

Andy shrugged. "It's his name."

Rachel smiled. "What, do they tell you their names?"

Andy raised his head and smiled back at her. "As a matter of fact, they do. How else would I learn them?"

Rachel laughed. "Okay, Catboy. Do me a favor and clear the table. Then go finish your homework after you call Dr. Crane to see how your cats are doing, since I know you're dying to do that."

"Okay."

Andy started clearing the table. Rachel pushed back her chair, stood, and stretched. She had her own homework to do. The due date of the project she'd been working on had been pushed up. She sighed and went down the hall to her office, listening to the clatter of Andy's steps on the stairs. When this project was done—that would be a good time. She was always so darned busy. Rachel switched on her laptop as she sat down at her desk. As soon as things calmed down, she'd have that talk with him.

Andy rode his bike to Coreyton Animal Hospital. He went straight back and saw Matti with his bright blue cast standing near the cages where Zohar and Regel lay dozing. He gritted his teeth as he saw the tubes and bandages. Saunders did this. Saunders and his stupid dogs. Andy's Magelight flared at his thoughts, and he forced himself to put the rage he felt out of his mind.

"How are you this morning?" he asked Matti.

"I'm fine. This friend of yours won't let me stay here with them," he said angrily, glaring at Dr. Crane.

"You don't need to stay here," Dr. Crane told him. "I set your leg, and it should heal quickly. So you're out of here. Andy can take you home with him."

"No. If I can't stay here, I'm needed at the Compound."

"The Compound?"

"That's where the Catmages live," Andy told him. "It's out in the country."

"How's he going to get there with a broken leg?"

"Good point," Andy said. "I'll ask a friend." Andy called Mr. Velez, who agreed to drive Matti to the East Woods after Andy's work day was finished. He and Teresa arrived just after closing time.

"Thanks for doing this, Mr. Velez."

Mr. Velez waved his hand. "It's nothing. I feel bad for the poor kitties."

"Don't let them hear you calling them that, Mr. Velez," Andy said.

"Which one is Matti?" Teresa asked.

"Here he comes now," Andy said as Dr. Crane came out of the back with a struggling British shorthair.

"Don't make me scruff you," Dr. Crane said. "Don't think I won't do it. Or find a carrier to stick you in."

Andy laughed as he heard Matti swearing at the vet. "Let me guess. You grew up in a human house too?"

"Language, Matti, language!" Dr. Crane said as Matti struggled in his arms.

"I lived six months with a breeder who liked to call us human baby names. You try hearing 'How's my wittle kittle?' over and over again without going crazy. She's lucky I didn't bite her big, fat—"

CHAPTER SIXTEEN

"Okay, we get the picture," Dr. Crane said, chuckling. He set Matti down carefully. "Look, Matti, don't worry about Zohar and Regel. I promise you, I'll take really good care of them. And Andy will bring them home as soon as they're ready."

"All right. I'll go. But if they need anything, you call me, Andy. I'll come right back."

"I will."

"You better tell me, Andy," Matti said, rearing up on his hind legs and putting his good paw on Andy's thigh.

"I said I would," Andy replied irritably, pushing Matti away. "You're bigger than Letsan. Go lean on a tree or something that can't feel it." He held the door and waited for Matti. "See you, Dr. Crane!"

Matti fretted aloud the whole drive to the Compound. Andy was relieved when Mr. Velez pulled the truck over to the side of the road. He opened the door for Matti. "Do you need me to go with you?"

Matti swore again. Andy laughed. "All right. Don't worry about Zohar and Regel. Dr. Crane is the best. And I'll send you a message if anything changes. I promise."

"You better. And thanks, Andy." Matti slapped him with his tail as he climbed over Andy to get out of the SUV.

Andy yawned. "It's been a long day. Thanks for bringing me, Mr. Velez."

"*De nada.* Let's take you home now, huh?"

"Yeah. Thanks."

Letsan checked on Zohar every day. He left the house before Andy was out of bed most mornings. The techs got used to seeing him waiting by the door and let him in. Letsan quickly became a popular visitor, although he never spoke to anyone but Dr. Crane and Andy. He was also invaluable at directing Zohar and Regel on how to act like dumbcats so they wouldn't raise suspicions with Dr. Crane's staff. Andy wasn't completely sure all of his coworkers were satisfied with the explanations given, especially because of the expressions on Dr. Crane's face when Letsan was speaking to him. More than once, Andy had to tell Letsan privately to stop drawing so much attention to himself when he was around the doctor.

"Well, I can't help it," Letsan said. "Dr. Crane wants to learn everything he can about Catmages, and it's a good idea to have someone like him on our side. So when he asks, I answer."

"Well, try not to do it during business hours," Andy sent. "It's starting to look weird."

One afternoon Andy came over to check on Zohar and stayed to help Dr. Crane after everyone else had gone home. Letsan entertained them with stories of the first few months of his life with a cat breeder, who had no idea that Letsan's mother and father were Catmages.

"So this woman who breeds Maine Coons has two Catmages living with her and doesn't know it?"

"Yes. Almost none of them do. A fair number of Catmages like my parents are happy living with humans. But it was their duty as Catmages to send me and my siblings to a Compound to learn how to master our powers."

"You just up and left one day?" Dr. Crane asked.

"When my parents summoned a Seeker to take us away, we were out of there like dust kitties to a vacuum cleaner," Letsan said. "We couldn't wait to start learning spells."

"And how did the people who lost valuable Maine Coon kittens react? You know you guys can fetch a fair amount of money, especially show cats."

Letsan raised his head. "You see, Andy? I told you I was special."

Andy grinned.

"Of course they looked for us, but we were miles away by morning. They weren't the sharpest tools in the drawer," Letsan said with a glint in his eye. "We've been hiding among you for thousands of years, after all. We're quite good at it."

Dr. Crane shook his head. "I still can't believe you've been here right under my nose. Then again, you're a cat, using human expressions, and you're talking to me. That takes a lot of believing."

"You get used to it," Andy said.

"It's my upbringing," Letsan said. "I spent a lot of time watching TV. It fascinated me when I was little."

"It fascinates you now," Andy said. "You're always watching TV with me."

"I have to keep up with the news of the world."

"Yeah, there's lots of news on the cartoon channels," Andy said.

"Hey! I watch nature shows, too."

"Because you want to catch the birds."

"Who wouldn't? Tasty, delicious little things. You haven't lived until you've had a sparrow."

Andy shuddered. "I'll pass."

Dr. Crane finished writing in the chart he was working on. "Well, let's go take a look at your boy and Regel. I think they're almost ready to get out of here."

"Excellent!" Letsan said. He jumped off the desk and raced into the back room.

On the day that Zohar and Regel were released, Letsan couldn't contain his excitement. Dr. Crane decided to bring them home himself. He told Andy to come around near closing time and they'd go to the Compound together. Dr. Crane said it was because he wanted to make sure they were okay, but Andy thought the real reason was so he could see the East Woods Compound for himself. Andy couldn't blame him. Being around Catmages for a couple of years hadn't jaded him to the marvels of intelligent magical cats.

"Catmages," Letsan corrected. "And you need to control your thoughts better. Zahavin would not be happy if she caught you projecting like that."

"Okay, okay," Andy sent. "Can't we just be happy for a little while? Zohar's going home!"

Letsan leaped onto the chair next to Andy, where they sat waiting for Dr. Crane to finish up some paperwork. He rubbed his face against Andy, who scratched his ears and smiled. "Dr. Crane says cats and dogs adapt really well to the loss of a limb. You'll see. Zohar and Regel will be fine."

"I know. And I didn't lose him. You saved his life, Andy. I'll always be grateful to you for that."

Andy shrugged. "I wish I knew what I did so I could do it again if I need to."

"It doesn't matter. What matters is you saved Zohar. And here he is!" Letsan said, jumping to the floor and leaping excitedly around Zohar, who walked slowly across the floor, Regel a few steps behind.

"It will take a little while to adjust, but you'll be fine," Dr. Crane said, watching the two carefully as they made their way toward Andy. "And listen, if either one of you notices anything funny about your wound—if it feels hot or smells bad, you let me know at once! We don't want those wounds getting infected."

"No offense, doctor, but I'd better be at death's door before I come back here again," Zohar said.

"None taken. Do you want to walk to my car or do you want Andy and me to carry you?"

Zohar gave him a withering stare and stood in front of the door. His Magelight flashed and the door swung open. He and Regel walked unsteadily through the door and stood next to the car, pointedly waiting for the humans to take them home.

"Yeah, he's going to be fine," Andy said as he opened the door for the Catmages. He got into the passenger seat and waited for Dr. Crane.

"You're in for a real treat," Andy told him. "You're going to love the Compound."

"Can't wait!" Dr. Crane said as he pulled out of the parking lot. Letsan lay on the back seat between his son and Regel, purring.

The guards had been instructed to let Dr. Crane through. They watched curiously as he and Andy followed Letsan and the two wounded Shomrim down the path to the meadow, then went back to their stations.

"How long has this place been here?" Dr. Crane asked.

"I never asked," Andy said.

"Since there was nothing but farmland and forest as far as the eye could see," Letsan said. "We moved it a few times as human towns grew closer and closer."

Dr. Crane pushed a branch out of his way. Andy noticed that he was watching Zohar and Regel closely. "They're going to have to adjust to their new gait," he said. "It would actually have been easier if they'd lost a hind leg. Cats put most of their weight on their front legs."

"We've noticed," Zohar said.

"We're Shomrim. We'll manage," Regel added.

"You guys are doing great," Andy said.

"They sure are!" Matti said, sprinting toward them and nearly bowling over Zohar and Regel with his enthusiastic greeting. Behind him was a large group of warriors, including Zohar's squad. Within moments, the two wounded Catmages were engulfed. It seemed like everyone wanted to sniff them or rub shoulders or lash them with their tails.

"Enough!" roared Razor as he made his way through the crowd. "All of you, back to your duties. Zohar and Regel need rest."

"No we don't," Zohar said. "We've been resting for too long. What we need is to work with our squads." Regel growled assent.

Razor looked at the two thoughtfully. "All right. Report to your squads and get back to practice. But take it easy. I'll see you later today." The Shomrim cheered as they headed toward the practice grounds together, leaving Andy, Dr. Crane, Razor, and Letsan.

"Another human," Razor sniffed. "Good First Law observation in this place."

"Desperate times call for desperate measures," Andy said.

"We're not desperate."

"It's a saying. Geez, Razor, can't you ever be nice to anyone? Dr.

174

Crane has saved a lot of Catmages over the years, including Goldeneyes and Leilei. It's because of him that your nephew is going to be able to live a full, happy life even with only three legs."

"It's okay, Andy," Dr. Crane said. "There are a lot of dogs and, uh, dumbcats—is that the word?—that don't like me either. It goes with the profession."

"I didn't say I don't like you," Razor said. "I have to get to know you before I make that decision."

Dr. Crane laughed. "I appreciate that. So, can I look around the Compound or do we have to go home?"

"I'll take you," Letsan said.

"I'll do it," Razor said, surprising them all. "You go watch your boy and make sure he doesn't overdo it. Andy, you come with us."

They showed Dr. Crane everything from the Teaching Rings to the ma'on and the bayits. He was fascinated and impressed, stopping to chat with as many Catmages as would talk to him. Razor said little, but observed everything. After about an hour, Dr. Crane and Andy said their goodbyes and headed back to the car. Razor went with them to the outer guard post.

"You're not half bad," he told Dr. Crane as he and Andy turned to leave. "I'll let the guards know you can be passed through."

"Thanks, Razor," Dr. Crane said with a smile. "See you around."

Back in the car, Andy fastened his seatbelt and chuckled.

"What's so funny?"

"That was Razor's version of a compliment. He likes you, Dr. Crane. It took him two years to decide whether or not he liked me."

"I'm sure you're exaggerating."

"Maybe. But it's still pretty special."

"Good to know. Now let's get you home."

The disastrous outcome of the Halloween battle haunted Goldeneyes. Every time she saw Zohar walking on three legs, her heart ached. She knew it wasn't logical, but she thought that if she only had more power, perhaps she could have been more help. Perhaps Zohar and Regel would still have all four legs.

She kept these thoughts to herself around Letsan. The last thing he needed right now was having to tend her wounded feelings when his son was recovering from actual wounds. But there was a solution, one that Letsan couldn't help her with. She would have to do this on her own.

A few days after the battle, she found Hakham on the edge of the Compound meadow chatting with Methuselah. They greeted her warmly.

"Zahavin, excellent," Methuselah said. "We need you to settle an argument about your grandmother. This old coot says that he was her senior by a moon. I say he's going senile and that she was born two whole seasons before Hakham."

"They were in the same Teaching Ring, Master Methuselah. Have you forgotten?"

"By the One, you're right! I guess it is me who's going senile."

Hakham laughed. "You haven't forgotten, Master, as we were in your Teaching Ring together. You were the first of us to recognize Nafshi's greatness."

"But not the last," Methuselah said. "Well, what can we do for you, my dear? You didn't come here to listen to two old Catmages prattle on."

"No sir, but since you brought up Nafshi, I—" Now that it came down to it, Goldeneyes was hesitant to say it out loud.

"Yes?" Methuselah said kindly.

Goldeneyes took a deep breath. "I think it's time I underwent the ritual of Avdei Ha-Or," she said.

Her words were met with silence. Hakham and Methuselah looked at each other, their ears twitching slightly. At last Hakham spoke.

"It is a huge step," Hakham said. "I admit I hadn't expected you to ask for another cycle or two. In fact, I expected you to wait until I decided you were ready."

"I'm ready now," she said.

"Is she?" Methuselah asked.

Hakham thought long before he answered.

"Yes. Yes, I think Zahavin is capable of the ritual."

"That is not what I asked."

"I know what you asked."

"And you know I am ready!" she insisted. "I am the same age as Nafshi was when she performed the ritual. You told me yourself that she was only a few moons behind you."

"Yes, I did. But she worked tirelessly in the moons leading up to the ritual, and you have not been practicing for Avdei Ha-Or."

"No. I have only been practicing for—and fighting in—war with the Wild Ones these last three cycles."

"Still, it is a completely different kind of training, Zahavin."

"Hakham, you know I can do this. Am I not of the line of Nafshi? I created my Magelight while most Catmages are still in their Teaching Rings. I have been working for this my whole life. I see now that Nafshi put me on this path from the time I left the Teaching Rings and she began tutoring me. With all due respect, Hakham, she was the greatest teacher in living memory."

"She's got you there, Hakham," Methuselah said, laughing. "Nafshi was the best of us."

"I do not deny it. The question is not how good a teacher Nafshi was. The question is whether or not Zahavin is ready to join us in Avdei Ha-Or. You know what happens to those who are not ready."

Methuselah was silent.

"My life is mine to risk, Hakham."

"Why now, Zahavin? Why the sudden rush?"

"Because we need more power. No, *I* need more power! You were at Saunders' house when our warriors were beaten like half-year kittens. If I had had the strength of a Magi like you and Nafshi, maybe Niflah's Wild Ones would not have cut through our Shomrim like a claw through a leaf. How many more must we lose to Saunders and his evil plans? Every time

I see Zohar and Regel, all I can think is that if I had been stronger—if *we* had been stronger—they would still be whole."

Hakham blinked at her. "Ah. Now I see." He stood and moved over to brush shoulders with his apprentice. "Zahavin, what happened was not your fault. Matti went behind our back, and with insufficient forces. He fell into a trap. By the time we got there, most of the damage had been done. Blame Matti for not being truthful to us. Blame Razor and me for not seeing through his ruse. But don't blame yourself."

"If I had had more power, Nafshi would still be alive," she said.

"If, if, if," Methuselah said. "If it rained fish instead of water, we wouldn't have to forage for food."

Goldeneyes glared at the old Catmage. "Are you mocking me?"

"Yes, my dear, I am mocking you. Zahavin, you are many things, but you do not carry the weight of the world on your shoulders. That is my job, and Hakham is helping me with it. And doing a terrible job, I might add."

In spite of herself, Goldeneyes laughed.

"Master Methuselah, I want this. I want to be ready for anything the Wild Ones spring on us. I want to be as powerful as Nafshi was—as you and Hakham are. I am ready for the ritual."

Methuselah's tail twitched. "I think you are *almost* ready, Zahavin. You're right, you have been practicing for war. But you know how dangerous the ritual can be. Those who do it wrong the first time rarely get a second chance to do it right."

"I understand. I'm willing to try."

"Perhaps we can reach a compromise," Hakham said. "Let us practice specifically for Avdei Ha-Or for the next few moons. There's nothing outside the Compound that can't wait. Winter is about to set in. The Wild Ones will have to battle the elements as well as us if they attack in the snow."

"That is an excellent idea, Hakham," Methuselah said. "Zahavin, you will train with Hakham. And if you like, I will assist as well."

"I would like that very much, sir," she said. "Nafshi would be very pleased to know that you're helping me."

"Then it's settled. We will work with you until we think you are ready. But you agree to let us decide when that is."

Goldeneyes thought it over. "Done," she said.

"Good. Then come spring, you will join us as a member of Avdei Ha-Or."

Or die trying, Goldeneyes thought privately.

SEVENTEEN:
TRAITOR, TRAITOR

Razor paced back and forth in front of his bayit. Someone had betrayed them. Someone had told the Wild Ones exactly what to expect and when to expect it. That was the only explanation. Razor had a few ideas, but he needed proof. The word had gone out that he wanted a full report of everything that went on during the days before the battle. All of the guards had been examined by Razor and Letsan. None could remember anything out of the ordinary—until Regel came back to the East Woods and heard that Razor was trying to piece together the reasons for the disaster.

Razor stopped pacing as Regel and Matti approached. "How are you?" he asked, trying not to look at his legs.

"Not too bad, sir," Regel replied. "I barely miss it. I can still beat Matti in a race."

Razor grunted. "A half-year kitten can beat Matti in a race. He runs like a fish with legs."

Regel laughed as Matti reared on his hind legs and leaped at Razor, who ducked aside. "What can I do for you?" Razor asked.

"The Captain says you want information on the days leading up to the attack."

"What have you got for me?" Razor asked.

"Well, sir, the day of the attack, my squad was the last one to leave. Matti sent us out a few squads at a time, remember."

"I remember. Go on."

"You also know that Wild One, what's his name, Kel?"

"Yes."

"I saw him as we were heading into town. He was in the brush on the other side of the road, just watching us. I knew he was spying on the Wild Ones for us. I thought he was on his way to report to you, so I didn't think any more about it. But he definitely saw me and my squad."

Razor's gaze grew chill. "Thank you, Regel. Why don't you take off and leave Matti and me to talk this over?"

"Sir."

Regel disappeared from view, and Razor swore loud and long. "The next time that little Wild One shows his face around here will be his last."

"Is there any chance he really was coming to talk to you? Could we be wrong about him?" Matti asked.

"If he were, I would have talked to him. It's a bit funny, isn't it, that he was here just before the attack and suddenly the Wild Ones knew exactly what we planned? Your Shomrim were busy with preparations, and mine had orders to let Kel in. They wouldn't question him being around the Compound. It's the most likely explanation."

"It is," Matti said, growling. "Let's find out. If it was Kel—"

"Yes," Razor said. "Pass the word to the guard to bring him to us the moment he reappears."

"It will be my pleasure." Razor watched Matti leave and gazed after him for a few moments. Then his Magelight flared and a large chunk of the tree in front of him flew off the trunk.

"If it was you, Kelev," he growled, "Roah will be the least of your problems."

Razor had to wait a week before Kelev came back to the Compound. Katana sent a message from the guard post when he returned. She brought him to Hakham's bayit, where Razor, Matti, Methuselah, and the Elders waited in a semicircle. Kelev crouched low on the ground, blinking furiously.

"I didn't expect to see so many famous Catmages," he said. "To what do I owe this great honor?"

"Drop the act, Kelev," Razor said. "We know you told the Wild Ones about our attack on Saunders' house."

"What? No! I don't know what you're talking about!" he said, his body trembling. "I didn't even know you were going to attack!"

"You were here the day the order was given," Razor growled. "You were seen watching our squads leave the Compound. And worst of all, you are Bett and Roah's offspring! You've been spying on us from the beginning."

"No, I swear by the One, I didn't do it."

"Then how do you explain the Wild Ones knowing exactly when and in what force Matti would arrive at the house?" Hakham asked.

"Kill him!" Matti said. "He caused the deaths of many of our best warriors. And my friends!"

"Not to mention the maiming of my eldest son," Letsan added. "I'm with Matti. Kill him before he can betray us again."

"Blood will tell," Razor said. "He's a Wild One through and through. I told you it was wrong to trust him."

"You can't blame Patches and Leilei for trying," Silsula said. "Isn't there any other way to handle this? The poor thing isn't responsible for his birth." She looked to her sister. "Zahavin, what do you think?"

Goldeneyes studied the trembling Wild One lying on the ground before them. She felt pity, but she also felt anger at the loss of still more Catmages to the evil that Saunders had brought into their world.

"I don't see any way around it, Kelev. You were seen in the road watching our warriors head into town. Admit that you told Roah what was happening. Or must we tear the information from your mind?"

"No!" Kel said. "It wasn't me. It was Velvel! He told my father

182

about the attack. I heard him!"

"Velvel?" she asked, taken aback.

"Yes. He's been working with the Wild Ones since he arrived. He only pretends that he's on your side. I'm telling you, Velvel is working for Roah and Saunders. He laughs about it all the time. He says you're all so blind and stupid it's like dealing with kittens."

Razor growled. "Show us proof," he said, "and maybe we'll believe you."

"The Magelight can't lie. Let me show you."

"If this is a trick—" Matti said.

"It's not. Let me show you what I saw and you'll see who the real traitor is."

"Matti! Letsan! With me," Razor said. "Zahavin, Hakham, Silsula, be ready. If he makes a wrong move, kill him."

"Sit up, child," Zehira said. "I'm tired of looking at you slinking down there like you were already found guilty."

Kel slowly rose to a sitting position, still trembling. He looked down at the ground, still blinking.

The others moved closer, their Magelights beginning to brighten.

"Show me," Razor said. "Show us all."

Kel closed his eyes. His Magelight flared with the effort of projecting his memory to the Catmages surrounding him.

Kel crouched on a thick branch of a tree high above the path, all but hidden in its dense leaves. Below the tree he saw Roah and Velvel a short distance away.

"You're back from the Compound. Have you good news for me?" Roah asked.

"I did exactly as you told me. When Matanya heard that the house will be empty and unguarded tonight, he couldn't wait to start planning an attack."

"Are you certain he will come?"

"Absolutely. They think we are all here at the Compound. He couldn't wait to gather his forces, especially after I told him the dogs would be locked up. Everything is coming together as you had hoped."

"Not hoped. Planned. Hope is a thing that fools depend on. This is good, news Velvel. We can eliminate a threat and dishearten our foes at the same time. Will Razor be joining him?"

"I doubt it. He thinks tonight is a trap."

Roah laughed. "And so it is. I knew having Razor forced out of the Shomrim would be good for us. They will leave their best warrior and strategist at home when they face us."

"I couldn't stay long enough to find out all their plans," Velvel said. "But I knew you'd want to know. They will attack tonight. I'd stake my life on it."

"Good. Good. I will tell Saunders. He will be pleased. Kfir is in town. Send a message to him. Tell him to prepare our warriors. I will meet him in town."

"At once, Roah."

"One moment. They still do not suspect you are working with us?"

Velvel laughed. "If they did, I'd be dead." He trotted away down the path, and Roah disappeared from Kel's sight.

The scene ended. Matti and Razor's ears went back and growls rose from their throats.

"That's why I was seen near the wood," Kel said. "I was on my way to warn you. But I got there too late—my siblings found me, and I didn't dare come here."

Razor stared at Kel, unblinking.

"This is my fault," Matti said. "You were right, Razor. I sensed there was something off about Velvel, and I ignored my instinct."

"Well, he had me fooled, too. I thought he was just a Seeker." Razor's tail lashed.

"What will we do now?" Goldeneyes asked.

"Now," Matti said, "we find our friend Velvel. Doubtless he'll show up here again for more to tell the Wild Ones."

"For now, Kel stays here—under guard," Razor said. Kel left surrounded by Zehira, Silsula, and two of the Shomrim.

When they were out of sight, Matti turned to Razor and Hakham. "I resign as Captain of the Shomrim. I failed my fighters and I failed this Compound. Razor, it would be a relief to me if you'd take command again. I'll speak to what's left of my warriors." His head drooped as he thought of the friends lost in battle.

"I accept, with one condition," Hakham said.

"What condition?"

"That you serve as Razor's lieutenant. I need the both of you in our battle with Saunders."

Razor growled an affirmative.

"Done," Matti said gratefully.

"I have another condition," Razor said. "Nobody outside this circle knows that I'm in charge now. We don't know if Velvel was the only traitor. Let's see if we can smoke out any more Catmages working for the enemy."

"Oh, Razor, your paranoia is an example to us all," Letsan said.

"Brother, my 'paranoia' has kept me alive all these years. And you too, for the last few."

"And my legions of fans are grateful to you."

Razor snorted. "Now for Velvel," he said. "I think I have a way of getting him here, and it's going to involve Kel. He can bring the traitor here to us. It's obvious Velvel was lying about not being allowed out of the Compound."

"Brother," Letsan said, purring approvingly, "you are the second-smartest Maine Coon alive."

"You being the first?"

"Naturally."

Razor rubbed his shoulder against Letsan's. "You got the brains. I got the brawn. We make a good team."

CHAPTER SEVENTEEN

"Velvel will find out just *how* good," Letsan growled.

The two brothers and Matti left to find Kel. They found him in a bayit at the farthest edge of the meadow, guarded by the Shomrim. "Bring him out," Razor said. One of the guards went inside and came back with Kel.

"You have a reprieve," Razor said.

"And a way to prove yourself," Matti added.

"Name it!"

"Get Velvel here. Make something up. We don't care how you do it. But get Velvel back in this Compound. If you do that, we'll start to believe you really mean it when you say you want to help us," Razor said.

Kel stood up straight. "I can do that, sir. You'll see. I'm with you, I swear!"

"Get that traitor over here, then."

"And Kel," Matti said, his hackles rising, "if you cross us, there is nowhere you can hide. Someone is going to pay for all those deaths. Pray that it isn't you."

Trembling, Kel was escorted out of the Compound by his guards. Razor and Matti watched as they took him away.

"Well, that probably did the job," Matti said cheerfully. "I can't tell if Kel's more afraid of me or you."

"Doesn't matter. So long as he does what's needed."

Kel shivered as Matti's Shomrim guards watched him cross the road. That was a close one. True, he hadn't betrayed their plans to Roah—Velvel had done that—but he was still in danger of being caught, especially if he couldn't produce Velvel. He tracked down a meal while he thought about what to do. He found a mouse that moved too slowly back to its hole, and feasted on the way back to the West Woods Compound. By the time he was done washing his face, he had a plan. When he reached the Compound, he went straight to Roah's bayit. Two of Kfir's largest warriors, a pair of black cats, stood guard on either side of the entrance.

"What do you want?" one asked.

"I need to speak to Roah," Kel said.

"Why would Roah want to talk to a runt like you?" the other said as the pair of them laughed at him.

"I have important information for him!" Kel said, getting annoyed. He was tired of the bigger ones picking on him. He had every right to talk to his father. He stepped forward and the first guard moved to block him.

"Step aside," Kel said. The two guards laughed uproariously.

"Make me, kitten."

Anger and fear surged through Kel. If he couldn't talk to Roah, Matti's guards would get him eventually, maybe even Matti himself. Before he knew what he was doing, his Magelight flared and a light dagger flew at the guard in front of him. He leaped aside, but the jet caught him on the tail. The smell of singed fur filled the air. The other guard laughed loudly.

"Good job, Garev! You let a pint-size Catmage take you out. I'm sure Kfir would love to hear about this."

Garev growled and turned to face Kel. "You got your shot, kitten. Now it's my turn." His Magelight began to glow.

"Let him come." Garev turned to see Roah's eyes glowing from within the shaded bayit. "It seems my son has some of my fire after all. Garev, get back to your position." Garev turned to obey. Roah's Magelight sparked and a jet of light seared the tip of Garev's ear. He yowled in pain.

"Let that teach you to be a better guard. Expect the unexpected. If anyone ever gets the better of you again while you are guarding me, I'll kill you."

Garev blinked at Roah and sat back down beside the entrance, not even glancing at Kel as he went inside.

"Why are you here?" Roah asked.

Kel glanced around nervously, blinking. He made sure he was only communicating privately with his father. Nobody else could know this. "I need to tell you something. Hear me out. Please."

"Proceed."

CHAPTER SEVENTEEN

Kel told Roah about the time he had spent ingratiating himself with the Catmages. He told him how Patches and Leilei were completely taken in by his story of being an outsider. And he told Roah what had happened that day, how the Catmages thought he was the traitor, and how he had instead placed the blame on Velvel.

"You were spying on me that day?" Roah asked when he finished.

"Not on purpose, Father. I didn't know you would be there. I was hiding from my siblings."

"You have not yet earned the right to call me father. You are weak. You should not hide. You should fight."

"They gang up on me every time!"

"Why do you not lie in wait until they are alone and punish them singly? You are stupid as well as weak."

Stung, Kel stood straight up and fluffed out his fur. "I am not stupid *or* weak! I have worked my way into Razor's confidence. No other Wild One here can say the same, not even Velvel!"

Roah stared unblinking at him until Kel lowered his head. "You do have some spirit. Perhaps you are my son after all. Now I must decide what to do."

"They'll kill me if I don't send him to them," Kel said.

"We can always get another Seeker," Roah said. "Velvel has been exposed. He is no longer useful. I will send him to them. You will continue to curry favor with the enemy. But from now on you will come to me after every visit to their Compound."

"Yes, Roah! Thank you!"

"And Kelev—"

"Yes?"

"Learn how to defeat your siblings. I expect to hear that you have vanquished them before the next full moon."

"Will you help me, sir? Will you teach me how?"

Roah was silent again, watching steadily as Kel dropped his gaze and crouched low.

"Yes. Come see me tomorrow after sunrise. I think it is past time I took over your education."

Kel raised himself to a sitting position and forced himself to look his father straight in the eyes. "Yes sir," he said. He left as swiftly as he dared. On the way out, he heard Roah telling his guards to send Velvel to him. Kel hurried away. Perhaps he could find one of his siblings alone tonight. It had been a good day.

The next day, Velvel strolled casually past the two Shomrim guards near the road. He hadn't been back to the East Woods Compound since the night of the attack, and Roah had asked him to gather information on the aftermath. This would be easy, he thought. All he had to do was show his concern for the well-being of his fellow Catmages, and he'd be able to collect everything Roah needed. As he neared the Compound, three of Matti's largest Shomrim headed his way. None of them looked the worse for wear. That would go on his report. He was about to say hello when they surrounded him.

"If you'll come with us, please," Atzel said. "Matti wants to see you."

Velvel had little choice but to go with the Shomrim, though their formality puzzled him. They led him to the meadow, where the East Woods Council was arranged in a formal semicircle with Hakham at its center. Matti and Razor sat between the arms of the half-circle, facing him. A large group of Catmages looked on. Velvel realized that there were no kittens in the crowd, and fear struck him. The crowd parted as the guards marched him forward until he stood before the two captains.

"What's going on?" Velvel asked.

"Remove his Magelight," Hakham said. "Cut it off and bring it to me."

"Let me have the pleasure," Razor said to the guards. With a flash of his Magelight, he cut the leather straps, and Velvel's Magelight fell to the ground. Razor picked it up and floated it over to Hakham, dropping it in front of the Council.

"Velvel, you are charged with betraying this Compound to the enemy, leading to the maiming and deaths of many of our warriors," Hakham said.

A hostile murmur came from the crowd. Ears flattened and tails lashed as Hakham spoke.

"Ridiculous!" Velvel said. "I am one of Kharoom's most trusted Catmages. He'll hear about this from me, you may be sure."

"He won't," Razor said.

"Are you threatening me? Hakham, Razor has never liked me. Is he the one who said I betrayed you? He's lying!"

"It wasn't Razor who informed us we had a traitor in our midst," Hakham said. "Now be silent!"

Velvel looked from face to face, and could not find an ally. His heart started thudding.

"Residents of the East Woods," Hakham said, and the last of the crowd's murmuring ceased. "We have evidence that Velvel betrayed our plans to the Enemy last moon. You know that Matti led his Shomrim to the Enemy's house, expecting there to be no Wild Ones. Yet soon after they arrived, Wild Ones poured out from their hiding places and assailed our warriors. The dogs that were supposed to be locked up were loose, and you can see the results of their work on Regel and Zohar." Many in the crowd looked over to the three-legged Catmages, murmuring. "Many died. These deaths are not only on the Wild Ones, but on the one who falsely told us the house would be empty. That one is Velvel!"

The murmurs grew into shouts and hisses as the crowd turned its attention to Velvel.

"I didn't know!" Velvel cried. "I thought my information was sound. I didn't know the Wild Ones were in hiding in town."

"Liar!" Matti said, fur bristling. He moved forward until he was inches away from the Seeker. "Shall I show him, Hakham?"

"I will do it." There was a pause while Hakham closed his eyes and concentrated deeply. Soon everyone in the crowd saw the scene that Kel had showed the Council. Even through his fear, Velvel couldn't help but marvel at the power needed to present those memories to what looked like the entire Compound. The rumors were true. Hakham was a Magus. How could Velvel use this to his advantage? He needed time to think.

"This is not what it appears to be," he said.

"The Magelight can't lie!" shouted someone in the crowd.

"That is correct," Methuselah said. "Magelights can only show memories. They aren't a human picture show."

There were scattered chuckles at that remark.

Velvel panted. He tried to collect his thoughts and slow his breathing. "If you'll give me a chance to explain," he said. "I told you what I believed to be true. I didn't know Roah's forces were lying in wait. You know I have to pretend to be with the Wild Ones. I had to keep up appearances so that they wouldn't know I'm working for Kharoom—and for you!"

"If you were truly on our side, you wouldn't have betrayed our battle plan to the enemy!" Matti roared. Without warning, he leaped at Velvel, biting, clawing, and growling. The guards stepped away and watched as the crowd roared.

"Enough!" Hakham boomed over the crowd. "Matanya, cease!"

Matti got up, spitting out cream-colored fur. Velvel was bleeding from his face and chest. Matti turned his face from Velvel and walked over to Razor, who bumped him with his shoulder.

"Nice job," Razor said for all to hear.

"Thanks."

"We are not Wild Ones," Hakham said sternly. "We will follow our rules. Matanya, you will not attack Velvel again unless you are authorized to do so."

"Yes, Hakham."

"It is our custom to hear the charges against the accused and give him a chance to defend himself. We have done so. Now, the Council will vote. Please come forward and state whether you think Velvel is innocent or guilty."

CHAPTER SEVENTEEN

One by one, the Council stepped forward.

"Methuselah."

"Guilty."

"Zehira."

"Guilty."

"Silsula."

"Guilty."

"Letsan."

"Guilty."

"Then it is unanimous. Guilty," said Hakham. A growl rose from the crowd.

"What—what are you going to do to me?" Velvel asked.

Hakham ignored him and addressed the assembly. "Velvel the Seeker has been found guilty of betraying the East Woods Shomrim to the enemy. We cast him out. He is no longer a member of this Compound, or of Catmage society. We will destroy his Magelight. Razor, Matti, you may join us. Zahavin, please make sure the shards are contained."

The five members of the Council and the two warriors sent daggers of light into the Magelight lying on the ground. It exploded into pieces that crashed harmlessly against the walls of a golden ball of light cast by Goldeneyes. The ball faded, and the shards fell. Velvel screamed long and loud, collapsing on the ground and shuddering.

"Rarely have we ever had to dispense this kind of justice. The Fifth Law set down by Neshama is *Do Not Harm Catmages*. But by decree, Velvel is no longer one of us. Velvel's actions caused the death and wounding of many of our kind. The penalty for violating our Laws is often banishment. If we banish Velvel, what then? He will simply rejoin the Wild Ones and continue working against us. Therefore, Velvel must die."

Gasps and murmurs erupted from the crowd.

"No!" Velvel shouted. "No, you can't! Kharoom will hear of this! I am one of his most trusted Catmages! You're making a mistake, I didn't know what was going to happen!"

Razor laughed out loud at the mention of Kharoom. "Don't worry, Velvel. We'll send Kharoom your ears and tail when we tell him of your fate."

"We most certainly will not!" Silsula said. "Are we Wild Ones or are we Catmages?"

"He didn't mean it, sister," Goldeneyes sent privately. "It's just Razor being Razor."

"Take him away," Hakham said. Regel and Zohar joined the three guards in shouldering a howling Velvel through the parting crowd. "Council members, follow me. You too, Razor, Matti, Zahavin. Come with us."

They made their way through the dispersing Catmages to Hakham's bayit.

"We've never executed anyone in this Compound before," Silsula said when everyone had settled. "I haven't the faintest idea how to go about this, and I'm not so sure we should."

"I'm sure," Razor growled. "You voted to find him guilty. Are you changing your mind?"

"No. He was guilty of betraying us. But—death? Is that a just penalty for what he did?"

"What other choice have we?" Methuselah said. "Hakham is right. If we allow him to live, Velvel will only rejoin the enemy and work against us."

Silsula sighed. "Well, I'm not going to be any part of the execution. You do whatever you want. I'm going to find my kittens and forget that Velvel ever set foot in this Compound."

"She has a point," Goldeneyes said as she watched her sister go. "There hasn't been an execution in the East Woods in living memory."

"I have witnessed a few," Methuselah said, "and so has Hakham. The criminal is taken to a private place and executed by a group of Catmages. I suspect you will have no lack of volunteers for this," he said, eyeing Razor and Matti.

"No," Letsan said, "they won't. I'm coming along."

CHAPTER SEVENTEEN

"When do you want us to do it?" Matti asked.

"It would be cruel to make him wait too long," Methuselah said. "Gather a group of your Shomrim and take him far into the woods, where no Catmage goes. Bury him there when you are finished, and put no marker above his grave."

"We'll return when it's done," Matti said. He left the bayit, followed by Razor and Letsan.

Methuselah sat down with a thump.

"Are you all right, Master?" Hakham asked.

"Yes. I'm just saddened that it has come to this. Catmages should not kill one another."

"No, they should not. But these are the times we live in, and that is what we must work to end."

"If you don't need me any longer, I'm going to find Silsula and join her," Zehira said wearily. "Zahavin, what about you? Are you coming with me?"

"I have lessons," she said. "I'll visit my nieces and nephews later."

Goldeneyes was still with Hakham when Razor and Matti returned later that afternoon.

"It's done," Razor said. "Velvel will not betray us again."

"Kharoom is going to want to know about this," Matti said.

Razor laughed harshly. "Feel free to tell him. I'm not wasting any energy on that fool. He's the one that saddled you with Velvel in the first place."

Matti gazed off into the distance. Then he shook himself and bumped shoulders with Razor. "Never mind. Let Kharoom ask me about Velvel if he cares so much for his pet. I'd much rather get our warriors in shape for the next attack. And this time our plans won't be betrayed to the Wild Ones before we can implement them. We'll get the Tilyon yet, Razor."

Razor growled an assent as they took their leave.

EIGHTEEN: HISTORY REPEATS

Niflah yawned and woke from a midday nap. He stretched and yawned again, leaped off the sofa and padded into the kitchen for a drink of water. Alef sat in front of the cellar door as if he were guarding it.

"What are you doing by the door?" Niflah asked.

"Sitting."

"So I see. Why are you sitting in front of the cellar door as if you have a secret behind it?"

"I don't know what you're talking about. I want to sit and think. So I sit here and think. Is that too difficult to believe?"

"Yes, when it is you doing the thinking," Niflah said.

Alef's ears went back. "Very funny, old one," he said acidly. "You and Patches would have made a great pair."

"Why are you here?" Niflah asked again. "You don't move a whisker without Roah's orders. What is behind that door that you don't want me to see?"

"Nothing."

"Then you won't mind if I take a look?" he asked, walking to the door. Alef remained where he was, blocking the way.

"Step aside."

"You must not go down there," Alef said. "Roah is busy and must not be disturbed."

"So he *is* down there, and he's doing something he doesn't want me to know about? Again I say, step aside."

"I may not. And I would not proceed if I were you."

"You are not me, and I will not be left out of anything! I am supposed to head the new Council!" he thundered.

Niflah shoved past Alef and thrust the cellar door open with his Magelight. As he climbed down the stairs he stopped midway. Six of Saunders' dogs were caged in kennels. Roah stood in front of them, Magelight glowing. He was projecting loudly, and Niflah could hear his thoughts. But the astonishing thing was he could hear rudimentary thoughts coming from the dogs. No, that couldn't be right. He stopped and listened hard. He wasn't imagining it. The dogs were talking back to Roah!

Must not hurt cats. Cats are friends.

"Yes," Roah said. "We are your friends. We will help you. But there are bad cats that you can hurt. We will show you. Good cats. Bad cats. Learn the difference."

Good cats. Bad cats.

"I am a good cat. Roah is your friend."

Roah friend.

"What in the name of the First is going on here?" Niflah asked. "What are you doing with these dogs?"

Roah's Magelight went out and he turned, growling.

"You fool! I am in the middle of an important training session. Get out!"

Bad cat? We will kill bad cat! The largest dog growled.

"No, Shadow, good cat," Roah said. "Just immensely stupid at the moment."

Stupid cat. What is stupid?

Roah laughed. "Someone who does not do as he is told. That is enough for today. Shadow, you did well. Good dog."

Good dog. Dog good.

Roah went up the stairs without waiting to see if Niflah followed.

When they were both inside the kitchen, he slammed the door shut with his Magelight and faced Alef, tail lashing.

"I told you I was not to be interrupted," he said.

"I tried to stop him. He did not listen."

"What—what are you doing to those dogs?" Niflah asked.

"Making them smarter."

Niflah was stunned. "You have been manipulating the intelligence of the dogs?" he asked incredulously. "Is that even possible?"

Roah's tail switched impatiently. "It is obviously possible. We have done it. You have seen it. They are the key to defeating the Shomrim."

"It is forbidden Do you not remember the Seventh Law? *Do not use magic to harm other creatures!*"

"Yes, and *Do not harm Catmages* is the Fifth Law. You didn't seem to care about that so much when you were battling your brother and his warriors. We have been breaking the Laws since before we joined with Saunders. It's a little late to grow a conscience, old one."

"This is different. You are interfering with the natural order of things. The One made dogs as dumb as we used to be for a reason!"

Roah was unmoved. "We need the dogs. We can direct their attacks better if they are smarter. And we will not have to keep valuable fighters at the rear to control them. It will turn the tide of battle. Or are you so trapped by your old ways that you will hinder us with your resistance?"

"It is—difficult to change the habits of a lifetime," Niflah admitted. "I wish you'd involved me from the very beginning. I'm not sure it's wise to teach another species to think."

"They do not think as you and I do. Their thoughts are rudimentary. But it will do. Rest easy on that count."

Niflah was still trying to absorb what he'd just seen and heard. "But how—how did you even get the idea for this?"

"You do not reach high enough. That is why Hakham became head of the Council and you did not. The only true restriction to our power is lack of will. If you can think it, you can do it. That is the true reason I was

197

cast out of our society. The other Catmages fear their power. I embrace it. Jealousy is the root of their hatred for me."

"That, and your cruelty to other Catmages and lesser creatures," Niflah said.

"The strong take, and the weak serve the strong. One way or another. It is what you want, is it not? You wish to take charge of the Council. You are willing to join with a human and outcast Catmages to do so. Our methods, old one, are not that far apart. Let us not pretend your paws are clean. You cannot defeat your brother without using the resources available to you. Whether those resources are Wild Ones or dogs makes no difference."

"I—I suppose so. But still, how did you come to this plan?"

"Saunders suggested it. His ancestor did it first and recorded it in his journal."

"I should like to hear it for myself."

Roah stood. "Then let us go find Saunders." He turned to Alef, who had stayed silently by the door during their conversation. "You may go. I will remember your failure today."

Alef slunk away, his look back at Niflah boding ill, but the old tabby was too busy watching Roah to notice.

They found Saunders in his office. Open books and papers were scattered across his desk. He raised his eyebrows as the two Catmages entered.

"I'm busy."

"Niflah has learned that we are training the dogs."

Saunders frowned. "If you're here to try to convince us to stop, you can save your breath. Roah and I are of one mind about this."

"No, Saunders, that isn't why I'm here. Roah says that your ancestor discovered these methods. I should like to hear how he did it. I should like to be part of everything, and I am not happy that this has been kept from me."

Saunders relaxed. "I don't see why not. Perhaps you will be able to discover something that could move our work along faster. My dogs are getting smarter, but they can't yet think on their own. They still have to be carefully controlled in battle. The latest test proved that."

"The latest test?" Niflah asked. "What test? Who have they been fighting? Do you have some captive Catmages that I know nothing about?"

"Don't be absurd, Niflah. I don't want my Dobermans getting hurt in training. We rounded up a group of—as you say—dumbcats. The dogs practice on them."

"I see," Niflah said quietly, closing his thoughts completely to the others. There were some things about Saunders' methods that he was beginning to regret having to do. He pushed those feelings aside. If this book held useful information that would help them defeat the Shomrim, then the sooner the Council was overthrown, the sooner Niflah could stop Saunders and his brutal methods. He could regret the death of innocent dumbcats later. For now, he must stay with Saunders and Roah to achieve his goal.

Saunders opened a desk drawer and withdrew a box fastened with a combination lock. He spun the lock, opened the box, and removed a small book with an ancient, cracked leather cover. He flipped carefully through the pages and read out loud:

The leader of the Magickal Cats is an all-black male whom it amuses me to call Lucifer, though of course I am most careful about saying his name out loud, as it has become clear to me that some of the villagers do not believe the reasons I give them for venturing often into the Forest. Last week I posited an experiment, mentioning it to Lucifer after we had spent several hours in the wood so that he could shew me the various practices behind the Ceremony of the Making of the Lights. It was a great disappointment to me to learn that he would not be making a Light then and there, due to the extreme energy it takes to create one and also because his Light had been created some years ago, although it was destroyed when he was cast out, and he had to make another.

I discussed with Lucifer and with his mate and assistant, a striped female whom I have designated Little Tiger for her fierceness and for the sharp-ness of her tongue, whether or not they thought that a Man could wield a Light. We conversed at length, I naturally insisting that with the proper instruction and practice that a Man would be able to use a Light as well as a Cat, though I did concede that at first the Cats would have to teach a Man before he could use a Light for himself. Little Tiger was of the opinion that no Man could be-gin to come near the abilities of the Cat Mage, and would not budge from her assertion no matter how I made my case.

We then went on to discuss the intelligence of our two species, the Cats insisting that their kind had gone farther than any other species by the Grace of God, whom they call The One Above Us All. I asked them if there were any way to improve any of the other animal species; not to the point of allowing them to have Lights of their own, but would there be a way, perhaps, of improving a dog's intelligence, or even a cat that was merely a cat. They laughed long and hard about both suggestions, but at the last they admitted to me that they found it very easy to manipulate the will of a lesser species such as rabbits. Lucifer confessed that he had on occasion forced dogs away from him and his kind, and that it probably would not be a very difficult step from controlling a canine to making it understand a different way of looking at things. Lucifer was certain that he could create a smarter breed of dog if he and his companions wished it so. We determined to try it at once, and that when I returned on the morrow I would bring one of my dogs and get to work immediately to see if we could accomplish this feat.

Saunders stopped reading. "That was the first mention of experi-menting with dogs. One of the last entries my ancestor wrote concerned the results of his, ah, experiment. Suffice to say that it became our inspira-tion to work on my dogs."

"And you are succeeding?" Niflah asked.

"I told you that we were," Roah said irritably. "Do you doubt me?"

"No. But I am curious as to your methods."

"I teach them to think."

"That is not an explanation."

"It is all the explanation you will get," Roah sniffed. "I told you, if you can think it, you can make it so. If you can't believe that, you will never defeat your brother."

"Then it's a good thing we have you, isn't it?" Niflah said sarcastically, stung by the chastisement.

"Arguing is a waste of time. Accept that this is part of our plan. We chose you for a reason, Niflah. We have need of you."

Niflah thought back to the day that Roah had asked him to join his effort to take over the Council.

He had walked out of a meeting with Hakham and some of the other Council members, angry that once again, his suggestions had been ignored in favor of his brother's.

A black-and-white tuxedo cat stepped out from behind a tree as Niflah approached.

"Roah!" Niflah said. "You shouldn't be here. I heard you were banished."

"So the Seekers have brought the news here, then. Yes. I am banished," Roah said derisively. "Flung out of proper Catmage society, my Magelight destroyed, my shame made public for all to know." He laughed. "So what? Do you know how long it took me to make a new Magelight?" The gem in his collar flashed brightly. "It took me three suns to recover my strength. And I will make another, and another, and another if I must. The Council is full of impotent fools, including your brother."

Niflah's ears twitched and he looked around furtively.

"*I* am on that Council, Roah. Shall I stay and listen to you insult me? I am not one of those poor souls you talked into joining your cause and getting banished with you," Niflah said. "I follow our people's laws."

"Our laws," Roah said scornfully. "They are not laws. They are suggestions that have been codified and sanctified to keep power in the hands of the few and away from the many. Your brother is one of the few. Why are *you* not head of the Council, Niflah? You have every bit as much power and wisdom as Hakham."

Niflah looked around again, heart pounding. "I will not listen to this."

"No one will see or hear us," Roah said. "There is no one around. I've been planning this day for a long time. You and I have much to talk about."

"I don't think so," Niflah said, turning away.

"I can help you get out from under the shadow of your brother. Don't pretend you don't want that."

Niflah froze in mid-step.

"You should be leading the Council," Roah went on. "He has always taken what should have been yours. Your wisdom and your powers are needed. You should not be kept down any longer."

Niflah turned back toward the younger Catmage. "Whatever you think you know about me—"

"I know you have watched silently while your brother gets the accolades. I know he has the position that you have always deserved. We both know how Nafshi swayed the vote that made him head of the Council over you. She used her influence to persuade the weaker members. You were littermates. Everyone knows you are at least as powerful as Hakham, but because of Nafshi you have come in second in the eyes of the others. There are many of us who believe you are the stronger one—and that you should rule in his stead."

Niflah tilted his head, his ears flattening. "It doesn't matter what a Wild One thinks of me. What matters are the Council members who vote for my brother time after time. And speaking of time, you are wasting mine." He turned again to leave.

"No, Niflah, I am *not* wasting your time. They exiled me because they fear me. I speak of new ways of living, of doing things differently from our ancestors—and they cast me out because they are afraid of change."

"They cast you out because you have broken our laws! You tried to recruit other Catmages to rebel against us!"

Roah laughed again. "Yes, that is what they would say. It is what they have been taught to say. Change is bad, tradition must be maintained. Nonsense! Niflah, listen: I have met a human. He knows about Catmages. He will help us! He found a history of an ancestor who worked with Catmages many cycles of the sun ago."

"You have been making contact with humans?" Niflah asked, shocked. "Are there *any* laws you haven't broken?"

"Listen to me, Niflah. This human can help us."

"How?" Niflah asked. "How did he even know you were a Catmage? We look exactly like dumbcats."

"Dumbcats do not wear the collars we wear. His ancestor's book has drawings of them. I have seen it."

Niflah sat down, his tail twitching at the news. "You have spoken to a human. You have exposed us! We are at risk! I must tell the Council."

"No, you must listen," Roah told him. "The human and I have talked many times. He is wise. He is powerful! He can help us. Niflah, think about it. We could change Catmages for all time. Humans have strengths—and weapons—that we can't even dream of. Think of what we could learn!"

"It is forbidden," Niflah whispered. "Secrecy is the first of the Seven Laws."

"The precious Laws!" Roah said scornfully. "They are cords that bind us to the Councils. If we stay away from humans, we can never harness their power, never partner with them for the betterment of all. You have been indoctrinated, Niflah. Free yourself from the Council's control! Come with me. At the very least, come meet the man who offers us aid. What harm could there be in talking?"

Niflah hesitated.

"It's only a few days' journey from here. Come with me." Roah stepped forward and rubbed his shoulder against Niflah. "Just think of what you could do in your brother's place." Roah paused, giving Niflah time to think. "I tell you, this human can help us. Come meet him." His mind-voice dropped to a whisper. "Picture yourself at the head of the Council. Think of all you could achieve. How much disappointment have you had to swallow because your brother and his faction would not hear the good sense of your words?"

Niflah's ears twitched. The tip of his tail beat a pattern against the ground while Roah waited.

"All right," he said at last. "I will come with you. As you say, there is no harm in talking."

"None at all!" Roah said happily. "But won't you need to make an excuse to be out of the Compound?" he asked slyly.

"I am a grown Catmage and a member of the Council. I explain myself to no one."

"My apologies. Then let us leave now."

"Where are we going?"

"Into the town that lies near the East Woods Compound. He will be very happy to meet you."

"Does this man have a name?"

"Saunders," Roah said. "His name is Saunders."

Together, they trotted down the path.

Roah thought back too to that fateful day and their first journey together.

Saunders had been right about Niflah, Roah thought. All they'd had to do was dangle the bait of replacing his brother in front of him, and one of the most powerful Council members was theirs. One was all they needed, Saunders said. They could take care of the rest later.

Roah had guarded his thoughts carefully as they continued toward the town. His companion was not doing nearly as good a job. Roah could hear Niflah's thoughts, and they were all about what he would do if he were head of the Council. Roah chuckled to himself. Yes, Saunders was a good judge of character. He had chosen the perfect Council member for their plan.

Roah pushed his thoughts back to the present and watched Saunders replace the journal in the lockbox. Niflah was mollified for now. "He is still useful to us," Roah sent privately to Saunders, who nodded curtly.

"Perhaps Niflah can help you speed the training," Saunders said aloud.

"We shall see. For now, I think we should continue as we were. Niflah still has the boy to teach."

Saunders shrugged. "As you wish. Now, both of you get out of my office. I've work to do."

Roah and Niflah went out the door and down the hall.

"I'm hungry," Niflah said. "I'm going out to hunt. We'll talk about this later."

Roah watched the old one trot down the stairs. He sat down, the tip of his tail thumping the floor. "Yes, you are still of use, old one," he thought. "For the present."

NINETEEN: TEACHER, TEACHER

Jack Straight paced back and forth in front of Saunders' desk. "I told you Taylor couldn't handle my AP History class. He's barely scraping by with a D after two marking periods. If he doesn't bring his grade up, he's going to get kicked off the football team."

Saunders sat behind his desk, face expressionless, watching Jack pace. "And I told you, cousin, that you must find a way to make sure he passes your class. Are you not tutoring him?"

"Yes! I've been helping him since the beginning of the school year, and it's not working." Jack stopped and kicked the chair in front of the desk. "Nothing is working. Taylor doesn't do well with authority figures. Except for you, apparently. Why is that?" he said, looking suspiciously at Saunders.

"I have no idea. Perhaps he respects me more than he respects you."

Fears you is more like it, Jack thought.

Saunders stood, stretching his long, thin arms and yawning. "Resolve this," he said, fixing Jack with a cold stare. "If Mr. Grant fails, you will have failed me. You know how little I would like that."

Jack thought of the times in the past when Stan had decided Jack had failed him. He swallowed. "Fine. I'll think of something."

"Yes, you will."

Jack hurried out of the office and strode quickly through the halls. He got to his classroom a few minutes before the period was about to start, and sat thinking. By the time the students filed in for class, he knew what to do.

When the bell for the end of class rang, Jack asked Becca to remain behind. "I'll be with you in a moment. Taylor," he said. "Wait a minute." He spoke a few quick words with Taylor, who hurried away when they were finished.

"I have a big favor to ask you," he said as he came back into the room. "Taylor needs a tutor, or he's going to fail this class."

"No offense Mr. Straight, but why is he here in the first place? You and I both know he shouldn't be."

"That's not the point, Becca. The point is, I need someone to help Taylor. I've been tutoring him myself, but I think he'd relate better to another student."

"He doesn't like me. And I don't like him, either. He's a bully and a jerk. You know he used to pick on Andy all the time. And that fight two years ago? It started because Taylor insulted me. Andy got in trouble, but Taylor didn't. Why is that?"

Jack sat down on the edge of his desk and crossed his arms. "I can't say. I'm not the principal. Look, Becca, I know Taylor's not the nicest kid in the school, but I'm not asking you to be friends with him. I'm asking you to help him pass this class. You don't know everything about him. He's got some … issues at home."

"You mean his stepbrothers picking on him?"

"You know?"

"Yeah, I saw them once on Parents Night. But so what? That's no excuse for Taylor to pick on other kids."

Jack frowned. "No, it isn't. But it should make you understand that it might not be as simple as it looks. I don't think he's all bad. He's been trying hard to keep up in this class, but I can't seem to get through to him.

I think he needs one of his peers helping him. That's where you come in."

Becca shook her head. "I don't know."

"I'm willing to give you extra credit. You do this, and you won't have to turn in a paper at the end of term."

Becca's eyebrows rose. "Really?"

"Really. You're a straight-A student, Becca. I know you grasp the subject well. I don't need you to write a paper to prove it to me."

"How about getting out of final exams?" she asked. "After all, I have such a good grasp of the subject."

Jack grinned. "Nice try. No. But think about how good this will look on your college application—helping a student who was about to fail and saving the football team at the same time."

Becca nodded. "All right. How often will I have to work with him?"

"That depends on how well you do tutoring him. You'll have to figure that out yourselves." He looked up at the clock. "I told Taylor to hurry up with his lunch and come back here. I'll tell him you're taking over for me, and have him contact you to arrange some tutoring sessions."

"Okay. I better run to lunch myself," she said, moving toward the door.

"One last thing: You can't tell anyone Taylor is failing. If anyone asks, say that I asked you to help him get through a rough spot."

"Okay, I guess," she said hesitantly.

"No guessing. You don't tell Andy or anyone else. This is confidential information that only Taylor and his parents are allowed to share."

"I won't tell anyone," she promised.

"Thanks, Becca. You have no idea how much I appreciate your help."

She nodded and turned to the door. Jack watched her leave and sighed with relief. He had a good feeling about this. He'd found a way to help Taylor and keep Stan off his back. Becca could definitely be counted on. If only Taylor could be!

"So what did Mr. Straight want with you?" Andy asked when Becca joined him, Teresa, and Mike at the lunch table.

"He wants me to tutor Taylor."

They all gaped at her. Then all three of them spoke at once.

"You're kidding."

"No way!"

"Are you crazy?"

"So, I take it none of you thinks my tutoring Taylor is a good idea?" Becca asked, grinning at Teresa, Mike, and Andy.

"Worst. Idea. Ever!" Mike said. "How can you even stand to be around that moron?"

"You can't do it, Becca. Tell Mr. Straight you changed your mind," Andy said.

"No."

"Taylor is the enemy!" Andy said, his voice rising. "How can you possibly want to help that creep after all the rotten things he's done to me? And to you!"

"It's complicated," she said.

"No it isn't. Go tell Mr. Straight you won't do it."

"You don't tell me what to do," Becca said, eyes flashing. "I'm going to tutor him. So get over it and get used to it." She stood, picked up her tray, and moved over to the empty seat next to Teresa. She left as soon as she was finished eating, and didn't look back as she hurried out of the cafeteria. She saw Taylor in the hall as she went to her next class.

"I just saw Mr. Straight," he said. Taylor seemed embarrassed. "You're gonna help me with history, huh?"

"Yes. When should we start?"

Taylor shrugged. "I don't know. Today, maybe."

"Okay, where should we meet?"

"Mr. Straight's classroom, I guess. That's where I've been meeting him."

"Okay. See you after school, then."

"See you then."

Taylor walked away quickly. Becca shrugged to herself and continued on to her next class.

Taylor and Becca met in Mr. Straight's classroom for lessons several times over the next few weeks, while Mr. Straight graded papers. She laid down the law on the first day and told Taylor that if he caused any trouble with Andy, he'd find himself a new tutor.

"Okay, okay," he said. "I have bigger problems than Cohen, anyway. Can we just never mention him?"

"Fine by me," Becca said.

Taylor's grades started to tick upward. Becca was pleased and a little bit surprised. But he was actually pleasant during the tutoring sessions, and she found herself feeling guilty for almost liking him. One Friday at the end of the lesson, he walked up to her as she put her books in her backpack.

"Can you tutor me over the weekend, too?" he asked. "Monday's three days away, and I forget this stuff sometimes. I mean, I try to study on my own, but it's not so easy. I think if I had one more lesson with you I'd do better."

"That's asking a lot, Taylor."

"I know. But I feel like we're really close to my getting a handle on this subject."

Becca frowned as she thought it over. She could imagine Andy and Mike's reaction to this news. Well, what they didn't know wouldn't hurt them, and anyway, Andy worked at the vet on Saturday morning. He'd never know.

"Let's try it this Saturday morning and see what happens," she said.

"Thanks, Becca!"

"Your house or mine?"

"Nobody's going to be home at my place Saturday morning, and I can't get a ride to your place."

"Okay, I'll talk to my dad tonight and text you." She picked up her things. "So long."

"Thanks, Becca!" Taylor picked up his backpack and followed her out the door.

Becca told her parents about Taylor's request that night at dinner.

"I don't like that kid," her father said.

"Yeah, I'm not very fond of him either. But he's been nice to me since I started tutoring. And maybe I can talk him into being nicer to other people while I'm at it."

"You mean Andy?" her mother asked.

"Not just Andy. Taylor picks on a lot of kids. Well, I haven't seen him do it lately, but he used to."

"Why would he just stop?" her father said.

"I don't know. Now that I think of it, he's a lot busier this year than last year."

"You may just have hit upon the perfect anti-bullying strategy: Make the kid so busy he doesn't have time to pick on anyone."

Becca smiled. "Well, whatever the reason, he's not bothering Andy anymore. Maybe because he thinks I'd quit tutoring him if he did."

"That's a good reason," her mother said.

"So can I tutor him on Saturday?"

His parents looked at each other. Her father shrugged. "Okay. But you text me if you feel the least bit uncomfortable, and I'll come get you right away."

"I will."

Becca looked out the car window at a small, brown colonial house that had definitely seen better days. Her father walked her to the front door and waited as Becca rang the doorbell.

Taylor opened the door and said hello. He seemed surprised to see Becca's father.

"I wanted to make sure everything was okay before I left my daughter here," Mr. Jefferson said, his eyebrows drawn together.

"Yeah, everything's fine. You want to come into the kitchen and see the study area?" Taylor said.

"No. I'll see you in a couple of hours," he told Becca, not taking his eyes off Taylor.

"Bye, Dad."

They watched him leave and then closed the door and went inside. Taylor didn't seem to be wearing the Magelight necklace, which was a relief. It was bad enough she argued constantly with Andy over tutoring Taylor. If Taylor started flaunting the Magelights, it would only lend fuel to Andy's case that she shouldn't be anywhere near the "enemy."

He led Becca through the house to the kitchen. She was glad to note his books were open on the table. "You've been studying already?" she asked.

"Yeah. Figured I could use it," he said with a half-grin.

"Well, you're not wrong."

"Why is it so much easier for you?" Taylor wanted to know. "This stuff is hard. Heck, regular history is hard enough without all this extra stuff!"

"It doesn't come easy," Becca said. "It never did. I had to learn how to study. Didn't your parents help you when you were little?"

Taylor flushed. "My parents divorced when I was six. Then Mom remarried a couple years later. She's always too busy. And my stepdad says it's not his job to do my work for me."

Becca frowned. She'd seen Taylor's stepfather at school events from time to time, especially football games. Even then it was noticeable that he favored his sons over his stepson.

"Well, you don't need their help," she said. "What you need are good study habits. This is history, not calculus. You don't have to grasp difficult concepts. Well, okay, you have to learn all the different political systems. But it's mostly learning what happened, where, and when. Look at it this way: If you can learn how to keep all those football plays straight in your head, you can learn history."

"I never thought of it like that," he said.

"How do you learn the plays?"

"Coach goes over them during practice, gives us a playbook, makes us learn them. But football is a lot easier than history."

"Is it? Or is it just that you like football and you don't like class-work?"

"Wow. I didn't think of it that way, either." He grinned at Becca. "You really are smart."

"Maybe. But let's see what we can do about helping you learn all about how the Habsburg dynasty became Europe's ruling class."

Two hours later, Becca put her books in her backpack as Taylor gathered his from the kitchen table. "Nice work today, Taylor," she said.

"Thanks. Are you hungry? My mom makes really good cookies."

"Sure. My dad's going to be here any minute, though."

Taylor went over to the counter and opened a plastic container. "Then have a couple to go," he said, coming back to the table and holding the container out to her.

"Thanks," she said, reaching for one.

The back door opened and in walked Taylor's stepbrothers.

"Hope we're interrupting," Nick said.

"Cookies for me? Sweet!" Matt said, reaching rudely past Becca. Taylor swatted his hand away.

"Wait your turn. Becca's a guest."

Nick shook his head. "You should not have done that, stepbro."

Matt grinned. "What he said." He moved between Becca and Taylor. Becca backed away. Matt moved menacingly close. "How many times are we going to have to teach you manners, stepbro?" he asked, poking Taylor in the shoulder. Taylor stepped backwards at each poke.

"C'mon, Matt, back off," Taylor muttered, glancing down at the floor. He seemed to shrink in on himself as Becca watched.

Becca froze. She couldn't think what to do. If she stuck up for Taylor, would his stepbrothers turn on her? She was beginning to regret agreeing to meet here. Her phone buzzed and she glanced at it. The text was from her father.

I'm outside.

Taylor's stepbrothers weren't paying her any attention, but Taylor could see her. She replied to the text quickly.

Ring the doorbell. Fast!

"Um, Taylor?" she said, making up her mind. All three heads turned toward her. *Good*, she thought, *they're distracted*. Then she heard the sound she was waiting for—the doorbell. "Oh. That must be my dad," she said.

Taylor looked at her gratefully. "I'll walk you out," he said, moving before Matt could react. They hurried away from the kitchen.

"Thanks," Taylor said quietly as he opened the door for her. Becca's father was standing at the door.

"Well?" he asked his daughter.

Nick and Matt came through the hallway to stand behind Taylor and Becca. The looks on their faces boded ill for their stepbrother once his visitors left.

"Oh," Becca's father said, frowning as he studied the two older boys. "Hey, Taylor, do you need a lift anywhere? Becca and I aren't in any kind of rush."

"Taylor has to stay home," Matt said. "He's not allowed to go out without permission."

"Really?" Mr. Jefferson said. "Does that apply to you two?"

"We're seniors."

"But you're not his mother. So I'm guessing Taylor could, say, text her and find out if it's okay to come with Becca and me?"

Taylor grinned and reached into his pocket for his phone and texted his mother while his stepbrothers watched sourly. "Yep, Mom says I can go with you. Thanks, Mr. Jefferson. I'd love a lift to Pete's house. Let me go get my stuff." He pushed past his stepbrothers, who both wore sour looks. Taylor came back shortly with his jacket and backpack.

"See you later," he said to his brothers as he followed Becca and her

214

father to their car.

"Thanks Mr. Jefferson," he said as they pulled away from the curb, his stepbrothers glaring at them from the doorway.

"Don't mention it. To me, anyway. You might want to mention it to your mother."

"There's nothing to mention," Taylor said, looking out the window.

Becca's dad glanced at Taylor and shrugged. "Suit yourself."

Taylor said nothing more until they dropped him off at Pete's house. "Thanks again. See you around, Becca." He waited until the car was out of sight, then walked down the sidewalk back the way they had come. He didn't tell them that he knew Pete was out with his family for the day. Taylor didn't really have anywhere to go, but at least he wasn't home alone with his stepbrothers. He wished his mother didn't have to work so much. Things were better when she was around. While he was at it, he wished she'd never married his jerk of a stepfather and brought his two jerky sons into Taylor's life. He couldn't wait until summer. They'd both gotten football scholarships and would be leaving him in peace for the first time in years. Meanwhile, maybe he should start planning more lessons with Niflah to keep him out of the house more often. Yeah, that would be a good idea. Taylor settled his backpack and took off in the direction of Principal Saunders' house to see if anyone there would have time for a lesson.

A short while later, he went through the front gate and down the sidewalk to the porch. He lifted his hand to knock on the door when it swung open. Grinning, Taylor stepped inside, knowing that one of the Wild Ones had opened the door for him.

"Kitchen," Roah sent.

Taylor went down the hall and found Roah sitting in the kitchen window in the afternoon sunlight.

"How did you know I was at the door?" Taylor asked.

"Cats have much better hearing than humans. You walk loudly on wooden steps."

"Oh."

CHAPTER NINETEEN

"Why are you here?"

Taylor shrugged. "I had a little extra time today so I thought I'd get another lesson in. Is Principal Saunders here?"

Roah gazed at him. "No."

"Well, is Niflah here?"

"He is at the Compound today. No one is here. Just me and the dogs." Roah dropped his head and licked his shoulder.

Taylor was a little afraid of Roah. He'd seen him discipline the Wild Ones who failed him. But maybe Roah would teach him. "Well then, can—can you give me a lesson?" Taylor asked. "Would that be all right?"

Roah stopped grooming his shoulder. "Perhaps. But you are hiding something. Why are you here?"

Taylor hesitated.

"Tell me the truth. I have no wish to teach a boy who does not trust me."

"Because it sucks to be in my house!" Taylor shouted. "My stepbrothers are always picking on me and it's worse when my mom's not around. And she's never around because my stepfather is a drunk who can't hold onto a job for more than a few months so she has to work double shifts to make enough money to pay the bills while he goes out drinking when he's not working! *Anywhere* is better than home!"

Roah watched Taylor unblinking

"You are weak," Roah said.

"I am not! Matt and Nick are bigger and stronger than me, and they almost always come at me two at a time."

"You have Magelights."

"That I can't use. What do you think Principal Saunders would do if my stepbrothers discovered my Magelights? He told me to keep them secret!"

"You do not think. You could use your Magelights to cause harm to your stepbrothers without their ever knowing it was you who did it."

"What?" Taylor said. "What do you mean? How?"

"Would you like me to teach you how?"

"Yes!"

"Then I want something from you."

"Anything! Name it!"

"I want to learn how to count."

"What?"

"Teach me human numbers."

"But—why?"

"That is none of your concern. Here is what I offer: You will teach me to count, and tell no one—*no one*—and I will teach you how to make your stepbrothers regret ever harming you."

"It's a deal!" Taylor said, reaching out his hand. Roah stared at him. "Uh, sorry. Humans shake hands when they make a deal." He dropped his hand back to his side as Roah continued to stare.

"Numbers first, now, while no one else is around," Roah said. "Then Magelight lessons. And I warn you, I've no patience for any student who doesn't give me his full attention."

"Got it," Taylor said. He sat down at the table and took out a notebook and pen. "Come over here and I'll teach you how to count to ten, to start."

Roah jumped down from the windowsill and leaped onto the table. He sat next to Taylor. "I am ready."

Half an hour later, Taylor put away his notebook and pen, marveling that he'd just taught a cat how to count. "You did good," he told Roah.

"Yes. Now I will teach you some things. You cannot use the Magelights directly on your brothers. But you can use your Magelights to make things happen to them."

Taylor's expression brightened as he realized what Roah was saying.

"You catch on quickly. Good. But you must remember that you cannot allow your brothers to see the light that emanates from your Magelights. You will have to find a way to do things without them realizing it is you doing them."

CHAPTER NINETEEN

"You mean like knocking something off a shelf onto their heads," Taylor said, grinning widely. "Roah, you're a genius. I am going to have *so* much fun doing this." He laughed out loud.

"You will be discreet. Remember that Saunders will take away the Magelights if you are not."

"No chance of that," Taylor said, shaking his head. "I know a good thing when I've got it. I'm hanging onto these Magelights for good. Besides, you need me to help counter Cohen."

"That is true," Roah said. "But it is also true that Saunders could replace you if need be."

"Not gonna happen." He glanced up at the kitchen clock. "I have a little time before my mom gets home."

"Then we shall work on your using the Magelights without letting anyone know you are doing so."

That was a lot harder than Taylor realized. After an hour of trying, he'd mastered the art of making something move, but not of doing it with only one Magelight.

"If you can separate the Magelights and use only one at a time, it will be easier to hide the telltale glow," Roah said. "Work on that for next time."

"I will," Taylor promised. He gathered up his backpack and headed out the front door. His head was spinning with ideas about things dropping on his brothers. There were so many medals and trophies in their room from their years in sports. Yeah, this was going to be a lot of fun. Laughing, Taylor went through the front gate and turned down the street toward home.

TWENTY: TILYON TROUBLES

Fall grew into winter, and snow covered the streets of Coreyton. Andy found that being friends with someone like Mr. Velez was useful on many levels. He didn't mind driving Andy out to the Compound on the weekend, and he gave Andy a cover story of spending the day with Teresa, Mike, and Becca. It was true, too, as they went regularly with him to the Compound.

Becca spent her spare time reading war and strategy books, looking for ways to help Razor and the Shomrim. Mike learned to dial back his clowning in Razor's presence, thanks to a lot of prodding by Teresa. He spent a lot of time with the kittens and younger Catmages and became quite a favorite of theirs. Andy trained hard with Zehira when he wasn't practicing with Zohar and the Shomrim.

Goldeneyes was too busy for him these days. Her time was taken by private lessons with Methuselah and Hakham. She didn't speak much about the lessons, but she was tired a lot, and Andy noticed that on the rare occasions when he saw her in the bayit she shared with Letsan, she was asleep or resting.

It took Zohar and Regel some time to learn to adjust to having three legs. By Midwinter they were so used to their new gaits that they got around almost as well as they had before. But it still bothered Andy to see them. It made him work harder when he was training with Zohar, and the Shomrim were heartened as Andy improved. Many of them started calling him the Son of Aaron to one another.

"We should give you a Catmage name, Andy," Zohar said at the end of a particularly satisfying practice. His suggestion was met with shouts of agreement from the Shomrim around them.

"How about Yaacov?" he said. "It's my Hebrew name, just like your Catmage names."

"Yaacov! Yaacov! Yaacov!" the Shomrim chanted.

"Let's go back to the meadow," Andy said, quieting his friends, but grinning broadly. "I have to get home for dinner."

"Yaacov, eh?" Razor asked gruffly as he strolled toward them as they made their way down the path. "Not bad. What does it mean?"

"I don't know," Andy said. "I was named for my grandfather. It's a Jewish tradition to give your kids Hebrew names."

"Humans," Razor said. "If you were a Catmage, you'd know what it means."

Not even Razor's teasing could bring down Andy's mood. "And if you were a human, you'd know how to do this," he said, reaching down and scooping up a handful of snow, which he quickly shaped into a snowball and threw at Razor. Razor gave a harsh bark of laughter as he diverted the snowball's path toward a nearby warrior, hitting him in the flank. But while he was looking away at the warrior he had hit, Andy got him with another snowball. Suddenly, there was dead silence as the other Shomrim stopped still in their tracks. *Uh-oh*, Andy thought. Then Razor let out a roar of laughter, which was quickly joined by the rest of the Catmages.

"Good shot, Yaacov. Good tactic, getting your target while his attention was diverted." He shook the snow off his coat. "Just don't ever do it again." He fell into step with Andy as they returned to the meadow.

"I'd really just like to be called Andy."

"That was a good practice, Andy."

"Thanks." *Wow.*

"My brother wasn't wrong about you."

Double wow.

"I'm feeling better and better about our odds these days. You keep studying and working this hard, and Saunders is going to regret ever having messed with us."

"I'm trying," Andy said. They reached the meadow during a study break. Catmages of all ages were sitting in groups or bouncing around. Andy saw a large group near Mike and Teresa, their Magelights flashing on and off.

"What's that clown doing?" Razor wondered.

"Knowing Mike, something silly and fun," Andy said.

Mike saw them and shouted for Andy to join him.

"What's up?" Andy asked.

"Well, we were playing ball, but they kept getting lost in the snow. So I'm teaching the Cat Kiddies something else," Mike said. "Watch."

He bent down to make a snowball and flung it in the air. The apprentices were taking turns batting it around with their Magelights.

"More games," Razor said disdainfully.

Three more Catmages batted the ball. The last one knocked off a chunk of snow.

"You're out!" the others shouted. The ball bounded around as the next few had their turn.

Razor glanced over at Andy. "Don't even think it, boy."

"I wasn't."

"I was." Razor's Magelight flared, the snowball's course changed, and smacked into Andy's chest before he could duck. Mike and the youngsters burst into laughter. "Now we're even."

Andy shook his head and brushed snow off his jacket. "C'mon, Mike, get the others. It's time to go."

Principal Saunders sat behind his desk observing Taylor Grant, who was facing the wall and attempting to send him a message via his Magelights.

CHAPTER TWENTY

It was a test of sorts. Saunders enjoyed throwing these little challenges at the boy. It kept him on his toes, and it also encouraged him to practice. So far, Mr. Grant was proving to be very adept. During this exercise, he was not allowed to speak. Having him face the wall removed the temptation to open his mouth. And it enabled Saunders to practice as well, though that was something he'd never admit to a child. Or to one of those cats.

"Mind-voice only, Mr. Grant," he sent. "You will stay there until I'm happy with your results. Practice makes perfect. Roah tells me you're quite good at this."

Taylor couldn't get over how much like his speaking voice Saunders' mind-voice was. "I am good at this," Taylor sent. "But can I take a break? I have to go to the bathroom."

"Very well," Saunders sent back. "But be quick. I bore easily, and if you want a ride home tonight, you'd better make sure I'm not bored."

"Yes, sir!" Taylor. He hurried out the door and down the hall to the nearest boy's bathroom. Moments after he left, Mario Velez appeared.

Mario Velez walked down the empty hall. He had just finished cleaning the boys' locker room. One of them had thought it would be funny to stuff a notebook down a toilet. If he found out who did it…

He wheeled the mop and bucket down the hall toward the custodian's closet. There was a light on in the principal's office at the other end of the hall. Mario had seen Saunders leave hours ago. *Maybe he left the light on. I better check.* He left the mop and bucket and walked softly until he could get a look inside the room. Saunders was sitting behind his desk, alone. Mario's eyebrows shot up. The principal had come back. And he was wearing that necklace the kids wanted—the one with the cat on it. He bet Andy would want to know about this. He turned and went back down the hall as quietly as he could, taking his phone out of his pocket on the way. When he was out of earshot of the office, he stopped to send a text message.

TILYON TROUBLES

Goldeneyes and Letsan lazed on Andy's bed. She was taking a break from her lessons, and they were both in town for a change. It was nice having them around again. Letsan said it was to keep an eye on things, but Andy was pretty sure it was because he liked the comfort of a heated house.

Andy's phone buzzed on the night table. His mother was working late. It was probably from her, telling him she would be even later. He stretched, saved the paper he was working on and reached over to get the phone.

"You know, good friends would have passed the phone over to me," he said.

"Yes, but good Catmages never needlessly expend magical energy," Letsan said, yawning. "So you'll just have to settle for taking two whole steps to get your phone. Poor boy. Zahavin, do you think we'll have to heal him after expending all that power?"

"We just might," she said. "Andy, shall we call Dr. Crane to check you over?"

"I'm a boy, not a Catmage," he said. "Dr. Crane's a vet." He looked down at the phone. "It's Mr. Velez," he said. He read the text and gasped.

"What is it?" Goldeneyes asked.

"Saunders is alone at the high school, and he has the Tilyon! Mr. Velez says if we hurry, we might be able to get it back!"

Letsan and Goldeneyes leaped up, eyes blazing. "How many guards are at Saunders' house?" Goldeneyes asked.

"At least four," Letsan said.

"Call two of them to join us. Andy, your bike—can you sneak out?"

"Mom's not going to be home until late. There's no sneaking about it. Come on, let's go," he said, putting his phone in his pocket and grabbing a heavy sweatshirt on the way out the door. Letsan and Goldeneyes were at the garage door before he was on the ground floor. He stopped to send a text to Mr. Velez asking him to leave a door open for them. Andy saw the flash of an orange light from Letsan's collar as he sent a message to the Shomrim on duty across town. He hurried to get his bike out and the two Catmages settled in the basket. Then Andy took off down the road, pedaling furiously, his sweatshirt trailing behind in his wake as they rode.

When he got to the school, they waited by the door until he regained his breath. Andy texted Mr. Velez that they were there and asked if Saunders was still in his office. He received a one-word response: *Yes.*

"Now what?" Andy asked. "Do we wait for the others? Do we go in now?"

"We wait," Letsan said. "We do this right. Let me think about how we're going to do this."

By the time Taylor came out of the boy's room, Mr. Velez was already out of sight down the darkened hall. Taylor hurried back to the office.

Saunders stopped paging through a website on his laptop as the boy came through the door. "I'd like to see if you can send a Magelight message. Go to the stairwell at the end of the hall. Message me from there. You should have no difficulty, as it's a short distance. You keep telling me how much better you are than Mr. Cohen. Prove it."

"Yes, sir!" Taylor said. He hurried out into the darkened hallway in the opposite direction that the janitor had taken. At the end of the hall, he stepped through the open door and stood just inside on the landing. Niflah had told him the best thing to do was visualize what he wanted to send. So he thought of himself waving at Saunders. He took several slow, steady breaths. Then he closed his eyes and concentrated on sending the message. He felt his Magelights grow warm. He opened his eyes and saw a multicolored light shoot out of his necklace and down the hall. He stopped himself from whooping with joy, knowing it would make Saunders angry. He settled for grinning hugely and pumping the air with his fist. Taylor thought about going back to the office, but Saunders hadn't told him to come back yet. So he stayed put, waiting.

"Katana and Atzel are on their way," Letsan said. "They'll be here soon."

"Mr. Velez should get out of there," Andy said. "Saunders will fire him if he thinks he's helping us. I'm going to text him." He waited until he received a return message. "Okay, he's leaving. His car's on the other side of the building, he says."

"Andy, you're not going inside," Goldeneyes told him.

"What? Why?"

"Because Mr. Velez isn't the only one who can get in trouble if he's caught. In fact, I want you across the street and hidden behind that parked car," she said, indicating where she wanted Andy to go.

"But you need me!"

"No, we don't," Letsan said. "Zahavin is right. We'll have four well-trained warriors against one partly-trained human with no aura. Get out of here, now. If we need you, we'll call you."

Furious, Andy got back on his bike and did as he was told. "I thought you said I was making great progress and ready to fight," he sent as he crossed the street.

"I did," Goldeneyes responded, "and you are. But now is not your time. If we manage to retrieve the Tilyon, we still have eleven Magelights to get back. And you still have to be in a school run by Saunders."

"You sound like my mother," Andy grumbled. He said nothing else while he waited for the other Catmages to arrive. A few minutes later, he saw the flash of a yellow Magelight as Goldeneyes pushed open the unlocked door. The Catmages went inside, and Andy waited restlessly.

Taylor's cell phone buzzed. *Very good,* said the message from Saunders. *Another.* Taylor grinned and wondered what else he could send as a message. Somehow, he doubted Saunders would want an image of Taylor pummeling Cohen. Or maybe not. He stuck his head out the doorway to see if there was anything he could create an image of to send. Taylor gasped as he saw four cats moving slowly toward the principal's office. They weren't any of the cats he was used to working with. "Hey!" he shouted. "What are you doing?" His shouts echoed down the empty hall. A jet of light burst out of a Magelight and Taylor ducked quickly back into the stairwell.

"No!" he heard one of the cats say. "He's just a boy! Leave him! He can't hurt us! It's Saunders we want."

Suddenly, the office door slammed shut. The cats were outside. "What's going on?" Taylor sent. "What should I do?" There was no response.

He peered cautiously out the door. The four cats were standing outside, their Magelights glowing. He heard the lock on the door clicking. Principal Saunders must be holding the lock shut. *Think, Grant, think!* he told himself. Then he closed his eyes, breathed deeply, and clenched his fists in concentration. A multicolored message flew out of his Magelight necklace, down the hall, and out the crack in the outside door. Taylor was overcome with exhaustion and had to sit down heavily.

Back at Saunders' house, Roah and Alef sat on the back porch, waiting for Saunders to get home. Alef had returned from the West Woods Compound that afternoon. Roah was pleased with his report and had allowed Alef to sit in on his latest session with the dogs.

"They will be a formidable weapon when they are ready," Alef said. "We must take care that they do not become a weapon to be used against us."

"That will not happen. I will kill any dog that attacks Wild Ones."

"Good."

Their ears twitched as they listened to the night sounds. A many-colored message light appeared at a distance, zooming toward Roah.

"It's an attack on Saunders at the school!" Roah said, leaping off the porch. "Hurry!"

Alef was right behind him. They ran full speed to the school.

Saunders had enough presence of mind to leap up at Taylor's shout and hurry to the door. He saw the four Catmages, recognized Goldeneyes and Letsan, slammed the door in their faces and locked it. He laughed grimly.

TILYON TROUBLES

They hadn't expected such a simple trick. His laughter died as he realized they were trying to open the lock with their Magelights. Saunders gripped the lock and held on tightly. *We'll see who's stronger, me or the kitties*, he thought. The lock held fast in his hand. Saunders loosened his hold on the lock to let them think they were getting the upper hand. Then he slammed it shut again, laughing.

"Go home, kitty cats, before you find yourself in much deeper than you want," he said.

"You have no dogs and no Wild Ones to help you this time," Gold-eneyes said. "We will have the Tilyon back. It's only a matter of time."

Saunders frowned. They were right. There was only so long he could hold the lock in place before his hand tired. He had to think of something, but what?

Taylor wiped the sweat from his forehead. His strength was coming back, but he felt like he'd just finished football practice on a hot summer day. He looked around the corner. The cats were still outside the door. Taylor didn't know what to do. At least one of them was ready to hurt Taylor if he tried to get to Saunders. Better stay put. He moved away from the door and put his back against the wall.

"Where are you?" Roah's voice said in his head.

"The stairwell outside Saunders' office! He's being attacked!"

"I know, fool, I got your message. Tell me what's happening now! We are outside his office window."

"Four Catmages are in the hall outside the office. Saunders is keeping the door locked. They haven't been able to open it yet."

"Show me."

Taylor concentrated and sent a mental image to Roah.

"Stay there until we call you."

Outside, Roah and Alef had found the open door. They charged down the hall, firing at the Catmages outside the principal's office. Roah's jet took the grey-and-white Catmage in the leg, causing her to yowl in pain. Letsan threw up a shield and deflected Alef's light dagger. Growling, he turned to face the Wild One, firing three times in quick succession. Alef danced aside and dodged the first two. The third one clipped his tail. The smell of burnt fur filled the air.

"There are only two!" Goldeneyes said. "Take them, then we get the Tilyon."

The four Catmages stopped trying to force the door open and faced the new threat. Colored light daggers flew up and down the hall, some finding their marks. Taylor quailed inside the hallway. His lessons hadn't begun to cover anything like this.

"Now!" Roah shouted. The office door opened, and Saunders launched an office chair at the Catmages, who dodged quickly. The chair hit Atzel, who grunted and whirled, protecting his flank from the Wild Ones. Letsan called the others to him. The four of them ranged themselves against the two Wild One and Saunders, who stood back, grinning.

"I've been doing some practicing lately. Would you like to see what I can do?" Saunders asked. The Tilyon flared, and suddenly Katana cried out in pain, blood dripping from her ear. Saunders' laughter echoed through the hall. "Lovely! Let's see how Zahavin will look with a slash on that pretty face." The Tilyon flashed again as Saunders clenched his fists. Letsan jumped in front of Goldeneyes, pushing her aside. Blood poured from his shoulder, and he growled.

"This isn't going to work," he said. "We can't ignore Saunders. He's mastered the Tilyon. Katana, Atzel, Zahavin—time to go."

"No!" Goldeneyes said. "We can take it back!"

"No we can't. On my mark, shields up, run past the Wild Ones, and get out of here. Katana, tell Andy to get going home and we'll catch up with him. Zahavin, that's an order. Do it! Now!"

The Wild Ones moved aside as they charged, and the Catmages turned, backing down the hallway until they were near the door. Roah and Alef kept firing until they left. Saunders' laughter echoed down the halls as they fled.

TILYON TROUBLES

"You can come out now," Roah told Taylor. He hurried over to them.

"Is everything all right?" he asked Saunders. "Roah told me to stay put. I'm sorry I couldn't help you fight."

"The boy sent us a message when you were attacked," Roah said. "If he had not, you would have lost the Tilyon this night."

"I see," Saunders said. "Mr. Grant, you did well. *Very* well."

Taylor flushed at the praise, smiling. "Thanks, Principal Saunders."

"What puzzles me, though, is how they knew I was here tonight." His eyes blazed. "Did you say anything to anyone? Did you mention it to Mr. Cohen while you were in class, perhaps?"

"No! I didn't even tell my mom. She thinks I'm studying with Becca!"

"Then how did they find out?"

"Let it go, Saunders," Roah said. "We will figure it out later. I think we should leave this place. They might come back with greater force."

Saunders glared at Roah and Alef. "You're right," he said. "Let's go. Mr. Grant, gather your things and I'll drive you home."

As the shutting door echoed down the hall, Mario Velez stepped out of the shadows. His SUV was parked on the other side of the building. Principal Saunders wouldn't know he was there. Not today, anyway. Frowning, Mario walked past the principal's office. It was time to go home.

"I thought he was alone," Andy said. They had stopped to tend to their wounds, which weren't serious. Letsan and Katana healed themselves.

"So did we. Mr. Velez must not have seen Taylor. He was at the end of the hall when we got there. And he seems to have learned how to send messages."

"I saw a strange, many-colored light after he shouted at us," Atzel said. "And you stopped me from hurting him! He is the enemy!"

"He's just a boy!"

"What?" Andy said. "He can send messages? Already? I only just learned how to do it myself this year."

"You don't have five Magelights," Letsan said. "This is news that must be shared with the Council. I'm going to the East Woods tonight. Katana, Atzel, are you fit for guard duty still?"

"Yes. We'll head back to our posts."

"I'll make sure Andy gets home safely," Goldeneyes said.

"I don't need a babysitter!"

"No you don't, but I am still going home with you. I'm staying there tonight."

"Oh."

"Be careful, Zahavin," Letsan said.

"You too. I will see you in the morning."

Andy waited until she was in the basket, then took off for home. He was still furious. They'd come so close to getting back the Tilyon. Once again, Taylor had made Andy's life difficult. He gritted his teeth as he pedaled down the street. *Someday, he's going to pay for everything.*

TWENTY-ONE: SPRING BREAK

The first day of spring break dawned gloriously. Andy, Becca, and Mike decided to take full advantage of it. Mike and Becca rode their bikes to Andy's house and found him waiting for them on the front porch.

"What's on the agenda for today?" Mike called to Andy as they wheeled up his driveway.

"Becca says she has some ideas she wants me to work on."

"Would they have anything to do with all the different balls in my backpack that Becca made me bring?"

"No, I just wanted to see if you'd bring them for me," she said.

"What?"

"I'm kidding. Yes, I need them. You brought all kinds, right?"

"Ping-Pong balls, bouncy balls, sponge balls, baseballs, everything I could find. So what am I going to do while you guys are playing catch?"

"Razor will find something for you to do."

"Great," Mike grumbled. "I get to work with Grumpy Guy."

"Welcome to my world," Andy said.

"Although—" Mike said. "You know, I may have something else Razor will be interested in. Hey, Andy, do you have some heavy string or rope and maybe some canvas or leather?"

"Rope, yeah. Canvas, I don't know."

They searched the garage and found an old canvas beach bag and fetched a bundle of heavy cord. Mike cut off a few squares, measured out the rope Andy gave him, cut holes in two squares and threaded the cord through them. Then he bundled it all into his backpack.

"All done," he said. "I think Razor is going to be very pleased when he sees this." Andy got his bike, and the three of them were soon on the road out of town, Andy in the lead.

They arrived outside the Compound and hid their bikes in the hedge. The guards recognized them and let them pass unchallenged. Andy tried to avoid the muddiest parts of the path as they headed to the main meadow.

"I love spring, but I'm not all that fond of mud," Mike said. "Not since I was six, anyway. Remember, Andy?"

"You mean the mud pies? Yeah. Our moms got so mad at us that day."

Becca's eyebrows rose. "I don't think I know this story."

"Oh, Mom and I were over at Mike's after it had been really rainy. They let us go out in the yard to play, and we decided to make mud pies. And then Mike decided making mud pies was too boring."

"Uh-oh."

Andy grinned. "Yep. He started throwing them at me. So I threw them back. Mom says the only parts of us not covered in mud were our eyes."

"My mom hosed us down in the yard outside before she let us back in the house."

Becca started laughing. "I can just picture it. No chance your moms took an actual picture, is there?"

Andy shrugged. "I don't know. You can ask."

"I'll ask at the Passover Seder," she said mischievously. "Maybe your mom will start passing around your baby pictures."

Andy groaned. "You do that, and I'll make sure your mom brings *your* baby pictures."

Rebecca put her hands up. "Okay, okay, I won't ask."

They reached the Compound and split up. Mike went to find Razor. Andy grinned as he saw Leilei sprinting over to them.

"Zahavin said I can help Becca train you today!" she said happily.

"You're both training me? Is that what are the baseballs for, Becca?" Andy asked.

"Yep. If Catmages can shield themselves and fire at the same time, you can, too."

"I've been trying during my classes with Zehira. I can't do it."

Becca brushed that off. "Yes you can." She dumped the bag of balls on the ground and picked a Ping-Pong ball out of the pile. "Don't catch this. Try to bounce it away with a Magelight shield." She threw it at Andy's chest. As he produced a shield to deflect it, Leilei's Magelight flashed and another ball flew at Andy.

"Fire at it, Andy!" Leilei said.

Andy's shield disappeared and the second ball bounced off him.

"I can't do it," he said. "It's like trying to rub your stomach and pat your head at the same time!"

"You mean like this?" Becca said, grinning as she did exactly that.

"Not helping."

Andy stood still while Becca and Leilei tossed two more Ping-Pong balls at him. The second one bounced off his chest. They tried again and again, but Andy couldn't seem to get the hang of deflecting one ball with the Magelight while firing a light dagger at the other.

"Andy, you can do this," Leilei said. "Auntie Zahavin says that the secret to casting spells with a Magelight is limited only by your imagination."

"And Andy has a great imagination. So imagine you're holding, say, a shield and a sword."

Andy bent his left arm and closed his hand around the strap of an imaginary shield. His right hand gripped an imaginary sword. The Magelight stayed dull. He frowned and concentrated.

CHAPTER TWENTY-ONE

"Nothing," he said.

"Well, wait until I throw something," she said. She conferred quickly with Leilei. Becca tossed a sponge ball at him. At the same time, Leilei launched a second ball. Andy deflected the first one. The second one hit him in the stomach.

"Ow!"

Becca sighed. "Drastic times call for drastic measures," she said. She nodded to Leilei.

"What's that supposed to mean?"

"This." She leaned down, picked up a baseball, and threw it with all of her might at Andy's face. Leilei used her Magelight to send a second baseball at his chest. He flung out his left arm, which was still holding the imaginary shield, and chopped downward at the ball with his right. His Magelight flared. The first ball bounded away. The second ball was knocked to the ground as a long, sword-shaped green light flared out of Andy's right hand. Becca beamed at him while Leilei leaped around them in a fair imitation of Patches.

"You see? You *can* do it!" Becca said.

"But that was really hard. I don't know if I could do that in the middle of a battle."

"Concentrate, Andy. I know you can do this," Leilei told him. "You're wearing Nafshi's Magelight!"

A memory came suddenly to Andy. He was in Saunders' cellar with Nafshi, asking her how Catmages made their magic.

It's all about concentration and focus. Imagery is the easy part.

Andy took a deep breath, closed his eyes, and concentrated. Then he opened them and said, "I'm ready. Let's do it again. Leilei, fire a light dagger. We need to test me for real."

"I don't know, Andy—"

"I can do this. Both of you, do it!"

Becca threw a baseball at him full speed while Leilei fired a dagger. Andy jerked up his arm with its imaginary shield. His Magelight flashed and the dagger bounced off the shield and fell harmlessly to the ground. At the same time, his light sword flashed and cut downward. The baseball fell to the ground in two halves. Becca and Leilei stood still for a moment, looking at the smoking halves of the baseball on the ground. Then Leilei cheered, laughing as she ran to examine the ruined ball.

"You did it!" Becca said, running to him. Andy jumped up in the air and ran to meet her. He grabbed her by the waist and spun her around, whooping. He set her down and they stood, grinning at each other, his hands around her waist. Andy was struck by how pretty her eyes were. His breath caught and they leaned toward each other.

"Andy! Becca! Wait 'til you hear. This is so cool!" Mike called as he ran across the field. They moved hastily apart and saw Mike heading their way, followed by Razor, Matti, and Letsan.

"Wait until you hear what we did!" Leilei said.

"Aren't you late for your lesson with Zehira?" Razor asked her.

"Oops. I'd better run. Bye, Andy! Bye, Becca!" She ran quickly across the meadow.

"What's so cool?" Andy asked, wishing Mike had given him one more minute with Becca.

Mike was swinging the rope-and-canvas contraption he'd made at Andy's house. "I showed them what I could do with a sling," he said. "Razor liked it."

"Yes, until it fell apart after a few tries," Razor said.

"That's because I have to sew the canvas on. I didn't have the time to make one the right way. I wanted to show you the concept. I told you I could be useful against the Wild Ones."

Razor grunted. "Maybe. I'm not convinced it's your place to fight with us, boy. The Wild Ones play for keeps."

"That's why you need us," Mike said. "Andy's going."

"Andy has a Magelight."

"Well, I have a sling. And rocks. And a great throwing arm."

"I don't think we belong in the middle of the fight," Becca said,

235

"but I'm glad you're here, Razor. I want to discuss some more battle strate-gy and tactics I've been reading about."

Razor stopped in front of Becca, who leaned down to scratch his torn ears. Razor turned his head from side to side, purring softly. Mike and Andy glanced at each other in shock.

"If you're smart, you won't say anything," Letsan sent privately to the two boys.

"What's the topic for today?" Razor asked.

"Encirclement. You told me you want to take the fight to Saunders. If you really mean it, there are ways to do it. And I think we could talk Mr. Velez into helping us with reinforcements."

Razor grunted. "My bayit. Letsan, get Zohar and meet us there. Matti, with me." They went back the way they came, leaving Mike and Andy standing by themselves in the field.

"Was it something I said?" Mike asked.

Andy laughed. "It's always something you said. Go on after them, keep your mouth shut and listen. Razor's not going to let you do anything until you show him you can be quiet and serious."

"Roger that," Mike said, saluting sharply.

"Yeah, that's not something you're going to want to do in front of Razor."

Mike waved and headed after the others. Andy shook his head and went to wait by the Teaching Rings until Goldeneyes arrived, apologetic at being so late.

"Methuselah was helping me through a very tricky spell," she said. "I needed to rest and regain my strength."

"I don't mind. The more you know, the better we'll be when we go after the Tilyon."

Goldeneyes purred. "I've got some good things to impart to you, as well. Let's go find a more private place and get to work."

Andy followed Goldeneyes as she led him into a small clearing in the woods. "And wait until you see what Becca and I were just practicing," he said happily. Things were definitely looking up for the good guys.

"I need to talk to you, Andrew," she said.

Uh-oh. She's going all formal on me.

"Yes, I am, because this is serious. Do you remember Hakham explaining Avdei Ha-Or to you?"

"Yeah, that was the thing Nafshi did that embedded her Magelight under her skin. I remember."

"Well, I'm going to undergo the ritual."

"What? When?"

"Soon. Methuselah and Hakham think I'm ready."

"But—but you could *die*," Andy said. "If you don't do it right, it will kill you!"

"You just said that you were happy I was learning more with Methuselah."

"That was before I knew you're putting your life in danger!"

"Yes, Avdei Ha-Or is a risk. But I have no intention of dying."

"No one does, but they still die," Andy pointed out.

"That's enough," Goldeneyes said. "Andrew, you have no say in this matter. I'm telling you because you deserve to know. I am done speaking of it."

"Then you shouldn't have told me at all. How am I going to concentrate now when all I can do is worry about you?"

"This will be a good time for you to learn how to clear your mind of major distractions then, won't it? Close your eyes and do your breathing exercises."

Andy sighed. She was going to do this? Fine. Then Andy was going to work hard, too. It was time Saunders was stopped once and for all.

The rest of spring break rushed by. Friday night, the first night of Passover, arrived. As always, Becca and her mother showed up early to help with the cooking and getting the Seder table ready. Andy bore his chores with good humor as the house filled with delicious smells, especially since their mothers were liberal about taste-testing the food.

Andy and Becca put the china on the table as their mothers finished cooking. Becca glanced toward the kitchen and lowered her voice. "So, how many 'cats' is your mom allowing this year?"

Andy glanced upstairs. Goldeneyes had made it through the Avdei Ha-Or ritual a few days ago, but it had taken a lot out of her. Letsan came to town to get Andy and his bike so she could recuperate with him. She let him feel the lump of her Magelight in her neck beneath the collar. It made him think of Nafshi. Goldeneyes was getting stronger every day, but she was not quite back to normal.

"I'm fine," she sent from his room. "And your thoughts are bleeding out everywhere. Close your mind!"

Andy rolled his eyes. He caught Becca's look and grinned. "Not you, Goldeneyes. She and Letsan are the only ones here this year. Leilei's too busy studying. And no way on earth would I ever let Patches come to something like this."

Becca grinned. "Yeah, he'd probably bounce all over the table and spill the wine and grape juice."

"Wouldn't be the first time," Andy said, returning her smile. "It's not Passover if someone doesn't spill something."

"Where are they?"

"In my room. They're steering clear until the Seder starts."

"Anybody home?" Mike called, pushing through the front door and rushing to the kitchen. His parents and brother entered with more decorum.

"Dining room!" Andy said. Mike, his brother Kenny, and his father joined Andy and Becca. Not long after, the door opened again for Becca's father, who stopped briefly in the kitchen to drop off another dessert. He and Mike's father were soon deep in conversation about the Red Sox.

The table was ready, the soup was warming on the stove, and the sky was darkening. Andy answered the doorbell and welcomed Teresa and her grandfather. "I got this for you," Mr. Velez said, handing Andy a Passover cake. "Found it in the supermarket. I hope it's okay."

"Thanks, Mr. Velez, that's really nice of you," Andy said, leading them to the dining room. He showed them to their seats and put the cake on the sideboard. "Any time now," he sent to Goldeneyes. He heard a thump on the floor upstairs.

"If that's Letsan, someone's getting fat," Mike said.

Andy laughed as Letsan let off a string of human swears to all of them.

"Temper, temper!" Mike said.

"What?" Kenny asked.

"Nothing."

"Then why did you say anything?"

"Shut up, Kenny."

"Michael!" his mother said as she entered the room.

"Sorry," Mike muttered.

Letsan and Goldeneyes came into the dining room just ahead of Andy and Becca's mothers. They took their seats on the extra chairs against the wall. Andy's mother smiled at them and said, "Well, now that everyone's here, let's begin."

"You'll explain things to me, hey, Andy?" Mr. Velez said.

"I can do that, sir," Letsan sent to him and Andy.

Mr. Velez laughed out loud. "Sorry, I'm just happy," he said when everyone turned to stare.

He looked on with interest at all of the rituals, wondering at the Seder plate with its symbolic foods, enjoying the dipping of the vegetables in salt water, the breaking of the matzo, and drinking the cups of wine. He nodded knowingly when they read about the ten plagues and the Hebrews leaving Egypt. His and Teresa's eyes met and they glanced toward the cats sitting near the opposite wall. Letsan blinked at them and their smiles widened.

The Seder dinner was thoroughly enjoyed by all. Letsan and Goldeneyes stuffed themselves on turkey. Goldeneyes refused Mike's offer of a bit of horseradish. "You are playing with fire," Andy said softly.

"No, *she* would be," Mike said. Teresa kicked his foot under the table.

"Hey!"

"You deserve it, trying to play a mean trick like that."

"Oh, like Goldeneyes would really fall for it."

"He's right, I wouldn't," she said. Mr. Velez chuckled.

At the other parents' looks, he said, "I'm still happy," he said, shrugging. "Growing up Catholic and in Mexico, I never got a chance to be at a Seder."

"Well, we're very glad you're here tonight," Andy's mother said, raising her wine glass.

"Hear, hear," said the others. Glasses were raised and clinked, the table was cleared, and desserts brought. When nobody could hold another bite, they took out the Haggadahs once more, opened the door for Elijah, finished the last two glasses of wine, and said all together, "Next year in Jerusalem!"

Letsan and Goldeneyes decided to get out from underfoot and went upstairs to Andy's room. Andy, his mother, and Mike walked Teresa and her grandfather to the door. "This was one of the best nights I ever had," Mr. Velez said. "Thank you for having us, Mrs. Cohen."

"Call me Rachel, please."

"Then you call me Mario."

"We were happy to have you, Mario. Happy Easter to you and Teresa."

"Thanks, Mrs. Cohen," Teresa said. "Good night!"

Andy and Mike stayed on the porch, waving as Mr. Velez drove off. The door opened and Becca joined them. "Tonight was really nice," she said.

"Yeah," Andy agreed. "If only getting ready for Passover was the biggest problem in my life these days."

"All things must end," Goldeneyes said from the window above.

"Someday, this *will* be the biggest problem in your life again."

"I hope so," he said. "C'mon, guys, let's get back inside. I have to work at the vet's tomorrow." They followed Andy back into the house, where they helped their parents finish cleaning up.

At last, Andy and his mother walked the others to the door and said goodnight. He made his way upstairs as the dishwasher hummed in the kitchen and his mother turned off the downstairs lights. Andy changed into his pajamas, brushed his teeth, and got into bed. Goldeneyes and Letsan joined him as he turned out the light.

"You're really better?" he sent to Goldeneyes.

"I really am," she said, yawning. "Now go to sleep."

TWENTY-TWO: BATTLE PLANS

Spring break was over and school was back in session. The day of the planned attack on the Wild Ones drew nearer. Andy was out at the Compound every chance he got. Becca and Mike joined him when they could, but Mike's schedule was hectic due to his theater group obligations, and Becca was still tutoring Taylor. She and Andy had come to a tacit understanding of never mentioning Taylor. It still rankled Andy that she was helping his long-time antagonist, but when it became clear that Becca was not going to stop, he gave up arguing. Taylor was showing uncommon tact as well by leaving Andy and Mike alone. He wondered if that was part of the deal she made. It didn't really make a difference. Andy couldn't stand Taylor, and he never would.

One sunny Saturday afternoon, Andy went straight to the Compound after a quick lunch. Goldeneyes had gone back to the Compound a few days after the Seder, declaring that she was fully recovered and felt better than ever. Letsan was at the Compound as well, working hard with Razor and Matti. Razor and Letsan wanted him to work with the Shomrim in the weeks leading up to the attack. They were determined to beat the Wild Ones this time.

Andy hid his bike in the bushes and waved at the guards as he passed. He hurried to the practice grounds, where he found Zohar and his squad and joined them.

Razor watched from the trees as Andy practiced with Zohar. Attack, deflect. Attack, deflect. They were almost lulled into a rhythm, but Zohar decided to test Andy and secretly signaled Regel to double up against the boy. Andy grinned at the new tactic and widened his shield as they both attacked, then shot two light daggers, one at each Catmage. Regel had to leap aside quickly to avoid getting hit.

"Nicely done," Razor said. Andy looked around quickly and saw the scarred Maine Coon strolling out of the tree line. "Don't take your eyes off your enemy, boy!" he barked as Regel used Andy's distraction to fire another jet. Andy flung up his arm, and a Magelight shield deflected the bolt.

"Enough!" Zohar said. "This is practice, not target practice."

"Yes, but a good burn will teach Andy a lesson like nothing else," Razor said.

"A good burn will raise more questions than anything else," Zohar said, "especially from the humans. Andy is not going to be on the front line. He's going to stay back and support us as needed. He's more than ready for his role."

"I agree," Razor said, startling Andy. "And I need the boy, so you and Regel finish practicing without him. Come," he said to Andy without waiting to see if he followed.

Puzzled, Andy moved quickly after Razor. "Uh—am I in trouble?" he asked.

Razor laughed. "No. I wanted to talk to you privately." Razor stopped in the middle of the path. "Sit," he said. Andy sat down on the dirt.

"Becca and Mike want to take part in the fighting."

"I know," Andy said. "I'm torn about whether or not they should."

"I'm not. They're not Catmages. They'd be defenseless against Magelight attacks."

"So you're saying no?"

"No. Methuselah has a better idea. He says the humans should stay here and defend the Compound in case the Wild Ones discover that most of our warriors are gone and try an attack."

"Um—won't they still be defenseless against Magelights here, too?"

"Yes, but their job will be to protect the young ones, and they'll have guards with them with specific orders to protect Becca and Mike as well as the kittens. I can't spare any of my Shomrim for that when we go after Saunders."

"That's a great idea!" Andy said. "Razor, that's perfect! I'll bet I can get Teresa and Mr. Velez to come along, too. They helped on Halloween, don't forget."

Razor grunted. "Velez is okay. He can come. But what can the girl do?"

"Anything Becca can do, pretty much."

"That's a lot. All right. Ask them."

"I will! Thanks, Razor." Andy rose and dusted off his jeans. "Anything else?"

Razor gazed up at Andy before he answered. "Yes. Make sure you don't let anything distract you when you're in the real fight. Don't get hurt, or Letsan will have my tail. And I wouldn't like it, either." He turned and trotted off back to the Compound, leaving Andy standing stunned and open-mouthed. Then Andy started laughing. Razor liked him after all. *Wow.*

The next day Andy and Becca met Mike and Teresa at the Velez house to tell them about Methuselah's idea.

"I want to be in the main battle," Mike protested. "I'm ready!"

"You should be happy they're letting you do anything," Andy said. "And really, Methuselah is right. You and the others will be a huge help if the Wild Ones decide to attack the Compound. Most of the warriors are going after the Tilyon, and they'll be practically defenseless here."

"Great idea," Mr. Velez agreed.

"Yeah, okay," said Mike, but I wanted—"

"There are a couple of litters of kittens, you know. You'll be helping protect them."

Mike brightened. "Good point. From now on, my title is Mike Murdoch, Defender of the Wee Ones!" he said, saluting. "We shall not fail to guard the fluff!"

"Come on, Wee Defender, I'm hungry," Teresa said, grabbing his arm and pulling him toward the kitchen. She and Mike were staying behind while her grandfather drove Becca and Andy to the Compound.

"See you later," Andy said as he got into the front passenger seat, relieved that Mike had lightened up. He turned to look at Becca, who put her backpack carefully on the floor.

"He'll be fine," she said. "And if anything goes wrong, Mr. Velez can drive us to Saunders' house to help."

"So, are you all ready for the big day?" he asked.

"What big day?" Mr. Velez wanted to know.

"Becca's been working with Razor and some of the others on a battle plan for months. Today's the day she presents it to all the Catmage leaders. Most of them know pieces of it, but only the East Woods Council knows it all."

"I made some charts to show them," she said, grinning. "I have my laptop with me. It'll be the first time in the history of the world that cats are going to learn by PowerPoint."

"Don't let Goldeneyes hear you call them cats," Andy said.

"She don't get mad at me when I say it," Mr. Velez said.

"You know, you're right. I wonder why?"

"Because she likes him better than she likes you," Becca said with a grin.

A few minutes later, Mr. Velez pulled his SUV onto the shoulder near the East Woods Compound. Teriya and Temura showed themselves briefly as they entered the wood, then returned to their guard positions as Andy and the others went down the path. They bypassed the meadow and went straight to Hakham's bayit, where they found Goldeneyes and Letsan waiting outside.

"Change of plans. Too many people and Catmages to fit here," Letsan said. "We're meeting in the woods." He led them to a fallen tree where the others were already assembled.

"This is perfect," Becca said. She put the backpack on the ground and removed her laptop, setting it on the trunk of the tree. "Ready when you are, Razor," she said to the scarred commander.

"Right. Most of you have attended enough meetings to know about the tactics we want to deploy. Becca says encirclement is a good tactic for this battle. She's going to take over now. You will give her the same attention you would give me or Matti."

He stepped back and waited. Becca took a seat on the log. Andy and Mr. Velez sat on the ground behind the Catmages.

"The Wild Ones held their force in reserve on Halloween," Becca began, "and came at our fighters from the backyard. We're going to take advantage of that this time by deliberately leaving the back of the house open. We'll send our fighters in the front and sides, attacking from the neighbors' yards when the time is right. Our spies report that they keep almost no Wild Ones in the house. Most of them are out here in the woods across the road from us." There were growls at that reminder. "When the Wild Ones detect a large group of Shomrim approaching the house, they'll panic and send for help. We're keeping our full force in reserve until we're ready to swoop in and surprise them. Razor will be sending the warriors into town a squad or two at a time over a period of several days, secretly, late at night. The Wild Ones at the Compound will think the Shomrim are here. When the ones at the house send for help, they'll empty out the West Woods. We're hoping we can get in and out of the house before they get to town, but if we can't, their fighters are going to be tired from having to hustle into town, while ours will be fresh and lying in wait for them."

She pulled up a diagram on the laptop. "This is a plan, uh, a sort of picture of the house. These shapes you see are the shapes of the rooms. Here, here, and here are where you'll be," she said, pointing to the screen. "There's only one way the Wild Ones can get in without having to fight.

They'll think we made a mistake or that we didn't have a large enough force to cover the rear, and they'll pour into the backyard. Then we bring in our reserve force behind them and they'll fall right into our trap. They'll be surrounded on all sides. This time, the surprise will be to their disadvantage."

Andy saw the Catmages watching Becca with rapt attention, and felt prouder of her than ever.

"I can take some of you to town in my car today. You can stay with me for a few days," Mr. Velez said.

"That would be very helpful," she said. "I was going to suggest that the squads hide around my house, Andy's house, and Mike's house if they can. Your house would be better still, because you and Teresa already know about Catmages."

"As many as you want. I got lots of room. Teresa will love it," he said with a smile.

"Thank you, Mr. Velez," Letsan said. His thanks were echoed by the Council and the captains.

"This is what you get when you work with humans," Letsan told Goldeneyes and Andy privately. "I told you they'd come in handy."

"Pay attention," Goldeneyes said. Andy dared not look at Letsan for fear he'd burst out laughing. But something was bothering him. He caught Becca's eye.

"Do you have a question about the preparations, Andy?"

"Well, not for you, for Razor. What do we do if the Wild Ones cast an aura spell on the Compound? Won't they find out that a lot of Catmages are missing?"

"That won't be an issue, Andy," Hakham said. "The spell is not difficult to cast if you're near a Catmage. But the longer the distance, the more difficult it becomes and the more energy it demands. It took me many days to find Nafshi's aura two cycles ago, and the only reason I found yours was because you and she were in proximity. No Catmage would cast the spell without good reason. The Wild Ones, like us, rely on their senses to keep watch. Our patrols will make sure no Wild Ones come near enough to discover our ruse."

"Good," Andy said.

"Is this clear enough that you can explain it to your squads?" she asked. The assembled captains and squad leaders answered affirmatively.

"It's a good plan," Matti said.

"It's a great plan," Razor growled. "Becca's the smartest human I ever met."

"Stop it, Razor, you're going to make me blush," she said, but she was smiling. "Are there any questions?"

"Are you fighting with us?" Katana asked.

Becca hesitated, and Hakham answered for her. "No. I will not allow it. Only Andy will come with us to the Evil One's house. Becca and Mike will be here helping to protect the Compound if it comes to that. Even Andy will act in a support role rather than taking part in the battle."

Andy felt bad for Becca, but Hakham was right. Saunders and the Wild Ones had already proven they had no consideration for youth or weakness. Look what they did to Patches and Kel. And him! And then there were the dogs. They could do serious damage. No, Hakham and Razor were right. Becca should stay far, far away from that house.

"Are there any questions?" Razor said, looking around and waiting for an answer. "No? Good. Captains and squad leaders, you will teach this plan to your warriors. The captains have the assignments for each squad. Zohar, you and Atzel will roust your squads and go into town with Velez today." Razor paused and leaped onto the log, turning to face the waiting Catmages. "This time," he said, his tail switching and his ears flat on his head, "the Wild Ones will be the losers. This time, they'll be the ones that need a human vet!" The captains cheered. "All right, Shomrim, get out of here. Make me proud. Dismissed!"

The Shomrim scattered swiftly. The Elders left more slowly. Hakham stayed behind with Methuselah, Goldeneyes, and Letsan. Becca shut down her computer and packed it away.

"Do you really think this will work?" Andy asked.

"Yes, Andy," Methuselah said. "We have more warriors, our strategies are sound, and even a young, fit Catmage will be exhausted after running the distance between here and town. That last part was brilliant," he said, glancing at Becca. "It might make the difference between victory and defeat."

"Good, because I'm really sick of watching my friends get hurt or die."

"So are we, Andy. So are we." The Catmages headed toward the Compound, followed by Andy and Becca. On the walk over, Andy found himself next to Silsula.

"Is Leilei going to fight?" he asked.

"No, dear," she said. *Chirrup.* "She and Patches won't be going."

"Why not?"

"Leilei is not a warrior and she hasn't asked to train with the Shomrim," Goldeneyes said. "Patches is—well—Patches."

Andy grinned. "He sure is. But won't they want to fight?"

"They haven't shown any desire to do so yet."

"So they'll stay here with Becca and Mike and protect the Compound. Good."

They split up when they reached the meadow. Mr. Velez hadn't had a chance to look around when he'd brought the bodies out to the Compound the day after the Halloween battle, and during the winter he had just dropped Andy off and picked him up. He was delighted to be shown about by Andy and Becca. The grin never left his face as he explored the Teaching Rings and the bayits. He even poked his head inside the ma'on, which was mostly empty in the middle of the day.

"You say the cats, they built this?" he asked.

"Yeah, I was here the day they did. It was really cool."

Mr. Velez shook his head. "They're pretty smart."

Letsan and Goldeneyes caught up to him and Andy as they were about to leave. Mr. Velez told them what he thought about the ma'on.

"Well, we did get the idea from watching humans," Letsan said.

"Don't tell Zahavin," he added in a stage whisper they all could catch. "She might get the idea that humans are okay after all."

Goldeneyes pretended not to hear him. "Andy, have you got a ball on you?" she asked.

"Always," he said, putting his hand in his pocket and holding out a small sponge ball.

"Thanks," she said. Her Magelight flared and the ball soared straight at Letsan, who jumped but not in time. It hit him in the flank.

"That's the way it is, is it?" he said, grabbing the ball and flinging it back at her. She deflected it with a light shield, and it bounced onto the grass near a litter of kittens, who bounded after it. Andy, Becca, and Mr. Velez burst into laughter. Letsan fluffed out his fur and leaped at Goldeneyes, who went up on her hind legs to meet him and batted at him until he fell back down, laughing.

"Someone's in a good mood," Leilei said as she and Patches trotted toward them.

"Letsan wants to play? Patches will play with Letsan," he said, leaping toward them in his trademark four-legged hop.

"Not now, Patches," Letsan said. "Razor is expecting me."

"Razor is mean to Patches."

"Razor is mean to everyone," Letsan said. "Look at it this way. Be very, very worried if he's ever nice to you."

Patches tilted his head, trying to decide if he should be worried about that. Letsan trotted off, still chuckling.

"That wasn't funny," Patches said. "Now Letsan is mean to Patches."

"Patches is too sensitive," Goldeneyes said in a tone that sounded a lot like his.

Andy did a double-take. "You really are in a good mood," he said.

"Because for the first time in a very long time Andy, I'm feeling hopeful."

By the time they were ready to leave, Zohar and Atzel's squads were waiting. "It's a good thing you have an SUV," Andy said. "That's a lot of Catmages."

"Zohar can sit on my lap," Becca said with a smile.

"Let's go," Mr. Velez said. He shook his head. "A house full of magical kitties. Teresa is going to be the happiest girl in the whole school."

"And she can't talk about it with anybody but us," Becca said.

"She knows. I know."

When they reached the SUV, Andy waited until all of the Catmages were settled in before he took his seat in front. "No standing up to look out the windows," Andy said. "We look really weird already, and I can't think of a cover story to tell a cop if we get pulled over."

"Everybody ready? Okay, here we go," Mr. Velez said as he pulled onto the road. "Don't worry, Andy, I'll go slow and careful."

"Next time we do this, let's make sure it's dark out."

"Here's hoping there won't have to be a next time," Zohar said.

The humans held a war council of their own that evening over dinner at Mr. Velez' house. Andy wanted to be sure that everyone was prepared. So between bites of pizza, they discussed who would be where the night of the attack, and what they'd be doing. Becca, Mike, and Andy would tell their parents they were having dinner at the Velezes, which would be true. The attack would happen sometime after dark, and Andy figured they'd be back home before curfew.

Zohar, who was staying at the Velez house, was with them in the dining room to answer questions. He declined an offer of pizza. "That stuff smells like three-day-old dead squirrel," he said.

"That's the garlic, Zohar. Really, you'd like it. Or maybe just the cheese," Mike told him.

"No thanks. Not unless you want to try raw sparrow."

"Pass. I have to have my sparrow cooked or it's no deal."

"No cooking sparrows in my kitchen," Mr. Velez said.

"Hey, I have something to show you all," Mike said, reaching into the backpack behind his chair. He held up a hunting slingshot. "Look what I got. It's way better than my homemade slings."

Andy whistled. "That thing looks nasty. Where'd you get it?"

"Bought it online. Well, Robert Gunter bought it for me. His dad is a little looser about stuff like this than mine. I couldn't think of an explanation for buying it that would get me anything other than a big fat no."

"Is that even legal in this state?" Becca asked.

"Yep. Got the ammo for it, too. Any Wild Ones come after the kittens, they're gonna feel the wrath of The Wee Defender! You guys can have my slings."

"Here's hoping we won't need any of this stuff!" Becca said.

"Hear, hear!" Andy said, raising his can of soda.

"Speaking of here, can I leave this with you, Mr. Velez? I don't want to take the chance of my brother Kenny finding it. Or my parents."

"Yeah. I'll keep it safe for you."

"Thanks."

Mr. Velez drove them home, leaving Andy for last.

"You think the plan is gonna work this time?" he asked.

"I hope so. I don't see how it can fail."

"Well, I hope so too. That Saunders, he's a bad man."

"I know." Andy was thoughtful during the last minutes of the drive. When Mr. Velez pulled up to his house, Andy put out his hand. "Thank you for everything you've done for the Catmages, Mr. Velez," he said. "You're a really good guy."

Mr. Velez grinned as he shook Andy's hand. "Thanks, Andy." He nodded toward the door. "Get out of here. See you in a few days."

The next week seemed to take forever. Andy found himself watching the second hand tick by during class and got called out by more than one teacher for inattentiveness. He didn't dare talk about the plans during the school day, and he stopped Mike cold if the subject came up with a terse, "Not here." His heart nearly thumped out of his chest at lunch one day when Mike tried to mention the Compound as Taylor passed their table.

"I don't want to talk about compound fractions at lunch," he said.

"What?" Mike asked.

Andy kicked him under the table.

"Hey!"

"What do you want, Grant?" Andy asked as Taylor lingered nearby.

"Nothing. I have everything I need light here—I mean, right here," he said, scratching his chest over the Magelight necklace.

"Wearing it all the time now, huh?" Andy said. "Big deal." He clenched his right fist, feeling his Magelight grow warm.

"Temper, temper, Cohen. You want to *lighten up.*"

"Get lost, Grant."

"As soon as I talk to Becca about something."

"I'll be right back," she said, rising. She left the table with Taylor as Andy seethed.

"I told you not to say anything during school hours," Andy hissed at Mike. "Just keep your mouth shut about it unless we're home."

"All right, all right. Sorry!"

Becca came back to the table and sat down.

"Well?" Andy asked.

She shrugged as she took a bite of her sandwich. "He wanted to know if I was free Saturday for another lesson. I told him I had plans."

"Do you think he suspects?"

"No, I think he wanted me to tutor him this Saturday, like I've been doing a lot of Saturdays until now. Andy, just calm down and finish your lunch. If you keep acting like this, everyone's going to think there's something up with you."

"Yeah. Calm down, man," Mike said. "Be cool like me."

"Okay, okay. But I wish this week would hurry up and be over."

The week did end. Squads of Shomrim left the Compound under cover of darkness to join their compatriots in town. Andy hid several squads under his porch. Letsan and Goldeneyes came back to the house to help. Mr. Velez went to the Compound to save Hakham and Methuselah the long walk into town and hosted them at his house. The day drew closer. On the night before the battle, Andy sat on the porch with Letsan and Goldeneyes. Many of the Shomrim were out hunting. Several of them were nearby, keeping watch.

"Nervous?" Letsan asked.

"A little. Tomorrow's a big day."

"It is," Goldeneyes said, "but worrying won't help."

"I know, but it's hard not to."

"Then do what I do. Think of Nafshi."

Andy smiled. "I already do, a lot. She was really special." His Magelight glowed, and he was suffused with warmth. "Sometimes I think she's still with us."

"Of course she is!" Goldeneyes said. "Her Magelight is right there on your wrist."

Andy raised his hand to look at it. "Yeah. And she's in our hearts and memories, too."

"Yes. She always will be." Goldeneyes blinked and leaped from her perch on the railing to Andy's lap. He stroked her head. The porch light snapped on.

"That's my cue to go inside," he sent. Goldeneyes jumped off his lap as Andy stood.

"One more day," Letsan said.

"One more day," Andy repeated. He shut the light off as he went inside.

That same night, Kel trotted, tail held high, across the road that separated the Compounds. The moon rose above him as he made his way through the trees. Roah was visiting West Woods. Now was a perfect time to nose around the East Woods. There had to be something worthwhile to report back to his father. The Catmages had been quiet for too long. Everyone at West Woods was sure they were going to try something, but nobody knew when—or how. But Kel could find out. Then Roah would acknowledge him in front of everyone, including his siblings—and Alef.

He slowed as he neared the sentry post, made himself small, lowered his tail, and put on a fearful attitude. He kept walking until he was challenged by the guard. It was a calico who he didn't recognize.

"H-hello," he said, cowering.

"You are Kel," she said coldly. "What do you want?"

"I have news," he said. "Razor told me to let him know when anything important happens at the Compound."

"Well?" she said impatiently.

"Can I talk to Razor?"

"Razor is too busy to take a message from a Wild One like you," the calico sneered.

"What about Matti?"

The calico laughed. "You think that Captain Matti will have time if Razor doesn't? They're both extremely busy."

"Well, then is Katana around?"

"No."

"Well what about Zohar?"

"Tell me what you came to tell Razor, and I will pass it along."

Kel blinked at her and crouched low to the ground. "Roah is in the West Woods," he whispered. "He must be here for a reason, because he spends most of his time at the house with Saunders."

The calico gazed long at Kel. Then she turned her head and sent a private message to a nearby guard. When the silver tabby arrived, she told Kel, "Wait here," she said, "and be quiet." The silver tabby took her place, watching Kel with a steady gaze.

Kel blinked again and stayed where he was, thinking. He was puzzled by the guard's answers. Zohar and Katana were both gone, and Razor and Matti were too busy to speak to him. Something was up for certain.

A short while later, the calico returned. "You can go back to the Wild Ones now. Razor was unimpressed with your news."

CHAPTER TWENTY-TWO

"But—"

"Go. Or do you want me to escort you?" she said, eyes glittering.

"N-no," Kel said. "I'll leave." He turned and slunk through the woods, not daring to look back until he was sure he was out of sight. Roah would definitely want to know about this, but what information did he really have? That a couple of Razor's captains were not in the Compound and Razor and Matti were too busy to talk to a spy?

"By the First!" Kel said to himself. "They're leaving the Compound! They're up to something!" He hurried across the road back to the West Woods. This was big news. Roah was going to be very happy.

Kel found Roah in his bayit. This time, the guard let him in without question. He told his father what he had learned.

"Are you certain?" Roah asked. "They are leaving the Compound?"

"I think so, sir."

"You *think* so?" Roah's eyes flashed. "I do not act on imprecise information. Did you cast an aura spell?"

"No sir. I thought they might see my Magelight flash and be suspicious."

Roah sat in silence as he thought things over. "They may be planning an attack on Saunders."

"That's what I thought!" Kel said. "What will we do?"

Roah ignored him and spoke to the guard outside. "Find Stav. Bring her here, quickly."

Garev came back with a small white cat, who blinked at Roah and sat down.

"Stav, I want you to cast an aura spell on the East Woods. Kel thinks they are moving Catmages out of the Compound. Find out if he is right."

She blinked again. "I'll need to be closer. Kel can come with me to the edge of the road. He can protect me while I cast the spell, then send you a message while I recover."

"Then he will do so."

Kel's heart leaped at being given a task by his father. "It is my honor, Roah," he said as he left. When he was gone Roah called for Kfir, the captain of his army, and told him what he had learned from Kel.

"Stav is confirming Kel's report now. If it is true, we need to get our warriors to the house. How many Tzofim are at the hidden base in town?"

"Two or three squads. Most of us are out here training."

"Then you will go back to town with your warriors. Hide them at the vacant house until Razor and his Shomrim make their move. Then rush them over to Saunders' and rid me of those Shomrim once and for all."

Kfir's tail switched. "We must wait until we know for certain. If Razor is moving his fighters out now, Stav will see them. We don't want my Tzofim to run into Razor's forces on the way into town—unless you want to start the fight early."

"Then go into town yourself and use your reserves," Roah said. "Why have we been keeping them in hiding if not for situations like this?"

"I will remind you that it was my idea to have a secret base," Kfir said, "and that my tactics worked beautifully last fall. If they've emptied the East Woods, they've left it vulnerable. I'd like to send a force over there. We can destroy their headquarters at the same time we defeat their warriors. They may never recover from such a blow."

"Perhaps," Roah said, "but it's likely they've left little more than kittens, yearlings, and mothers. It seems a waste of effort. I would rather send the bulk of our strength at Razor and Matanya."

"We can take the kittens and raise them in our ways."

"That is a good point. Very well. You may send a few squads to take the East Woods. And Kfir—don't make me regret this."

"You won't."

At that moment, Kel's message flew into Roah's Magelight.

"Kel's information is sound. Stav found very few Shomrim at the Compound."

"I will pass the word to my captains," Kfir said. "We'll leave after moonset."

Kfir left, and Roah sent out another message. Alef and Bett arrived shortly. He told them the news.

Alef purred. "It is past time we eliminated Razor and his friends. Niflah will be pleased."

"Not as pleased as we will be," Bett said. "When do we leave?"

There was a noise outside and Kel hurried through the door. Alef and Bett glared at the interruption.

"What are *you* doing here?" Alef asked.

"Reporting to Roah, as instructed," Kel said. "Sir, Stav is resting comfortably, well hidden in brush. I thought you might need me so I came back as fast as I could."

"We were just assigning duties. You will stay here," Roah said. "You will join the attack on the East Woods. Kfir will assign you a squad."

A squad! He was being given command of a squad, and in front of Alef and Bett! Kel stood up straight, his tail curled over his back. "Yes, father," he said. Roah did not correct him.

"We go to town tonight," Roah told Alef and Bett. "On the way I want to hear about the progress you've made with the dogs." He nodded to Kel. "You may leave now. Alef, Bett, with me."

The four of them left the bayit.

On the morning of the appointed day, Matti and Razor led the last of the Shomrim squads out of the Compound. They planned to march at a leisurely pace and rest through the afternoon and evening. Silsula, Patches, and Leilei watched them go, along with the remaining Catmages and the apprentices who were too young to fight.

"May the One above us all guide your paths," Leilei said softly as she watched the last tail disappear into the trees.

"He will, sweetling," Silsula said. "But it doesn't hurt to pray." She licked Leilei's ear. "Go join the guards at the main path, both of you. We don't want any Wild Ones coming after the kittens."

"Patches will not let that happen," he said, fluffing out his fur and growling. "Come with Patches, Leilei. Protect the babies!" He hurried off,

Leilei at his heels. When they reached the guards, they were shown to separate spots and told to lie quiet and keep alert.

"Patches, make sure you stay quiet," Leilei sent privately. "We won't be able to hear anyone sneaking up on us if you make noise."

"Patches will be very quiet," he whispered. "Watch."

To her surprise, he kept to his word. The long day wore on with nothing worse than a few squirrels and a snake making their way through the underbrush. Leilei found her mind wandering and forced herself to pay attention. Guard duty was serious business!

As the afternoon melted into evening, Leilei was startled by the sound of a human shouting. She sprang up, astonished, and looked to the older guards for advice.

"Keep still!" Teriya told her. "We're not expecting Andy or his friends. We don't know this human. We must assume he is a danger to us."

"Methuselah!" the human shouted.

Leilei and Teriya exchanged shocked glances. The human knew Methuselah? He knew they were there? He knew!

TWENTY-THREE:
ONCE MORE INTO THE HOUSE

On the day of the attack, Mr. Velez waited for Andy and the others a few blocks away from school. They got quickly into the SUV and drove to his house, where they spent the afternoon nervously going over their tasks for the day. Zohar and Atzel had their squads rest through the afternoon. Several other squads had joined them until the house was teeming with Catmages.

Andy talked it over with Becca and Mr. Velez, and then made a phone call to Dr. Crane to let him know that his services might be needed later.

"Why?" Dr. Crane wanted to know.

"I can't go into details. But there's going to be a fight."

"Andy—"

"I can't stop it, Dr. Crane. Please, can you just be ready tonight? I'll text you."

"All right. But I'm not happy about this at all."

"Neither am I," Andy said.

"Maybe we won't need him, Andy," Becca said. "We're a lot more prepared this time."

"Yeah, it's Catmages as far as the eye can see," Mike said as he glanced out the window and around the room. "Boy, I'm glad I don't have to change their litterboxes."

"They don't use litterboxes," Andy said.

"Still."

They would stay inside until dusk, then Mr. Velez would drop Andy off a block away from Saunders' house on the way out of town with the others. The Shomrim left a few at a time, making their way to their designated spots before nightfall. Andy wished them luck as they left the house. It seemed too quiet as they ate Chinese takeout for dinner. Mike tried to keep the mood light, but his jokes couldn't cover the tension they all felt. When it was finally time to leave, Andy found his heart racing.

"Nervous?" Becca asked as they left the house.

"Yeah. I've been down this road before."

"I'm scared, too. But this time will be different. You'll see."

"I hope you're right."

"I am." She reached out and hugged Andy briefly. "Take care of yourself," she said softly.

"You too."

They piled into the SUV. Now even Mike was quiet as Mr. Velez drove across town. He stopped the car out of sight of Saunders' house and Andy got out.

"Good luck, *amigo*," Mr. Velez said. "Watch your back."

Andy nodded, waved, and shut the door. The streetlights came on as he headed down the block.

Harry had sat at his kitchen table that same day, lingering over lunch. Methuselah had been gone for months, and there was no knowing when he'd return. Would it be so hard for him to get some kind of message to Harry? There was that boy, Andy. Methuselah could have found a way to get the boy to reach out to him. But no, that ungrateful cat had not so much as thought of him since the fall, he'd bet.

Even as the thought occurred to him, he knew it wasn't true.

261

Methuselah had been his constant companion for years. He must miss Harry as much as Harry missed him. If he wasn't sending messages, he was too busy. But maybe he could be a little less busy?

Harry had filled the lonely days searching for any mention of the Tilyon, but so far, he'd found nothing worth reporting. He'd been going through the shelves methodically, and last night he'd found a batch of books that seemed promising and decided to start fresh in the morning. He finished his tea, cleared the table, and went to the library, where he pulled a pile of books off the shelf and put them on his desk. He bent over and began leafing through them.

Hours later, Harry picked up a handwritten leather-bound book—a previous librarian's notebook. He scanned the yellowed pages of routine reports about stories inscribed, names of the Safrans the librarian worked with, and other minute details from a century ago. Yawning, Harry wished that his predecessors had had the forethought to categorize, or at least include a table of contents. Would it have killed them to make an index? Harry rubbed his eyes beneath his glasses, then he turned the page and kept reading. A passage caught his eye, and he sat up straight. He placed a bookmark on the page and snapped the book shut. "Ach," he said out loud. "It looks like I'll be driving out to Coreyton to see that walking hairball today."

As Harry got into his car and pulled out of the driveway, he was overcome by doubt. Maybe he was worrying over nothing. Well, it would be nice to see Methuselah again, no matter the reason.

The sun was low in the sky by the time he reached the shoulder of the road where he'd brought Methuselah last fall. Harry put the book in his sweater pocket and walked carefully through the field to the hedge where Andy had hidden his bike the day they met.

"Methuselah! I know you're in there!" he shouted. "I need to see Methuselah immediately. Tell him Harry's here!"

There was no response.

"Don't play games with me, you stupid cats! I know you can understand me. One of you go get Methuselah or I'm going to stand here shouting until he comes out."

Leilei and Teriya looked at each other. "He's calling for Methuselah!" Leilei said. "I don't think he's working with the Wild Ones."

"We have our orders," Timura said. "No one comes into the Compound."

"He's not asking to come in. He wants Methuselah to come out."

"We don't talk to humans. Have you forgotten the First Law?"

"The First Law says don't practice magic in front of humans. It doesn't say you can't talk to them." Before Teriya could react, Leilei raced out of the thicket to where Harry stood shouting.

"Come back! By the First's whiskers, Leilei, I'll have your ears for this!"

Leilei ignored her. Her heart leaped as she heard another Catmage behind her. She glanced back and was relieved to see Patches joining her.

"Patches will go where Leilei goes," he said.

"Let's go see who this human is."

They slowed to a walk and crept forward until they could see the man and he could see them.

"I need to see Methuselah," Harry said irritably. "I'm an old man, and I hate waiting. Go tell him Harry's here."

"Methuselah isn't here," Leilei said.

"Well, where is he? I have something important to tell him."

"He went into town. He's kind of busy."

Harry frowned. "Doing what? What could make him go into town? He's too old, he shouldn't be walking through the streets like that. He gets tired too easily. Where is he? I have to find him."

Patches and Leilei looked at each other. "I don't know if we should tell him, Patches. We don't really know him."

"He is a good man. He is worried about Methuselah. Patches likes Harry." He said it out loud so Harry could hear him. "Patches *likes* Harry!" Then he leaped his four-legged hop toward Harry, hopping around him in a circle. Harry chuckled.

"All right, Patches, is it? Stop going around me like that or I'll get dizzy and fall trying to watch you, and then where will we be?"

Patches stopped. "Methuselah went to the Evil One's house," Patches said in a low voice. "Patches is afraid. Saunders is mean. Wild Ones are mean. Methuselah might get hurt."

"What?!" Harry asked. "Where is he? Tell me! I'll give that Saunders something if he tries to hurt my Methuselah!"

"We could take him there," Leilei said.

"Razor will be mad at us."

"Not if we don't interfere. We can show Harry how to get there and stay back out of the way. Razor can't get mad at us for that."

"Who is Razor?" Harry asked. "Never mind, I don't care. If you know where Methuselah is, and you can take me there, let's go!"

"It's a long walk," Patches said.

"I have a car."

"Hooray! Patches likes riding in cars. What do you think, Leilei?"

She glanced back at the guards. "Well," she said, "I think we're in trouble no matter what we do. Let's go."

Patches cheered.

"This way," Harry said. Patches and Leilei followed him to the car. They leaped into the front seat as he held the door open for them. "Where to?" he asked.

"Do you know how to get into town?" Leilei asked.

Harry shrugged. "I guess so. You mean Coreyton?"

"Yes, that's what Andy calls it."

"Then let's go."

He drove slowly toward the town, wondering how his two passengers were going to be able to give him directions once he got there.

"Oh, Patches can show you," he said.

"You heard me thinking?"

"You think very loudly. Patches is loud too, mostly. But Patches can be quiet," he finished in a whisper. "See?"

Harry smiled. "I've never met a Catmage quite like you," he said.

"Patches is unique," Leilei agreed.

Patches showed Harry how to get to Saunders' house by putting images in his mind. It took Harry a while to adapt to a cats-eye-view of the streets of Coreyton, but he managed. "Extraordinary," Harry said. "All these years Methuselah has been with me, and he never did anything like this."

"We don't do it very often," Leilei said. "We talk to each other just like humans, only we talk with our mind-voices."

"So you do, my dear. Well, I am quite enjoying myself with the two of you, or I would be if I weren't so worried about Methuselah."

"Patches likes Harry. Harry is a nice man!"

"Thank you, my boy. Now, in between telling me how to get to the house, can one of you explain to me what's going on?"

"How much do you know about the Tilyon and the murder of the Council two cycles ago?" Leilei asked.

"Methuselah told me everything he knew, but I haven't seen him since the summer. I'm behind in the news."

Leilei spent the rest of the drive telling Harry what she knew about the plan to attack Saunders' house. The more he heard, the more worried Harry became. His friend was in danger, that was obvious.

"Are we near the house yet?" he asked when Leilei finished speaking.

Patches was standing on his hind legs looking out the window. "Whoops! Yes! Very close. Next street, go this way," Patches said, pointing with a paw. "Street after that, other way!"

Harry drove down the block and pulled over to the side of the road.

"Why are you stopping?" Patches asked. "We are not there!"

"I need to think a moment," Harry said. "If there's a full-scale battle going on, we need to be careful about getting in the middle of it. We don't dare jeopardize our friends."

"It's full dark out," Leilei said. "The plan was to wait for nightfall and then attack. They must have already begun."

"I don't know what to do!" Harry said. "If Methuselah were here—"

"We need to help!" Leilei said. "Harry, please, just go! Once we see what's happening, we can decide what to do."

"All right," Harry said. He pulled away from the curb and raced down the block toward Saunders' house. He stopped the car underneath the big oak tree in front of number 19 and opened the door. There were two boys at the gate of the house. He thought he recognized one of them.

Andy moved slowly down Oak Street. Razor wanted him in position on the far side of Mackie's house, where he could keep an eye on what was happening without being seen himself, and where he could get in quickly if needed. As he glanced at number 19, Andy saw a light on in a second floor window. He wondered if Saunders was home or if he'd just left the light on.

"He's home," Letsan's voice said in his head. "There are a few Wild Ones in the house, no more than two squads. Everyone else is in hiding until the signal is given." He poked his head out from under the porch two doors beyond Saunders' house.

"Shut up, you two," Razor said. He was crouched on a branch in the oak tree in front of Saunders' house. "Andy's bleeding into everyone's heads again."

"Sorry!" Andy said hastily. He closed his eyes and did his breathing exercises to calm himself and imagined a wall around his head. It wouldn't do to let the Wild Ones know what he was thinking.

Night fell. Andy waited for the signal. When it came at last, the Shomrim started moving toward the front yard. The gate was flung open and several squads of Shomrim streamed inside. The front door to Saunders' house flew open as they swept up the porch and into the house. One of the spies in the neighbors' yards flashed out a warning. "Wild Ones are coming in through the backyard!"

"That's too soon," Razor said. "How did they get to town so fast?"

"Maybe they were somewhere nearby already," Matti said. "How many are there?"

"We can handle them!" the warrior said.

"Good. Let's move it, Matti."

Andy could barely keep still, but he had his orders. He was to stay where he was until told to move in. Razor, Matti, and their squad leaders would take care of things at the house. And they had Hakham, Methuselah, Letsan, and Goldeneyes, too. Things were looking good so far.

Matti and Letsan led the Shomrim into the house while Razor stayed outside in the tree, observing and barking orders from above. They heard the warning about the Wild Ones coming through the back and set their defensive lines. "Cover every doorway!" Letsan shouted. "We won't let them pull the same tricks again!" The Shomrim set themselves and waited for the assault. But the Wild Ones in the yard didn't come inside.

"What are they waiting for?" Matti asked.

"I think they were waiting for me," Kfir said as he came charging down the stairs at the head of a group of Wild Ones. Matti growled and his fur rose. "Surprised to see me, Matti? What's the matter, is Razor too afraid to come after me himself this time?"

"Shut up, traitor!" Matti said as he braced himself to meet Kfir's charge. Magelights flashed and the air filled with jets of light, growls, screams, and yowls. The back door crashed open as Kfir's Tzofim in the backyard joined the fight.

"Oh, dear," Kfir said. "You weren't expecting that, were you? Outnumbered again."

Matti laughed harshly. "Second wave!" he shouted to Razor. The Shomrim hiding at the neighbor's on either side of number 19 cheered and knocked some of the boards in the fence loose. They swept through the holes, one half pouring into the backyard and hitting the Wild Ones from their rear, the rest barreling through the front yard. Razor dropped from the tree and called two more squads to join him, racing through the front door behind the second wave. Hakham, Methuselah, Goldeneyes, and Letsan made their own formidable squad. The wrath of two Magi together was a sight to behold, but Goldeneyes and Letsan fought so fiercely that they nearly equaled the old ones.

"I should have undergone the ritual ages ago," Goldeneyes said as she and Letsan paused for a moment, breathing hard and shielding themselves against stray shots.

"Power becomes you," Letsan said as he felled a Wild One with a light dagger. The fighting continued thick and furious. Methuselah and Hakham stood side by side, forcing back the Wild Ones in their path. Others on their side were not so lucky. Some of Razor's Shomrim lay on the ground along with the Wild Ones.

"Something's wrong," Matti said. "Why aren't they tiring faster? How can they be this fresh if they had to come all the way from the Compound?"

Kfir heard Matti, and he laughed long and loud. "You underestimated us again," he said. "My Tzofim didn't have a long journey at all. Really, Razor, your spies are a joke. They see what we want them to see. And what they don't see is going to cost you. Now!" he said.

The cellar door flew open and half a dozen dogs raced up the steps, barking and growling. Matti couldn't believe his eyes. Roah, Alef, Bett, and Niflah *were riding on the backs of the dogs*. They dug their claws into thick pads connected to leather harnesses as the dogs dashed through the Shomrim, biting and snapping. Yowls of pain erupted where the dogs found their prey. The four Wild Ones shot dart after dart of light at the Shomrim.

"Hello, brother," Niflah said as the dog he rode approached Hakham. "It's past time we stop killing one another. Call off your forces and we'll let you live."

Hakham leaped aside as Niflah fired at him. "Ever the betrayer, brother," Hakham said, deflecting the arrow with a blazing shield. "Give us back the Tilyon and we'll call off the fight." He sent a light dagger at the dog. Niflah deflected it at the last second, but a dart from Methuselah aimed at the dog's leg hit true, and the dog dropped, throwing Niflah off its back. Niflah twisted in midair and barely landed on his feet. He slid across the floor into the wall, recovering quickly to turn and face his enemies.

The other dogs were making inroads into the Catmage forces. Razor watched in horror as one of them grabbed a warrior, crunched down on bone and shook it from side to side. The Catmage slid to the floor, dead.

"We can't handle the dogs in close quarters!" Razor shouted. "Everyone out! Front, back, sides, retreat!"

The Shomrim scrambled to do as he said. Hakham and Methuselah conferred quickly, then used their Magelights to grab a painting off the wall and crash it into a dog. Roah leaped from the dog just before the painting hit. The dog yelped and ran. Alef and Bett saw what was happening and fired together at Hakham and Methuselah. The two Magi deflected the darts but had to back away. The Wild Ones could reach them more easily from their vantage point on the dogs, while the Shomrim had to fire high to reach the riders. Most of their shots bounced harmlessly past the Wild Ones.

"We need to distract them while our Shomrim retreat," Letsan said. "Zahavin, shield me!" Letsan got as close as he dared to one of the riderless dogs, tempting it to try to bite him. Goldeneyes threw a light shield in front of him as the dog's jaws tried to lock around his body. Its jaws couldn't penetrate the shield. Letsan fired a jet into the dog's eye, blinding it. Yelping, it backed away.

"Now! Outside with the rest of them!"

Once outside, the battle raged all around Saunders' house. Razor was astonished at the number and freshness of the Wild Ones. They had nearly as many fighters in their force as Razor did. Once again, they'd been utterly wrong about their enemy's strength. Once again, Razor had failed. Another warrior fell in front of him, and Razor's fury and rage overwhelmed him. Suddenly he was all over the battlefield, growling, biting, clawing, firing off light daggers. He saw a large rock lying on the ground as he moved across the yard. "Matti!" he yelled, lifting the rock with his

Magelight. Matti knocked it at one of the dogs with all his strength. It hit the dog's leg with an audible crack, and the dog went down.

Not far from Razor, Zohar and Atzel formed their squads into a semicircle, backs to the fence. Wild Ones tried without success to break through.

"Not bad for a three-legged fighter, am I?" Zohar said as he watched a Wild One fall. "I wouldn't mind a shot at the dog that got my leg."

"Maybe later!" Atzel said, ducking as a green jet flew close enough to singe his whiskers. "Right now let's just take care of the Wild Ones."

Razor stopped to gauge the battle, his sides heaving. His forces in the front yard were holding their own. Hakham and Methuselah covered the yard, helping wherever they were needed. A large force of Wild Ones stayed just inside the front door, firing from cover into the Shomrim. Hakham and Methuselah were conferring about how best to handle them.

"Letsan! Zahavin! Form up with me. Dalet squad, to me!" Moments later, Razor raced around the right side of the house. They met no Wild Ones until they reached the backyard, where a battle raged between the Tzofim and the Shomrim. Razor's warriors came out behind a group of Wild Ones, surprising them from the rear and dropping more than a few of them. Razor laughed harshly as the Wild Ones fled through the loose boards. A number lay dead or wounded on the ground. He scanned the yard and signaled his warriors to follow him to the other side of the house. They flushed out the last of the Wild Ones, once again surprising them from the rear. But Razor didn't have enough spare fighters to guard against their returning to the rear of the house. He needed another plan, but he couldn't very well call time out and chat with Hakham and Methuselah. Damn those Wild Ones! Razor led his force back to the front yard and arranged defensive positions to watch the sides of the house. He had to get to Matti and figure out what to do next.

Andy shifted from foot to foot, wishing he could leave his spot. He could hear growls, yowls, and yelps. His imagination began to run away with him. He wanted so badly to see what was going on, but he'd promised.

He heard the sound of footsteps coming down the sidewalk and quickly withdrew further into the shadows. Maybe whoever it was wouldn't notice the noises coming from Saunders' house. Andy peered out at the person as he walked by and gasped. Taylor? What was *he* doing here?

Taylor hurried past and stopped just shy of the gate in the front fence. Andy saw the glow of colored lights as Taylor prepared to do something with his Magelights.

"Oh no you don't!" he shouted, running out of his hiding place and clenching his fists. "If you touch them, I'll kill you!"

Taylor turned quickly. "So you made it to the big fight, but you're hiding out here? What's the matter, too chicken to get involved?"

"Shut up, Taylor."

"Make me."

They were standing face to face now, about three feet apart. Taylor still towered over him. But he didn't scare Andy anymore. "It's just you and me now, Tay-Tay," Andy said, hoping to get Taylor mad enough to distract him. He didn't know what Taylor had learned over the past months. Maybe he could taunt him into revealing himself. "Have you learned how to pick up anything heavier than a piece of paper with those things yet?"

"You think you're so great," Taylor said. "So smart. So different. You don't have to work hard to keep up in class. You get someone like Becca without even trying. And you think you're so special because you have a Magelight. I have to work hard for everything I get. Nothing comes easy to me. But you know what, Cohen? My hard work paid off. You're going to love what I can do with these," he said, hand on the Magelight necklace. The five lights started glowing again, and suddenly a multicolored arrow headed straight for Andy. He swung his right arm in a shielding motion and the arrow bounced off and dissipated.

"I have a Magelight because Saunders killed Nafshi," Andy said between gritted teeth. "She gave it to me before she died. You're wearing the Magelights of Catmages that Saunders murdered. And you've been helping

CHAPTER TWENTY-THREE

him all this time. Don't think I don't remember who lied to my mother about where I was the night Saunders hit me over the head and stuck me in the cellar."

"Aw, poor baby. Damn straight I'm with Saunders. He's powerful, loser. And thanks to him, I'm powerful too." Taylor fired again, and Andy deflected the bolt.

"Try harder, Tay-Tay. Show me that hard work you're bragging about!" Andy said with a smile.

Taylor's face reddened and his brows drew together. "Fine, Cohen. You want more? Have some of this!"

The lights grew brighter than they had before. Andy braced himself to deflect another bolt. But he didn't expect Taylor to fire a light dagger from three separate Magelights. Andy managed to deflect two, but the third sliced open his cheek. Taylor laughed harshly as he saw the blood in the glow of the streetlight.

Andy gaped as he reached up to his cheek. Blood ran through his fingers. His heartbeat throbbed in his ears as his anger grew. *Whoosh. Whoosh. Whoosh.* Taylor was laughing, just like he'd done all those times he'd bullied Andy. Rage filled him, took him over. *Whoosh. Whoosh. Whoosh.* Andy flung out his right arm, fist clenched. A wave of green light shot from his Magelight, covering Taylor from head to foot. He flew backward through the gate, arms flailing vainly, and landed heavily, his head smacking the ground. He lay still. Andy, gasping, froze in horror at what he had just done.

Saunders stood at the office window on the second floor, watching the battle. He clenched the Tilyon in his hand, cursing every time he heard one of his dogs cry out in pain. Roah had assured him that this time they could protect the Dobermans. Saunders was furious, but it was better that he stayed out of the fight for now. Let the kitties take the brunt of the damage. He would sweep in later and help mop up. The Tilyon glowed brightly. He held it so tightly it cut into his skin.

ONCE MORE INTO THE HOUSE

Wait a moment. He peered at the yard next door. Was that—Andy? Yes, and there was Taylor. Oh, this should be interesting. Andy had no idea how far Taylor had come this year. Saunders released his grip on the Tilyon and watched avidly.

"We can't beat them," Letsan said, gasping. The Shomrim were gathered in the front yard in defensive positions. "At best we're fighting them to a draw. That's not going to get us the Tilyon."

"We can't give up!" Razor said. "We keep fighting until we win!"

"That's the spirit!" Kfir said. "Keep fighting, even though you're going to die."

"Show your face outside the door and we'll see who's dying today," Razor growled. "Scared, Kfir?"

"No, smart. We have one more surprise for you." He stood aside as the three unharmed dogs leaped through the door. Alef, Bett, and Roah rode them. Behind them were three more dogs without riders, snapping and charging at the Shomrim in the yard.

"Let's see how fast they can run!" Razor said, tearing off in front of a dog and racing around the side of the house. The dog followed instantly, and two other Shomrim picked up on Razor's tactic. They led the riderless dogs on a wild chase around the yard. Matti split off two squads to head down the other side of the house and surprise the dogs. The yelps and whines coming from the side of the house told him that the Shomrim were hitting their marks.

Roah, Alef, and Bett had to work hard to stop their dogs from joining in the chase. Matti laughed. "You can't hit us while you're trying to control those dogs," he said, firing at the riders as he spoke. Cheering, the Shomrim joined in. Niflah led the Wild Ones out of the house in a mass charge. The yard was in chaos when Taylor came crashing to the ground through the gate.

Goldeneyes saw Andy staring at Taylor in horror. Until that moment, she and Letsan had been standing shoulder to shoulder with Matti, pushing the Wild Ones back toward the house. Now they watched Andy.

The Wild Ones took advantage of their distraction to regroup into a defensive line. The Shomrim ranged themselves against them.

"Andy!" Goldeneyes shouted.

"Andy!" Harry called from the street. "What did you do?"

"I—I didn't mean to—I'm sorry—I—" He wiped the sweat from his forehead, not knowing what to say or do. His shoulders slumped.

"Well, well, Mr. Cohen." Saunders appeared on the porch and leaned against the doorframe, arms crossed and a slight smile on his face. "You've been a very naughty boy. What have you done to Mr. Grant?" The Tilyon shone from the chain around his neck.

All over the yard, the fighting paused. "The Tilyon!" shouted a Cat-mage. "He's wearing the Tilyon!"

Saunders looked for the Catmage that had shouted, and found him. "Yes," he said. "The Tilyon. Would you like to see what it can do?" Without waiting for an answer, Saunders sent a dagger at the Catmage, scoring its flank.

Patches and Leilei hid behind Harry.

"Saunders is a bad man," Patches muttered. "A very bad man."

"I want to leave," Leilei whispered. "Let's go, Patches. The dogs—I don't want to stay here."

"Something is not right about the dogs," Patches said.

"Of course not! They're being controlled by Wild Ones."

"No. Something is different. Their collars ... something is wrong."

"So you can wield the Tilyon," Hakham said. "That still doesn't make it yours."

"No, having it makes it mine. Niflah, I'm so disappointed in you. I thought you would have managed to kill your brother by now. Would you like me to take care of it for you?"

Now it was Hakham's turn to laugh. "You can try, Evil One. But unlike Nafshi, I am not caged and drugged. Do your best. I should be glad to duel with you."

"No, let me!" Goldeneyes said. "I owe him for my grandmother."

"I think not," Saunders said. His eyes narrowed as he scanned the yard. "You've cost me some of my dogs again. They are not easy to replace. And I don't believe in dueling with my inferiors." He uncrossed his arms and withdrew a pistol from his pocket. "Do you recognize this, Zahavin?" he asked.

Goldeneyes froze in terror. That was the pistol he had used to shoot her two years before when she was on a reconnaissance mission, and the one he had threatened her with last year when he stole the Tilyon.

"No!" Andy yelled. "I won't let you do it!" He leaped toward her, but she was halfway across the yard. There was no way he'd reach her in time.

"Oh, yes, Mr. Cohen," Saunders said, squeezing the trigger. "You can't stop me this time." Matti leaped in front of Goldeneyes and knocked her aside as the gun went off. The bullet hit Matti in his side and he fell, bleeding heavily.

"No!" Andy screamed. "Not again! NO!" He clenched his fists, the blood roaring in his ears. *Whoosh. Whoosh. Whoosh.* His Magelight flared. A wave of green light burst from him and over the entire yard, just as it had on Halloween, and flung the Wild Ones and the dogs aside like toys. Even Saunders staggered in the doorway and had to grab hold of the frame to stay on his feet. The Wild Ones fled. Saunders glared at Andy and stepped slowly toward him. As his foot touched the yard, a door slammed next door.

"Saunders! Damn you, this is the last straw. You and your dogs woke my boy *again!* I've had it. What did I tell you about shooting off fireworks? What is *wrong* with you? I called the police. I told you I would." Mackie stood on his back porch, his face flaming red under the light. Saunders swore and rushed back into the house. Once inside, he picked up the phone and hurriedly punched in a number.

"This is Stan Saunders. Oh, good, it's you, Gerri. Yes, Mackie told me. I assure you it's a simple misunderstanding. I can clear it up. About an hour will do. Thank you, my dear. You have a birthday coming up soon, don't you? Oh, I never forget my friends. Well, a dispatcher's job is a very important one, so I should let you go. Thank you."

Saunders went back to the front door and looked around. He heard his dogs whimpering in the backyard, which was full of Catmages helping the wounded. Andy Cohen sat next to the cat that he had shot. And there was a strange man kneeling next to Taylor Grant, touching his head. Saunders strode past them all, turned at the gate and paused.

"I will kill any cat still in my yard when I return," he said through clenched teeth. "And you had better be gone too, Mr. Cohen." They heard him climb the steps next door. "Mackie, if you'll just let me explain," he said. The door closed and they heard muffled shouting, then silence.

Matti lay dying. Goldeneyes sat near him, licking his ear. "You saved me," she said. "Oh, Matti, we can't stop the bleeding. We tried."

"It was worth it," he said. "Where's Razor?"

"Right here," Razor said. "You didn't duck fast enough. Told you you weren't as fast as me."

"Beat them," Matti said, his voice getting weaker. "Razor, get the Tilyon back."

"We will, Matti. May the First bless your steps to the world beyond."

Razor bowed his head as the light went out of Matti's eyes.

TWENTY-FOUR: GOODBYE TO YOU

Razor raised his head. "Time for the death song later. We have to get the dead out of the house. We can't let the Wild Ones get any more Magelights." He looked up at Andy, who brushed the tears from his eyes. "You and Harry, come with me. Letsan! Zohar! Methuselah, I need your help."

Andy sniffled and rose. He and Harry followed Razor into the house. The Wild Ones were nowhere to be found. Andy and Harry picked up Catmages at Razor's direction. They commandeered towels from the kitchen and a bathroom. It didn't take long. Razor used his Magelight to cut off the collars of any dead Wild One they found as well. "No use giving Saunders any more Magelights to misuse," he said.

When they were finished, they left the house. Taylor was nowhere to be seen. He had gone as soon as he could walk steadily, Hakham told them. Andy texted Dr. Crane that he'd be coming to him with wounded Catmages. Harry said he'd drive them. They loaded the dead and wounded into his car. Andy took one last look around the yard. He found Patches at the side of the house, crouched a few feet away from a dog.

"Is it dead?" Andy asked.

"Yes," Patches said. "But it is still wrong. The collar is wrong."

"Patches, I don't have time for this," Andy said. "We have to go."

Razor noticed Andy standing near the fence and strode over to him. "What's going on? We need to leave."

Andy shrugged. "Patches says there's something wrong with the dog. Or the collar."

"Magelight. Magelight! Dog is wearing Magelight on collar!" Patches shouted. "That is the reason dogs are so smart! Saunders gave them Magelights! Dogs should not have Magelights!"

Razor stared thoughtfully at the dog. It was one of the dogs that the Wild Ones rode into the battle. His Magelight flashed and sliced the collar. "Bring that with us, Andy. We'll check it later, when we have time," he said.

Andy picked up the collar. Another death you could chalk up to Saunders. Rage coursed through him. He took a deep breath. "Let's get the hell out of here," he said, stalking out of the yard.

Later that evening, after Dr. Crane had taken care of the worst wounded, Harry drove Andy and the others back to the Compound. He pulled over onto the shoulder of the road and opened the doors for the weary and battered Catmages. "Methuselah, would you and Hakham stay with me a few minutes, please?" he said as they made their way to the ground. They waited until the others were out of sight.

"What is it, Harry?" Methuselah asked.

"I found something in one of my predecessor's journals that you need to know about. It's just a few lines, but when I read them, I thought about your boy Andy. And that Saunders, who has all those Magelights." He pulled the book out of his pocket, adjusted his glasses, leaned against the car and started reading.

On this the Twelfth day of September in the year Seventeen Hundred and Thirty-Nine, I write this in the hope that my successors will pass along the knowledge that I put here in these pages. I do not know the full story, as the Catmages who were involved live a long distance away, and we have only received the information second-hand from another who heard bits of the story but couldn't be brought to me to tell it in its entirety. The Catmage that I spoke to about this seemed most anxious that I make a note and pass this along to future generations. This is the warning that they wanted me to impart: Under no circumstance is a Catmage to use another's Magelight on the death of its owner. While it is true that for the most part, the deceased Catmage's Magelight is destroyed, let it be known far and wide that it is perilous to do elsewise.

Harry stopped reading.

"Is that it?" Hakham asked. "Isn't there anything more?"

"No. Isn't that enough? Something obviously happened when a Catmage used another's Magelight nearly three centuries ago. Look what he did to that other boy tonight. Did you see it? He went through the air like he'd been thrown."

"I've been troubled since I met Andy," Methuselah said. "Do you recall that he recognized me, yet we had never met?"

"Yes," Hakham said. "And he is casting powerful spells that are clearly above his level. I did not expect Zohar to live after the Halloween battle, yet Andy cured him."

"Andy brought him back from near death," Methuselah said. "That is Magus-level healing."

"You think that Nafshi's soul in the Magelight is influencing Andy," Hakham said.

"Don't you? The Magelight held her *neshama*. It was not destroyed."

"No. And maybe it has nothing to do with Nafshi's soul. Maybe Andy, as the boy in the prophecy, has always had Magus-level strength. Perhaps his use of Nafshi's Magelight augments his own natural powers. We don't know, Methuselah. And the book Harry brought tells us almost nothing."

Methuselah laughed harshly. "You're right, the information is useless. A boy who has been studying barely two years exhibits the same level of power as a Magus who has practiced and studied for decades. It must be because he is the one prophesied to help us defeat the Darkness. Yes, it's a completely likely explanation. Never mind that Andy could barely float a leaf last year. It's his aura. That must be the answer."

Hakham bristled at the sarcasm. "We know nothing for certain," he snapped, "and until we do, say nothing to the boy. Or to anyone else."

"Not even Zahavin?"

"No. This requires more study. We will keep it among ourselves. Thank you, Harry, for letting us know. Methuselah, are you coming with me back to the compound?"

"No. I'm going home with Harry. I've been here long enough. I told you I wouldn't stay forever."

"We still need you, my old friend."

"And I will come back. But for now, I'm going home. I want to sleep in my own bed and eat in my own kitchen."

"You mean my bed and my kitchen," Harry said.

"Our bed. Our kitchen." Methuselah twined himself around Harry's legs.

"Cat hair. Always with the cat hair," Harry muttered. But he was smiling.

"Farewell, then. I'm going to get some rest in *my* home."

"Goodbye, Hakham. Until next time!"

Hakham watched them get into the car and drive away. Then he turned and headed down the path to the compound. Harry had given him much to think about. And he was already heartsick over their losses. Well, it could wait at least until he ate and rested. If only Nafshi were here to share his worries with. But then, if Nafshi were here, Andy wouldn't have her Magelight, and this would be one less problem they'd have to deal with.

Hakham strode slowly, his soul and body weary. The Shomrim guards watched him pass without speaking. The Catmages and kittens he encountered gave him a wide berth. Word must have gone around by now about Matti's sacrifice. There would have to be a ceremony, but he couldn't face it just now.

GOODBYE TO YOU

When he reached his bayit, Razor was sitting in front of the door. "Is there something you need, Razor?" he asked. "Because I want nothing more than to sleep right now."

"Patches was right. There was a Magelight in the dog collar, under the largest stud. It was one of the Council Magelights. Zehira recognized the aura."

"What did you do with it?"

"It's destroyed."

"So they're down to ten Magelights."

"And the Tilyon."

Hakham sat heavily. "Razor, my friend, this has not been a good day."

"There's more," Razor said. "The Wild Ones left a reserve force. They attacked the Compound while we were in town."

"What? Why did no one tell me? Is everyone all right?"

"Come see," Razor said.

They went to the meadow, where Mr. Velez and Andy's friends were in the middle of a large group of the Catmages who had stayed behind. Most of the kittens bounced happily around Mike, who was tossing a series of balls around for them to chase.

"What are they saying?" Hakham asked as they got closer.

"Wee Defender," Razor said. "That's what they're calling Mike. He told them he was the Defender of the Wee Ones."

Hakham surprised himself by laughing long and loud. "By the One, I needed that. Why the title?"

"Because Mike and the others held off the attack. That slingshot he brought? Nasty. Effective. Between our Shomrim guards and Andy's friends, we sent them back with their tails between their legs. Silsula and Zehira were amazing, I'm told."

"I hope you're not surprised," Silsula said as they drew near. *Chirrup.* "After all, I *am* of the line of Nafshi." *Chirrup.* "Hakham, where is Andy?"

281

CHAPTER TWENTY-FOUR

"Isn't he here with everyone else?"

"He was. No one can find him. We thought he was with you."

"No."

"I'll tell Zahavin," she said. She left them and went to find her sister. Goldeneyes and Letsan were with Becca. They were filling one another in on the details of the night. Patches and Leilei sat near, listening.

"Andy is missing," Silsula said. "Have any of you seen him?"

"No," Goldeneyes said, "but I have an easy way to find him. Patches, will you please locate Nafshi's Magelight?"

"Easy!" Patches said, leaping to his feet. "Not even have to concentrate. Andy is in practice field."

"That's where they're burying Matti," Letsan said. "And the other Shomrim that died tonight. Come on, Zahavin, let's go find him."

They found Andy sitting on the ground with Zohar and a large group of warriors. The gathering was breaking up. Some of the Catmages greeted them as they passed. Soon only Andy and Zohar remained. Zohar nudged Andy's hand. "Let's go, Andy."

"Is that it?" Andy asked. He was holding Matti's collar, which no longer held his Magelight. "That's all you're doing for them?"

"No," Zohar said. "There will be a memorial service. Come back tomorrow."

"No," Andy said.

"No?"

"No. I can't. I just can't." He noticed Becca, Goldeneyes, and Letsan watching him. Andy stood, clenching his fist around Matti's collar. "I'm done," he said. "I can't stand watching my friends die anymore. I quit."

"What do you mean, you quit?" Letsan said.

"I quit. I'm out. I'm done!" Andy shouted, rising. "I can't do this anymore. Every time I try to help, I make things worse. Nafshi's dead. Matti's dead. I almost killed Taylor tonight!"

"You what?" Becca asked.

282

GOODBYE TO YOU

"You saw it," Andy said, nodding at Letsan and Goldeneyes. "You were there. He hit his head on the ground. What if there had been a rock? He could have died, and it would have been my fault. So that's it. I'm done. I quit."

"You can't quit!" Goldeneyes said. "You're the Son of Aaron! We can't win without you. Andy, I know you're upset, but just take some time and calm down. You'll feel better in the morning."

"I don't want to feel better in the morning!" Andy roared. "I don't ever want to feel better about what happened tonight! I don't want to keep fighting, and I don't want to keep watching my friends die. Or lose their legs," he said, glancing at Zohar.

"Andy, you saved Zohar," Letsan said. "He would have died if not for you."

Andy shrugged. "So what? It was my fault he was there in the first place. I messed up from day one. If it wasn't for me, Nafshi would still be alive, and Saunders would never have gotten the Tilyon. So I'm quitting before I hurt you guys even more."

He rushed past them, his Magelight glowing, and ran through the woods. They could see the green light as he ran.

"I'll talk to him tomorrow," Becca said. "He just needs time to calm down."

"You're probably right," Goldeneyes said. "Let's go. It's time Becca and the others went home."

They went back to the meadow. Andy wasn't there. Letsan and Goldeneyes waited as Becca, Mike, and Teresa gathered their things and left the Compound. They found Andy waiting by Mr. Velez' SUV. He said little on the ride home, and the others let him be. Mr. Velez dropped Andy off at his house and surprised him by getting out and walking him to the door.

"You're a good kid, Andy," he said. "You been doing lots of good things with these cats. The bad stuff, it's not your fault." He reached out and gripped Andy's shoulder to give it a squeeze. "Just remember that.

283

You're a good kid."

Andy shrugged. Mr. Velez shook his head and turned away. Andy turned out the porch light and went inside.

"He'll be okay tomorrow," Becca said, but she didn't sound too sure.

"Yeah, he'll be fine. And if he isn't, I'll *make* him fine," Mike said.

Teresa looked sadly out the window. "None of you understands," she said softly. "He won't be fine tomorrow. He won't be okay for a long, long time."

The SUV drove away. Andy stood in the darkened hallway looking out the window beside the door, watching the truck disappear down the street.

"I quit," he whispered and went up the stairs to bed.

ABOUT THE AUTHOR

Meryl Yourish attended the Clarion Science Fiction and Fantasy Writers' Workshop at Michigan State University, which led to her first fiction sale.

After spending most of her life in northeastern New Jersey, Meryl moved to Richmond, Virginia in 2002. She spent her first six years in Richmond teaching fourth graders in religious school at a local synagogue. Although a teacher really shouldn't play favorites, the hero of The Catmage Chronicles was named after one of her students (he thinks it's cool).

Today she spends her time writing and lives with her two cats, one of whom looks suspiciously like Letsan.

Find out more about Meryl, her writing, and her cats at www.merylyourish.com.

ACKNOWLEDGMENTS

It's hard to believe I'm at the halfway point of the series. I would like to thank the people who helped me get there.

Once again Sarah Getzler was a vital part of the process as she played my sounding board whenever I was stuck, and gave me constant encouragement.

Thanks to Janet Platt and Chris Hlatky for their friendship and assistance.

Special thanks to Dr. Tom Haney (a.k.a. Dr. Crane), Dr. Lipstock, Dr. Cloman, and Dr. Cline for answering my many questions about cat injury and repair, and to the wonderful staff at Bon Air Animal Hospital, who tend to my cats with loving care.

To my beta readers: Sarah Getzler, Cathy Henry, and Janet Platt. Thanks to Mike Scher and Drew Wheeler, for catching the things we all missed. Thanks to Neil Clarke for his friendship, support, and ebook formatting. And thanks again to my editor, Bridget McKenna.

To Larry Felder, who is always ready to lend an ear and give me encouragement when I need it the most.

A very special shout-out to my loyal Facebook fans: Gian Cagampan, Kathy Pritchard, Robert Gunter, Vicki Reed, Debra Franklin, Cindy Lopez, Dave Mac, Ryka George, and Kathy Greathouse. Your encouragement is worth more than I can say.

Cover revised by Gerard Gorman
Cover design: Camille Murphy Bugden

Made in United States
North Haven, CT
15 February 2022

16149626R00176